MY MADE-UP LIFE

Born in Bradford to Irish parents, Anne-Marie O'Connor moved to Dublin in 2000, an experience that formed the background to her first novel, *Everyone's Got a Bono Story*. She now lives in Manchester, where she spends her time writing. She has written plays for both theatre and radio. *My Made-Up Life* is her second novel.

Also by Anne-Marie O'Connor

EVERYONE'S GOT A BONO STORY

ANNE-MARIE O'CONNOR

MY MADE-UP LIFE

Tivoli
An imprint of Gill & Macmillan Ltd
Hume Avenue
Park West
Dublin 12
with associated companies throughout the world
www.gillmacmillan.ie

© Anne-Marie O'Connor 2005
0 7171 3607 8

Print origination by TypeIT, Dublin
Printed and bound by Nørhaven Paperback A/S, Denmark

The paper used in this book is made from the wood pulp of managed forests. For every tree felled, at least one tree is planted, thereby renewing natural resources.

All rights reserved. No part of this publication may be copied, reproduced or transmitted in any form or by any means, without permission of the publishers.

A catalogue record is available for this book from the British Library.

1 3 5 4 2

This book is a work of fiction. Names, characters, places and incidents are either the product of the author's imagination or are used fictitiously. Any resemblance to actual events or locales or persons, living or dead, is entirely coincidental.

To Donal

Acknowledgements

I would like to thank everyone at Gill & Macmillan for all their hard work. Alison Walsh and Deirdre Nolan for their help, enthusiasm and great editing. Michael Gill, Cliona Lewis, Dearbhaile Curran, Nicki Howard, Anita Ruane, Aoileann O'Donnell, Peter Thew, Paul Neilan and Chris Carroll (who does a great tour of Dublin if anyone's interested).

Tana French, for her brilliant, eagle-eyed editing. Geraldine Nichol, for everything she has done. James Holland, for his reading and feedback and for being responsible for most of the colons in this book. Jane Chapman, for the same. Fiona Behan and George Browne for their help and advice; hurry up and teach those daughters of yours to read so that they can join in. Dave Haley, for his accountancy, which, contrary to popular belief, involves slightly more than free booze and slap-up lunches; well, every now and again it does. Caz Boaz, for knowing the Stone Roses and for giving me a nosey into the world of advertising, along with Matt Crosby and Rich Sorensen. (Making things up off the top of your head for a living! What sort of a job is that?). Don Callaghan, for the house and the Communion tree. Claire McGettrick and everyone at Adoption Ireland (adoptionireland.com) for giving me an insight into how they work, helping to make the difficult and emotional process of tracing birth parents and children given up for adoption more bearable. Helen Gallagher at UCD, for her help with admissions information. Terry Carberry and all at the Eason's warehouse, and all the booksellers of Ireland. Danny Brocklehurst, for advice on writing and general fun and silly stories (there's your reference). All of the Irish Girls, for your advice, warmth and lovely food – especially Sarah Webb, who has been so kind.

My family, for their support and for always being at the other end of the phone. The Byrnes, for their kindness and hospitality. My friends, for being supportive, caring and funny (you're not all *that* funny, so don't go trying stand-up or anything).

Donal, for everything – especially for listening to me drivelling on about all the different ideas I have. (You're right: the story didn't warrant a boy wizard.)

Prologue

This wasn't the first time Ciara had found herself at the end of an evening that should have drawn to a close at around midnight, after a few sociable glasses of wine, but that had instead degenerated into tequila-slamming mayhem. It was, however, the first time she had found herself being swung by her ankles from Dublin's Millennium Bridge at four o'clock in the morning. At the back of her drunken mind she knew she should be terrified, but she was actually quite enjoying herself.

'Put me down!' she squealed, giggling as the blood rushed to her head.

'Tick-tock, tick-tock,' Scott said as he swung her from side to side. Through the railings, Ciara could see Laura stomping towards them, her face like thunder.

'Scott, what the hell do you think you're doing? You'll kill her.' Laura grabbed one of Ciara's ankles and began to yank her unceremoniously back over the railings. 'Yes?' she snapped at a group of young men who had gathered to see what exactly was going on.

'Ow!' Ciara drunkenly objected, as her chest scraped against the railings. 'That hurts.'

'Well, it's better than ending up in the Liffey.'

Scott grabbed Ciara around the waist and hoisted her back onto the bridge. 'We were only messing,' he complained, like a scolded child.

'Yeah, well, there's messing and there's acting like irresponsible idiots. You could have dropped her, and then what?'

Ciara felt a giggle welling up in her chest. She attempted to stifle it, but Laura's narkiness and the silliness of the situation were too much for her: she exploded into fits of laughter.

Laura threw her a look of disdain. 'Oh, forget it. I'm going home. Throw her in the river for all I care; you're as stupid as each other.'

'Ooh!' Ciara and Scott said in stereo, pulling imaginary handbags up to their chests and falling about laughing again. Laura stormed off.

'Laura, don't be like that!' Ciara shouted after her. But it was too late: she had stomped across the bridge and disappeared behind Eliza Blue's.

'Come on, let's get you home,' Scott said, heading in the same direction.

'I don't live that way. I live over there in Smithfield,' Ciara said, pointing.

'Oh, OK. Well, I'm off back to Ranelagh. You'll be OK walking on your own, won't you?'

'Yeah, of course.'

Who said chivalry was dead? Ciara thought, as she wandered alone towards her apartment. Not that there was anything for Scott to be chivalrous about. He was just a regular in the bar where Ciara worked; and, besides, she lived with her boyfriend Declan. Scott was just good for a laugh and always ready for an impromptu night out. He could still have walked her home, though, Ciara thought. She hoped Declan would be awake when she got in. She rummaged in her coat pocket for her mobile and sent him a text: 'Hi Dec, on way home, I love you xxx.'

Her phone beeped almost immediately and she grabbed it, glad that Declan was awake.

'It's 4 in the morning, where have you been? I've an early start tomorrow so be quiet when you get in.' Ciara winced: *I'm in the doghouse, again.* 'P.S. Who's www, why do you loud them and what's a gheab?'

Ciara read it three times before deciding to check the message she had sent him. It read, 'Gheab, on way good, I loud you www.'

Damn predictive text, Ciara thought as she wobbled her way back home, hoping that Declan wasn't in too much of a mood with her.

1

Ciara was home. Manchester, England. But this was not the triumphant homecoming she had always envisaged for herself – far from it. Standing by the baggage carousel watching the neatly packed cases roll past, she shifted uncomfortably. She couldn't believe that people had actually had the forethought to put coloured ribbons on their bags in order to differentiate them from all the others. Not having had the time or the forethought even to zip her bags up properly, never mind adorn them with haberdashery, she waited impatiently, foot tapping, for the overstuffed, lumpy backpacks containing the material sum of her life in Dublin to emerge.

After about twenty minutes all the other passengers from Ciara's flight had reclaimed their bags, leaving her alone to watch a suitcase apparently left by an evacuee during the Second World War make its way past her for the fifteenth time. Her bags were lost, Ciara concluded, just before they lurched – apologetically last – through the flaps towards her.

She dragged them onto her trolley and, taking a deep breath, headed towards the Customs exit marked 'EU countries'. She knew that, if she thought about what she had left behind and what she was about to face, she might spontaneously combust into a teary heap.

The doors opened into the arrivals hall. There was something very dramatic about airport doors, Ciara thought, something a bit *Stars in Their Eyes* ('Tonight, Matthew, I'm going to be a complete fool!'). She scoured the hall for a familiar face. She needn't have worried: there were six of them waiting for her.

She saw her eldest sister, Maeve, first. *What the hell is she doing here?* Ciara thought. *Shouldn't she be sewing up some multi-million-pound business deal or inventing a cure for cancer or jetting off to South America?* Maeve, of course, looked immaculate. Ciara always complained that Maeve had got all the alpha-female bits from the family gene pool: she was five foot nine, with full lips, a perfectly straight nose and cheekbones you could hang a coat on.

The rest of the Coffey children, although they resembled Maeve, all had their little flaws. Her own were plain to see, Ciara thought mournfully: her nose was slightly crooked, her eyebrows were too thin and she always felt a foot shorter than Maeve – who was looking at her with a mixture of pity and fake bonhomie that made her want to vomit.

Next to Maeve was their mother, Margaret. The look of worry on her face was criminal; she was wringing her hands as if she were awaiting delivery of a body bag rather than a daughter. Beside her was Ciara's father, Sean Coffey, his arms crossed, his feet firmly planted on the floor. He was wearing a stoic look – one that Ciara couldn't quite read and that frankly scared her to death. Next to him was Anthony, Ciara's younger brother, frantically texting someone and paying no attention to what was going on around him.

Then there was Claire, Ciara's other big sister. When Ciara and Claire were younger, they had been close; even though they had grown apart as they got older, in times of crisis Claire was still the member of the family whom Ciara was most likely to confide in. She wanted to hear Claire tell her that everything was going to be all right and not to mind what that nasty Maeve had to say. Ciara nearly broke into a run to get to her, but the last face she saw kept her to a walk. It was Michael, Maeve's perfect husband – *Perfect wanker*, Ciara thought as her heart, which had done its fair share of sinking over the past twenty-four hours, fell from her knees to her feet. *What's he doing here?*

Claire hurried towards Ciara and hugged her tightly, whispering in her ear as she pulled her close, 'Whatever's happened, it's going to be OK.' The words made Ciara well up; she felt hot tears falling down her cheeks.

Her mother hugged her briskly, rubbing her back as if trying to wind a child, then held her at arm's length to get a proper look at her. 'Is this it, then? Are you back for good?' She was immediately scolded by a look from Claire.

Ciara shook her head in shock. She hadn't really thought about it properly, but as she allowed the reality of what she was doing to sink in, she realised that she couldn't be back for good. This had to be temporary: she had a whole life in Ireland that she'd just left behind.

Sean nodded. 'Ciara,' was all he said by way of acknowledgement. Ciara felt as if she was in trouble, but that was how she always felt when her father was around. He squeezed her shoulder, which made her feel slightly better, before taking one of her bags and nodding in the direction of the car park.

Then it was Maeve's turn. 'Ciara, I am so, *so* sorry that you and Declan have split up,' she gushed, with such ferocity that the backdraft nearly nailed Ciara to the revolving doors. Hearing Declan's name made her feel as if she had been kicked in the stomach, but she didn't have much time to think about it: she was immediately and dramatically buried in her sister's DKNY-wrapped bosom. As she pulled her head back for air, Michael clasped her hand and kissed her on the cheek. *Bleurghh! Get off me!* Ciara wanted to scream.

'Shall we?' Sean asked, rallying the troops. Ciara nodded, and everyone followed him in uncomfortable silence. Ciara hung back, with Claire linking her arm; Anthony slipped his mobile in his pocket and joined them.

'All right, sis?' he asked. Ciara looked at him. He was seventeen now, and he looked great, she thought, half envious, half admiring. She wished she were seventeen again. In fact, she realised, at that moment she wished she were anyone or anywhere but herself and here.

'Not really.' She tried to smile, and Claire squeezed her hand.

'You're better off without him,' Anthony said matter-of-factly.

Hearing her little brother have a grown-up opinion sparked something in Ciara. 'Do you think so?' she asked, intrigued. Anthony had met Declan a few times, and Declan had told Ciara that they'd always got along famously. They'd gone to a football match together, been to Laser Quest; Declan had even taken Anthony out for his first pint, in Dublin.

'He was all right and everything, and he took me

out and that – but, well, I just thought…' Anthony paused, gathering his thoughts.

'Go on,' Ciara urged.

'Well, actually, I was going to make something up to make you feel better, but he was dead sound.'

Ciara sniffed wryly. *Great,* she thought. That was Declan all over: everyone thought he was great. *He's not great!* Ciara wanted to shout at Anthony, or anyone else who would listen. *He's horrible, low-life scum!*

'Well, I wouldn't want you to be nasty about him on my account,' she said instead.

'What's happened, then? Why's he done your head in so much?'

'It doesn't matter, Ant. It's a long story.'

Anthony raised an eyebrow and looked away. Ciara could tell that long stories about his sisters' ex-boyfriends weren't his favourite topic. Claire squeezed Ciara's arm, and they walked in silence to the car.

The car ride home was fairly uneventful. Margaret informed Ciara that two people she had never heard of had died: 'You *do,* you know Mrs Callaghan; you do. She used to always hang around with Mrs Fitzpatrick – you *do,* she was the nosey one with the hat. Well, her husband died.' Ciara begged Claire, with her eyes, to make their mother stop talking, but there wasn't much chance of that. Margaret didn't like uncomfortable silences, and she was intent on filling the air with anything that came to mind – as long as it didn't touch on the reasons for her daughter's sudden and unexpected homecoming.

Ciara sat back and let her mother's monologue wash over her. Her father had the car heater on full blast, making her shuffle uncomfortably. Margaret fanned herself with a leaflet from an operatic event at a nearby stately home, and everyone, including Sean, looked as if they were having a particularly difficult menopause, but Ciara couldn't be bothered to ask him to adjust the heat. She was relieved that Maeve and Michael weren't there to add their twopence-worth, but she was sure that was something she could look forward to when they got back to the house.

Maeve and Michael were following Sean's Rover in their Mercedes SLK, Michael's new toy. 'What do you think of the beast?' he had asked Ciara in the airport car park. Claire had kicked her.

'It's nice,' had been all Ciara could manage. Michael had been visibly disappointed that she hadn't been so excited that she straddled the bonnet and writhed uncontrollably, like something out of a Mötley Crüe video. What she had really wanted to say was, 'Yeah, Claire told me you'd swapped the Lexus, and she also said she'd seen you at the gym wearing trunks, which is frankly unforgivable and points towards a mid-life crisis,' but of course she hadn't. She was as guilty as anyone of keeping up the paper-thin veneer of civility that prevented her from being honest with family members.

The journey home took less than fifteen minutes. Ciara stared out at the familiar sights of Manchester – the white, imposing pharmaceutical-company building that marked the beginning of Didsbury; the painfully cool shops of Burton Road, full of overpriced knick-knacks and unusable *objets d'art*. 'Look at this road,' Claire said, nudging her, trying to cheer her up. 'You could open a shop selling turds, and people would buy them because it's in West Didsbury.' They passed the pubs and restaurants of leafy Lapwing Lane and drove along the tree-lined Palatine Road. Ciara grudgingly admired the surroundings. She always forgot how green Manchester was in parts; she was happy to perpetuate the myth, to people who'd never been there, that it was a dreary Lowry painting of a place and wetter than the Brazilian rain forests.

Sean swung the car into the drive. 'Here we are: home sweet home,' he bellowed. Ciara felt strangely lonely. It might be home, but she wasn't altogether sure what she was doing there. She climbed out of the car and looked up at the house. It was a huge, five-bedroom terraced house in Withington, an urban village about four miles from the city centre. The ivy was still crawling up the walls and over the original stained-glass windows. Ciara peered into the back garden, and there stood the four trees that the Coffey children had planted on their Communion days. Ciara noticed that hers was still the weakest of the four; it looked like a bundle of twigs with a few leaves taped to it, whereas Maeve's was like a particularly voracious redwood.

'Come on, then,' Sean instructed, 'let's get you in the house.'

'I'll put the kettle on,' Margaret said. Ciara shook her head and looked at Claire; their mother believed that the world's problems could be smoothed over with a cup of PG Tips.

'Where shall I put my stuff?' Ciara asked, as Claire held open the front door. There was one thing about home, she noticed, that never changed: the smell. It was a mixture of washing powder, cooking and the central heating, which was always on, even in the middle of summer. Usually, when Ciara came home, she felt quietly comforted by this smell; but now it had the opposite effect. It made her wonder if her flat in Dublin had its own smell, and this in turn made her think about Declan and where he'd been wafting his aroma the previous night... Before she knew it, she was angry and upset again.

Ciara realised that Claire was watching her with curiosity as she stood at the bottom of the stairs, sniffing the air like one of the Bisto kids. 'Sorry – home always smells the same,' she explained. Claire nodded, but Ciara knew that she could have licked the wall and said, 'Ah! Home – the walls always taste the same,' and Claire would have nodded to keep her happy.

'Where shall I dump my stuff?' she asked.

'Your room, I presume.'

'Come on, Claire, my room's not been *my* room for six years.'

It was true. The wheels of the plane taking Ciara to Ireland for the first time had barely lifted from the runway before Margaret had chintzed the room up beyond recognition. Gone were Ciara's posters and Mod target bedspread; in had come a graveyard for yellow pelmets and frills and borders. Lace doilies the world over had apparently got wind of this abomination and made their way there, salmon-like, to claim a fitting resting-place. Ciara threw her bags on the floor anyway. She sat down slowly on the edge of the bed and took in her surroundings, trying to believe that this really was her home – yellow or not.

Claire sat down next to her and put a hand on her knee. 'Come on, then; spill it. What's happened?'

Ciara took a deep breath and prepared to tell her sister why she had left Ireland and Declan so suddenly. After being dragged out of bed at two o'clock that morning by a panic-stricken phone call, the least Claire deserved was a decent explanation.

2

Declan slammed the door shut behind him and shuddered as he stepped onto Camden Street. He strode purposefully in the direction of the Liffey and Smithfield, where his own apartment was waiting for him.

Declan felt terrible. The fact that, over the past forty-eight hours, he had drunk enough pints to kill a small cow wasn't helping; but he felt awful for another reason. He hadn't been home for two nights. The first had been fairly innocent – an advertising awards ceremony that had gone on till the early hours – but last night…

He popped into a café to grab a coffee and clear his head. The girl behind the counter smiled at him as he ordered a cappuccino. Declan was used to girls smiling at him, and usually he smiled politely back; but today he just didn't have it in him. Guilt was rampaging up and down his veins like a herd of elephants, and he wanted it to go away. He wanted to rewind back to last night, call Ciara and ask her to meet him. Then they would have gone home together and everything would have been fine…

But Declan knew, deep down, that it wouldn't have worked out like that. Things had been bad between him and Ciara for a long time. If he had invited her into town, they would have begun arguing after an hour in each other's company. This had been the pattern for at least the past six months, and Declan was sick to death of it.

He accepted the coffee, weakly acknowledging the girl behind the counter. Then he sat down, pulled out his mobile and dialled Ciara's number.

'This is a recorded message from Eircom. The number you have dialled is unavailable…'

'Bollocks!' Declan sighed, shaking his head. 'Answer your bloody phone, Ciara!' A pang of guilt gnawed at his stomach, but he quickly drowned it with cappuccino. After redialling her number four times and getting the same message, he assumed that Ciara was probably in a complete fouler with him for not coming home last night. He gulped the rest of his coffee and thought, with the self-righteousness of the guilty, that she had no reason to be in a mood with him; she was out more than he was.

He dialled the apartment and beckoned the waitress for the bill. She brought it over just in time to see the blood drain from Declan's face. It had also drained from every other part of his body. The mild panic of the previous moment was nothing compared to the full rigor mortis of being found out.

There had been no reply, and as the answering machine clicked into motion, Declan had become agitated by Ciara's familiar voice at the other end of the phone – he wanted to speak to her, not to some machine. She had insisted on changing his Roy Keane message for a more sedate one: 'Hi, you've reached Declan and Ciara. We're not here to…' And then Declan's thoughts had come to a shuddering halt as he realised that what he was hearing wasn't the usual message. Far from it.

He could tell immediately – from her tone, and from the fact that her Manchester accent, which was usually quite soft, had reached Liam Gallagher levels – that Ciara was extremely annoyed.

'Hi, you've reached Declan. I'm not here to take your call because I'm out shagging the arse off this cow named Laura, who's meant to be my ex-girlfriend's friend. If you'd like to leave a message, please do so after the beep.'

Throwing a five-euro note onto the table, Declan ran out of the café and down South William Street, almost knocking over a handful of posing girls who weren't used to having their daily pouting disturbed. He shouted an apology over his shoulder and kept running. He ran onto Dame Street and through Temple Bar, and only stopped at the traffic lights by the Ha'penny Bridge because he thought his lungs were going to collapse. He had to get home. There had to be something he could say that would make things all right. Ciara always came round in the end… But he'd never slept with someone behind her back before. *How the hell did she know?* Declan thought, outraged. The only time he'd ever done anything like this, and she had to find out.

Declan wanted to kick himself. Last night had been terrible. Laura was a friend of Ciara's; they'd worked in the same city-centre bar for the past two years. Declan had arranged to meet her because he'd wanted to talk to someone who knew Ciara, who knew about their relationship. He'd needed some advice. He knew they were growing apart, and he'd thought that talking about it with Laura might help him understand what was going on in his girlfriend's head.

It hadn't. They had both got very drunk and ended up back at Laura's flat, and, judging by the hazy snapshots that were persistently flashing through Declan's mind, he had slept with her – no, not even slept with her; just had sex with her. He had woken up on the settee, trying to work out where he was. Laura's bedroom door had been bolted shut. She had reluctantly come out to see Declan as he was leaving; they had spent five minutes squirming in each other's company, talking about anything other than what they had done only hours earlier, before he had finally made a break for the door.

Declan couldn't believe what he had done. He lived with his girlfriend, and he loved her. He didn't shag her friends; apart from anything else, it was tacky. How had he got himself into this situation? And how on earth did Ciara know? She couldn't possibly – not for sure. She'd probably found out somehow that Declan had stayed at Laura's, but she couldn't know what had actually happened there. There was no way Laura would have said anything; she was equally mortified. Declan wanted to talk Ciara round, to convince her that it hadn't really happened. He didn't want to admit to it because he didn't want to hurt her.

He decided on a story. He would tell Ciara that someone had spiked his drink, and that he'd gone to Laura's flat because he'd bumped into her and she lived near town. He knew the alibi had holes – their own flat was so near the city centre that he could jump out of the window and land in the Liffey – but he didn't have much time or material to work with.

Pulling open the door of the apartment block, Declan tried to gulp down the feeling of foreboding that was lodged in his throat. When he got to the pub that evening he would tell his best friend, Barry, that he felt terrible because he loved Ciara;

but he wouldn't be sure if he really meant it. Things had been so bad between him and Ciara recently that he wasn't sure what he felt any more. All he knew was that, if things were finally going to come to a head, he didn't want it to be because of his own foolish indiscretion.

By the time he got into the flat, Declan was so wound up that it came as a minor relief to discover that Ciara wasn't actually there. Almost immediately, though, he began to panic again. He wanted this over and done with. He didn't want to wait around until Ciara had calmed down enough to come back and confront him.

Making his way into the bedroom, Declan immediately sensed that something wasn't quite right. He ran to his wardrobe and flung the doors open, his imagination whirling with visions of Ciara hacking his clothes to ribbons and poisoning the dog he didn't have; but everything was as he had left it. Breathing a sigh of relief, he sat on the bed to take off his shoes. He was still in his clothes from the previous evening, and he smelled like a brewery. He needed a shower, but the logistics were too much for him. Falling back on the bed, Declan pulled the pillows under his head and stretched his arms out like the crucified Christ, which he considered very apt under the circumstances.

As he turned his head, though, he noticed something that made him leap from the bed like a scalded pup. Ciara's wardrobe was empty. He checked the cupboard where she kept all her photographs: nothing. He ran into the bathroom: her make-up and lotion bottles were gone. He hunted high and low for some kind of note, anything, to tell him where she was: nothing.

In the bedroom again, he picked up a picture of himself and Ciara. For a moment he wondered why she hadn't smashed it, but that wasn't how Ciara was. She didn't slash clothes, she didn't throw pictures across the room – and she didn't pack up all her belongings and vanish unless, Declan thought, sliding down the wall into a self-pitying heap, unless she meant it. He looked at the picture: him and Ciara standing by a slab of Neolithic rock in Newgrange, grinning. She looked gorgeous. Her blond hair was pulled back from her face, and her bright blue eyes were sparkling out at him as she laughed.

Declan wanted to cry – it would do him good, he thought morosely – but he couldn't. The tears wouldn't come. He knew he should feel loss or something, but the only real feeling he had, at that moment, was confusion. Maybe he was in shock, he thought. He did know that he needed Ciara, and that he had to find her and sort this out.

Where could she be? he thought, over and over. He rang Barian, the bar where Ciara worked, but they said she wasn't expected in that day. He rang a couple of Ciara's friends, but nobody knew anything. He tried Jimmy and Róisín, old college friends of hers, but Róisín asked warily why he thought she might have seen Ciara, and he realised he was grasping at straws. The last time Ciara and Róisín had met hadn't exactly been an episode of *Friends*.

He thought of hanging around in Sin nightclub for half an hour – he was bound to bump into some acquaintances of Ciara's in there; but she wouldn't have turned to any of that shower for help. He would have called Laura, but the only way Ciara would have gone there was if she was planning to suffocate the girl with a rucksack full of clothes.

The only other people he could think of were Ciara's sisters. One of them might have an idea where she was. Pulling out the Golden Pages, he found the Coffey family's numbers scrawled on the front page.

Declan looked at the numbers. Just the idea of dialling any of them filled him with dread. He couldn't do it. He would sit it out, he thought: give it a couple of hours to see if she contacted him. Then, if she didn't, he'd call Claire and see if she'd heard anything.

Declan slid himself across the wooden floorboards towards his DVDs and reached for his favourite film, to take his mind off the shambolic mess he had got himself into. He thought maybe he should call Laura and warn her that Ciara knew, but he couldn't be bothered. He wanted to hide in a hole and make it all go away. He didn't want to admit, even to himself, what he had done. He was utterly ashamed.

Gazing at his DVD collection, Declan forgot all the bad times he and Ciara had had lately. He could think of her only as someone without a bad bone in her body – until he opened the *Goodfellas* case and discovered the disc wasn't there. He grabbed *Scarface* – gone. *Fight Club* – nowhere to be seen. Declan riffled through his hundred-strong DVD collection, his pride and joy, and realised there wasn't a single disc left.

The good cry he'd been wanting came to him with sudden ease. He sat among his DVD boxes, thinking of Ciara, and sobbed into the collector's-edition case of *My Cousin Vinny*.

3

Ciara sighed and looked at her sister. In the early hours of that morning she had called Claire, who had just been dropping off to sleep, and sobbed incoherently. She had been so snotty and upset that she could barely get her breath, but she had managed to convey that she would be on the first flight to Manchester in the morning, and that Declan was the biggest arsehole on the planet. In the morning she had texted Claire to say that she would be in at nine o'clock, and could she come to collect her?

'Listen, sorry about the entourage,' Claire said, 'but I was dead upset. You weren't really making much sense last night. So I called Mum – which was stupid, I know, because she overreacted, like she does about everything, and dragged everyone in on it. When she said Maeve was coming, I thought, *Ciara's going to kill me.*'

Ciara shook her head. 'It's fine. It was nice to see everyone, in a really weird way – even Maeve. I wouldn't have thought she'd come, though; she probably just wanted to show off the car.' She smiled, then took a deep breath. 'So…where shall I start?'

Claire shrugged her shoulders.

'OK,' Ciara began. 'You know Laura?' Claire shrugged again; Ciara often talked about an ever-changing cast of friends in Dublin.

'She worked with me in the bar. Well, anyway, last night she slept with Declan.' Ciara welled up as she heard the words come out of her mouth.

Claire put her arms around her. 'I can't believe it,' she said quietly.

'I know…' Ciara began to sob uncontrollably. She had been holding back the tears; she didn't want to be a weeping heap.

'It's fine. Go on; just tell me when you're ready.'

'Right.' Ciara took a deep breath and, gripping a frilly cushion to steady herself, rushed to tell Claire the gist of what had happened, before she thought about what she was saying and the tears began again. 'I couldn't get hold of Declan – he'd been at some advertising awards ceremony the night before and stayed at his friend Barry's, and' – she took another breath – 'he had his phone off. And things haven't been too good, as you know, so I just thought, *Fuck him*, and went to the gym. When I got back I had a glass of wine and was going to just go out and meet a few people, but then my mobile rang and it was Declan's number. I answered it and said, "Where the bloody hell have you been?" – I was really angry with him by now – but he wasn't actually on the phone; he'd just knocked it and called me by accident. And I could hear him...' Ciara's voice began to crack. 'And her. It was Laura, I'd know her voice anywhere, and they were...' She broke into sobs again.

Claire held her head to her shoulder and stroked her hair. 'It's OK,' she soothed. 'You're home now. It's going to be fine.'

'It's not, though, is it?' Ciara sat back, streaky-faced and wild-eyed. 'I heard my boyfriend shagging someone else last night!'

'Look, Ciara,' Claire began tentatively, 'are you absolutely one hundred per cent sure that's what you heard?'

'Of course I am!' Ciara shrieked. 'Do you think I'm stupid?'

'I'm sorry.' Claire looked as if she wished she'd never opened her mouth. 'I'm sorry – I shouldn't have said that.'

Ciara flushed, feeling foolish. 'No, I'm sorry. I shouldn't be taking your head off; I know you're trying to help. But yes, that's definitely what I heard.' She put her head in her hands. Claire put her arms around her sister again, and Ciara sobbed, feeling as if her heart was breaking.

'Hi,' Ciara said sheepishly, pushing open the door to Anthony's room.

'Hi,' he said, swinging around on his bed to face her.

'I suppose you heard all that.'

'Heard what?'

Ciara smiled – he obviously didn't want to have an embarrassing conversation about his sister's caterwauling – and pulled a carrier bag from behind her back. 'Anyway, never mind that. I've got something for you.'

'What is it?' Anthony opened the bag to reveal Declan's DVDs. 'Wicked! Where'd you get these?' he asked, pulling them out one by one. Then a grin of realisation broke across his face. 'Ohhh... Cheers, Ciara!'

'No problem,' she said, smiling back. But she didn't really feel like smiling. She had expected to feel some sort of triumph – *Ah-ha! Got you back, bastardo! Don't cross me again!* – but she didn't. The sound of her boyfriend having sex with her friend was ringing in her ears, and all the DVD redistribution in the world wasn't going to change that.

She headed downstairs, peering over the banister: her dad was sitting at the dining-room table, reading the *Irish Independent* and sipping a cup of tea. It was now or never, she thought. She was going to have to give her parents some form of explanation. She went into the dining room; Sean looked up from the paper.

'Feeling any better?' he asked, giving Ciara the intense look that he used to give her when she got nine As and one B and he wanted to know where the B had come from.

'A bit.' Ciara nodded. 'Look, Dad, I just want you to know I'm really grateful that you've all been so good – coming to get me this morning and all that.' The words were sticking slightly in her throat. She hated grovelling to her father, for two reasons: first, she wasn't very good at it, and second, it didn't wash one little bit. 'Well, anyway, I think you deserve an explanation of why I've come back like this.'

Sean folded his fingers into a steeple, placed his elbows firmly on the table, and waited for his daughter to get to the point. Suddenly, Ciara realised that she really hadn't thought this through. She was going to have a hard time being completely truthful about the nature of her return to Manchester.

Her parents lived in a liberal urban area, but that was a coincidence, not a lifestyle choice. Back in the 60s, they had liked the look of the big Victorian terraced house, but that didn't mean they had transformed into the left-leaning urbanites who became their neighbours over the years. The Coffeys' personal philosophies on life, as far as Ciara could see, were as near to the Pope's as was possible. Sean was the head teacher at the nearby Catholic high school, and Margaret was a part-time secretary at the northern office of the Catholic paper, *The Light*.

If Penny, the daughter of her parents' neighbours – Lou the social worker and Colin the housing officer – had come home and told them she had caught her boyfriend *in flagrante delicto* with her so-called friend, they would have hugged her and told her that it obviously wasn't meant to be and that she needed space to get over it and time to get to know herself. Sean and Margaret, on the other hand, didn't even realise Ciara had had sex with Declan, never mind lived with him. The concept of him having sex with someone else was completely beyond the realms of their reality.

As Ciara was trying to shape her open-mouthed stuttering into something coherent, her mother came into the dining room. 'How are you?' she asked, pushing Ciara's hair back out of her face.

'She's just about to tell us what's driven her back from home.' Ciara stiffened. Her father always did this. It was fair enough that he called Ireland 'home' – he had been born there, even if he had been living in England for thirty-five years – but he had the habit of referring to it as everyone else's home as well, as in, 'Margaret, did you see that on the telly there – wasn't Nelson Mandela home the other day?'

'Well, I thought you'd tell us in your own time,' Margaret said, wiping her hands on the tea-towel draped over her shoulder.

'Yeah, well, you deserve to know.' Ciara paused. 'I've split up with Declan.'

Sean and Margaret looked at her and waited for the real explanation.

'And – well, the thing is…' She grabbed at thin air, wanting, as always, to give her parents an explanation that fit into their paradigm of the world and how it should be. 'The Irish economy's not been great recently, and they had to let a lot of people go at work, and I' – she took a deep breath and looked down at her hands, which she was wringing in her lap – 'I was one of them.' Where was this coming from?

'And so you just upped sticks and left? Just like that?' Margaret asked, incredulous.

'Yeah. It wasn't quite that straightforward, but I just needed to get away for a while.' Ciara knew, as she so often did when she tried to explain anything to her parents, that she was digging a huge hole for herself and she was going to regret it as soon as the conversation was over.

Margaret sighed. 'Well, I don't know what to think. I'd have thought there was everything in Dublin for you. You've got a great degree, from a great university…'

Ciara shifted uncomfortably in her chair. 'Well, I didn't say I was definitely staying, did I?'

'You've just said there's no work in Ireland. And you've turned up here with little or no warning, bringing most of your belongings, from what I can gather. I just assumed you were staying.'

Ciara folded her arms defensively. Margaret seemed disappointed. Ciara hated disappointing her parents and duly went out of her way to avoid it – which often led her to tell them things that weren't, strictly speaking, true. 'Well, I can't help what you assumed,' she sniffed.

'I will not have you talk to your mother like that.' Sean smacked the *Irish Independent* against the table like a man who meant business.

'I'm sorry, Dad.' Ciara felt herself tremble under her father's disapproval. 'I'm just upset, and I came back because...' She needed her father to say that she was doing the right thing; and she knew that, for him to do that, she would have to pull something out of the bag, and quickly. 'I missed you all. I think I was getting fed up in Ireland.'

Sean softened slightly, much to Ciara's relief. 'Well, if you missed us, you only had to call and we could have arranged this a bit better.'

'I know,' Ciara nodded, 'I know. But I'm here now.' She shrugged and half-smiled at her father. Once again she had tried, momentarily, to be adult and truthful with her parents – and once again she had failed miserably.

He smiled back approvingly. 'Well, first thing Monday morning, why don't you go into town and sign up with some recruitment agencies?'

Ciara swallowed hard and tried to disguise her alarm. 'I hadn't really thought about that – I was just going to...' She broke off weakly.

Just going to what? she thought. *Wallow in self-pity for a while and then go back to my bar job in Ireland and work alongside Laura? Not likely. Go back in a screaming rage, tackle Declan and Laura head-on, and hope everything will be all right and I can pick up where I left off?* After this disappearing act, she wouldn't even have a job to go back to; she had already been on her last warning after ringing in sick once too often.

And she wasn't sure where she could turn for support in Dublin any more. If she had been, she wouldn't have flown to the highly demanding bosom of her family. Most of Ciara's good friends in Ireland, friends she had made when she first went to university, had got themselves onto the career and property ladders, now that they were all twenty-five – and, as far as Ciara was concerned, they had become boring and sensible way before their time. They sat around talking about the brutal house prices and the fact that they couldn't even afford a turf shed in Sallins, rather than about where the next all-night party was going to be.

'That's a great idea,' Margaret said. 'In fact' – a thought suddenly occurred to her – 'that's what

Michael does, isn't it, Sean? Maeve's Michael – he's a recruitment consultant. You can ask him. They should be here by now; I wonder where they've got to.'

Ciara groaned inwardly. *Not Michael*, she thought, a fake fixed grin of joy plastered across her face. Michael helping her get a job... *What a thoroughly depressing idea*, she thought, just as Maeve popped her head through the patio door.

'Hi! Sorry we're late. We took a bit of a detour; Michael decided we needed to stop off at that knick-knack shop in Didsbury to buy this.' She produced her purchase from a painfully cool carrier bag.

'What the hell is that?' Sean asked.

'It's a Philippe Starck lemon-squeezer,' Michael explained.

'Looks like an implement of torture,' Sean said, unimpressed.

'It's a design classic.'

'Well for it,' Sean said, slipping his glasses back onto his nose and returning to his paper. Ciara smirked.

'Do you need to talk about anything?' Maeve asked. Seeing that Ciara had been crying, she pulled her into their second bear hug of the hour.

Ciara winced. Maeve wasn't very good at offering sympathy; she was like someone trying to stroke a baby's head with a mallet. On top of everything, she had their parents as the approving audience to this sisterly concern.

'No, no. Really, Maeve…' Ciara pushed her sister away, gently but firmly. 'I'll be fine.'

'Do you need me to do anything?' Maeve asked.

'No, Maeve, seriously. I'm just really upset about Declan, that's all.'

'Well, if you do, you only have to give me a shout.'

'I know,' Ciara said firmly. 'I said I'm fine.'

'Will you just come upstairs with me a minute?' Maeve asked. She smiled at their parents.

Ciara felt her heart sink – she was sure Maeve just wanted to prove what a fantastic eldest daughter she was. When they were younger it had been exactly the same: Maeve knew best – or at least she thought she did; she always wanted to help Ciara solve her problems, even if she didn't have any. But she wasn't doing it out of the kindness of her heart. Ciara firmly believed that everything Maeve did in life was a competition. At school, it didn't matter what Ciara achieved – winning sporting medals, public-speaking contests and writing competitions, gaining top grades in her exams; it always seemed that Maeve had already been there, done that and bought the T-shirt. Teachers went all dewy-eyed at the mere thought of their ex-star pupil. Ciara was always 'Maeve's sister'. Claire had never been compared to Maeve in the same way; Ciara put it down to the fact that there was little family resemblance between the two, but the difference wasn't just physical. Claire had rarely been dragged into the self-imposed family competition when they were growing up – she had always preferred to do her own thing. Even her decision to become a teacher had had nothing to do with following in her father's footsteps; it had been because of a genuine liking for young people. Ciara wished she could be more like Claire.

Despite herself, she gritted her teeth and followed obediently behind Maeve. *What pearls of wisdom will the blueprint for perfection have for me today?* she wondered.

Maeve sat down at the top of the stairs, her head cocked to one side in concern.

'What's this? Kilroy?' Ciara asked.

Maeve straightened her back and laughed, a quick, staccato laugh. 'No, I just thought we'd be out of earshot. We can go in one of the bedrooms if you prefer.'

Ciara shrugged. 'Here's OK. Look, Maeve, I've had a shitty few days, that's all – nothing any of you lot can do anything about. I'll be OK.'

'And what's happened with Declan?'

Ciara looked away. 'Nothing. I don't want to talk about it, OK? He's just been a shit, that's all.'

'Well, I'm sure you're better off without him anyway,' Maeve said. 'You're home now. You can get yourself a proper job over here and you'll be fine.'

'What?' Ciara spat.

'Don't raise your voice, Ciara. I'm only saying—'

'What is it with you? "You're home now,"' she mimicked in a screechy voice. 'In case you haven't noticed, I live in *Dublin*! And as for getting myself a "proper job" – what, as opposed to the pretend job I had in Ireland? I worked as an account handler for an advertising agency – is that not *proper* enough for you?' She glared at her sister, daring her to argue. 'We can't all be accountancy robots, Maeve. Sorry to disappoint you.'

Maeve was, in fact, under the impression that Ciara had had a good job in Ireland. Ciara had told her family that she was working in an advertising firm, just like Declan. She would have said she was an astronaut or a horse whisperer or something equally talented and unachievable, but this way kept the lie manageable. Every time she came home, she had added to the story; by now it was probably a surprise to all of them that the Irish advertising industry was able to manage without the magical Ciara touch.

Maeve got to her feet and said, keeping her voice low, 'I wasn't saying your job wasn't a good one. I'm just saying that you can get an equally good one here, if you want – if you're going to stay, which I presumed you were, seeing as you turned up at the airport laden down like a packhorse.'

'Don't talk to me like a child! You're not my boss, Maeve, just because you're older than me.'

'If you snap at me like a child, I'll treat you like one.'

Ciara was on her feet at the top of the stairs, jabbing a finger in Maeve's direction. 'Sod you and your proper jobs! You're just a stuck-up cow, and—'

She didn't have a chance to finish her sentence: Maeve grabbed the top of her arm in something like a Vulcan Death Grip. 'Listen to me, you spoilt little shit...' Her usual Received Pronunciation had dropped away into harsh Mancunian tones.

At this point Claire flew up the stairs and jumped between her sisters, holding them apart at arm's length.

'Maeve, stop it! She's really upset; can't you see that? You can discuss this later.'

'Well, I tell you what: that is the last time I drag myself out of bed on a Saturday morning to come and get *you* from the airport,' Maeve said huffily, as if her last few hundred Saturday mornings had been filled with trips to Terminal 2.

'Get out!' Ciara shouted.

'I'm going!' Maeve hollered over her shoulder on her way down the stairs.

'What's going on here?' Sean demanded, as she flew past him.

'Leave it, Dad,' Maeve said sternly. 'Michael, come on – we're going.'

'What, now?'

'Yes, now. I've had about as much of her as I can take for one day.' Maeve stormed out of the front door. Michael followed, lemon-squeezer under arm.

'What's happened?' Margaret's voice quavered up the stairwell. 'You're only back two minutes and there's war!'

'Aargh!' Ciara shouted, exasperated.

'You didn't even ask Michael about getting you a job –'

'I'll be down in a bit, Mum!' Ciara shouted. 'Tell her I can't hear her, Claire, I've gone deaf.'

Claire rolled her eyes as Ciara slammed her bedroom door. Outside, the screech of Mercedes tyres could be heard pulling off along the road.

4

Declan was utterly fed up. After kicking his DVD boxes around the room for a while, he had given himself a good talking-to; then, in a futile attempt to regain a semblance of normality, he had put them all back in alphabetical order again. He was now busy pacing round the flat.

There had been no sign of Ciara, and he was nearing his wits' end. Her phone was off – it wasn't even going to voice-mail. Declan couldn't for the life of him think where she might have gone.

Suddenly he lunged for the phone and dialled Laura's number. This was his fifth attempt, and this time he wasn't going to put the phone down before the first ring.

'Hello.' Laura's voice made his mouth dry up and a violent, thudding dread pulsate in the pit of his stomach.

'Hi...hi, Laura. This is Declan.'

'I know who it is.' Her voice was clipped.

'Yeah, yeah – well, em...' Declan grappled for words. 'The thing is that last night – well, it was great and everything...' He winced at his own lie. 'But I just – well, it's Ciara. She, em, she hasn't come home and—'

'Please spare me the "It was great" line, Declan,' Laura sighed. 'And, before you start, you don't have to tell me not to say anything to her. I'm hardly about to tell a friend that I've stupidly slept with her boyfriend, am I?'

Declan pulled his hand desperately through his short black hair. 'I wasn't, Laura. I was ringing to see if you'd heard from her.'

'Well, I haven't,' she snapped.

'And to tell you that she's found out somehow, I don't know how – but she knows, or so she says.'

'Shit! No, no, no!' There was a rising panic in Laura's voice. 'Tell me you're lying, Declan. Shit, this is fucked up! I am such an idiot... What the fuck was I doing – what the fuck were *we* doing?'

'Yes, she knows.' Declan let out a heavy sigh as Laura unravelled at the other end of the phone. He didn't have time for this. 'I just thought you should know.'

'That's big of you. Do you know how low I feel,

Declan? And it's your fault...' Laura was about to say something else, but Declan didn't want to hear it. He hung up.

'Shit!' he screamed in frustration, throwing his mobile across the room.

Once he had calmed down a little and his face had returned to something approaching its normal colour, Declan picked up the phone and called Barry. He desperately needed to see his best friend right now.

Barry and Declan worked together as a creative team at JMSS&A, Ireland's most successful advertising agency. Between the two of them, they had managed to convince the general public that drinking stout was akin to having an orgasm, buying flat-pack furniture was better than two weeks in the sun and fizzy orange juice was the new black.

Declan had trained in graphic design. When he met Barry, he had been working in a pub in Phibsboro and trying to piece together his portfolio. Barry had been desperately trying to get into copywriting, but the nearest he had got was unpaid work experience making cups of tea for other copywriters, at a small back-street company that dreamed up tag lines for leaflets advertising double-glazing and budget European food stores. They had put their heads and portfolios together, and – after a lot of broken promises and rejection letters from smug London agencies – pure luck had come to their rescue. The man charged with setting up the Dublin branch of JMSS&A had been drinking in the bar where Declan worked, and they had struck up a conversation about Dublin. This had eventually led to an interview for Declan and Barry, and they had been offered the position of creative team.

'Well?' Barry said, when he got to Declan's flat.

'Well, yourself?'

'Ah, you know the way. Story?'

Declan shrugged. 'This and that; you know how it is.'

'Out on the batter again last night?' Barry helped himself to a beer from the fridge. 'Want one?'

'No, thanks, I couldn't; my guts are in bits.' Declan rubbed his stomach. 'Yeah, I was on the lash all right.'

'Where'd you go? We were in Slattery's, of all places.'

'I was in Doheny's for most of the night.' Declan rubbed his hands over his face.

Barry sat down in the armchair and opened his can. 'Where's herself?' he asked, absentmindedly flicking the TV on.

'She's not here.'

'At work?' Barry flicked through the music channels and stopped on a video of Justin Timberlake. 'What is it with this yoke? He's just some little pubey-headed young fella. Just because he's shaved his head now, women are throwing their knickers at him from a five-mile radius.'

'I know.'

'Maybe I should shave my head?'

'Yeah, and have the belly surgically removed.'

Barry laughed and rubbed his ample stomach. 'All bought and paid for, this little beauty.'

They sat in silence until the end of the video; then Barry began channel-surfing again. 'What were we saying there?'

'When?'

'Before Pube-Head.'

'You were asking if Ciara was at work.'

'And is she?'

'No.' Declan put his head in his hands. 'She's gone, Barry.'

Barry sat up straight and left the Discovery Channel to its own devices. 'What – *gone*, gone?'

'I think so. All her stuff's gone, everything. And she's switched her phone off.'

'Ah…' Barry waved his hand dismissively. 'She'll come back. What did you two argue about this time?'

'We didn't argue. I shagged Laura, her mate from work.'

'You fucking eejit! You did *what*?' Barry looked at Declan as if he'd lost his mind.

'I know. And somehow she found out and left me this.' Declan played the answering-machine message for Barry, who bit his bottom lip and shuffled uncomfortably in his seat. 'Go on, laugh it up – I know you want to!' Declan shouted.

'I'm sorry – it's just… Well, that's pretty funny. For Ciara.'

'Ciara *is* funny!' Declan protested.

'All right! Jesus Christ. She fucks off and now you're defending her? I'm just saying that that message is pretty funny, under the circumstances.'

'What am I going to do? How am I going to find her?'

'Have you tried ringing her ma and da?'

'I was going to, but there's not a chance. They don't even know their precious daughter lives in the same flat as me.'

'What?'

'I've told you that before.'

'It's news to me.'

'I have. They're like throwbacks from the 1950s. The pair of them left Ireland, and their brains haven't moved on since they got on the boat.'

'A bit "Fields of Athenry", are they?'

'Jesus, and the rest. They go to céilís.'

'Go 'way.'

'I swear to God. And the only music the father listens to is Phil Coulter and the Fureys.'

'Jesus, even my old man's not that bad.'

'I know. Time-warp stuff. Anyway, Jesus, I couldn't care less about them; it's their daughter I'm worried about. She could be anywhere.'

'Have you tried ringing round?'

'I have, of course, but no joy.'

'Did you use your mobile?'

'What's that got to do with the price of fish?'

'Just answer the question.'

'Yes.'

'Well, press redial on the land line; Ciara might have used it before she went.'

'You genius!' Declan said, running over to the phone. To his surprise, it connected him to the Ryanair reservations line.

'Shit.' Declan stood, open-mouthed, as the penny dropped from a few hundred feet up. 'She must be back in Manchester.'

'Call them.'

'I can't, Bar. I haven't the nerve.' Declan thought of the clannish disapproval he would face if Ciara's family thought that her return home had anything to do with him.

'Well, if you're not going to call them, my friend, the only thing you can do is wait.' Barry pushed himself up from the chair.

'Just sit here?'

'No, you big gom – come with me and wait in the pub. That way, when you get home she might have come back, or at least called you – and, if she hasn't, you'll be too pissed to care.'

'I don't know…' Declan shook his head, feeling terrible.

'All right, what are you going to do? Sit here and watch *The* bleeding *Godfather* till she decides to come home?'

Declan raised an eyebrow. 'All right, so. I'll get

my coat.' Barry had a point – not that he was about to tell him that Ciara had taken his DVDs. If Barry had thought the answering-machine message was funny, the DVDs would probably give him a coronary. Declan grabbed his jacket and headed out of the door.

5

Mass had been the riot Ciara remembered it to be. The priest, Father O'Neill, seemed to have a link to immortality, if not to the Fountain of Youth. He had been shuffling around the altar, bent over in a ninety-degree angle, mumbling incoherent words of half-hearted praise, for as long as Ciara could remember. She tried to catch Claire's eye, but Margaret threw her a glance and she quickly faced front. Even at twenty-five, Ciara wasn't allowed to sit next to Claire at Mass for fear they would burst out laughing.

Anthony surreptitiously fumbled in his pocket, trying to locate his mobile phone, and received a weary look from Maeve. Michael was leafing nervously back and forth through the hymnbook. Margaret and Sean had no need of hymnbooks or Mass booklets: they knew the script verbatim. Margaret sang each hymn in a voice that sounded as if someone were coshing Charlotte Church over the head with a bag of pennies, and Ciara saw Anthony biting his lower lip to stop himself from laughing.

Then, to top it all off, Father O'Neill's slow, monotonous voice launched into a sermon about the day's gospel: the return of the prodigal son.

'He did not turn the child away, though he had been a squandering, debauched fool who had taken his father's love and support and thrown it back in his face. No! On the contrary, he welcomed the son with open arms. An odd thing to do, you may think...' Ciara was sure she saw Maeve's eyebrow twitch empathetically. *Please, someone, get me out of here...* 'But no! Not at all! For the father's love was unconditional! And it did not matter to him that his son was a wastrel, for he was *his* wastrel.' Well, at least the topic of the Sunday-lunch conversation was covered, Ciara thought grimly.

She felt numb. She looked at the altar, thinking about the last few days, and tried to connect everything that had happened with her belief in God – if she had such a thing. She wasn't sure she did – she'd never really thought about it; she just went to Mass when her parents did. She knew He was supposed to move in mysterious ways – but at this particular moment, Ciara decided, He was moving around her like a complete and unrelenting arsehole.

'Well, that was nice, wasn't it?' Margaret said, pulling a mountain of roast potatoes from the oven with her Ed the Duck oven gloves. Ciara stood next to her, stirring the gravy.

'What was?' She was quite sure that her mother wasn't referring to the Eminem CD that had been screaming out of Anthony's room until Sean snapped it in half. (Then he had run downstairs, shouting, 'There'll be no "motherfucking" in this house!' to throw the offending object into the bin. Anthony, who had been following him and objecting vehemently to the destruction of his property, had been so delighted by this line that he had held his nose to stop himself from laughing and run back up to his room.)

'Mass, of course,' her mother said, putting the joint of beef on top of the cooker, ready for Sean to calm down and carve it as he always did. 'All of us being together. And seeing Father O'Neill – I bet you haven't seen him in ages.'

'Yes, it was nice,' Ciara agreed automatically. 'And you're right, I hadn't seen him in ages.'

'He's a good man, Father O'Neill; he's always been very good to us.'

'So you've said.' *A thousand times,* Ciara thought.

'He did a nice sermon. It's funny how these things can be so relevant to your everyday life.'

'I'm not a wastrel, Mum. I haven't been off for years squandering the Coffey coffers in exotic lands.'

'And we've not killed the fatted calf, either,' Maeve's voice said over Ciara's shoulder. 'Need any help, Mum?'

'No, we're fine,' Ciara replied curtly.

'You're Ciara; that's Mum,' Maeve said, smiling tightly.

'Thanks for that, Maeve; I don't know how we'd manage without your input,' Ciara snapped. There was no way she was going to be the one to initiate a truce.

'I was only asking if you needed any help.' Maeve glared at her.

Ciara spun round, gravy spoon in hand. 'Well, I'm only telling you we're fine.'

'Will you two stop arguing? You're like little children!' Margaret protested. 'You've only been home a day and you're at it.'

'She started it!' Ciara sulked.

'How did I start it? Grow up, Ciara,' Maeve sighed, turning to leave.

'Me? You're thirty-three.'

Maeve ignored her and went back into the living room.

Margaret shook her head. 'Can't you two think of something nice to say to each other, for once?'

Ciara shrugged. She knew she was being petulant, but she was quite enjoying it. 'Do you want the vegetables served up?'

'So, Ciara, what's the plan for this week?'

Under her father's gaze, Ciara felt as if she were being lasered to her chair. 'Plan? Em, well…I was going to go into town tomorrow – you know, like we talked about yesterday – and get a job, or at least try to. After that, I don't really know.'

'See?' Sean poked a spud-mounted fork at Anthony. 'This one doesn't let the grass grow under her feet.' Ciara squirmed guiltily.

'What you on about?' Anthony screwed up his face. 'How am I letting the grass grow under my feet? I'm doing my A-levels. Should I be out winning a Nobel Prize or something?'

'I won't have cheek!' Sean bellowed. Anthony sighed and rolled his eyes, shovelling food into his mouth. Ciara looked on with grudging admiration. She would never have the nerve to speak to her father like that.

'Drop in to me at work. We'll find you something,' Michael offered. He was sitting back in his chair, at a forty-five-degree angle to the table, with his legs open, as if there wasn't enough space in the dining room for the girth of his groin. 'Your mum told me you could do with a little help.'

Ciara winced. 'Well, what I'm looking for is quite specialised…' she lied. *If someone followed me around, all day, every day, and heard some of the rubbish that comes out of my mouth, I'd be certified.* Ciara hated talking about her supposed career. It meant having to trawl her memory and remember exactly what she had lied about.

'We've loads of ad-agent clients: we've a whole media section,' Michael said. 'I'll tell one of the girls to pencil you in for tomorrow afternoon. They can look over your CV in the morning, and then you can come in and talk to them. You do have your CV, don't you?'

'Yeah.' Ciara put far more energy than was necessary into shovelling a pile of carrots onto her fork and avoiding Michael's gaze. 'It's on disk.'

'You wanted me to look over it, didn't you?' Claire interjected.

Ciara sighed with relief. 'Yeah, that's right.'

'Well, we'll do that first, and then you can e-mail it to Michael's work. You can't give out a CV that's two years old.'

'Very true,' Michael agreed.

'Well, wouldn't it be better to have Michael look at it, Claire?' Maeve said, pushing her food around her plate thoughtfully. 'I mean, don't get me wrong, but, as a teacher, do you know much about business CVs?'

'I'm the bloody careers adviser for the sixth form!'

Maeve pulled a face. 'Oops! Silly me. Sorry.'

'It'd be great if you could set up a meeting for me, Michael. Cheers for that,' Ciara lied.

'So how's work treating you, Maeve?' Sean asked.

Ciara watched Maeve intently, hoping she was going to say, 'Hopeless, terrible, I'm useless at my job – in fact, I haven't got a job; I'm actually a crack addict.' It might have made her feel slightly better about her own situation.

Of course, she didn't. 'Really well; great, in fact. We've a huge new client who's throwing business at us, which is great for me, but it means I haven't a minute to myself.'

Sean nodded his approval. 'Good girl.'

'I haven't been a girl for a good fifteen years, Dad.'

Ciara's eyes widened, with horrified delight, towards Claire. Maeve back-chatting their father? She must be having a bad week.

Sean arched an eyebrow, his face set sternly. 'All right, Maeve: good woman.'

'Thank you,' Maeve said tersely.

'She's so busy at work that I'm beginning to forget what she looks like,' Michael interjected. Ciara detected a note of tetchiness in his voice as well. *Maybe all's not well in Paradise*, she thought with undisguised glee.

Then she saw something out of the corner of her eye that knocked any minor family skirmishes straight out of her mind. A dark-haired man had just walked past the window, not daring to look in, and was heading for the front door. Ciara felt a sharp pinch of nausea: it was Declan.

The doorbell rang, and she jumped to her feet.

'I'll get it!' Her rising panic drew stares from her family. 'It's just…it's…' she stammered, 'it's Declan, and I don't know what he's doing here. I'll tell him to go away.'

'You'll do no such thing!' Margaret protested. 'You'll invite him in. Whatever you two argued over, I'm sure you can talk it through. Your father and I had many a falling-out when we were courting.' She put down her knife and fork matter-of-factly. 'We didn't run off to a different country; we sorted out our differences. If he's had the decency to come all the way over here from Ireland, then you bring him in. You can talk to him, at least.'

Ciara threw a look of sheer panic at Claire, who shrugged her shoulders helplessly. The doorbell rang again.

'Well, off you go,' Sean instructed her.

Ciara opened the door and stared at Declan standing there. A sheep couldn't have looked more sheepish. Idling in his hand was a bunch of drooping flowers that looked as if they'd been stolen from a graveyard.

'Ciara,' he said helplessly, his voice cracking, 'you've had me worried sick. What's going on? I got back the other day and there was some random message on the answering machine about me' – he lowered his voice to a whisper – 'shagging Laura. What the hell is going on? Are you completely paranoid?'

Ciara couldn't believe he was trying to lie his way out. 'Don't try and act all innocent, Declan.'

'I'm not trying to act innocent; I just don't know what on earth is happening.'

She pulled the door closed behind her and joined him on the step. Seeing Declan in the flesh made her think of what she had heard on the phone, bringing back the anger and hurt, pushing away any lingering positive memories and feelings.

'Happening?' she spat through clenched teeth. '*Happening?*' She modified her speech to a whisper; she didn't want anyone hearing what was bound to become an altercation. 'I want you out of my life, Declan, you scumbag. That's what's happening.'

'Please, Ciara, listen to me!' Declan threw down the flowers and grabbed Ciara's arm. She gave him a look that made him take his hand away.

'What do you think you're doing, showing up here? This big grand gesture with the flowers and—'

'Ciara, I need you to listen to me,' Declan broke in. 'I don't know what you think went on the other night, or why you got on a plane back to Manchester…' Ciara waited in silent disdain, allowing Declan to lie himself into a hole: *He doesn't know for certain that I know, or how I know*, she thought. 'Nothing happened between me and Laura. I got drunk and stayed over at her house – end of story. I just want you to come home so we can sort this mess out.'

'Nothing happened? Is that right?' she asked, her voice icy.

'Nothing, I swear to God. I bumped into her in Doheny's, and I got locked out of my brain; I think someone spiked my drink. I was all over the place, and Laura took me home to her flat because we ended up in the Modern Green and her flat's only crawling distance from there, and I fell asleep. That's it, Ciara. You have to believe me.'

'You sat on the phone, you utter dick. I heard everything.' Ciara felt an alien bitterness solidifying in her chest. 'You know how you always end up ringing me by mistake when you've forgotten to lock your phone? Well, it's landed you right in the shit this time, Declan. I heard you shagging Laura, and I heard her shouting your name like someone had rammed a poker up her arse, and I don't know how long it went on for, because I had to switch it off because I couldn't listen to it any more.' Her voice cracked.

Declan stood in stunned silence, his mouth flapping open, like a fish drowning on air. When he finally found his voice, it was panic-stricken and pleading. 'Ciara, you have to listen to me. Shit…' He grabbed Ciara by both arms, begging her to look at him; she shrugged his grasp away. 'I need you to listen when I tell you this – and you have to believe me. It meant nothing. Nothing at all.'

'Oh, fuck off! Listen to yourself, Declan; you sound like something off the telly. Of course it meant something. It meant that we are finished. And I swear to God, if I see you again I won't be responsible for my actions.'

'Ciara, you have to listen to me. I love you. I've never felt so bad about anything as I do about Friday night, and I want to explain. I didn't want to lie about it, but I thought if I came clean you'd finish with me – and now it looks that way anyway!' Declan tried to keep his voice down. 'Even if you won't forgive me, I'd like you to at least hear me out.'

Ciara dropped her shoulders, which had been somewhere up near the back of her head, and exhaled a sigh. She looked at Declan and wanted him to leave her alone. He had hurt her so much that she felt almost removed from the situation. She was exhausted with thinking about it. Had this happened a year or even six months earlier, she would have wanted an explanation, and in it she would have found whatever she needed to forgive him. But there had been too much bitching and bickering between herself and Declan over the past six months.

She looked at Declan, his face set in defiance, and knew that, after coming all the way to Manchester, he wasn't going to leave without some sort of reward for his efforts.

'OK, I'll talk to you, but not here. And then I want you to go.'

Declan threw himself against the wall, holding

his arms in the air like a man awaiting the firing squad. 'Whatever you want.'

'I want my boyfriend not to shag other people.'

'Jesus Christ, Ciara, will you give it a fucking rest until I get half a chance to explain? You're straight at my throat…' Declan paused, realising that they had an audience. Margaret was holding the door open.

'Will you two not come in off the street? And, Ciara, get this poor man a cup of tea, if he's come all the way from Ireland.'

Ciara glared at her mother.

'Now then, Declan, how have you been?' Margaret ushered him into the dining room. 'We haven't seen you in an age.'

'Well, Declan. How are you?' Sean proffered a hand.

'I'm good, yeah, good. Yourself, Mr Coffey?' Declan shuffled nervously from one foot to the other.

'Ah, you know yourself. Have a seat. Anthony, get Declan a chair from upstairs, will you?' Anthony, who had been watching Declan warily, pulled a face and pushed himself away from the table.

'I'll get it, Anthony – it's fine…' Declan said, his face reddening.

'No, it's OK; I know where it is,' Anthony said over his shoulder. He returned moments later carrying Sean's office chair, which looked like the contestant's chair from *Mastermind*.

'Is there not a better chair than that, Anthony? Dear me!' Margaret said.

'No, that's fine, honestly, Mrs Coffey. Ciara and I were just going to go out for a little walk in a while anyway.' Declan sat down. His nose was at table-height. He planted his feet firmly on the floor in an attempt not to swivel uncontrollably.

'It's a bit unpredictable, that chair,' Sean noted.

'No, it's fine,' Declan assured him, looking decidedly uncomfortable.

Anthony stifled a laugh, and Ciara saw Maeve nudge Michael. She glared at her. *She loves this,* she thought.

'Trifle, Declan? You'll have a bit of trifle?' Margaret asked.

'Em, yes, that would be lovely.' Declan looked at Ciara; she glanced away.

'So, Declan,' Maeve said, with what Ciara thought was delicate derision, 'what brings you to Manchester?' Everyone stiffened.

'I've come to see your sister.'

'OK…' she said dubiously, one eyebrow lifting.

'Maeve!' Ciara warned.

'Ciara, I said, "OK", that's all. You don't need to snap at me!'

'Right – that's it.' Ciara got to her feet. 'We're going out. Come on, Declan.' She turned to her mother, who was holding two of her best cut-glass bowls filled to the brim with trifle. 'I'll have it later, Mum, thanks.'

'But I've just served it out.' Margaret looked forlornly at the trifle.

'Ciara, this is ridiculous. Sit back down and finish your dinner, and then you can go out for your walk.' Sean didn't even raise his voice; he simply delivered his instruction with such menace that Ciara and Declan both did exactly as they were told.

After a moment, Declan leaned forward in his chair and smiled an appeasing smile at Sean. Ciara knew that look. Declan was aware that he was going to be there for at least the next half-hour, so he might as well make things as comfortable for himself as possible. 'Sean, did you see the hurling the other day?'

Ciara rolled her eyes. Declan had about as much interest in hurling as she had in mud-wrestling. She jabbed her spoon into her trifle, heaped a bite into her mouth and looked wretchedly over at Claire, who was smiling sympathetically.

Ciara stood at the end of the tree-lined road that led to Withington village, her hands on her hips. She had finally managed to escape, taking Declan and his charm offensive with her. The hour of listening to him wax lyrical about hurling had only aggravated her feelings towards him, but she had waited until they were out of earshot of the house before she told him exactly what she thought of him.

'I want you to go back to Dublin and forget you ever met me.'

'Jesus Christ, Ciara, I just want to sort this out!' Declan threw his arms up in despair. 'I didn't mean to do it!'

Ciara looked at Declan; his eyes were pleading with her to believe him. She felt her resolve waver, but she steeled herself in time and said, 'Oh, it just slipped in, did it? You accidentally fucked her brains out?'

Declan screwed his face up in disgust. 'Jesus, do you have to say it like that?'

'Disgusts you, does it? It didn't disgust you too much on Friday night.'

Declan shook his head and took a step back. 'Look, I'm not going to argue with you.'

He always did this, Ciara thought. He whipped her into a frenzy; then, halfway through the argument, he began to look exasperated and told her he'd had enough of arguing. But he wasn't going to get away with it – not this time. She was going to have her say and he was going to listen, whether he liked it or not. 'No, you're not. You're going to get out of my sight and my life, or I'll—'

'You're not listening,' Declan interrupted. 'There's no point in even talking to you when you're like this.'

'What's there to listen to? I want you to go.'

'Don't be so ridiculous, Ciara. You can't just run away from your entire life. We've been through too much to split up over this.'

She looked at him, and suddenly her anger dissipated. She *could* run away from her life in Dublin, she realised, because it amounted to very little. She had a crappy job in a pretentious bar, and the good friends she had made had all fallen away, as they settled down and she continued to party as if she'd been given two months to live. The friends she had made in the meantime weren't *real* friends; they were just people to go out with. If they had been real friends, she would have called them instead of getting on the first plane home. Ciara felt a bitter taste in her mouth as she admitted to herself that she had no one left to turn to in Ireland. One thought knocked against the next like dominoes tumbling, sparking another realisation: her entire time in Ireland had amounted to nothing. In the whole time there, she had never managed to finish anything that she had started. If she was running away, she wasn't running away from much.

Ciara turned to Declan and said quietly (which, she noticed, took him slightly by surprise: he had been expecting more shouting), 'No, Declan, we've been through too much to stay together after this. Now, I'm going to go back home, and I want you to go away and leave me alone.' She moved slowly away, hoping that her resolve would at least see her back to the door.

'You just don't listen!' Declan shouted after her.

'I come all the way here, and you won't even hear me out!' He stormed off down the street. Ciara turned just in time to see him rounding the corner, shoulders slumped.

As she walked back to her parents' house, she realised there was a distinct possibility that this was the last time she would see Declan. She was enveloped by a feeling so strong that she didn't want to acknowledge it at all. It was fear – fear that she had just made the biggest mistake of her life.

As she sombrely pushed open the door, she was greeted by her mother nearly falling on top of her. Margaret had obviously been hovering around the letterbox, trying to figure out what on earth was going on.

6

October 1999

Ciara hauled her rucksack up onto her back and grabbed the bin-bag full of pans that her mother had insisted she bring with her. Feeling like the Saucepan Man from the Enid Blyton story, she clattered her way towards the taxi rank at Dublin airport. She had spent the last few weeks telling her friends back in Manchester that she couldn't wait to get to Ireland, but, now that she was here, she was scared witless by the prospect of starting life in another country. She was nineteen years old. She had thought that the year she had spent working, after leaving school, might make her feel more mature, but at that moment she felt like a little girl.

She waited in line patiently for ten minutes, and then impatiently for another ten, until she was at the front of the queue. The taxi driver didn't budge from his seat as Ciara, struggling with her bags, told him she needed to go to Rathmines; instead he waved over his shoulder, indicating that the boot was open. When she had finally managed to dump her bags in the boot and climbed into the car, he snapped, 'What have you in there? A dead body?'

'No,' Ciara said, shocked by his rudeness. 'Some pans.'

'We have pan shops over here, you know,' he said, putting the car into gear and screeching away.

'My mum gave them to me.'

'Typical.'

Ciara leaned forward in her seat. She wasn't having this. 'What do you mean, "typical"? Have you met my mother? Are you *au fait* with her pan-pushing?'

'*Au fait?*' the man said mockingly, looking at Ciara in the rear-view mirror. 'Big words for one so young.'

Ciara blushed, slumping back in her seat. *Just my luck to get the rudest taxi driver in Dublin,* she thought.

'You a student?'

'Yes,' she said shortly.

'Thought so.'

Ciara was about to ask him what that was

supposed to mean when he shouted, 'Jesus Christ!'

'What?' Ciara asked, looking around wide-eyed.

'They've only gone and torn the road up. Great.' He pulled the steering-wheel around like a rally driver; Ciara found her face pushed up against the window like a stick-on Garfield. 'We're going to have to go the other way.'

'OK,' Ciara muttered. It didn't matter to her which way they went; she had no idea where she was.

The taxi driver's mood didn't improve. By the time they hit gridlocked traffic in the city centre and three drops of rain struck the windscreen, he was complaining vehemently that the weather was terrible, the traffic was terrible, and Ciara and her pans might be better off going back from whence they came.

'You know what?' Ciara said finally. 'I think you need a holiday.'

'Oh, that's a great idea,' he said sarcastically. 'With my leg?' Ciara had no idea what he was talking about and no desire to find out. She sighed and looked out of the window as the traffic snaked down O'Connell Street towards the Liffey. There was a sculpture of a woman lying in what appeared to be a bath; 'Anna Livia' was engraved on the side.

'That's the Floozy in the Jacuzzi,' the taxi driver said, perking up for the first time in the journey.

Ciara laughed. 'Did you think that up?'

'No, that's what everyone calls it. Do you know the Molly Malone statue?'

'That's near Trinity, isn't it?'

'The very same. Well, that's the Tart with the Cart.'

Ciara smiled; he seemed to be cheering up. As the car neared the traffic lights on O'Connell Bridge, she looked up at a large statue and said, 'What do you call him, then?'

'Him? We call him Daniel O'Connell, that's what we call him,' the taxi driver snapped, before falling back into silence. Ciara arched an eyebrow and slumped in her seat. She didn't have the energy to tell him that she knew exactly who Daniel O'Connell was — no one grew up in Sean Coffey's house without knowing everything there was to know about Ireland, from Fionn MacCumhaill to the Good Friday Agreement — and that she had just been making conversation. In stony silence they drove around the outside of Trinity, and Ciara looked nervously out at the sweeping, crescent-shaped wall surrounding the entrance: this was where she would spend the next four years.

At last the driver passed along a grand Georgian square, turned into a smaller square of newly built houses, and pulled up. Ciara paid him and got out of the car, dragging her bags from the boot herself. As she turned away to lug her bags up the steps of her new home, the driver sped off, spattering mud up the backs of her legs.

'Fantastic!' Ciara shouted at no one in particular. Things could only get better — at least, she hoped so. She hadn't expected to be greeted by a ticker-tape parade, but a bit of common courtesy wouldn't have hurt.

As she was struggling up the stairs, the door flew open and six or seven gabbling women and children spilled out onto the street.

'Now I've left you the bed linen, and that nice bread I bought, and those washing tablets,' one woman was shouting over the throng to a young woman at the back of the crowd. 'You know how to use them, don't you? And the iron – don't put it through that nice shirt I bought you; it needs to be on a cool temperature…' The woman looked down the steps at the bedraggled Ciara, who was trying to make her way to the front door. 'Oh, hello! Are you moving in here? Well, come here – let me help you! Girls, will you help the poor thing?'

Ciara was surrounded by the group, who grabbed her belongings and hoisted them up the stairs.

'I'm Nadine.'

'I'm Shauna. Who are you? Are you going to be living here?' demanded an eager-looking teenager.

'I introduced myself first,' Nadine objected. 'God, Shauna, you are self-obsessed.'

'No, I'm not!'

Ciara began to panic: the agency had placed her with a family of lunatics… Then the red-faced young woman who had been receiving the helpful ironing tips grabbed one of Ciara's bags and said,

'Hi, I'm Róisín. I've just arrived, as you can tell. And this is my embarrassing family.'

'We're not embarrassing!' 'Shut your face, Róisín.' 'Yeah, Róisín, we've come half way across the country for you.'

'Hi, I'm Ciara.'

'These are my sisters, and that's my mum, Mary.'

'Pleased to meet you all,' Ciara smiled, as they all helped bring her and her belongings in out of the rain.

'And they were just heading off.'

'She's full of the charm, isn't she, Ciara? We were heading off, but now you're here we might stay for a cup of tea,' Mary said.

'Mum!' Róisín pleaded.

'Yeah, Mum. We want to go shopping!' Shauna complained.

'All right. Keep your hair on! We're going. Now, if you need anything, just pick up the phone. That's all you have to do.' Mary rummaged for her car keys. 'And don't mind her funny ways, Ciara – you'll get used to them; she is house-trained.'

'Mum! Go home!'

Ciara laughed. The girls ran to the car to avoid the rain, arguing about which shop they were going to first.

As they all piled into the people-carrier, Róisín waved goodbye; when they finally disappeared around the corner, she slammed the door shut, holding her back to it. 'Thank God! I've been waiting eighteen years for that. I thought they were never going to go!'

'They seem lovely.'

'You should try living with them!'

Ciara laughed.

'Help yourself to a room,' Róisín said; 'we're the first two here. I'll get you a cup of tea.'

'That'd be great,' Ciara said. She was warming immediately to her new housemate.

She showered and changed, and put a few of her belongings around the room to make it feel more like home. She tacked up a dog-eared Stone Roses poster that Maeve had given to her when she was eleven, some photos of her friends back home – her favourite was one of her and her best friend Rachel, grinning at the camera as Ciara held it at arm's length – and finally a picture of her family that her mother had insisted they have taken by a professional photographer; Maeve said it made them look like a cross between the Waltons and the Beverley Sisters. Then she wandered downstairs and joined Róisín.

Róisín handed her a cup of tea. 'So what course are you on?'

'BESS. That's economics, to a normal person,' Ciara said, rolling her eyes, as she always did when she mentioned the subject.

'Me too!'

'Really?' Ciara said, delighted.

'That's great; we can register together,' Róisín said. 'Are you bricking it?'

Ciara laughed. 'Yeah, I suppose I am.'

'I am, and I'm still in the same country. If I'd had to get here on a plane, I'd be beside myself by now.'

Ciara smiled and sipped her tea. She felt relaxed with Róisín. 'I'll be fine, I'm sure.'

'Do you know, I've only ever been to Dublin twice in my life before today,' Róisín informed her. 'But I've always wanted to come to college here. Isn't that mad, when you think about it? I think I just wanted to get as far away from my mad family as possible. They're great, but they're so full-on all the time. Comes with having a house full of girls, I think.'

Ciara laughed. 'I bet you fight in lumps about borrowing each other's clothes.'

'It's a nightmare! I haven't had a pair of knickers that I could guarantee are my own for years! Have you brothers and sisters?'

'Two sisters, Maeve and Claire, and a younger brother, Anthony. Thankfully both of my sisters are older than me, so the cast-offs tend to come my way.'

'What made you come over here for college?' Róisín asked, offering Ciara a biscuit.

Ciara nibbled it thoughtfully, feeling slightly thrown by the question. 'Em, I suppose it was because my dad came here and he said it was a great place to study.' She shrugged, feeling slightly sheepish. 'It's not very rebellious, is it?'

Róisín smiled. 'Is your father Irish?'

'Very.' Ciara laughed.

They spent the rest of the day and the evening together. Ciara found Róisín funny and irreverent, just as ready and willing to launch herself upon Dublin as she was herself. That night they got dressed up and went out on the town; they staggered home at four o'clock that morning, sworn friends.

The next day they walked into town to register at their new university. In spite of the fact that they were both dying with hangovers, Ciara and Róisín were giddy with excitement as they walked through the archway into the manicured grounds of Trinity. Ciara might have felt as if she had been transported into another, more genteel era, were it not for the fact that three skateboarders with metal piercings hanging out of every available piece of skin were trying a bone-shattering experiment on the steps of the dining hall, while being shouted at by a security guard.

'This is amazing!' she said. 'I can't believe I'm actually here.'

'I know. It's deadly.' Róisín looked around the large, square courtyard. 'Where do we go now?'

Ciara grabbed her information pack from her bag. 'We sign up over here, I think.' She linked Róisín and they followed a makeshift sign saying, 'Registration this way'. Ciara was so happy she felt like yelping. In Manchester, she had always been envious of the students there – living on their own, not having to answer to anyone – and here she was, doing exactly the same thing. It was very liberating – as was the realisation that nearly every man she had passed on campus was good-looking.

As they went into the registration hall, Ciara whispered, 'Is it me, or is every guy on campus fit?'

'There's not too many bad-looking ones, it has to be said,' Róisín said, with a serious look of contemplation on her face. She caught Ciara's eye and they began giggling. *I'm going to enjoy it here,* Ciara thought, smiling at her new friend.

7

Maeve had been at work since seven o'clock. She liked getting into the office early: she got through more work in those first two hours than in all the rest of the day.

Maeve was a partner in one of the larger accountancy firms to grace Deansgate; on one side her office looked out over the sprawl of Manchester towards the Lowry Hotel, on the other past the glass boat-bow edifice of the new million-pound apartments. Maeve gazed out of the window, watching people scurrying about on the street below; it made her think that, while they might not have the lorry-load of work that she had, they didn't have offices like this, either.

Today was going to be chaos; she could feel it already. She was pencilled in for three meetings – none of them billable – when what she really wanted to do was get stuck into her new client, a German firm called Zala that had revolutionised airport security with a fancy new scanning system; they were sending people over to meet her in four days. Maeve had been fighting to win their business for eighteen months. She'd come up against stiff opposition from colleagues, who had urged caution and pointed out that there was a big risk attached to a company that had grown almost literally overnight, but she had managed to convince her superiors that even an idiot could see this wasn't some two-bit enterprise with 'boom and bust' written all over it.

Having won their approval, Maeve had then had the job of competing for Zala's business with the rest of the accounting world. However, once she secured a face-to-face meeting with the board of directors, it was almost a done deal. She had prepared so thoroughly that she would have been very surprised had someone else won the business. The chief auditor had been eating out of her palm from the word go, and there had been a number of sly comments from her male counterparts, to the effect that he'd been as impressed with her appearance as with her ability; but Maeve had taken them on the chin, as she always did. She knew that a good haircut and a nice pair of legs didn't ensure multi-million-pound deals, but she had also worked in this industry long enough to know that complaining about the remarks would get her nowhere. The only way to gain her colleagues' respect was to consistently out-perform them – which she did.

As she scrolled through the list of contacts on her laptop, her PA appeared at the door.

'Hi, Becky. What've you got for me?' Maeve liked and trusted Becky, who had worked for her for over two years and was so highly organised, even by accountancy standards, that it beggared belief. She knew where everything and everyone was at any given moment – a bit like God, Maeve had told Michael, but with more words per minute.

Becky sat down opposite Maeve's large oak desk and went through her list of appointments for the following week, starting with the dinner party on Wednesday for the new recruits straight out of college. Maeve berated herself: she'd completely forgotten about that. *All those poor, fresh-faced things – they should be off travelling the world,* she thought. It made her sad to think that, in their early twenties, they were signing themselves up for a career. There was a sizeable bit of Maeve that wished that, upon receiving her qualifications, she'd just packed everything in and gone off somewhere to pick coconuts, or at least gone somewhere where she wouldn't have to look at an Excel spreadsheet for at least a month.

Maeve sighed. There weren't enough hours in the day for her to get through her 'to do' list. She knew she was guilty of not delegating as much work as she should, but she often thought that it was quicker and easier to do things herself.

'And, of course, your good friend Dirk Willerman is coming over from Germany on Friday. He was asking if you were free for dinner.' Becky smirked.

'Thank you, Becky.' Maeve wanted to put a stop to any innuendo flying around the office about the chief auditor's imaginary penchant for her. 'Anything else?' she asked briskly.

'Yes, you told me that I wasn't to allow you out of this office until you'd made an appointment with the bank manager,' Becky said, 'so that you can, and I quote, "rip his head off".'

'Oh, yeah – that's right.' Maeve was ready to swing for someone at the bank. She'd received a couple of snotty letters that didn't match up with her finances, and she wanted to sort it out once and for all. And if she got there and the bank manager was some fourteen-year-old jobsworth who was afraid of his own shadow – as had happened the last time she'd visited her branch – then she might not be accountable for her actions. 'Is that it, then?'

'Yeah, those four hundred and eighty things are about it for now.' Becky smiled. 'Fancy a coffee?'

'Yeah – strong and black, thanks.'

'Oh, yeah, there is something else: Nicole's

coming in at lunchtime. She's bringing the new sprog. It's a month old.'

Nicole had been a young administrative assistant until she had – as her own mother had so eloquently put it, when she called Becky to explain why her daughter wouldn't be coming back – 'got herself knocked up'. Maeve had taken Nicole under her wing, which wasn't something she was renowned for. She'd brought her out for lunch, bought her presents for when the baby was born – always being careful not to overstep the bounds of professionalism – and urged her to return to work when the baby was old enough. She felt sorry for the girl, she told Becky: only seventeen, and her life was being mapped out for her.

Maeve felt a sudden, unexpected lurch in her stomach. She had been so busy at work, she hadn't spoken to Nicole since before the baby was born. Now she wished she had.

'You all right, Maeve?' Becky bent forward to catch Maeve's eye.

'Yes, I'm fine. What?'

'Sorry. I thought – well, I thought you were about to cry, that's all.' Becky let out a little laugh of embarrassment at the preposterous notion. 'It'll be great to see her again, won't it?'

'Yeah, it will.' Maeve blinked. 'The pollen count's through the roof again. So what's she called the kid?'

'You're not going to believe it.'

'What?'

'Britney.' Becky gulped back a laugh.

'No!' Maeve burst into helpless laughter. 'I bet that was her mad mother's idea.'

'I'm telling you, she's called it Britney. Now, don't be laughing when she comes in. I know you're not the cluckiest person in the world, but still, find something nice to say about the kid.' Becky pushed herself up from the chair. 'I'll be about five minutes with the coffee.'

'Thanks,' Maeve said, smiling.

But, as the door closed behind Becky, she felt an overwhelming rush of sorrow wash over her. Her phone was ringing, but she ignored it; she was too busy fighting back tears. *What am I doing?* she thought. *This is ridiculous. I don't cry. I must be overworked. I'll hand off a few of the smaller accounts, and then I'll be fine.*

By the time Becky came back, Maeve had managed to compose herself and was sitting at her desk, her chair swivelled to face the wall, pretending to talk on her mobile. Becky set the coffee down on the desk and left. As the door closed, Maeve pulled a tissue from her top drawer and wiped her face purposefully. This had been just an isolated, uncharacteristic incident. She had work to do. And it wasn't going to do itself.

8

The following day, Ciara was sitting in the foyer of NPV Consulting, crossing and uncrossing her legs repeatedly in a bid to look at ease. She was dressed up to the nines in a pristine Planet skirt-suit, a cast-off of Maeve's that she'd found at home. Ciara hadn't had to wear a skirt for work since the last time she had worked in an office, which, if her memory served her correctly, had been over two years ago. Not that this was immediately apparent from the complete, unabridged fairy story, entitled 'Ciara Coffey – Curriculum Vitae', that she was holding in her hands.

'Hi, Ciara. I'm Sally Thompson. Would you like to come through?' The girl thrust a business card into Ciara's left hand and shook her right with such gusto that she nearly took Ciara's arm out of its socket. Ciara could only assume that Sally had just returned from a month-long sales-cum-brainwashing course.

Sally glanced over the work of fiction, asked Ciara if she had managed to find the office OK and declared her love for Ireland (after exploring the cobbled, touristy streets of Temple Bar on a hen weekend, apparently, she felt that she could definitely live there). Then she got down to business. 'So I see you were an account handler at Peabody, O'Neill and Sachs for two years; that sounds quite impressive. Tell me all about it.'

Ciara winced inwardly. She might as well have written that she was third in line to the English throne. She wasn't sure she could follow through with a lie of such magnitude; but there was no way Michael was going to find out that she was anything less than she had always claimed to be.

She took a deep breath. 'Sorry – I hope I didn't mislead you there. I worked *with* account handlers; I wasn't, strictly speaking, an account handler myself.'

'Oh.' Sally looked down at the CV again, slightly confused. 'I'll have to make a note of that. Could you tell me a little about Peabody, O'Neill and Sachs? I've never actually heard of them.'

That's because those are the surnames of the partners in the bar where I actually worked. 'They were small – boutique, actually.' *What am I on about?* 'They offered a bespoke service to a select client base.' *And I, Sally, as you may have noticed, have swallowed a dictionary.*

'And what was your role there, exactly?'

Ciara told her everything she knew about working alongside an advertising account handler. This was safer ground. Declan had complained regularly and vehemently about the account handlers in his office, calling them parasites and telling her exactly what they had done to rile him that week; and Ciara herself had once worked as the receptionist at JMSS&A for two weeks, covering the real receptionist's holidays at a time when Dublin was booming and temps were hard to come by. After seeing how the various people in the office worked, she had had to admit that, as pretentious as she sometimes thought Declan's job was, at least it had substance. She had marvelled at the account handlers. In Ciara's opinion, anyone whose job involved waving a box of tampons and saying, 'We need to look at marketing to men; we're neglecting fifty per cent of our marketplace,' had to be having a laugh.

'You seem to know your stuff,' Sally said, impressed. 'Tell me about the clients.'

Ciara stammered slightly. She hadn't seen that one coming. She wasn't sure why; it was an obvious question. She mentioned a few Irish and international companies, trying so hard to maintain eye contact that she felt Sally shuffle uncomfortably under her gaze. Once through this minefield, though, the rest of the interview was a breeze. She even managed to answer the 'Where do you see yourself in five years' time?' question without replying, 'Sitting on a beach.' By the end of the interview Sally was telling her that, pending references (another work of complete fiction) she didn't think she would have any problem finding her a position.

As they left the office, with joint-popping handshakes all round, Ciara breathed a sigh of what should have been relief, but was more like despair. Not only had she broken her promise to herself to be truthful now that she was back in Manchester, she had involved Maeve and Michael in her dishonesty.

'Well? How did you get on?' Michael had sidled up to her and was leaning an outstretched hand against the wall.

'Good, I think.' Ciara smiled awkwardly. Her eyes were strangely drawn to his dark-brown hairline, which had recently decided to march down the back of his head. She hoped to God that he wouldn't find out she had admitted to not being an account handler; then she decided he probably didn't know what that was anyway.

'Great! If anyone's going to get you a job, it's Sally; she's a great girl.'

Ciara felt her face crease in an involuntary spasm, but the 'girl' in question said, with a geisha-style flutter of her eyelashes, 'Oh, Michael, you flatter me!'

Michael winked at Sally, and she giggled. Ciara wanted to turn herself inside out with embarrassment. *Leave the horrible office flirting until I've gone, please — you're my sister's husband!*

'I'll be in touch very soon, Ciara,' Sally said, recovering.

'Yeah, great,' Ciara said, a little too breezily. 'Listen, Michael, I'd better get going. But thanks for your help; it's much appreciated.'

'No problem. See you soon,' Michael said, with an affability that Ciara was sure was more for Sally's benefit than for hers. Stepping into the lift, she checked her watch: she had ten minutes to get to her next appointment.

Ciara had flicked through the Yellow Pages to see which agencies specialised in the type of work she was actually looking for. She had decided to give CrazyTemps a miss, and she thought Le Temp des Temps sounded far too contrived (she pictured a tiny enterprise run by a purse-lipped Maggie Smith look-alike), but Sureplace Recruitment sounded OK; and the woman she had spoken to on the phone — Lisa Morris — had seemed very approachable.

Lisa turned out to be young and well-groomed. 'Have a seat,' she said, gesturing towards her desk. 'Now then, what sort of work is it you're looking for, exactly?'

'Just general admin – you know… Anything, really. I've done reception work and a bit of copy-typing, but nothing for a while. I've been working in a bar for the past two years.'

'OK.' Lisa looked over Ciara's CV – her real CV – and asked, 'You moved to Ireland six years ago, is that right?'

'Yeah, that's right. I've just moved back this weekend.' Lisa – like everyone else – had visited Ireland and liked it, but unlike Sally she had ventured further than Dame Street: she had spent a summer in Cashel. Ciara felt a lot more comfortable with Lisa than she had with Sally.

'So what made you move to Ireland?' Lisa asked finally, after they had discussed the recent boom in Manchester.

Ciara took a deep breath. 'I went to do a degree at Trinity College.'

'A degree?' Lisa looked at Ciara's CV again. 'I know you don't need a degree to do the type of work you're looking for at the moment, but it's always a good idea to put it on your CV.' She smiled. 'It just gives you that edge when we send your details to an employer.'

'It's not on my CV,' Ciara said quietly, looking down at her feet, 'because I didn't actually finish it.'

She felt a wave of shame as she made the admission. Smiling weakly, she took another deep breath and started to explain to Lisa why she hadn't completed her degree. If she was going to be honest, she might as well begin somewhere.

9

Ciara's first year in Dublin was everything she had hoped for and more. She got an average of four lie-ins a week, went to every club in Dublin and had lots of fun meeting men, but she wasn't bowled over by anyone in particular – she was too busy having a good time with her new-found friends. She and Róisín had been joined in the house by two other girls, Sinéad and Geraldine; they all got along well, but the fact that Ciara and Róisín had spent their first few days in Dublin together – and the fact that they were on the same course – meant that their friendship was somehow stronger. By the end of the first year, they were almost inseparable.

Ciara returned to Dublin for her second year of

college delighted to be back in a world where she could get out of bed whenever she pleased. She had spent the summer working shifts in a shampoo factory in Manchester, screwing caps on bottles and feeling the will to live drain from her on an hourly basis. She had hardly been out at all; instead she had flopped around the house, explaining to her parents that they didn't know what real work was. The second she was back in Dublin, she started making up for lost party time.

One night she had had a particularly raucous session at the Kitchen nightclub and had managed to lose everyone she was with, including Róisín, who had faded around midnight after one too many Bacardi Breezers. At three o'clock, after seeing the queues at the taxi rank and realising that she would have a better chance of hailing an African elephant, Ciara began the trudge home.

The shoes she had chosen to wear that evening were highly impractical high-heeled sandals. She had been walking for twenty minutes when she passed the Bleeding Horse pub and realised they had something in common: her right sandal had garrotted its way through her ankle and smeared blood all over her heel. Ciara bent down wearily and took the shoe off. This left one side of her a foot taller than the other. She bent down again in resignation and took off the other sandal.

As she hobbled up the cold pavement, she heard heavy footsteps behind her. *Great; I'm going to get murdered and thrown in the canal to top it all*, she thought.

'You all right there?' a man's voice asked.

Ciara spun round to see a tall, dark-haired young man bemusedly staring at her bare feet. 'Yeah, I'm fine,' she said, straightening and hobbling on in a decidedly not-fine fashion.

'I'm not so sure you are. Your feet are in bits.'

'Well, serves me right for wearing stilts.' Ciara smiled, and then remembered that she really should be more guarded: only a certified lunatic would want to stand around in the early hours discussing the state of her feet.

'Would you like to borrow my shoes?'

Ciara laughed nervously. *I've had it now*, she thought. 'And what are you going to do – walk in your socks?'

'Yeah. I'm not bothered; they're good woolly socks that my mammy makes me wear.' He smiled, and Ciara softened slightly. There appeared to be a possibility that he wasn't really an axe murderer – although it would be just her luck to be bumped off by a lunatic masquerading as a friendly, good-looking bloke.

'I can't borrow your shoes. Anyway, I'm nearly home.'

'Where are you going to?'

'Rathmines.'

'Well, so am I, so take the shoes.' The man slipped his shoes off and offered them to Ciara.

'Look,' she said, suddenly serious, 'I don't know you from a hole in the ground, and you're offering me your shoes?'

'That's correct.' The man nodded solemnly.

Ciara cocked her head to one side and looked him over. 'Why don't we compromise?' she said finally.

'In what way?'

'You take your shoes back, and I'll wear the socks. It'll stop my feet being cold but remind me that I'm an idiot for wearing these things.'

'Smashing,' the man said, removing his socks.

As Ciara tiptoed up the Rathmines Road, resplendent in her black belt of a dress and woolly socks, chatting with the young sockless man, she realised that her stomach was doing gleeful somersaults. As they neared her house, she wished she'd said she lived in Dundrum or Kimmage, or maybe Waterford, just so that they could have kept walking together.

'Well, here I am,' she said, coming to a stop outside her house.

'Is that right?' The man looked up at the house and back at Ciara.

'Oh, your socks,' she said, bending down to take them off.

'No, keep them – really. I'll come back round for them during the week, if that's OK?' He smiled, and Ciara felt her knees actually weaken. 'I'll expect them washed and ironed, though.'

'Of course; that goes without saying,' she told him, turning to go up the steps. 'When would you like them back?'

'Tomorrow night might be good. We could meet in town if you wanted. How about eight o'clock at Hogan's? My socks like it in there.'

'Yeah, that's a great idea.' Ciara grinned. 'Bye, then; see you tomorrow.'

'It might help if I knew your name.'

'Oh, God, sorry. My name's Ciara.'

'Well, Ciara, I'm Declan. Pleased to meet you.'

Ciara woke the next morning clutching a pair of black socks, which she immediately threw to the floor. It was one thing borrowing a stranger's foot attire; it was another cuddling it in bed all night.

She missed her lectures for the day – Róisín would cover for her and sign her name on the registers – and spent the afternoon faffing around excitedly. She went into town and bought herself a new pair of jeans and a simple black polo-neck jumper – she wanted something new, but at the same time she didn't want Declan to think she had gone to any special effort for the sock-returning exercise. Then, at eight o'clock that evening, she walked nervously along Wexford Street.

Declan was waiting at the bar for her, and he looked great. He was wearing a blue T-shirt and a pair of jeans, and Ciara knew that, even if she hadn't been there to meet him, she would have given him the twice-over.

'Hello,' he said.

'Hello, yourself.' Ciara put her hand – it was shaking with nerves – into her coat pocket. 'Your socks, sir. Thank you very much.'

Declan sniffed them. 'You washed them! I am impressed.'

They found a table that looked out onto George's Street. Ciara said, 'I haven't been in this bar in ages.'

'Well, you haven't missed much,' Declan laughed.

Ciara realised that she couldn't think of anything to say. She was so nervous that she was suddenly, literally speechless. 'I didn't go to college today,' she offered finally.

'No? Which college is it?' Declan asked.

'Em…thingy.'

'Thingy College? I've never heard of that one.'

'Sorry…Trinity.'

'Jesus! Well, I'm in the presence of a genius, so.'

'God, no.' Ciara blushed.

'What are you doing at Trinners, then?'

'A course.' Ciara gulped.

Declan furrowed his brow. 'A course. Right.'

Ciara panicked: he obviously thought she was being aloof. 'Economics and stuff.' She tried to regulate her breathing.

'So how's economics and stuff?'

'Rubbish.' Ciara felt as if she had been possessed by an inarticulate five-year-old.

'Rubbish?' Declan looked slightly perplexed.

'Em, yeah. Just going to the loo.' Ciara got up from her stool and headed for the ladies', banging into every table on the way, like a human pinball. By the time she was standing in front of the mirror she was puce with mortification. She splashed her face with water and looked at her reflection, mouthing, 'What are you *doing*?' She thought she wouldn't be surprised if, by the time she got back, Declan had drained his pint and disappeared. It was completely unlike her to be tongue-tied – usually there was no shutting her up. The most annoying thing was that Ciara knew why she was unable to string a sentence together: it was because she really fancied Declan. She was going to have to go back out and force herself to talk.

When she peeped back into the bar, Declan – much to her relief – was still sitting there, reading the back of a beer-mat.

'Look,' Ciara began, before she had even sat back down, 'I'm not acting like myself with you – and I need to, or there's no point in me being here. I just went into the toilet and splashed water on my face because I can't believe I'm unable to talk. And the thing is, I *can* talk; I do talk – I talk all the time.'

A smile was spreading across Declan's face. Ciara steam-rollered on: 'But I couldn't just then, when we came in, and it's because – well, it's because I fancy you, which I know is obvious, because I'm sitting here pretending that I'm delivering socks…' She was talking so fast that she was nearly squeaking. 'But it's obvious that there's more to it than socks. This is a date, isn't it? So I just need to get something out of the way, and then I might, just might, be able to relax.' She leaned forward and kissed Declan full on the lips.

Pulling back, she looked at him, trying to gauge his reaction. After a moment, Declan burst out laughing and shook his head. 'You're some woman for one woman.'

Ciara felt her face relax into a smile.

'Well, I don't know how to top that,' Declan admitted. 'Actually, no, wait…' He got up from the table and knelt on one knee, to the bemusement of the other customers in the bar. 'Ciara, will you marry me?'

Ciara burst out laughing as he unfurled one of the socks and tied it in a knot around her wrist. Then he sat back down and smiled at her. 'Do you want me to let you into a little secret?'

Ciara smiled, admiring her new armband. 'Go on, then.'

'I don't live in Rathmines.'

'What?'

'I'd been to a party on Clanbrassil Street, and I was heading home when I saw you hobbling along on those ridiculous shoes. I thought, *Your one is never going to get home*, so I followed you to see if you were OK. I'm not a lunatic; I just thought I'd see how you got on. Then you took your shoes off, and I thought, *Ah, here, her feet will be in bits.* That's when I came up to talk to you.'

Ciara was smiling cautiously.

'Seriously, I'm not a nutcase. It's just that…well, when I saw you up close, I thought I wouldn't mind walking with you a bit further. The truth is, I live on the North Circular Road.'

Ciara burst out laughing. Rathmines was south of the river, a good forty minutes' walk from the North Circular Road – which was, as the name suggested, north. 'No one's ever given me his socks *and* lied about where he lived so he could walk with me.'

'I find that hard to believe.'

'No, I swear. And, therefore, I think I might take you up on your offer of marriage.'

Declan beamed from ear to ear. 'Smashing,' he said.

10

Declan strolled through the expansive foyer of JMSS&A and waved hello to Jenny, the jobsworth receptionist who believed the company would implode if she so much as went to the toilet between nine o'clock and five-thirty. She glowered at him. Declan hadn't quite seen eye to eye with Jenny since she had cornered him at the last office party. He had slithered along the wall, trying to escape, as she followed him, breathing drunkenly, 'I've seen the way you look at me.' He had escaped the evening unharmed, but ever since then he had found himself the object of Jenny's vitriol when things weren't going her way. Today, though, he was safe: she was otherwise occupied with a busy switchboard.

Declan headed for his office. Barry was nowhere to be seen, which wasn't unusual; he usually turned up at about half past ten. He closed the door behind him. The company had an open-door policy and it was deemed irretrievably rude to close an office door, but today Declan couldn't care less. He wanted to be on his own, and he defied anyone to tell him he couldn't.

He slumped into his chair and grabbed the pile of bumph the account handler had given him for a potentially huge ad campaign. It was for a brewery based in the north of England. JMSS&A had been approached because of their previous successes with similar brands. Their English branch was up in arms about the fact that it was more or less taken for granted that Barry and Declan would be working on the project.

Declan stared at a picture of a pint of bitter. He couldn't think of a single way to make it sexy or interesting. He had been feeling cynical about his work for a while, but it seemed all the more hollow to him after the weekend he'd had.

He hadn't slept well the night before. He'd kept waking up, expecting Ciara to be there; each time he realised that she wasn't, he had felt bereft all over again. Eventually he had got up and paced around the flat. When he first realised that Ciara had left, he had really believed they could sort things out; but, after his trip to Manchester, he had a terrible feeling that it was over.

Declan decided to do something he hadn't done since he was twelve and his mother had forced him to have a pen pal in Kenya, whom she'd dug up through some missionary she knew from church. He decided to write a letter.

Dear Ciara,

I want you to read this from beginning to end – then, if you want to, you can throw it in the bin and never speak to me again, but at least hear me out.

Things had been wrong between us for a long time, and I was sick to death of all the arguing and fighting. I didn't mean to sleep with Laura – that looks shit written down, but I didn't, and the fact that I did it and I can't change it makes me feel awful. We actually went out because I wanted to talk to her about you. After that argument about shirt-ironing and bill-paying, when I walked out of the flat, I needed someone to talk to, so I went to Barian and saw Laura. We agreed to meet on the Friday. She said she was worried about you as well: you were going out and getting trashed all the time, you were beginning to hang around with a set of complete arseholes, and you were on your last warning at work – she thought you were going to lose your job. I went out with her to try and figure out a way I could repair things between me and you, and instead I ruined everything.

I should have come clean straight away, after I'd heard the answering-machine message, but I didn't want to hurt you. I thought that, if I denied it, you might believe me and we could sort things out. I wish to God I hadn't done it — I've never done anything like that before, and I would never do anything like it again. I just want you to know that it's the biggest mistake I've ever made. I don't know why it happened. I really don't.

I shouldn't have gone to talk to Laura about you. What I should have done is talk to you. I should have told you that I missed you when you were out at parties all the time, and that I missed you when we were arguing. I remember the first time I saw you; I fancied you more than I've ever fancied anyone. I miss that Ciara, the one I first met and was mad about, the carefree Ciara — not the Ciara who only cares about where she goes and who she sees, and who's created this made-up life that means she constantly has to lie to herself and everyone else. 'I can't tell my parents this, I can't tell Maeve that, don't tell So-and-so I work in a bar, don't mention this to So-and-so because they think I'm such-and-such…' I got to the point where I didn't know whether I was coming or going with you.

That's it, really. Rant over. I just want you to know that I love you, and that my life feels like it's fallen in around my ears and there's nothing I can do about it.

I hope you'll want to call me, but if you don't, then at least I've said my piece.

Declan

Declan had been staring at the letter for at least fifteen minutes when Barry came into their shared office. Declan quickly tucked the letter into his top drawer.

'Well, any news?' When he got back from Manchester, Declan had gone straight to Barry's apartment in Raheny.

'Nothing. I've written her a letter.'

Barry stifled a laugh.

'I *can* write, you know.'

'Why don't you draw her a nice picture and I'll do the writing for you?'

'Shut up, Bar.'

'Give me a look at it.'

'No. It's fine.'

'Give me a look, you gobshite. I'm not going to laugh at you.'

'Would you ever piss off, Barry? It's fine, and that's that.'

Barry raised an eyebrow towards Declan and switched his computer on.

'There is one thing, though.'

'What's that?'

'How do I sign the bloody thing?'

Barry looked down at Declan's scribble pad. It said, 'Yours, Declan', 'Best, Declan', 'Love, Declan', 'Always, Declan' and 'Faithfully'.

'Brilliant!' Barry exclaimed. '"Faithfully!" You know, I think you should go with that.'

'Shut up, will you?' Declan snapped, pulling the letter out of the drawer and getting up.

'Sorry.' Barry stifled a smirk.

'It's fine,' Declan said, heading for the door. 'I've just put "Declan". It'll have to do.'

'Safest option.' Barry nodded sagely, turning his attention to his list of new e-mails.

In the reception area, there was a commotion occurring. Jenny was shouting at a courier who, it appeared, was refusing to take back a huge box of gold and silver gel pens – which she, as she was insisting at the top of her lungs, had never ordered. 'I distinctly, *distinctly* said pink and blue. What is wrong with you people?'

'I can't just take them back,' gritted the courier. 'You have to send them back with a returns form.'

'Not if I don't sign for them, I don't!' Jenny waggled her head from side to side. The phone rang. 'JMSS&A, how can I help you?' she shrilled.

Declan only wanted an envelope, but his timing couldn't have been worse. As he leaned across the battle line of the reception desk to the stationery shelves, Jenny jabbed at a button and snapped, like an un-muzzled Rottweiler, 'Declan Murphy, what the hell do you think you are doing?'

Declan stopped mid-motion, like a child with his hand in the biscuit tin. 'I just wanted an envelope.'

'Jesus, you're some fucking wagon,' the courier said, shaking his head and cutting his losses: he scooped up the box of pens and headed for the door.

'What did you call me?' Jenny screamed after him. The courier stuck up his middle finger over his shoulder and marched out of the office, leaving Declan to take the brunt of Jenny's wrath.

'This place! If it wasn't for me, I swear to God…' She breathed heavily, attempting to regain her composure. 'Now then, Declan – an envelope, is it?' She handed one to him. 'Need it posting?'

'It's grand; I can do it myself.' Declan grabbed a pen and addressed the envelope. He only knew where he stood with Jenny when she was being narky with him; he wasn't used to her being helpful.

'No need for that – no need for that at all. I've a few letters that have to go in the next half-hour.'

'Well, if you're sure…' Declan stuffed the letter in the envelope and handed it over to Jenny. He wasn't about to refuse her anything, not when she was showing signs of psychosis.

'Of course I'm sure,' she said, pulling the envelope from Declan's grasp. The phone went again. 'JMSS&A, how can I help you?' Declan backed away towards his office, glad of the opportunity to end the conversation.

Jenny watched him disappear around the corner, her eyes narrowing. Then she put the call through and grabbed the letter-opener. She read the letter quickly, a glint in her eye; then she leaned back in her chair and, fielding another call, popped the letter into the shredder.

11

Maeve flopped through the door, exhausted. She threw a bag – a lasagna and a bottle of wine – onto the imported Italian leather settee and absent-mindedly flicked the TV on, kicking her shoes into the corner. Michael wasn't home, but that wasn't unusual; he often worked long hours. Michael loved his job. Sometimes Maeve was proud to have a husband who was so dedicated to his work; other times, when she felt lonely, she wished they could manage to be in the house together more than once a week.

The answering machine was flashing for attention. It was her mother. 'Hello, it's me. Just wondered if you've heard from Ciara. She's out and about. It was her first day at work, and I just wanted to know how she got on. Some temporary job. Only back a few days, and she's working – that's great, isn't it? I thought she'd be home for her tea, but…oh, well. Talk to you later.'

Maeve stabbed the machine off with a manicured finger and slumped into an armchair. Did her mother think she had nothing better to do? Maeve hadn't heard from Ciara all week, which hadn't surprised her in the slightest. The only reason Ciara would call, Maeve thought cynically, was if she needed something. And, as she was living at home and was apparently working, that probably wouldn't happen.

Maeve wished their mother would get it into her head that she wasn't her younger siblings' guardian – that she had a very stressful job and couldn't just drop everything like a stolen telly whenever Margaret wanted her to come around and attend to her younger sister. She knew the problem was that she never said anything like that to her mother. She just agreed with whatever her parents said, in order to make life easier. What they didn't know couldn't hurt them, she reasoned – and, after witnessing how they handled information that they *were* privy to, she was pretty sure it was better to leave them in blissful ignorance.

She flicked the TV off with an annoyed stab of her finger. The end titles of *Coronation Street* were rolling, which meant it was eight o'clock – and not only had she just got in from work, but Michael was late, yet again. *Where is he?* Maeve thought, suddenly irritable. They never managed to sit down and eat a civilised meal together – not that frozen lasagna was the pinnacle of civilised dining, but still, it would be nice to sit face to face and talk about their day. No sooner was this idea in Maeve's mind than she dismissed it, and herself, as ridiculous. She was a modern woman; she wasn't some helpless little lady making dinner for her very own hunter-gatherer as he roamed the plains of South Manchester sniffing for a sale to close.

Putting the kettle on and opening the kitchen window onto the beautifully landscaped terrace, Maeve decided that maybe she was spending too much time being introspective. Maybe she needed a hobby, something to calm her constantly racing thoughts. Just as she was thinking that yoga or Pilates – or a combination of the two, incorporating football and boxing, that she had seen advertised in the health-food shop in Didsbury village – might be the answer to her problems, she heard the front door open.

'Hi, babe! It's me.' Michael sounded very chipper, she thought suspiciously. He bustled into the lounge holding a bunch of flowers big enough for an Olympic ice-dance medallist. 'For you,' he said, giving her a kiss on the cheek.

'What are these for?'

Michael looked at her, wide-eyed. 'Because you're

the most beautiful woman in Didsbury and I love you with all my heart. Do I need another reason?'

Maeve stopped herself from raising an incredulous eyebrow. 'Well, thank you,' she said, putting the flowers to her nose. 'They're beautiful.'

'I got my bonus today, and let's just say it's not to be sniffed at.'

'How much?'

Michael grabbed her by the hips and kissed her full on the lips. 'A gentleman never tells. But I've booked a table at your favourite restaurant to celebrate.'

Suddenly the idea of soggy lasagna seemed a very poor alternative to an evening out, no matter how tired Maeve felt. She grabbed her husband around the neck and kissed him deeply. 'Great. Let me just quickly get changed.'

'OK, but we need to be quick; I've booked us in for half past eight.'

The restaurant in West Didsbury was very busy for a Wednesday evening; it was a few minutes before they were seated in the conservatory. Maeve loved this place. The last time she had been there had been for her birthday, six months before. She liked to save it for special occasions. Tonight, however, her resolve was weak and she was willing to take any excuse for a celebration.

'Hello, how are you?' the waitress asked Michael.

'Fine, we're fine. Drink, Maeve?'

'I'll go straight to wine.'

'Soave Superior?' the waitress asked.

Maeve looked up, taken aback: how did the waitress know Michael's favourite wine?

'Yes, that would be lovely.' Michael smiled curtly and looked intently back at the menu.

'Do you know her?'

'No. Why would I know a waitress?'

'Well, she seems to know you and your taste in wine.'

'That's because I've been here a couple of times for work.'

'Oh. You never said.'

Michael sat up in the chair and smiled. 'I never thought to. I have to schmooze clients, and this is as good a place as any. And, anyway, you can't talk. I seem to recall you ringing me from Frankfurt – and I didn't even know you'd left Manchester!'

Maeve smiled. He was right: she had gone over for the day on business, a few weeks before, and had completely forgotten to mention it to Michael. 'OK, point taken.'

'What are you going to have?'

'Not sure.' Maeve scanned the menu. 'Do you remember the first time we came here?' she asked, looking up at Michael, her eyes twinkling.

'Remember?' He laughed. 'I thought we were going to be barred!' It had been one of their first dates, and they had been sitting in a darkened corner. Michael had started playing footsie with

Maeve; one thing had led to another, and they had finished the night unashamedly kissing across the table.

'What was it that waiter said?'

'He shouted, "I think the gentleman at table ten might need a finger-bowl in a minute!"'

'God, I'm mortified all over again.'

'You weren't too mortified that night.'

'I know.' Maeve bit her lip, remembering. They had left the restaurant and jumped in a taxi back to Michael's apartment, kissing and pulling at each other's clothes all the way. Just remembering made her feel giddy; it had been so out of character. She wasn't the sort of person who got amorous in taxis. She was the sort of person who asked the taxi driver if he'd been busy and what time he had started. She looked at Michael and smiled, remembering how they'd been when they first got together. He smiled back and ran his foot up her leg.

'Michael!' she laughed, in mock shock. He had slipped his shoe off without her noticing.

He winked at her. 'Only kidding. Come on; what are you having?'

'I think I'm going to have the scallops to start, and the...' A loud bang from the next table derailed her train of thought. A woman was bouncing a young child on her knee; the baby had thrown his arms out, knocking his bottle onto the floor. Michael tutted, and Maeve threw him a look as she bent to pick up the bottle.

'There you go,' she said, putting it on the table.

'Thank you,' the baby's mother said. 'He's like a windmill at the moment; I should tie his arms down.' Maeve laughed and winked at the little boy.

'Might be an idea,' Michael said under his breath.

'Michael!' Maeve glared at him and glanced quickly at the woman, to check that she hadn't heard the remark. She hadn't; she was too busy trying to prevent a napkin from being shredded.

'What?'

'You know what. That was really rude,' Maeve whispered.

'Are you finally getting broody?' Michael smiled and placed his hand on her leg.

She stiffened. 'No, I'm not getting broody. I'm just being polite.'

Michael removed his hand. 'Fine. But I wasn't being rude. There's a time and a place for babies, and a restaurant isn't it.'

'Oh, OK. So what's the time and place for a baby? This coming from the man who is adamant he wants to be a dad,' Maeve said, shaking her head.

'I do. I just won't bring it to restaurants to fire things around, that's all.'

'It's not an accessory, Michael.'

'And I'm not stupid, Maeve. What's wrong with you? You're biting my head off. Christ, that's the sort of thing you'd usually complain about yourself.'

'No, it's not,' Maeve said quietly, looking down at her menu. After a moment she sighed and looked back up at Michael. 'Look, I'm sorry. I'm just very stressed and tired at the moment.'

'I know. You don't have to take it out on me.'

'I'm sorry. Shall we start again, Michael? I feel terrible now.'

'OK.' Michael nodded. 'That's fine. So what are you going to have to eat?'

Sated from their three-course meal, Maeve and Michael happily finished off a bottle of wine, their earlier tetchiness forgotten. Maeve felt a rosy glow and looked at her husband appreciatively. Things between them had been strained lately, but when they were having a nice time together – as they were now – she tried to forget the fractiousness. Marriage, she knew, had to be worked at.

Maeve and Michael had married six years earlier. A mutual friend had introduced them, and they had hit it off from the start. She enjoyed his self-assurance. They had fulfilled her parents' wishes by getting married at their parish church – Michael, who had been brought up Anglican, had had to take a course on how to be a good Catholic so that they wouldn't have to be married in (God forbid) a registry office, or, worse still (God strike her down), an Anglican church. Maeve knew that Michael thought her family was slightly mad sometimes, but she also knew that he envied their closeness. He had just one brother, who was living in the States, and his parents had moved to Surrey when he was twenty.

'Shall we get the bill?' Michael asked, taking a platinum card from his wallet.

'Is that new?' Maeve asked. She was sure she hadn't seen it before.

'What do you mean, is it new? It's my credit card.'

'You've got a BarclayCard.'

'I've transferred the balance.'

'Oh, OK.' She didn't want to make an issue out of it. 'Good idea.'

'I know.' Michael waved to the waitress for the bill.

The credit card had reminded Maeve. 'I'm going to see the bank manager tomorrow.'

Michael stiffened. 'What for?'

'Just to sort some things out. He seems to think we're overspending, and I want to tell him that I'm going to move my bank account. I mean, it's preposterous. How can we overspend? We hardly have *time* to draw any money out.'

'Well, I did take a big chunk out to cover my work credit card until my expenses came through…'

'Not again, Michael.' Maeve threw him a look of exasperation. She couldn't help herself: his lack of common sense with money always irked her.

'Don't "Not again, Michael" me, Maeve.' He

leaned across the table, his voice lowered. 'It was just a stopgap. I've got a three-grand bonus going in there at the end of the week.'

'That's all well and good, but we need to have some sort of consistency in our account; otherwise our credit rating's going to be stuffed. Again.'

When Maeve first met Michael, he had managed to accrue a level of debt that rivalled that of a small African country. He had taken her out most evenings, taken her away most weekends; he liked to live a life that, at the time, had been way beyond his means. Maeve had reined him in, telling him he didn't have to impress her with gifts and holidays, and between them they had paid off the debt; but Maeve was still wary of her husband's spending. Michael was a romantic, in every sense of the word. He thought that any problem could be solved by creating a rosy glow around it. Candles, chocolates, meals, flowers... He'd have jumped through their bedroom window dressed in black and carrying a box of Milk Tray, if he'd been sure he wouldn't be tackled by a vigilante neighbour convinced he was a burglar.

'Bollocks to that, Maeve! I try to do something nice, bring you out for a meal, and what happens? You start throwing the whole money thing in my face again.'

'I am not, Michael – that's not fair! I just need to know where I stand, that's all. And if you're taking money out of the account and I'm getting grief from the bank, then I have a right to know.'

'Fine. Whatever you say, Maeve.' Michael handed his card to the waitress and waited till she was out of earshot. 'You are money-obsessed; do you know that?'

'No, I'm not. I'm just cautious. I'm an accountant; I don't take risks.'

'Yeah, that's the problem with you,' Michael muttered, as the waitress came back with his credit-card slip.

'What was that?' Maeve wasn't sure she'd heard him correctly.

'Nothing.' Michael stood up. 'Let's go home.'

12

Ciara had had more exciting weekends when she was five. Friday night had been OK, in as much as she'd managed to have conversations with a few people who weren't blood relations: Claire had rallied a few of her friends, and they had spent the evening in a bar in West Didsbury. Ciara had been shocked to find out that the price of a pint in Manchester had skyrocketed recently; it was even more expensive than in Dublin. Claire and her friends didn't seem to be too ruffled by the astronomical prices, but then, they all had jobs – actual jobs, not like Ciara's.

Claire had been great – texting her frequently to check that she was OK, inviting her out and making sure that she didn't feel left out – but Ciara knew she couldn't expect it to be like this all the time; Claire was a great shoulder to cry on, but she was busy, and she had always done her own thing. And, anyway, Claire's friends weren't any substitute for her own. Ciara knew she was going to have to take matters into her own hands. She needed to call Rachel, but she kept putting it off.

One good thing had happened on Friday, however. Sureplace, the temping agency, had called to offer Ciara a couple of weeks' work at an office in the city centre, starting Monday. At least she wouldn't have to lie to her mother any more – not about work, anyway.

The rest of the weekend had involved another Saturday night in, another Vietcong-style grilling from her father, and another trip to Mass to watch the geriatric shuffle again. Now, as Ciara sat trying to read the Sunday papers (Sean was listening to a compilation entitled *Green Gold* that was making her ears bleed), she heard the front door open, and Maeve shouted an exuberant 'Hello!' into the house. Ciara groaned inwardly. That was all she needed.

'Hello!' Sean bellowed, over 'I'll Take You Home Again, Kathleen'. 'How's Maeve?'

'Maeve's fine.' She poked her head around the sitting-room door. Ciara nodded stiffly at her.

'No Michael?' Sean inquired.

'We're not attached at the hip, Dad.'

Ciara looked up. What was wrong with Maeve? she wondered. This was the second time she'd snapped at their father. Ciara glanced over to see his reaction.

'I didn't say you were. I was simply asking a question,' he said flatly.

'Sorry,' Maeve said quickly. 'Michael's away for the weekend, at a conference in Dublin, of all places – would you believe it, Ciara?'

'Really?' Ciara said, in a voice that sounded as if she wanted to yawn, put her feet on the table and fall asleep.

'Yeah,' Maeve said, unperturbed. 'They're staying at Clontarf Castle. Do you know where that is?'

'Clontarf,' Ciara said, going back to her paper.

'I guessed it might be in *Clontarf*,' Maeve said tightly.

'What's the matter with you, Ciara?' Sean demanded.

'What? She was funny with you a minute ago about Michael, but as soon as I say anything, you snap at me!'

'Dear Lord, I give up,' Sean said, raising his eyes to heaven.

'I'm just trying to read, that's all – when you've quite finished your chit-chat!' Ciara snapped.

'Actually, Ciara, I wasn't here for a "chit-chat",' Maeve said through gritted teeth. 'I just popped by to see if you'd like to come for lunch with me.'

Ciara folded the paper shut and eyed her sister

suspiciously. On the one hand, it would be more enjoyable to sit in and chew on her own leg; on the other hand, she didn't want to look like the refusenik of the family. Anyway, if she went out then Maeve would pay, and at least it would get her out of the house.

'Yeah, that'd be...lovely.' She was sure there had to be a more appropriate word.

Sitting in her sister's Mercedes, Ciara felt a grudging envy. As they drove, people turned to look at the car, and she would have enjoyed the attention if it weren't for the fact that it only served to remind her that she herself couldn't afford so much as a pushbike.

They had been driving for at least five minutes before Maeve broke the silence. 'So how's Manchester treating you?'

'Oh, OK. You know.'

'No, I don't know. Tell me.'

'It's all right; nothing special. What else would you like me to say?'

Maeve sighed. 'I just want to know how you are, that's all. Is Waterwall OK for you?'

'Where?'

'It's a wine bar on Beech Road.'

'Wherever. I'm not fussy.' Ciara shrugged and noticed, with a certain amount of delight, that her sister was shaking her head in despair.

The place was heaving, but they managed to get a table for two in a corner. They both grabbed menus and studied them carefully, which allowed them a legitimate lull in the conversation.

The waitress arrived at their table with a bored, weary look on her face. 'What can I get you?' she snapped.

'Eggs Benedict, please,' Ciara said.

'You?' She turned to Maeve.

Maeve looked over her shoulder as if to suggest that the woman's manner must surely be directed, at the very most, towards a small woodland creature. 'Oh, *me*? I'll have the eggs Benedict too.' She eyeballed the waitress, who refused to match her look and, grabbing the menus, stomped off to bully another table.

'Miserable cow,' Maeve and Ciara said in unison. Ciara shuffled uncomfortably and smiled a half-smile.

'I know it's busy, but you'd think she'd at least do us the honour of letting *us* be rude to *her* first,' Maeve said.

Ciara knew she was trying to break the ice, but neither of them had come here to gang up on the waiting staff. 'So, Maeve,' she said, glancing around the busy restaurant, 'what brings us here?'

Maeve leaned to the side to catch her sister's returning gaze. 'I just think we've got off on the wrong foot since you've been back, that's all. I wanted to straighten things out.'

Ciara nodded, watching a harassed, bespectacled father try to fold up what looked to be the Aston

Martin of the pram world. By the time he had finished, he had entangled himself so completely that only his feet showed. His eldest daughter, who looked about five, had to rescue him, much to his embarrassment. Ciara giggled.

'What's so funny?' Maeve asked sternly.

'God, Maeve, don't be so defensive. I was laughing at Houdini, not at you.' Ciara mock-glared at her sister. 'I think straightening things out is a good idea.'

'Great. I was thinking that, with you being back in Manchester, and us being sisters...well, we're pretty much stuck with each other.'

Ciara felt the hairs on the back of her neck bristle. 'Oh, that's about right, isn't it?'

'What?' Maeve asked, bewildered.

'We're stuck with each other, right?' Ciara said matter-of-factly; she couldn't even bring herself to sound annoyed with her sister any more. 'The only reason you want to spend any time with me, Maeve, is that you want to suck up to Mum and Dad. Well, your nose is brown enough as it is.'

'Ciara Coffey, will you listen to yourself?'

Ciara folded her arms across her chest. 'There you go, treating me like a child. I am a person in my own right, you know. I'm not just your little sister.'

'I know that, Ciara. I was just hoping that we could come out and talk, and maybe begin getting to know each other again, as adults.'

Ciara pulled a face as if she'd just sucked a lemon. 'Well, you might have thought of that when you never bothered to come and see me in Ireland.'

The grumpy waitress was back. 'Eggs Benedict!' she bellowed, plonking the plates down in front of them.

'Thank you,' they both snapped at her.

Maeve resumed the conversation. 'I came to see you once.'

'You were there for work.'

'No, I wasn't. I met someone *from* work when I was there. But I came to see how you were doing.'

'There you go again. To see how I was doing. Not to see me, not to spend time with me, but to *see how I was doing*. So you could report back.'

'Jesus, Ciara!' Maeve stabbed her fork into the soft egg-yolk. 'There is no reasoning with you. I never came to Ireland because you always said you'd see me when you came back here. We talked about this last Christmas, and you said not to worry about it if I was busy – and I thought that was really understanding of you, because I *am* always really busy.'

'Great.' Ciara played with her hollandaise sauce.

'No, it's not great; it's shit. But it's a fact. And another fact, for your information, is that I hate Ireland. *Really* hate Ireland.'

Ciara sat back in her chair. She hadn't been expecting that. Maeve was always the one who toed the family line; the fact that she was daring to say something so audaciously rebellious filled Ciara with secret glee. If her father had heard Maeve's confession, he'd have nailed her upside down to her Communion tree.

'What are you talking about? You – Miss bloody runner-up for Irish Dancer of the Universe five years running – you hate Ireland? You, the one who got sent there for the summer to piss about on Aunt Patricia's farm like the Rose of Tralee, while we all had to stay in Manchester and get jobs over our summer holidays?'

Maeve set down her knife and fork. She seemed to have lost her appetite. 'I went for *one* summer, when I was in sixth form. That was it.'

Ciara could sense that her sister had had just about enough, but she was enjoying herself. 'Yeah, you're a martyr, Maeve – really, you are. No one else got special treatment; we all had to work.'

Maeve threw her napkin down on her barely touched food. 'Let's get a few things straight, shall we, Ciara, before you get yourself a job on *Jackanory*? I did not get special treatment. If anyone in the family is handled with kid gloves, then it's you. I might have gone to Ireland for the summer, but you, oh chosen one, went to Ireland for university – and not just any old college, either; no, that wouldn't do. You went to *Trinity*.' Maeve paused for breath. 'And the best thing, the absolute icing on the cake, is that we weren't even allowed to come to your graduation, because you decided that graduations were... What was it? Let me get it right.' Maeve put her palms in the air, like a psychic receiving a message from the other side. 'Oh, that's it: "just for show" and "meaningless". You did Mum and Dad out of the one bloody thing they'd have given their right arms to go to, because of some bolshie ideal of yours that lasted three seconds. And then what do you do?' Maeve was wide-eyed with incredulity. 'You piss off to Ibiza for two weeks! And yet we weren't allowed to say anything, because you're Ciara, and everyone *expects* you to behave like a big hippie airhead.'

Ciara was scarlet. 'Don't make out like I'm their bloody pride and joy! You only have to stick your bloody Toni-and-Guyed head through the door and Mum and Dad are all over you like a rash.'

Maeve signalled the grumpy waitress for the bill.

'I haven't finished eating!'

'Well, I have.' Maeve threw fifteen pounds on the table. 'Keep the change and get the bus home. I give up.'

'The bus? Sod that! You can give me a lift home.' Ciara shovelled the remainder of her eggs Benedict into her mouth, dribbling egg-yolk down her chin.

'No, I can't,' Maeve said, and stormed out of the restaurant.

She had hopped into the car and torn away before Ciara got to the door. Running into the street, Ciara saw the Mercedes's brake-lights disappear at the end of Beech Road. She stood, open-mouthed, in the middle of the road, stranded and fuming.

Ciara walked home – there wasn't a direct bus route – making noises about Maeve under her breath all the way, sounding like Muttley from *Wacky Races*. As she walked along Nell Lane, past Southern Cemetery and around the new exclusive housing development ('exclusive' meaning that only landed gentry and Russian oil magnates could afford to buy anything there), Ciara thought about what Maeve had said. At first she was furious with her – didn't Maeve realise that she was an adult too? – but, by the time she had trudged all the way home, she was finding it hard to stay angry. She didn't have the energy.

There was no one home, which was unusual for the Coffey household. Ciara remembered that her mother had asked if she wanted to help out at the local fête. Margaret was in charge of the tombola. Ciara had gracefully declined. Her mother loved running the tombola, but Ciara didn't really understand the attraction of selling raffle tickets to people who got excited when they won a tin of dried prunes or some ten-year-old bath salts.

Ciara decided that she was going to do something useful. She was going to check her e-mail. She had been putting it off: if no one from Dublin had contacted her, she knew it would upset her.

As she logged on to her e-mail account, Ciara had butterflies in her stomach. It had been a week since she had seen Declan, but a bit of her hoped – ridiculous though she knew it was, after she had said she never wanted to see him again – that he would at least e-mail her, to try and apologise again. The truth was that he was the one person Ciara did want to see, but she knew she had to have the courage of her convictions. If she had heard about someone forgiving a cheating partner, she would have happily poured scorn on them, seeing it as a sign of weakness. But she had to admit, if only to herself, that she had been thinking about little other than Declan.

Her inbox informed her that she had seven new messages. Ciara breathed a small sigh of relief – at least she wasn't being completely ignored. She scanned the messages quickly for Declan's name. When she realised that he hadn't even used the easy option of e-mail to contact her, she became resolute again. *Declan Murphy is an utter wanker,* she told herself. She needed to adopt this as her personal mantra and get on with her life, as much as it hurt. *How could he put everything behind him so quickly?* she wondered dolefully, ignoring the fact that she herself was making valiant headway in that area, having actually moved country and broken all contact.

She scanned the e-mails absently. Her spam guard was performing its usual outstanding job: she was being offered three penis extensions, a sneak preview of some American dorm girls getting down to it and a way to make a million in a month. She was about to hit the 'Delete all' button when she saw that the last two e-mails weren't attempts to lure her into the world of hardcore porn: they were from acquaintances in Dublin. Ciara felt giddy at the thought that they cared. Suddenly, she was embarrassed that she hadn't thought of these people as friends – yet they were e-mailing to check she was OK, which was more than Declan had done.

The first was from Scott, the man responsible for dangling her over the Liffey. After seeing her ribs the next day, Declan had declared Scott a 'thoughtless wanker'. As she opened the e-mail, Ciara couldn't help gloating a little: he couldn't be that thoughtless if he had bothered to e-mail her.

Hi, Kiwi –

Missed ya this w/e. Where were you? Tried your phone – no answer. Had to get some other friends to go out and play with.

Just writing because I was wondering if you could lend me 100 euro till the end of next week. That's when I get paid for the flyering I've been doing for the clubs. We could have a bit of a session if you're on for it.

Let me know asap about the money.
Cheers,
Scott xxx

A feeling of dejection crept over Ciara. Who did he think he was, calling her Kiwi and asking for money? She smacked the mouse angrily to delete the message.

The other e-mail was from Toni, a part-time jewellery designer and full-time lunatic who hung out in Barian.

Hi, Ciara –

Went into Barian today to see if you were out and about and they said you'd gone back to Manchester!!! Scott says no one's heard from you. What's the story? Have you and your boyfriend split up?

Ciara smiled gratefully at Toni's concern.

Let me know what's going on, because if your apartment's free I want to rent it. Will you let me know who the letting agency is?
Toni xxx

Ciara couldn't believe what she was reading. She read it again and then deleted the e-mail. *Fuck you,* she thought.

She shut the computer down, turned off all the switches in the study (her father lived under the impression that, if every appliance wasn't completely disconnected from the national grid as soon as it wasn't being used, he would have a tinder-box on his hands) and wandered into her yellow bedroom.

When Ciara had first been in Dublin, she had

had a solid group of friends – Róisín, Geraldine and Sinéad. How had she managed to let them all go? The altercation with Maeve came back into her mind, and she began to realise that Maeve had seen what she herself had been ignoring: she was back in Manchester, and she was going to stay. This had obviously been apparent to everyone except herself – until now. Even though she had been in Dublin for years, she no longer felt any connection with the place. She had nothing to go back for; she had to make a new start in Manchester. Maeve, Ciara realised, wanted her to get on with things – and she had a point. Not that Ciara was about to credit her with this revelation; she was still annoyed about her earlier desertion.

13

Maeve arrived home and slumped into the nearest available chair. The kitchen clock ticked loudly, making her all too aware of the silence of the house. She flicked on the TV and sighed, thinking about Ciara. *She's unbelievable. Does she think she's the only person in the world who has problems?* After flicking through the channels for ten minutes without paying attention to any of them, she pushed herself up from the chair and trudged upstairs.

Maeve rummaged behind the vast shoe collection in her wardrobe and found what she was looking for – her laptop case. She put it on the bed and, ignoring the actual laptop, pulled out an envelope addressed to her at the office. She knew she shouldn't really have brought the letter home. Despite the fact that Michael was away, she felt guilty about it even being in the house. Carefully taking a letter out of the envelope, Maeve studied the words. She had already read it over and over again since she had received it on Friday. Becky usually opened the post, but Maeve had instructed her that anything from the Republic of Ireland was to be handed straight over to her.

The letter was about something she had thought about every day for the past sixteen years. Some days were worse than others; sometimes the secret felt too heavy to carry alone. In England, only her mother, her father and Father O'Neill knew about it; and, as far as they were concerned, the topic was definitely not open for discussion.

She really had wanted to tell Michael, but somehow it had never felt like the right time. When they first got together, she had felt that it might somehow put him off her; then, as the relationship progressed, she had felt that she had deceived him by withholding the information initially, and that he would never trust her again if he found out now. On another, more instinctive level, Maeve felt sure that he would judge her harshly; that he would see her as a different person. This wasn't part of the Maeve package he had met and married. She knew how Michael thought, and nothing about the information she held in her hand would fit into his life-plan.

Maeve pulled out the enclosed photograph and scrutinised it again, although she already knew every inch of the face: the blond hair, the shy laughing eyes, the rosy cheeks. She looked back at the letter and wondered how long the girl had agonised over the words.

Dear Maeve,

I can't tell you how much it means to me that I've finally found you. Thank you for answering my first letter. I'm sorry it was so cryptic, but it had to be, so that you would only understand if you actually were the correct person for me to be writing to. I am now called Catherine Maloney, but I was, as you know, Gemma Coffey. I am sixteen years old. And, from everything I've found out, you are my natural mother.

I've been trying to trace you since I was fourteen. I asked the nuns at the adoption agency if I could meet you, but they told me to come back when I was over eighteen. But I didn't want to wait. I kept on and on at John and Miriam, my adoptive parents – they've been pretty good about it – until my dad finally cracked and told me he knew your surname. On the day he collected me from the home, when I was a baby, he saw my original name on the cot. He'd never even told my mum about it until he decided to tell me; he thought it might upset her and make her think about you all the time. He only told me in the end because he realised I really needed to know who you were.

It's taken a lot of work to find you. I got information on tracing people from the internet, and then I followed it until everyone was sick of me pestering them. I got your birth certificate online; I also found out that you are married but don't have any other children. I hope you don't think I'm a mad stalker — I'm not. I just really wanted to get in touch with you. I've had to be very careful and follow all these guidelines to make sure that I didn't contact someone who wasn't my birth mother, so I'm glad you answered my first letter so quickly and confirmed that you are who I thought you were.

Thank you for agreeing to let me write to you. I don't really know what to say. There's so much I want to ask you. I've always wondered what you look like. I'm enclosing a photograph, and of course I'm wondering if I look like you at all.

I live in Cashel in County Tipperary. I'll be doing my Leaving Cert next year, and I want to be a doctor, but I don't know if I'll get the points. I hope so. I work in a bakery at the weekends; the money's OK. I really like music — not boy bands and stuff, real music like rap and rock. My favourite singer is 50 Cent. I have one brother who is twenty. He is also adopted, but he doesn't want to find out who his natural parents are — but that's just because he's a boy, and they think strangely, don't they?

There's so much that I want to say, but I'm nervous. Any information you can give me would be great, and if you were willing to meet me I would be delighted. But of course that's up to you. Thank you for taking the time to answer my last letter.

Yours sincerely,
Catherine/Gemma

Every time Maeve read the letter, she found something new in it that made her want to cry.

She went downstairs, found a piece of paper and sat down. There was so much she wanted to say, but it took five minutes of staring before she wrote the first words. She felt she owed the young girl a truthful explanation. Once she began writing, though, she found that the words came, not easily but certainly quickly.

Dear Catherine,

Thank you for your lovely letter. I'd like to start by saying that you're not the only one who's nervous. I am too. But I just want you to know that I am so happy you've contacted me. I've enclosed a picture of myself, so that you can see all my crow's feet!

I live in a place called Didsbury, in Manchester – it's a village four miles from the city centre. I work as an accountant in town and spend most of my days in meetings or travelling abroad.

Before I say anything else about myself, I think I need to give you an explanation of why I gave you up for adoption. I got pregnant when I was in the Lower Sixth form – the same as your Leaving Cert year, I think. I had been going out with your birth father for about eight months when I found out I was pregnant. I come from a very strict Catholic family, and I was so scared I didn't know what to do; so I did nothing. I just went about my business, pretending everything was fine. I'm not sure how long this would have gone on if I hadn't had morning sickness – but I did, and my mum noticed it. She asked me if everything was OK; I said I was fine, but she pressed me, asking me if there was something she should know. I just crumbled; I started crying and told her I was pregnant. I'll never forget how she reacted. She didn't hug me or comfort me or shout at me. She just shook her head and asked, 'Who have you told?'

It wasn't what I had expected. I had thought she'd ask how I could have been so careless, or tell me that I was a disgrace, but she just wanted to know who knew. I said, 'No one,' and Mum said, 'Right, we need to sort this out. I'm calling your father.'

That night, when my sisters and brother were in bed, Mum and Dad told me what they had decided was the best thing for me. I was to go to Ireland, stay with my aunty, have the baby there and give her – you – up for adoption. I felt guilty and dirty, and Dad just kept staring at me as if he didn't recognise me. And I know it sounds awful, and I don't know what it'll be like for you to read this, but I was relieved – simply because the decision had been taken out of my hands.

I spent four months at my aunt's in Tullamore, and that's where you were born. For most of the pregnancy I was convinced that giving you up was the right decision, that I wasn't fit to be a mother, that someone else would give you a better life. But in the last month my thoughts really changed. You were moving around inside of me; you were part of me, and I wanted you more than anything. When you were born, I held you and looked at you and I wanted to keep you so much. You were beautiful.

I screamed at my aunt that she couldn't allow this to happen, that I wanted to ring my mum and dad, but she just looked away and said, 'You have no choice; it's been decided.' And, stupidly, I let them take you. It's the biggest regret of my life.

I came home and went about my life, but I just felt numb. I did my A-levels, went to university, got a job and worked, but all the time I felt that you should have been there. When I was twenty-five I tried contacting you, but the nuns told me in no uncertain terms that there was no way this would be allowed to happen.

No amount of apologising I can do could ever make up for giving you away. I just hope that this letter goes some way towards explaining why I did what I did, and that you know how much I wish things had been different.

I would love to meet you. We should probably take our time, get to know each other a little by letter first – that way we'll both be less nervous when we do meet. Will you send me your telephone number and I'll call you, if that's OK with you?

Maeve

Maeve read over the letter twice. Then she placed it carefully in an envelope, attached two stamps and walked to the nearest post-box. As the letter left her hand, she felt enormously relieved.

It wasn't until she returned home that she realised she hadn't mentioned Michael once in the letter.

14

Ciara had been back in Manchester for a few weeks, and things were taking on a comforting, if slightly monotonous, normality. She was temping by day and going to a nearby gym at night, reading, spending time with Claire, and trying to banish Declan from her mind on a near-hourly basis. He still hadn't made any attempt to contact her, nor she to contact him.

For the past two weeks Ciara had worked in a different office almost every day, covering sick leave in the most unlikely environments – a school, a women's refuge, an old people's housing association, a dodgy sales company where she'd had her bottom slapped by a twenty-one-year-old salesboy who'd probably have full use of his hand again by Christmas. Her favourite assignment had been covering for the receptionist at a place called Equality Matters, which dealt with discrimination cases.

A kindly-faced woman called Joan had shown her the reception area and got her a cup of tea. 'Most of the people who come in are very agreeable; they genuinely need help,' she'd told Ciara. 'Just sit them down and call one of us through. We do have the odd regular, though – you'll know if you get one of them. Again, just give me or Sue a shout, and we'll come through and deal with them.' Ciara had wondered who would be a regular at an equality office.

A few hours later, she had rearranged the filing cabinet and asked if anyone needed anything typing, as she felt guilty just sitting there; one of the women had given her a back catalogue of *Hello!* magazines and told her to relax. Ciara had leafed through them for a few minutes, but there was a limit to the interest she could muster for collagen-injected, aristocratic women with surnames like Von Bismarck. She decided to check online for well-paid jobs waiting to be filled by unqualified failures.

Then the door had opened and a woman had walked in, carrying four heavy carrier bags. Her eyes had darted wildly around the room. There was a faint smell emanating from her that Ciara couldn't quite place, but she thought that if you left milk in direct sunlight for three days it might give off a similar odour. The woman scurried over to the reception desk and looked quickly around, checking that she didn't have an audience, before tipping the contents of her bags all over the floor. Ciara jumped to her feet, staring in disbelief at the mess: defrosted lasagne, tinned food of all varieties, and at least twenty bottles of shampoo, conditioner and shower gel, all smeared with mouldy fish and meat. *A regular, maybe?* Ciara thought.

'I want to see your boss because I'm being discriminated against.'

Ciara looked at the woman in disbelief. 'I'll get someone, but first, I just need to know why your month's shopping is on the floor.'

'Because they were all two for one!' the woman shouted, at the top of her lungs. Joan ran out of her office. 'Everything all right, Ciara? ... Ah, Mary. What can we do for you this week?' she asked, looking at the mess.

'You can take the supermarkets to court for me – all of them!'

'Right. Well, what we're going to do first is clear up this mess. Ciara will make you a nice cup of tea and we can talk about it in one of the private offices – what do you say?'

Mary smiled and began scooping the mess back into the bags.

When Joan emerged from her meeting with Mary and saw her safely into the lift, she explained to Ciara the nature of Mary's gripe. It appeared that

Mary felt discriminated against by every major supermarket and high-street chemist because, when they offered 'two for the price of one' deals, she felt compelled to buy whatever was on offer. It made economic sense, she argued. But she lived on her own and therefore fresh goods went off (she didn't believe in freezers), and she only used one bottle of shampoo a year – which, in Ciara's opinion, wasn't something to be bragging about. So, Mary had told Joan, she wanted a complete ban on two-for-one offers: they were unfair to single people.

Joan had sent her away, saying that she didn't think this constituted discrimination, but that she would look into it. Mary's visit was a weekly occurrence, apparently. 'Sorry, love, I should have warned you. She usually comes in on Fridays, though. Last week she was discriminated against because they wouldn't let her be a bus driver. She can't drive, and she's seventy-five.'

But Ciara had only been needed for one day at Equality Matters, which she thought was a shame; she had enjoyed it there. She had had a two-day assignment in an office where the woman working beside her refused to talk to her: 'No point in polite chit-chat, you're only here for two days.' And the last few days had been particularly difficult. She was working in a property consultancy run by a man who had missed his calling: not having been born into a country where totalitarian regimes were the order of the day, he had set up his own tin-pot dictatorship in the heart of Manchester's banking district. Ciara had considered walking out after her new boss had shouted – no, *screamed* – at her for the third time, for, as far as she could gather, no good reason. But she had decided against it. She had stopped running away from things, she told herself. She was going to deal with this like a grown-up: she would go to Sureplace and talk to Lisa about it. She had been asked to go into the Sureplace office that lunchtime anyway – they were having some get-together for all the temps. Ciara had originally intended to skulk in, stuff some sandwiches in her mouth and skulk out again; instead, she was going to skulk in, tell Lisa she wanted to work somewhere else, stuff some sandwiches in her mouth and skulk out again.

Ciara walked across Piccadilly Gardens, avoiding the skater kids who were throwing one another into the fountains, and through the door of Sureplace. The reception area was festooned with balloons, and before she had a chance to work out what was happening, there was a collective shout of 'She's here!' Party poppers were deployed, a small ripple of tepid clapping went around the room and Lisa thrust a bouquet of flowers into Ciara's hand. 'Congratulations, Ciara – you're our Temp of the Month!'

Ciara smiled weakly and looked around. There were a handful of people standing around, chewing on catered sandwiches, pretending to look elated that the temp before their eyes was *the* temp of the whole entire *month*, and obviously feeling as uncomfortable as she was. They were obviously the other temps from Sureplace, lured there by the promise of free food. The boss shook Ciara's hand and handed her an envelope. 'Book token,' she said, by way of explanation.

'Thank you.' Ciara smiled shyly at the small crowd.

Lisa took her to one side. 'We've had great feedback on you. I know you've had a difficult week, but I promise your next assignment will be better. I've got a position in a really nice office on Deansgate. Everyone's really laid back there; I think you'll like it. It's for a few weeks, as well, so you can get used to the place.'

Ciara, still reeling from the shock of being party-poppered, said, 'Sounds great.'

'It's to start tomorrow, if that's OK?'

'Brilliant!' Ciara was delighted that she didn't have to go back to the property consultancy.

'I thought you'd be better off somewhere else. To be honest, we've had nothing but complaints from anyone we've placed where you are now. I thought you might be a match for him.' Lisa laughed.

'Cheers,' Ciara said. That was a backhanded compliment if ever she'd heard one.

'The new position is helping out the PAs to the partners at an accountancy firm. Here's their card.'

Ciara looked down at the card, and the name of

the firm filled her with a feeling of impending doom. Williams Mackay. *That's where Maeve works!* she thought, panic-stricken. 'Great! Thanks, Lisa.' Her voice had risen several notches, as if she had been sucking one of the helium balloons adorning the office. She couldn't very well say no – not after all the trouble they had gone to with the sandwiches and the Battenberg cake and the ten-pound book voucher.

Ciara left the office with her flowers, still a little overwhelmed. She didn't know whether to be delighted or disgusted: Temp of the Month was the first award she'd won since the South Manchester Schools 110-metre hurdles competition when she was fifteen.

She hoped to God that she wouldn't be working anywhere near Maeve. They hadn't spoken since Ciara had been forced to walk home from Beech Road. Sean said that Maeve was spending a lot of time working away from home, but Ciara knew she had just been keeping a low profile – she was probably, and rightfully, embarrassed about dumping her so rudely, Ciara decided. She toyed with the idea of calling Maeve and informing her of her new job, but decided against it. She'd cross that bridge if, and when, she came to it.

15

'No fucking way!' Declan said for the umpteenth time that evening. He was cupping his pint glass like a soothsayer gazing into a crystal ball, and shaking his head into it.

'Dec, will you give it a rest?' Barry waved to the lounge boy, indicating that another two pints were required. 'It's not like you've just been given three weeks to live.'

They were sitting in Bowe's, a small bar tucked away at the non-Temple-Bar end of Fleet Street. Declan loved this pub, but their main reason for choosing to drink there this evening was that there was no chance of their boss, John Marriott-Smith, popping in for a pint. He preferred to stick to

Dawson Street. Declan didn't want John seeing his real reaction to the news.

'Might as well have been,' Declan said.

'Oh, Jesus, where's my violin?'

'*Manchester,*' Declan said with disbelief.

The day had started ordinarily enough. He had gone into work with new verve. It had been weeks, and Ciara hadn't replied to his letter, so he was just going to have to get on with his life and forget her. He even managed to raise a smile for Jenny the receptionist, which was proof enough for him that his mood was changing.

Declan had had three coffees, read the papers, checked his e-mail and waited for Barry to put in an appearance. When he'd finally shown up, John had asked them to come into his office. He wanted to talk to them, he said, about a project for a giant drinks firm in Manchester that wanted to make their bitter more appealing to the alcopop generation. JMSS&A's Manchester office had been open nearly a year, and Declan and Barry had been asked to mentor one of their creative teams in the past. It was a time-consuming job, which neither of them had enjoyed, and at the moment Declan really didn't want to liaise with Manchester every day; he wanted to forget about Manchester and all it contained. So it had come as something of a kick in the stomach when John had said, 'It shouldn't be for more than a couple of months. There's a lovely hotel in Didsbury, just spitting distance from the office, that I'll book you into. I want my best creative team on this one, and you've worked on similar projects before…'

Declan felt as if his life had just imploded. The last thing he needed was to be in the same city as Ciara.

'I'm going to bump into her, I just know I am,' he complained to Barry.

'Will you ever fuck off with yourself? Manchester's huge; you are *not* going to bump into Ciara.'

'It might be huge, but I know enough about the place to know that Didsbury's where her sister lives and that it's about ten minutes' walk from her parents' house. So actually, Bar, I think that narrows down the odds. Wouldn't you say?'

'I think you're overreacting. It'll be brilliant. We can go out every night and lash into the expenses.'

'Yeah, and it *would* be great – anywhere else in the fucking world, it would be fantastic!' Declan, realising that he had just scared the lounge boy who was delivering their pints, lowered his voice. 'Anywhere except Manchester.'

'You need to think differently, that's all,' Barry said, picking up the fresh pint and taking a sip.

'What are you talking about?'

Barry pulled a bookie's pen from his jeans pocket and, ripping the top layer from the beer mat, began to scribble on it. 'You need to do a re-branding exercise on your ex-girlfriend.'

Declan shuffled closer to the bar, curious.

'OK, so what have we got?' Barry asked, screwing up his face in concentration. 'Previously, Ciara was fit, funny, intelligent, enough of a woman to make you – quite literally the cock of Dublin – put it away and anchor your boat in one harbour, if you get my drift.'

Declan nodded wistfully. He also winced, ever so slightly, at Barry's description of him. It was true, though: until Declan had met Ciara, he could have given Julio Iglesias a run for his money in a bedpost-notch competition.

'Don't go dewy-eyed on me; I'm just giving you the contrast, good girlfriend versus bad girlfriend. That description I just gave is how you see her when you're remembering the good times. Now, stay with me. Recently, the last – what? six, seven months?' Barry asked. Declan nodded. 'She's been giving you royal grief, am I right?'

'Well, I suppose so, but I was as bad…'

'Don't be making excuses for her. Remember, we're re-branding her. So come on' – Barry poised his pen over the beer mat – 'give me ten words to describe Ciara. No mush, now. I want you to think of her at her worst.'

At about three in the morning, Declan woke up with a thirst that could have killed a camel. Dragging himself out of bed, he headed for the kitchen. He turned the light on, squinted at the brightness, and tried to remember how many pints had led to this level of nausea and thirst.

As he approached the fridge to find anything that resembled liquid, Declan saw a photo of Ciara – Barry had finally shamed him into admitting he was carrying it around in his wallet – taped to the fridge door. On her head, drawn in Biro, were devil-horns, and a pointy Beelzebub beard was scribbled on her chin. Underneath was the beer mat, covered with Barry's working scrawl:

Music – 'Satan' by Orbital loudly plays.
Voice-over, whispering and rising to crescendo: 'Argumentative, self-centred, argumentative, absent, argumentative, messy, argumentative, complaining, argumentative, owned a Westlife CD. Want to live with that for the rest of eternity?'

Declan smiled wryly as he opened the fridge door. He hadn't been able to come up with ten words to malign Ciara, but he had said that she was the most argumentative person he'd ever met, and that when they'd first moved in together her CD collection had contained a few stinkers. (Declan had managed to convince her to let him use them as coasters. He was continually amazed by the robustness of *25 All-Time Tearjerkers*.) He slugged back half a gallon of Coke and looked at the advert again. He liked it, he decided. He was going to keep it, to help him remain resolute should he feel any signs of wavering.

16

Maeve was in a restaurant somewhere in the wilds of Cheshire. One of her colleagues had recommended it as the best restaurant he had ever been in. *He must be mad,* she thought. Sitting opposite her was Jack Partridge, a Manchester-based client, who was complaining vehemently about the size of the portions – which, Maeve had to agree, were miniscule.

'Is this what they call *nouvelle coozeen,* is it?' Jack had asked the waiter, who had smiled serenely as he placed the starters on the table. *He's probably gone to put earwax in our desserts,* Maeve thought.

The main courses had just arrived (the waiter had asked, 'Duck?' and, to Maeve's acute embarrassment, Jack had ducked, guffawing. The waiter had smiled tightly). 'So, my little numerical beauty, where are we up to?' Jack asked, in his gruff Salford accent.

In the last fifteen years, Jack Partridge had become one of the wealthiest men in the northwest. In the mid-80s, he had backed a friend who owned a small technology company producing digital boxes that made satellite-to-TV communication possible. Everyone had told him that he was mad, and that the digital box would be the next Sinclair C5; but Jack had put the money in anyway, to help his friend out of trouble. Jack and Partridge Enterprises now had more money than they knew what to do with. Rumour had it that Jack's initial wealth had been gained in the 60s and 70s, when he had reportedly been a Salford gangster. Maeve thought there was probably a lot of truth in this. He was far more Reggie Kray than Bill Gates.

She started to explain what their latest audit would involve. Schmoozing clients could be hard work a lot of the time, but there was something about Jack Partridge, with all his bluff inappropriateness, that Maeve quite liked. Taking him to a pretentious restaurant and watching him moan about the food felt like light respite at the moment. Maeve had other things on her mind. Her workload was towering. She and Michael had had another falling-out about money – it had started when she innocently picked up his Visa bill, and had ended in a shouting match – and now he was away for work all week, so she would have to wait until Friday to sort things out. And then there was Catherine.

The meal ended, and Maeve shook Jack's hand. 'It was lovely to see you again. I'll be in touch.'

'It was lovely to see *you* again,' he informed her. 'You've got the best pins in the business.'

She looked at him and shook her head, smiling. Jack winked and climbed into his Bentley Arnage, leaving Maeve to resume the business of worrying about her life.

'Hi, Becky. What've you got for me?' Maeve asked, heading purposefully towards her office.

Becky swung around on her chair. 'Everything; you've got a shed-load of stuff.'

'Surprise me.' Maeve groaned.

Becky followed her into her office and dumped a file full of paperwork on her desk. 'I've done everything that I could do myself. You just need to sign what's in there. And there's a list of your appointments and your calls. Oh, there's another package from Ireland – I popped it in your top drawer.'

Maeve's eyes widened slightly, and she furtively slid the drawer open an inch. 'Thanks.'

'And Michael just called.'

'Did he?' Maeve raised an eyebrow.

'Yeah, but the reception was terrible. He sounded like he was a million miles away.'

'He might as well be; he's in Aberdeen on a conference.'

'Oh, and I do have a surprise for you.'

'Yeah, what's that?'

'I'll just get her for you.'

'Her?' Maeve asked, puzzled, as Becky left the office.

A minute later she was back. She had a sheepish-looking Ciara in tow.

'Hi, Maeve.'

'Well, hello! What are you doing here?' Maeve asked amicably – for Becky's benefit, not her sister's.

'I'm just, em, temping.'

'Really? Here? Well, isn't that a fantastic coincidence?'

'I'll leave you two to it.' Becky smiled at the family tableau.

As the door closed behind her, Maeve's eyes narrowed. 'Temping here? As what?'

'I'm just working with the partners' PAs, clearing a backlog, apparently.'

'It's hardly the heady world of advertising.'

Ciara shuffled uncomfortably. 'No need to have a dig, Maeve. Is that another way of asking why I haven't got a *proper* job yet? I've only been back a few weeks; give me a chance. At least I'm working.'

Maeve let out a sigh. 'All right, Ciara; no need to

be so defensive. Anyway, how come you're here, of all places?'

'It's just a coincidence,' Ciara said, glaring at her sister. 'I didn't beg to come here, believe it or not, and I'll be out of your hair as soon as possible.'

'I'm not having a go, Ciara. I'm just asking you.'

'Well, I'm *just telling* you.'

'OK, that's fine. How's everything?'

'What, since you left me stranded in the street?'

'Ciara, leave it, please. I've enough on my plate.' Maeve picked up the bulging file she had just been handed, by way of explanation.

Ciara shrugged. 'I'm OK. Actually, I was made Temp of the Month yesterday. How's that for embarrassing?'

'But that's good, isn't it?'

'Is it?' Ciara asked. 'Look, I didn't want to come here, but the agency didn't have anything else. I'm skint, so I needed the money. I didn't think I'd bump into you. I can't believe that, of all the offices in the building, I'm in the same one as you – and working next to your PA.'

Maeve sighed. 'It's not the end of the world, is it? Just get on with it. It's fine.'

'I will, but I'll keep out of your way. Wouldn't want to cramp your style.' Ciara hopped out of the chair and headed out of the office.

Great. That's all I need, Maeve thought: *my sulky sister cocking up the filing.* She looked at the pile of post and the 'to do' list that Becky had handed her.

It was all urgent, but it could all wait, she thought, sliding open her desk drawer and pulling out the parcel.

When she opened it, Maeve felt suddenly relieved. This was the first time she had heard from Catherine since she'd posted that letter. She had hoped dearly that it had come across as sincere and heartfelt, the way it had been intended – and it seemed, from the thoughtfully assembled contents of the package, that it had. Catherine had sent some more pictures of herself, another letter, a CD of her favourite songs, and a strawberry face pack with a note attached: 'For relaxing after work.' Maeve held the face pack as if she had just been given the Crown Jewels to look after.

This letter seemed more relaxed than the last. '…I'd love to meet up soon – but I know you're right and we should probably get to know each other first. Thanks so much for the picture, by the way. I think we do look a bit alike, which was a really weird feeling at first – good weird, though, not bad weird.' She went on to tell Maeve about her daily life, her friends and her family. At the end she gave a phone number and her e-mail address: 'If you ever feel like talking, give me a ring.'

Maeve put the number in her Palm Pilot, her heart thumping at the idea of dialling it.

17

Ciara had been standing in line for nearly ten minutes, wondering which exotic combination of sandwich fillings to get today. Once she finally reached the counter, of course, she panic-bought the first thing that came to mind: leaving the avocado and bacon sitting in their silver dishes and the smoked chicken and mayonnaise glistening in its ramekin, she plumped for ham and cheese. She needed a better game plan at lunchtime, she decided, looking at the soggy result.

As she paid, her phone began to ring, and she rummaged in her pocket for it.

'Hi, Claire.'

'I've got a surprise for you.'

'What is it?'

'It's not a what, it's a who,' Claire said, with undisguised glee.

'Who?' *Declan?* Ciara thought, with a mixture of alarm and excitement.

'I'll just put her on.' *Her? Not Declan, then.*

'Hi, Ciara. It's Rachel.'

'Oh my God!' Ciara let out a squeal, drawing disapproving looks from the people around her. She accepted her change and ran from the shop. 'Rachel, how are you? I can't believe it! Where did you bump into Claire?'

'We're at a mentoring conference together. I'm in charge of careers at my school now – I'm the person who says, "Whatever you do, don't go into teaching."' She laughed. 'So how are you? I can't believe you're back.'

'I know. I'm good, I think,' Ciara said.

'Look, how do you fancy meeting up tonight, if you're free? I can't believe I haven't seen you for two years.'

'Yeah, that'd be great! Where?'

Ciara was sitting at a table in the trendy bar where she and Rachel had arranged to meet. Looking around, she couldn't help being impressed. It was in Hulme, an area bordering the city centre. Ciara had thought Rachel was mad to suggest even going near Hulme; when they were younger, taxis had refused to drive through it. But a lot had changed since then. When Ciara had moved to Ireland, the first batch of new houses in the area had just been built; now it appeared that the cool people of Manchester were queuing up, if not to live there, at least to drink there. The bar was very busy.

Ciara gazed around at the walls decorated with graffiti art and sipped her beer, feeling a flutter of first-date nerves in her stomach. Since she had got back, she had been meaning to contact Rachel. But she had put it off, waiting for something mildly interesting to happen to her, so that she would have something to talk about other than the tale of despair that her life had been of late. Ciara wanted to be able to say how successful she was – to be like one of those women in *Hello!* magazine, reclining on her velvet chaise longue, stroking her pet Bengal tiger and bleating on about how painfully fabulous everything was – but she couldn't, and this had made it difficult to pick up the phone and ring Rachel. Now, though, she was really excited about seeing her. No matter how shabby her life might be at the moment, she decided, she really needed to get in touch with her old friends.

Rachel and Ciara had been at school together since they were eleven. They had met on the first day of upper school and immediately become close. As they moved into their teens, they had spent their evenings hanging around in Withington and Fallowfield until their nine o'clock curfew, laughing at the posh-voiced students and pretending they were older than they were, for the benefit of the boys who were also hanging around doing the same things. After passing their GCSEs they had gone to the same sixth-form college and swapped hanging around on the streets for hanging around in clubs. They had thrown themselves into Manchester's clubland like a pair of debutantes into London society – to the point that Rachel hadn't done too well in her exams, and had had to take whatever course she could get. She had gone to Bradford College. Ciara, who always had the fear of her parents' disapproval to balance any teenage folly, had made sure that, whatever state she got herself into, she did everything necessary to get the grades she needed to go to Trinity.

Ciara couldn't believe how long it had been since she had seen Rachel, or even spoken to her. If someone had asked her, when she was eighteen, whether there was any chance that she might someday go a day, never mind two years, without speaking to Rachel, she would have laughed at the idea.

Rachel came through the door at breakneck speed. 'Sorry I'm late.' She hugged Ciara tightly. 'Look at you – you look great!' She held Ciara at arm's length for inspection.

'So do you,' Ciara said, delighted to see her.

'Thanks. I don't feel too good, though; we've just had a bit of a mad one at home. One of my housemates is a complete fruitcake. We just had a house meeting and kicked her out, but she's refusing to go. I locked my door and left her screaming at Mark like a woman possessed – Mark's my other housemate. God, what am I talking about? You don't know any of these people.' She looked apprehensively at the two-deep crowd at the bar. 'I'll brave that in a minute. I should've picked you up in a taxi; I had to come through Withington.'

'It's fine. I went to Claire's after work and she dropped me here.'

'So…' Rachel squeezed Ciara's knee. 'How've you been?'

They had so much to catch up on that they could only touch briefly on everything that had happened over the past couple of years. Rachel said that she loved teaching, and that she had moved back to Manchester the previous summer – the last Ciara had heard, she had moved in with her boyfriend in Headingley and had been intending to stay in Yorkshire.

'Leeds was great, but it wasn't home. It might have been different if I'd gone to college there, but I didn't – and I didn't want to stay in Bradford; it was all right, but if you grow up in a big city it's a bit hard to downsize. When Craig and I split up, it just seemed obvious to come back here. And so far – fingers crossed – it's been great.'

'Well, home's home. Actually, my home's a little *more* home than I can deal with. My dad's on at me every three seconds. I'm nearly crawling the walls at this stage.'

'Move in with us!' Rachel exclaimed.

'What?' Ciara was slightly taken aback.

'You heard. We've a spare room, or we will once Lunatic Lady moves out. It'd be a laugh.'

'Ray, I haven't seen you for two years and now you want to live with me?'

'You don't have to sleep in my bed! It's just an offer. We've got to get someone in. The place is like a doss-house anyway – the rent's dirt-cheap, quite frankly, because the landlord's embarrassed by the state the house is in. But you're more than welcome to have a look at the room. And Mark's lovely.'

This sounded like a great idea, but Ciara knew that, if she moved in, she would be confirming to herself that she wasn't going back to Dublin. 'Thanks. Yeah, I'll come and have a look at the room, if that's OK?'

'Of course it is. So come on – what else has been happening in the wonderful life of Ciara?'

'It's not so wonderful.'

Ciara told Rachel about her and Declan breaking up, but it wasn't until her third bottle of beer that she disclosed the real reason.

Rachel's brow furrowed in concern. 'God, Ciara, I am so sorry. I just never would have guessed it.'

Ciara cocked her head to one side. 'Come on, Ray, Declan was the biggest flirt on the planet.'

Rachel shrugged. 'Yeah, but he was mad about

you. I'm so sorry. I really thought you two would stay together.'

'Well, we didn't.' Ciara shrugged. 'But I miss him like mad, to be honest.'

'Of course you do.'

'Look, I didn't come here to moan about Declan all night; that is definitely in the past.' Ciara smiled. 'So do you know any single men?'

Rachel laughed. 'Yeah, a few. Withington and Didsbury are teeming with them – I just can't seem to find a decent one, that's all.'

'Well, we can sort that out, can't we?' Ciara said, smiling. Rachel had always been terminally bad at showing anyone that she fancied him.

'I hope so. Things have been a bit barren lately.'

'Listen,' Ciara said, 'I need to apologise for being so crap about getting in touch.'

'Don't be ridiculous, Ciara. We were both as bad as each other. I was in Leeds and you were in Ireland. I did send you a few e-mails, but they bounced.'

Ciara winced. At one stage she had gone so long without checking her e-mail that, when she finally got round to it, her address had been shut down and she'd had to get a new one. She was ashamed to admit that she hadn't got around to giving the new address to her old friends from home. She had wanted to cocoon herself in Dublin and keep her two worlds as separate as possible. The fear that they might collide had always sent a cold fear through her.

'I'm sorry,' she said lamely. 'I'm hopeless.'

'God, it doesn't matter.' Rachel laughed. 'What matters is that I've got my best mate back.'

Ciara felt a sudden lump in her throat.

'What's up with you, soppy-arse?' Rachel asked.

Ciara shrugged. 'Nothing. I've just got someone to play with again, that's all.'

They both smiled. 'So,' Rachel said, 'what's the plan, now you're back? Are you going to get some high-flying job in advertising? Are there even any advertising firms in Manchester? I'm not very well up on these things.'

Ciara didn't miss a beat. 'Yes, there are some really good ones, actually,' she heard herself say. 'I'm not sure which one I'd prefer to work for…'

She was about to say that she needed to find a company similar to the one she'd worked for in Dublin, but suddenly she felt horribly ashamed. Here she was lying to Rachel, who wouldn't have cared if she'd been working on the bins… She felt a sudden confessional impulse. She was sick of all her lies, and Rachel was one person with whom she should have been more honest – the one person with whom she knew she *could* have been honest. She had never told Rachel that she hadn't finished her degree, and why; she had been too embarrassed.

'Ray, I've got something to tell you. I'm not sure what you're going to think, though…'

Rachel looked at her. 'Go on.'

'Well…' Ciara paused, trying to get the words

right. 'I don't know where to start to make this sound better…' Seeing the look of deep concern on Rachel's face, Ciara realised that she was over-egging the pudding somewhat. 'Oh, sorry, Ray – I haven't got some terminal disease, or anything. I've just been an idiot.'

'Thank God for that.' Rachel let out a sigh of relief.

'Look, the thing is…' Ciara took a deep breath. 'I cheated in my exams at Trinity, and I got kicked out.' Rachel was furrowing her brow; Ciara didn't know if she was confused or disapproving. 'And I lied and told everyone over here that I'd passed because I'm an idiot. There's nothing more I can say, really. And I've spent the past few years pretending that life in Dublin was a bed of roses, when actually I was working in a bar.' Ciara found that she was cringing, her hands over her face, looking at her friend through the gaps between her fingers. Rachel was staring at her.

'I'm really sorry,' Ciara said. Rachel shook her head. 'Say something, Rachel! I feel terrible!'

A grin slowly broke across Rachel's face. 'I can't believe it! You, Ciara Coffey, Miss High Achiever of the Century—'

'No, that's Maeve,' Ciara interjected, smiling wryly.

'You, runner-up for Miss High Achiever of the Century—' Rachel corrected herself.

'That's better.'

'—haven't got a degree. And you were kicked out of Trinity!'

'All right, don't rub it in! So…you're not angry with me?'

'Angry? No. "Chuffed" would be a better word to use. I don't want you thinking I'm being a bitch, but it's great to know that you're human like the rest of us.'

'Come on, Ray, be fair.'

'OK. I'm sorry.' Rachel paused, planning the best way to phrase her next question. 'How did you cheat? It's not that I'm having a go – I'm just curious.'

Ciara, shamefaced, told Rachel what she had done.

Rachel sipped her beer thoughtfully. 'And is it bad of me to ask *why* you cheated?'

Ciara shrugged. 'I panicked. I knew I was going to mess up, so I tried to wriggle my way out of it. And it backfired.'

'And I take it you lied because you didn't want to admit to your mum and dad…'

'Don't!' Ciara cried; the embarrassment was excruciating. 'That's exactly why I did it. Please don't say anything to them. I can't believe I've let it go on this long.'

Rachel raised an eyebrow. 'Ciara, I'm hardly going to pop round for tea and tell them, am I? But you're twenty-five; maybe you could tell them.'

'You know what they're like.'

'I know what *you're* like. You think your dad is this big ogre. What's he going to do if you tell him the truth about something for once?'

'He'd be so disappointed!'

Rachel laughed. 'And then what? Can you die of disappointment?'

'You just don't understand.'

'You know, I don't. And I never will. But they're your family, and it's up to you what you do and don't tell them.' Rachel laughed and shook her head. Ciara could tell that she truly didn't understand what all the fuss was about. Smiling impishly, Rachel added, 'I'm just thinking of all the times you came back, giving it loads: "I am having the *best* time." And then on the phone you said, "I'm not going to graduation; I don't believe in them."'

'Please, Rachel, stop it – it's killing me!' Ciara dived back into her hands.

'Come here, you big idiot! Give me a hug. It's great to see you. You in all your glorious Catholic guiltiness.'

'Shut up!' Ciara said, hugging her. She felt as light as air: finally, she had admitted her guilty secret to someone on this side of the Irish Sea, other than Claire. Ciara really was happy to be home.

Sean Coffey hit the top of the radio. No sooner had the station crackled into life than the signal disappeared again. 'Blasted thing,' he said, shaking his head. Ciara looked across at Anthony and rolled her eyes. This was a weekly, if not daily, occurrence: Sean trying to tune in to his favourite Irish radio station, with all the desperation of a jungle-stranded explorer trying to locate the BBC World Service.

'Dad, just put a CD on.'

'Looks like I'm going to have to.'

'I'm going upstairs,' Anthony said, knowing what was coming.

'What's wrong with him?' Sean demanded. 'He's been in terrible form for months. Can't get a civil word out of him.'

'He's seventeen.'

Sean huffed, as if to say that was no excuse, and pulled out a Wolfe Tones CD. Ciara decided that maybe this was as good a time as any to tell him that she would be moving in with Rachel.

'Dad, I'm moving out.'

'Moving? Back home?'

'No, West Didsbury. And anyway, Dad, can I just point out that Manchester is home, not Dublin?'

'Ah, you know what I mean.' Sean waved his hand dismissively. 'What does your mother make of all this?'

'I don't know; I haven't told her.'

'Well, I think she's the one you should be telling.'

'I will when she gets back from aerobics.'

'When are you moving?'

'Next week, I hope,' Ciara said. 'I've still got to see the place, though.'

'Who will you be living with?'

'Rachel's got a spare room in her house.'

'Rachel?' Sean's eyes lit up approvingly. 'Now there's a great girl. How's the teaching going?'

'Fine – yes, she's fine.' Ciara squirmed in her seat; she didn't want to get him started on how great Rachel was to be in the profession of the gods – which teaching was, as far as Sean was concerned.

'And any sign of something permanent on the horizon for you?' *Bingo*, Ciara thought.

Sean studied her, and she performed her customary under-scrutiny shuffle. 'No, but I won Temp of the Month the other day.' There was no way she was going to tell him that she was working with Maeve, and she hoped her sister wouldn't mention it in some snide form of one-upmanship. She didn't want to be the one to break it to her parents that Maeve was every bit as fantastic at work as she was in every other aspect of her life; she knew the words would stick in her throat.

'And what's that, then?'

'It means they think I'm the best temp they have, I think.' Ciara felt herself flush with shame. She might as well have been tugging at her father's coattails, saying, *Look, Daddy, see what I won! I'm the best, aren't I?*

'That's what I've always said about you. Out of all the family, you're the one who applies yourself. That's great news altogether.'

'It was just an excuse to get all their employees

under one roof for sandwiches,' Ciara muttered, ashamed that she had even mentioned it.

'There you go, Ciara, underselling yourself as always.'

She took a deep breath. *If you only knew,* she thought. 'Anyway, I want to try and find something permanent. I've been back a while now.'

For once Ciara wasn't just waxing lyrical for her father's benefit; she meant it. She knew that she was back in Manchester for good. She was moving into Rachel's, and she was going to start looking for a permanent job. There was something out there for her – a great, glamorous career with her name stamped on it. The only problem was that she didn't have a clue what it was, or where to start looking.

18

The moment Ciara walked out of the first exam at the end of her third year at Trinity, she had a sudden urge to vomit. She charged to the bin in the foyer and stuffed a ripped exam booklet into it; then she ran outside and gulped in the fresh air.

'Monetary and bleeding Welfare Economics.' Ciara spun around to see Róisín shaking her head. 'That was some shite, wasn't it?'

'It was nearly impossible. Have you got a ciggy?'

'Since when do you smoke when you're sober?'

'Since now,' Ciara said, greedily grabbing the cigarette that Róisín held out to her. As she accepted a light from Róisín's Zippo, she realised her hand was shaking uncontrollably.

'Jesus, Ciara, it wasn't that bad. Let's go get a pint.'

Ciara sucked at the cigarette and nodded in agreement, as Róisín moved in the direction of the Pav bar.

The following morning Ciara heard the phone ringing, but her banging headache refused to let her get out of bed and answer it. She heard Róisín's voice downstairs and willed the call to be for one of the other girls.

'Ciara, it's for you.'

God, she thought, throwing back the bedclothes and hauling her sore head and furry tongue downstairs.

'Who is it?' she mouthed to Róisín, who had her hand over the receiver.

'Someone terribly posh,' Róisín whispered, affecting a D4 accent.

'Hello?' Ciara said.

'Ciara Coffey?' a grand male voice asked.

'Yes.'

'This is Ulick Curran.'

Ciara felt the back of her throat close in panic. 'Hello, Professor Curran.' Ulick Curran was the head of the Economics department. Ciara had never spoken to him before; he was far too senior to deal with undergraduates in ordinary circumstances. This led Ciara to believe that the creek up which she was paddling was faeces-ridden.

'Hello. I'll keep it brief. An invigilator of the Monetary and Welfare Economics exam has accused you of cheating.'

Ciara felt the blood drain from her entire body.

'Do you have anything to say?' Professor Curran asked sharply.

'Cheating?' she said weakly. 'I don't know what you're talking about.'

'He believes that you deliberately destroyed an answer booklet to make it look as if it had been lost by university staff. Does this ring any bells?'

'I *really* don't know what you're talking about,' Ciara insisted, feeling her resolve returning. She was used to being defiant in the face of accusation, even if the accusation was wholly accurate. 'I'm more than happy to come in and discuss the matter with you.'

'That's good. Be here by four. I just need you to think about a few things before I see you. Firstly, how many answer booklets did you use?'

Ciara pretended to think about it for a moment. 'Two.'

'And can you remember the topics of the three questions you answered?'

Ciara paused again. 'Pareto efficiency, Keynesianism versus classicalism and its influence on modern monetary policy, and' – she gulped – 'the one about whether welfare economics can ever benefit from a *laissez-faire* approach.' *Was that even the question?* she wondered, panicking.

'In that order.'

'In that order,' Ciara repeated. If she was going to dig herself out of this hole, she would have to stick to her story.

'And there's absolutely nothing you would like to share with me, while I'm on the phone, before we have our formal meeting?'

'Nothing. I really don't know what you're implying, but I'll be more than happy to go through everything when I meet with you and the invigilator.' She could feel her empty stomach clenching, and it had nothing to do with the alcohol she had consumed the night before.

'Very well, Ms Coffey. I'll see you in my office at four.'

Ciara heard the phone at the other end being hung up, and she felt utterly exposed. She dropped the receiver on the floor and put her head in her hands.

'You OK, Ciara?' Róisín had edged out of the lounge.

'No, Róisín, I'm not. I'm absolutely fucked.'

Ciara was sitting on a bench in St Stephen's Green, crying hysterically, as Declan hugged her and told her that everything was going to be all right. It had been a year and a half since he had wrapped his sock around her wrist, and they had been almost inseparable ever since.

'That's OK for you to say!' she sobbed. 'You

don't know what the lecturers are like. It's not like your place, where everyone was really laid back. And anyway, you've got a cushy job where everyone sits around drinking coffee and going on about how fantastic they are – it's easy for you to say everything's going to be all right!'

Declan pushed her away. He had been trying to comfort her for over an hour, but she was too wild with panic to listen.

'Look, I'm only trying to help. That doesn't mean you can give out to me and sneer at my job.'

'Oh, God, Declan, I am so sorry!' Ciara was suddenly contrite. 'I didn't mean it. I'm just really scared that they're going to throw me out.'

'OK, Ciara, put aside all the bullshit, and what you think I want to hear, and what you told the professor guy on the phone. I'm going to ask you something, and I don't want you to go mad – I just want a simple answer, yes or no. Did you cheat in your exam?'

Ciara convulsed in involuntary, spasmodic sobs.

'Did you?' Declan said gently.

'Yes, but I didn't think it was really cheating,' she said finally, wiping her nose on her coat sleeve and looking at him.

'Come on – you can talk to me. Whatever you've done, I'm still going to love you.'

Ciara sniffled gratefully.

'Unless it's murder. You didn't bump off an invigilator, did you?'

Ciara let out a teary laugh. 'No, I didn't.'

'Good. So tell me what happened.'

Ciara took a deep breath and told Declan exactly what she had done.

'Oh,' he said flatly, when she had finished.

'Yeah, I know. "Oh" is right. I've had it, haven't I?'

'Well, not necessarily.'

'Ooh, you sound convinced,' Ciara said sarcastically.

'Look, Ciara, I think you should just go in there and tell them the truth. Tell them that you're really sorry, that there was so much pressure on you that you just panicked. Tell them whatever you have to – just come clean.'

'I know – you're right.' She ran her arms inside Declan's jacket and held him gratefully.

'What I don't get, though, is why you did it in the first place. I thought you were going to revise specific topics, and if they didn't come up, you were just going to accept your mark and sit the supplementals in September if you had to, and then work really hard all next year.'

'I was. I don't know what came over me, I really don't,' Ciara said, squeezing Declan's hand.

But she knew exactly why she had done it. She wasn't used to failing, and she hadn't wanted to lie to her family about doing badly again, as she had the year before. Now, though, she was facing expulsion from university – and that was worse than any number of failed exams.

There's nothing like a long wait to exacerbate guilt, Ciara thought. She had been sitting outside of Professor Curran's office for half an hour before he called her in. It was a large room, with a window overlooking a courtyard. Three walls were lined with books; the fourth was adorned with a tatty poster of John Maynard Keynes.

'Have a seat,' Professor Curran said, glancing up from his notes briefly to acknowledge Ciara's presence. His face looked as if he were wearing a Groucho Marx disguise – all facial hair, nose and glasses.

'Thank you, Professor,' Ciara said meekly.

'Now, I asked you to think about the telephone conversation we had earlier, but since then something has been brought to my attention.' He pressed a button on his phone. 'Joan, is Nigel there yet? ... Yes, send him through.'

After a moment there was a knock at the office door, and it creaked open. Ciara felt every muscle in her body tense. Standing there was a man whom she recognised as one of the invigilators from her exam. In his hand was an exam booklet, one corner torn away. Ciara felt herself gulp violently – she was sure it was audible – like a cartoon character who had just been pushed from a cliff and was suspended in midair, fully aware of the impending drop. She looked at Professor Curran. Declan had said she should tell the truth, and now she had no choice.

A smug-faced Nigel placed the dog-eared, torn exam booklet on the desk, giving Ciara an accusatory look. Avoiding his gaze, she looked blankly at the desk.

'Would you like to explain what you thought you were doing, Ms Coffey?'

Ciara shuffled in her chair, the colour draining from her face. She could feel a lump forming in her throat, but she forced it back – the last thing she wanted to do was cry. She felt like an utter fool.

'I'm so sorry...' she began, shaking her head. 'I really am. I just panicked.'

'This doesn't look like the work of someone who panicked, Ms Coffey. It looks fairly premeditated.'

'Honestly, Professor,' Ciara said, forcing herself to sit straight-backed, 'I hadn't planned on cheating...it just happened.' She knew it sounded feeble, but it was the truth. 'When I turned over the page, there were only two questions that I could even hope to answer. But I needed to answer three. I was just going to answer two and then walk out and accept that I'd messed up...' She swallowed. 'But while I was sitting there, panicking, I remembered this conversation I overheard in the Buttery a few months ago. These two girls were saying that, if the university loses part of your exam paper, or messes it up so it's illegible, then they just mark you on the answers that are left. I know it sounds so stupid, now that I'm saying it out loud...but I looked at the two questions and reckoned they'd probably be worth a 2:2. If I could make it look as if I'd answered three questions but the third one had somehow gone missing, then I'd get a decent overall mark for the exam; otherwise, I knew I might fail.' Ciara's voice cracked. 'But this is worse than failing one exam, isn't it?'

'Would you care to continue telling me exactly what happened?' Professor Curran asked, his voice neutral.

'I put my hand up and asked for another booklet. I wrote one line at the end of the first booklet, so it looked like I was starting another question. I attached the two booklets together. And then, when I thought there was no one looking, I pulled the second booklet away from the first, so just the corner was left. I made it look like it had been ripped away accidentally.' Ciara stopped, but the silence in the room forced her to continue. 'I stuffed the empty booklet in my bag, and then when I got out I panicked and stuffed it in the bin in the foyer.'

Her voice trailed off weakly as she realised that her only defence was no defence at all. 'I'm sorry, Professor – I really am. I've been a fool.' She looked at him, imploring. 'If I could just have another chance – I promise I'll never do anything like that again. I really don't know what came over me…'

Professor Curran took a deep breath and looked down at the torn paper, then back up at Ciara. 'Well, I'm sorry to have to say this, but I feel that under the circumstances I have no choice. The department – indeed, the college – takes a dim view of cheating, in any form. Anything that gives you an unfair advantage over your peers is cheating. And I'm afraid, Ms Coffey, that that is what you did: you tried to alter your mark unfairly to your advantage.' Ciara felt as if she were being given a sentence in a court of law. 'I have no alternative but to dismiss you from the course.'

Ciara gasped, stunned. 'But…but I can't… What will I… Is there nothing that I can do?' she begged.

'I'm sorry, Ms Coffey, but I cannot be seen to condone cheating in any form. If I allow you to remain here, I will be lowering the standards of the institution.'

Ciara got to her feet slowly; her legs felt like jelly. She glared at Nigel, who had such a glint in his eyes that she thought he would probably crack open the champagne that night. Then she walked out of the room, dazed.

She sprinted out of the building into the courtyard. Declan was on the bench where he had said he would be, nursing a polystyrene coffee cup. Her face drained of all colour, Ciara slumped down next to him, staring numbly at her feet.

'I've been kicked out,' she whispered quietly.

It took Declan some time to coax her into giving him any account of what had happened in the interview.

'I'm so sorry, Ciara,' he said at last. 'But

everything will work out in the end – you'll see. Maybe you can appeal his decision.'

She shook her head violently. 'Not a chance. There's no way he'll go back on what he said. And the college will back him up.'

'Well, whatever happens, it'll be all right. You can apply to UCD, do the same course there; there's no need for them to find out that you ever went to Trinity.'

'They'll never have me – not after this.'

'They might; you never know.'

'And what do I tell my parents?'

'Tell them what you want. Say you've switched because the UCD course is better, say you're taking a year out; say whatever. It doesn't matter what you say to your parents – they're in England; what matters is that you sort this out. And you can. I know things look pretty shitty at the moment, but I swear to God – and don't thump me when I say this – one day, you *will* look back on this and laugh.' Declan held Ciara's hand and stroked her hair away from her face.

Later, he ran a bath and filled a hot-water bottle for her. When she had soaked herself for an hour, he brought her into his bedroom and tucked her into bed. Finally he slid in beside her, holding her tight as she sobbed silently.

The next day Ciara dragged herself back to her house in Rathmines, to explain to Róisín what had happened.

'I can't believe you did that,' Róisín said, shaking her head.

Ciara scrunched her face up. 'Are you having a go at me?'

'No, I'm not having a go at you. I just can't believe you did something so stupid.'

'Well, thanks for the support.'

'It's not support you need. What you need is to cop on.'

'That's very good of you,' Ciara said, storming upstairs. 'I'm going back to Declan's.'

Róisín followed her. 'Look, Ciara, you can huff and puff all you want, but the fact is, you've done no work all year and, rather than take the consequences, you cheated.'

'I know that. You don't have to remind me.' Ciara fired clothes into a rucksack.

'Look,' Róisín snapped, 'it's awful that you got kicked out, really awful, but you've only got…' She shut her mouth quickly.

'Were you going to say, "You've only got yourself to blame"?' Ciara demanded. 'Well, were you?'

Róisín stared defiantly at her. 'Yes, I was.'

'Well, fuck you, Róisín.' Ciara shoulder-barged past her angrily.

'Ciara, calm down – don't be like this.'

But Ciara didn't calm down; she marched out of the front door, nearly removing it from its hinges with the ferocity of her slam. Then she stomped to the bus stop. She didn't return home for days.

19

Maeve stepped out of Terminal 3 and hailed a cab, thankful to be nearly home. On the flight she had been sitting next to a woman whose fear of flying appeared to have manifested itself as possession by an evil spirit: at the mere suggestion of turbulence, she had thrown herself around in the seat and bitten the headrest in front. Maeve spent so much time commuting by air that she found it irritating when people made a fuss of it. *There should be a pen at the back of the plane, to put all the jumpy lunatics in,* she thought.

As the taxi pulled slowly along the street, carefully negotiating the speed bumps, Maeve saw that a light was on in the lounge. *Michael must be home*, she thought. She felt a nudge of nervousness. The previous weekend, she and Michael had been distant and tetchy with each other. She had left on Monday morning with a cursory goodbye; at five o'clock in the morning, facing the prospect of a week's work in Germany, she had neither the time nor the energy to discuss the nature of their mutual annoyance.

On the plus side, the tetchiness had given Maeve the opportunity to read two books she had been meaning to read for the past three months. It had also given her a chance to try to sort things out with Ciara – except that, after her sister's performance in the wine bar, Maeve had decided that she was through with trying to make amends. She didn't have time for wondering when Ciara was going to grow up and stop behaving like the world owed her a living. Besides they had to work together now, so an air of civility had to prevail.

On the down side, Maeve had had time to brood over the problems she and Michael were having. She had magnified them in her mind until she couldn't tell how objective she was being. Without talking to Michael – and she didn't feel that she could – she couldn't get to the bottom of them, so she had put off thinking about them altogether: she had spent the week in Germany in a flurry of meetings and business dinners, only allowing herself to think when she knew that she didn't have long to dwell on her thoughts. Now, though, she was home and she had to face Michael. It was either that or carry on ignoring each other until one of them moved out or died of old age.

'Hi, I'm home!' Maeve shouted, throwing her bags into the hallway.

Michael popped his head round the lounge door and smiled. He pulled his wife close and kissed her deeply.

Maeve was shocked. 'What's that for?'

'Because I love you, and I've missed you, and I want to stop fighting with you all the time.' He smiled, kissing her again. 'You look great.' He ran his hands over her charcoal Armani suit, down to the hemline of her skirt. He moved his hand upwards, along the inside of her thigh, and Maeve caught his wrist before she had time to think what she was doing.

'What's wrong?' Michael looked wounded.

'Nothing's wrong; I'm just tired. I've had a busy week, that's all.'

Michael dropped his hands and stepped back. 'You're always tired, Maeve. I haven't seen you for nearly a week. I've cooked you pasta carbonara and got a nice bottle of wine, and all you can say is that you're tired. Well, you're not on your own, you know. I've had a knackering week too.' He shrugged despondently. 'I don't know what's happened to you. There was a time when you'd have been through that door and down on me quicker than a rat down a drain.'

'Don't be so bloody crude, Michael.'

'Don't be so bloody prim, Maeve. It doesn't suit you.'

Maeve sighed. She hadn't even made it past the hall, and she and Michael were enemies again. 'Look, I'm sorry. Just let me have a bath and get changed, and then maybe we can start again.' She lowered her hand to Michael's waistband.

He shrugged and stepped back. 'Yeah, OK. That's fine.'

But Maeve knew it wasn't fine. She'd blown it; and, if she didn't make amends as quickly as possible, tonight showed all the signs of being as hostile as the previous weekend.

Maeve lay across Michael's chest, and he curled her hair round his finger. She had managed to patch up the mess she had created, and they had shared a quiet, intimate evening, talking, skirting around anything that was potentially flammable. Then they had had sex, for the first time in weeks.

As she lay, Maeve thought about when she and Michael had first met. They had spent more time in bed than upright. Increasingly, however, the idea of sex had led Maeve to feign skull-drilling migraines, narcolepsy, a prolapsed uterus – anything. She tried to attribute this to the fact that she was under a lot of pressure at work, but work had little to do with it. This was a perfect intimate moment – the sort of moment, Maeve thought, that would be a good time to talk about her past; but she couldn't do it. It scared her even to think about broaching the subject.

'Well, do you think that might be the one that slips past the goalie?' Michael asked.

'For God's sake, Michael, you have such a way with words.' Maeve sighed wearily.

Michael wanted children. Maeve knew that. It wasn't that he went all gooey-eyed over children in the street, or began to lactate at the sight of anything under the age of two. It was just that he wanted to leave his indelible mark on the planet, and he made this very clear. Maeve was sure his mental image of men holding babies came from the framed 80s print, *L'Enfant*, that his mother had had on the dining-room wall when he was growing up.

A couple of months ago he had said, 'We really should have a brood, Maeve – five or six kids. What do you think?'

When Maeve had pulled her jaw off of the floor, she had asked him why. Michael had responded, 'Because there are enough scumbags around the place throwing out kids. Just think, we'd be adding some much-needed chlorine to the Manchester gene pool.' He had been too busy laughing raucously at his own joke to notice his wife's face fall. It was comments like these that chipped away at Maeve's once rosy and accepting view of her husband.

Michael also secretly harboured the idea that,

with his Formula One sperm, he might sire the next Wayne Rooney. He watched wistfully as men kicked balls around with their sons in Didsbury Park. It made Maeve's stomach tighten – not with affection, but with discomfort.

It was nearly seven months since, bowing to Michael's persistence, she had told him she'd stopped taking the pill. Michael had been delighted; but, as the months went on, he had become concerned that nothing was happening. Unable to believe that they hadn't conceived on their first attempt, he had started buying pregnancy tests at the rate other men bought porn. Maeve had asked him to stop: he was putting too much pressure on her, she said, and her body was reacting adversely to it.

'I've got a good feeling about this one, Maeve,' Michael said, stroking her hair.

'Michael, don't.' Maeve wriggled uncomfortably.

'What?'

'I can't have a "Did we? Didn't we?" post-mortem every time we have sex.'

'Sorry, I know.' Michael kissed the top of her head. 'It must be around the corner, though, mustn't it?'

Maeve grunted.

'I've been thinking of names.'

Maeve felt her gut lurch. 'And what have you come up with?' she asked, trying to sound casual.

'Reese if it's a boy, and Dorothy if it's a girl.'

Maeve sat up and forced a laugh. 'Michael, were you on King Street at the time?'

'What do you mean?' he asked, propping himself up on his elbow and looking at her.

'They're clothes shops. Reiss and Dorothy Perkins.'

'Oh, God.' Michael groaned and collapsed back on the pillow. 'I wondered how they came to me so quickly. Oh, well…back to the drawing board.'

He drifted off to sleep soon after, but Maeve lay staring at the ceiling for what seemed like hours. She finally drifted into fitful rest as daylight began to seep through the curtains.

Maeve woke, as she always did, at six o'clock. At the weekend she got up for half an hour, had a cup of tea, then went back to bed and forced herself to sleep. On her way to the kitchen she went into the study, as she did every morning, and opened the drawer of the desk. It was her desk, one she had owned since she was at school, and Michael never went near it. Inside was a jewellery box with a tiny ballerina inside it; she had once pirouetted in time to the 'Dance of the Sugar Plum Fairy', but she had stopped working years ago.

Maeve opened the box. The guilt she had felt a few months before had all but dissipated; this had become part of her routine. Carefully removing a packet of contraceptive pills, she popped the one marked 'Saturday' out of the packet and into her mouth. She checked over her shoulder before quietly replacing the box. Sliding the drawer shut, she went over to the bookshelf, pretending to scan the books – this, too, was part of the routine, just in case Michael happened to pop his head in. The house was silent; Michael was still in bed. Maeve turned around and headed towards the kitchen.

20

'And here is where the main fermentation process takes place,' the monotone voice informed Barry and Declan. Declan felt as if he were about to slip into a coma. They were into their fifty-eighth minute (and counting) of a tour of Turton's Brewery. From what they'd been shown, Ian Paisley would be easier to re-brand as sexy than Turton's Bitter.

Declan and Barry had been in Manchester for two days, and this was the first time Declan had ventured more than twenty metres from the hotel – John hadn't been exaggerating when he said the office was spitting distance away. When he first arrived, Declan had had an eerie dread that he might collide headlong with Ciara around every corner he turned. Had he *really* not wanted to see her, then Sod's Law meant she would probably have been driving the cab from the airport; but actually – although he told himself there was no way he would actually try to contact her again – he was secretly hoping that he might casually bump into her.

In the car park, Declan and Barry breathed a simultaneous sigh of relief. They climbed into the hired car they had been given for the duration of their stay, and headed for the motorway that would take them back to south Manchester.

'What do you make of that?' Barry asked.

Declan picked up speed as they approached the slip road. 'I'm never drinking a pint of bitter in my life.'

'Me neither,' Barry agreed. 'It looked like a vat of urine samples. I'm going to have to scrape the bottom of the word barrel for this one.'

'Come on, Bar, it'll be a piece of piss. We'll be home before you know it.'

Barry smirked and looked out of the window as the Manchester skyline neared. 'You think so, do you?'

Back in the office, Declan and Barry threw around a few ideas and then commandeered one of the upstairs meeting rooms for a chat with the other three creative teams. The offices of JMSS&A

Manchester were built in a Victorian mill-owner's house. From the outside, it had an air of decaying grandeur, but that had been part of the architect's brief. Inside, the place was more *Star Trek* than Dickens. There was a wide, open-plan reception area, with a video wall where a dozen screens played various channels. Next to this was a table shaped like a chair, and four surrounding benches shaped like long, thin tables. Above this *Alice in Wonderland* creation hung the company mission statement, etched in letters recognisable from their successful ad campaigns: 'Live Outside the Box', it instructed. A large spiral staircase led to the meeting rooms – which, much to Declan and Barry's amusement, were actually labelled 'Inspiration Zones'.

Declan went to the receptionist, who was flicking through this month's copy of *Face* magazine, and smiled his most winning smile. She looked up.

'I don't think we've been formally introduced. I'm Declan Murphy.' He offered his hand.

'I know who you are.' The girl smiled a perfect smile in return, shaking his hand.

'Bad news travels fast round here, then?'

The girl groaned and rolled her eyes, still half-smiling.

'Can I have an…' Declan cleared his throat and put on his best Sean Connery voice. '…Inshpiration Zhone, pleashe.'

The receptionist laughed and checked her room

schedule. 'Zone Three is free, Mr Murphy.' She maintained eye contact, daring Declan to look away first. He didn't.

'Fantashtic. Thank you, Mish Moneypenny.'

'Oh, sweet Jesus,' Barry groaned. 'Is he doing Sean Connery for you?'

'I'll have you know Sean Connery does me, not the other way round,' Declan announced, spinning on his heel to face Barry and winking conspiratorially.

'Oh, not the fantasy about Sean Connery doing you again,' Barry said loudly.

'Shut it, you gobshite,' Declan told him as they headed for the stairs.

'Gobshite, me? Who's the one pulling the ladies with a Sean Connery impression?'

Declan grinned. 'Yeah, but it's nice to see I haven't lost the touch.'

'Think you're in, then?'

'Think? I know.' Declan felt a dormant confidence rear itself. 'How long do you give me?'

'To get her in the sack?'

'Jesus, calm down. No, to get her to go out with me.'

'Two days.'

Declan bounced up to the top of the spiral stairs. 'I'll do it in one.'

As far as Declan was concerned, the meeting had gone well. Barry had other ideas.

'They hate us!' he moaned, as he and Declan sat in the beer garden of the pub across the road from work.

'They don't *hate* us. They're just suspicious of us. Look at it from their point of view: JMS has sent over two of his golden boys from the Dublin office to do a job that these people should be able to do standing on their heads.'

'So why didn't he let them do it standing on their heads?'

'Because there's a bin-load of money riding on it – nothing more complicated than that. As far as I'm concerned, I'm going to be as nice as pie to everyone in that building, do my job and go home. If they want to learn from us, fine. If not, that's their tough shit. Either way, I'm not here to make any enemies. In fact…' Declan rummaged in the back pocket of his jeans. 'I'm here to make friends.' He grinned, holding out a piece of paper with a telephone number scrawled on it.

'You smooth bastard,' Barry said, with grudging admiration.

'Either you've got it…'

'What's her name?'

Declan checked the piece of paper. 'Ashlyn. Nice ring.' He nodded approvingly.

'Easy!'

'The fecking name, not her.'

Barry snorted into his beer. 'Are you taking her out this weekend?'

'It might have escaped your attention, Bar, but we live in Dublin. Come Friday evening, I don't know about you, but I'll be on the first plane out of here.'

Barry shrugged his shoulders. 'Yeah, but I just thought…'

'Well, you thought wrong.'

'Did I?' Barry said mysteriously, taking a swig of his pint. 'I just thought you might be interested in seats at Old Trafford on Saturday, that's all.' He reached into his pocket and produced two tickets for the Manchester United game.

Declan stared in disbelief. 'Sweet Mother of Jesus,' he said, open-mouthed. 'Where'd you get them?'

'Let's just say I have contacts. Still going home for the weekend?'

Declan grabbed the rare specimens from Barry's hand. He had to touch them, to check that he wasn't seeing things. 'I am in me hole,' he said.

Declan was standing near the entrance of the large West Didsbury pub, feeling very pleased with himself. Having spent the afternoon in the Theatre of Dreams cheering on Manchester United to a 4–1 victory, he felt as if he were floating. He had worshipped them since he was a child, but he had never been to Old Trafford before, and the sensation of stepping inside the hallowed ground was indescribable. Had Barry not been at his side, watching his every move, Declan would have lain on the floor and wept with emotion. As it was, he had winked at Barry and said, 'You have your uses,' as a roar went up around the stadium, puckering his skin into goosebumps.

Now he was waiting for Ashlyn, whom he had arranged to meet at eight. He figured he might as well make the most of his weekend in Manchester; it was going to be his one and only, after all. The place was mobbed, and he wondered if he would be able to find Ashlyn among all these people.

He headed for the bar; he might as well get in line and prepare for a long wait. The bar service in England was absolutely terrible, Declan had decided. It might be an idea to advertise Turton's Bitter with the simple slogan, 'We'll serve it quickly.' *They'd make a killing,* he thought, as he watched the three bar staff shuffle around, each attending to one pint, while the sea of people waiting to be served grew and grew.

He looked around the pub and realised that, as well as looking for Ashlyn, he was keeping an eye out for Ciara. He wasn't sure if she was the first person or the last person he wanted to see. Declan scolded himself for allowing his mind to drift back to her, and told himself firmly that she was very much the last person he wanted to see.

'Hi,' Ashlyn said, tapping Declan on the shoulder. She was dressed in a crisp white shirt with jeans; her dark hair was pulled back from her pretty, olive-skinned face.

'Hi, how are you?' Declan smiled, pleased to see her and even more pleased with himself for having guessed correctly: she did look even better outside of work.

By ten o'clock Declan was propped against a wall, happily flirting with Ashlyn. Ciara had always said he was a shameless flirt; Declan didn't think that was necessarily the case, but tonight he was on form and was relishing the fact that it might lead somewhere. As he constantly had to remind himself, he was single now; he could do whatever he pleased.

Ashlyn headed up to the bar, leaving Declan to watch admiringly as she sashayed away. Suddenly he heard a laugh, behind him, that chilled him to the bone. There was no mistaking that laugh: it was Ciara.

Declan froze on the spot. If he moved, she would see him. But if he *didn't* move, she would see him. He wanted to bob down and crawl along the floor like a soldier under a scramble-net, smack Ashlyn on the ankle and point animatedly towards the door.

'No! You did *not*! Stop it. You are such a liar!'

Declan didn't dare turn around, but he knew Ciara was talking to another man. He could just picture her face, all wide doll-eyes and mock disbelief. She said *he* was a flirt, but Ciara could have flirted for England if she put her mind to it.

'I swear to God,' the man laughed.

Declan bristled. *Who is he?* he thought jealously. *Is she out on a date? God, she doesn't waste any time, does she?* It didn't occur to him that the pot was screaming 'black' at the kettle. He wanted to turn around, grab Ciara by the arm, snap, 'Let's get this straight: whatever I did, I did. OK?' and then march her out of the pub. But he knew that he had no right to say anything. Anyway, Ciara would kill him if he tried any macho tactics.

Ashlyn arrived back with the drinks.

'How do you fancy going into town?' Declan asked.

'Yeah, OK. Are you all right?' Ashlyn screwed her face up, puzzled by his sudden edginess.

'Yeah, yeah – I'm fine.'

'You look like you've seen a ghost.'

'Do I?' Declan asked, nervously pushing himself flush to the wall.

Then Ciara walked past them, heading towards the door. Fortunately, she didn't look back. She was laughing raucously at something the man had just said; Declan felt his stomach knot and wondered what nugget of comic genius could have amused her so much. He had been hoping that, at the very least, Ciara's new friend might look like the Elephant Man – but, much to Declan's annoyance, there was no resemblance. The man threw his arm around Ciara's shoulders. Declan felt ill.

'Declan? Hello?' Ashlyn said tetchily.

'Sorry.' Declan snapped back to reality. If he

carried on like this, he was going to be spending the rest of the night on his own. 'I thought I recognised someone, that's all.' He smiled, returning his full attention to Ashlyn.

By closing time, Declan had made amends for his earlier rudeness. He and Ashlyn were getting along famously. 'So where shall we go from here?' he asked, smiling.

'Didn't you say you wanted to go into town?'

'Actually, never mind town – we could go to the bar of the hotel where I'm staying. You have to see the place; it's amazing. And it's such a waste – that big bathtub and that quadruple bed, all to myself…' He let the words hang in the air, a mischievous grin playing on his lips.

Ashlyn smiled knowingly. 'Sounds good.'

'Great.' Declan threw back his drink and quickly sneaked a look through the window. Ciara was nowhere to be seen. *If you can't beat them,* he thought, *join them.*

21

It had been over a week since Rachel and Ciara had met for a drink, but Rachel had suggested that Ciara not set foot in the house until they had got rid of the troublesome housemate. They had finally ousted her (she was now threatening to put a spell on the house), so Rachel had invited Ciara around to have a look at the newly spare room and to meet Mark, her housemate.

The house was tucked away on a tree-lined street; it was a Victorian terraced house, much like Ciara's parents', except smaller. It wasn't much to look at – the sort of place an estate agent would describe as having 'huge potential' and any sane person would describe as 'ramshackle' – but Mark, on the other hand... Rachel had mentioned that he worked in computers, and Ciara had imagined a hump-backed, bespectacled geek-boy; but when Mark answered the door, he turned out to be tall, with short blond hair and piercing blue eyes. Ciara wondered why on earth Rachel hadn't told her about him; if she'd had a housemate who looked like that, she'd have taken out an ad in the *Manchester Evening News*.

'Hi,' she beamed.

'Hi, Ciara. I'll be conducting the grand tour of the house that Jack built; Rachel's in the shower.'

'No problem,' Ciara said, following him.

'This is the kitchen. One of the special features of the house is that only two of the kitchen cupboards have doors.'

Ciara held his gaze and smiled. 'You're not selling it to me, you know.' *I'm flirting – I think I'm really flirting!* she thought giddily, feeling as if someone had taken the stabilisers off her bike for the first time.

'I'm just telling you, warts and all, what the place is like.' He smiled back. 'This is the lounge.'

'It looks nice.' Ciara gazed around, impressed.

'Do not be deceived. This, too, is a dump, but Ray and I have managed to make it look presentable with throws and dim lighting. Basically, the deal is, we get to live in West Didsbury for a relative pittance. The landlord comes around every so often and pretends he's going to sell the house; we all nod and give him some rent, and off he pops for another two or three months. Ridiculous, but true. The shower will fall on your head if you don't hold it in place, but other than that it's all liveable – and the room you'll be in is really big and nicely decorated. Come on, I'll show you.' Ciara followed him up the stairs, lasciviously watching his bum move in his Levis.

Rachel emerged from the shower, towelling her hair, as Ciara was admiring the bedroom. 'What do you think? The kitchen's a tip, isn't it?'

'When can I move in?' Ciara was sold. The state of the house didn't matter: the rent was low and the bedroom was huge – and, most importantly, she immediately felt at home there. She just hoped that the inordinate number of butterflies that had been playing in her stomach since she clapped eyes on Mark weren't blinding her judgement.

'Oh, brilliant!' Rachel said happily. 'Today, if you want.'

'Give me a few days – I need to break it gently to my parents. I'll move my stuff in during the week, if that's OK?'

'Perfect. Listen, I'm meeting some friends in Didsbury village for food – we're going for pints afterwards, if you want to come along.'

'I'm joining them around ten,' Mark said. 'You and I could go for a drink together first, if you've nothing else planned.'

'Good idea,' Ciara said casually. Secretly, she was delighted.

Mark was waiting for Ciara outside the pub. She immediately gave him brownie points for this act of chivalry, thinking of the amount of time she had spent alone in crowded pubs waiting for Declan. Ciara had a secret double standard when it came to feminism and the art of waiting. She would argue to the bitter end for the equality of women, but ask her to wait inside a pub on her own and suddenly she had a misty-eyed affection for days of yore when men threw their coats in puddles for their lady companions.

Mark muscled his way to the bar, and Ciara positioned herself against a rickety side-table covered in the day's newspapers; there wasn't a chance they would get a seat. She was still feeling giddy about being out with Mark. She was willing herself to have a good time and to like him; but, as she watched him inch closer to the bar, a sense of dread began to descend on her. *What am I doing?* she thought.

Actually, she knew exactly what she was doing. She was trying to prove to herself that she could go out with someone good-looking, funny and smart – and, in some silly way, she was trying to stick two fingers up at Declan. Just as Mark arrived back from the bar, it occurred to her that doing this with her new housemate might not be the best idea she had ever had. She chose to ignore the thought.

'God, sorry about that – I thought I was going to be there all week!'

'I know. It's weird, after living in Ireland where all the bar staff are amazing, to come back here and watch them shuffle around...' Ciara trailed off, realising that she sounded exactly like Declan had when he used to talk about England. 'But, then again, Ireland's not brilliant if you want to get anywhere; the public transport there's nowhere near as good as here.'

She could have kicked herself. *Flirt, goddammit!* she thought. She was hardly going to melt the elastic on Mark's Calvins with this level of repartee.

'Anyway, I'm sure this is what you came out for tonight: a soliloquy on Irish public transport.' Ciara laughed.

'No, but I wouldn't mind knowing about your time in Ireland. Rachel was telling me about you going to Trinity...' Mark paused. 'Or not, as the case may be.'

Ciara felt rooted to the ground with mortification. She was going to strangle Rachel for letting that slip. She laughed – the kind of false, overly light laugh usually heard canned and accompanying radio comedy – and quickly checked the surrounding punters, to make sure that her father hadn't somehow decided to come in and stand behind her.

'I'm sorry. Ray was just saying that you were always the brainbox at school, and she thought it was amazing that you'd done something so rebellious.'

Yeah, get me – Che Guevara, Ciara thought, grinning fixedly. 'Anyway, never mind about that. What about you? Tell me all about *you*.'

Mark did just that. He told Ciara about his university days in Salford, about his job and his friends, and he did it amusingly – he made her laugh her embarrassing snorting laugh, which only came out on special occasions when she thought something was really funny.

'How do you and Rachel know each other?' she asked.

Mark looked away. 'Oh, we met ages ago. Then we both needed somewhere to live at the same time, so we found the house. And Nutcase made three – the landlord found her through the paper. Thank God she's gone.'

'Where did you meet? You and Rachel.'

'Friends of friends. God, look at the time!' Mark pointed at the clock behind the bar. 'We were meant to meet her about ten minutes ago.'

Ciara wasn't exactly a bloodhound when it came to detecting subtle nuances in conversation, but she felt that Mark was being evasive. 'Which friends?'

Mark laughed. 'Is this Twenty Questions? Joe and Paul.'

Ciara reddened. 'Sorry.'

'Don't be sorry. I just didn't think you'd know who they were.'

'I don't.'

'OK, then. Anything else you want to know?' He grinned.

Ciara squirmed. 'Inside leg measurement?' She knocked back the remains of her vodka and cranberry. 'Well, I'm ready.'

As they left the pub, Mark threw a friendly arm around Ciara. 'Welcome back to Manchester, new housemate. Good to have you here.'

Ciara was relieved. 'Thanks.' She smiled up at him. 'Thanks for having me.'

The evening went well. Ciara and Mark met up with Rachel and her friends, and they went into town, to the bars along Deansgate Locks. At about one o'clock, on their way from one bar to another, they passed the place where the Hacienda nightclub used to be; Ciara and Rachel had cut their clubbing teeth there, when they should have been concentrating on their GCSEs. They broke away from the group and stood on the pavement, looking up at the new flats that stood where the club had been.

'Look at that – sacrilege,' Rachel said.

'I know.'

'Do you miss it?' Rachel asked, linking Ciara's arm.

'What?'

'Going out all the time, like we used to.'

Ciara thought about it for a moment. 'To be honest, Ray, I haven't given myself a chance to miss it. I've been on the razz for the last seven years.'

'Come on, you know what I mean. I don't just mean a couple of nights in the pub every week – I mean leathering it like we used to.'

'So do I,' Ciara said sombrely. 'I've done that every single weekend for years.'

Rachel looked at her, open-mouthed. 'Come on, you must have had a bit of a rest from it. I mean, you were with Declan for donkey's years…'

Ciara nodded. 'Yeah, I was, but we still went out all the time. And when he complained about it, I used to tell him he was turning into an old fart and go out on my own.'

'On your *own*?'

'God, no, not on my *own* own,' Ciara said dismissively. 'I mean without Declan. I'd meet up with people from work.'

That wasn't what she'd done at all. If she had a night off and Declan was annoying her by insisting on having a quiet night in, she would go out on her own and hope to bump into someone she knew. She would start off by having a few drinks at Barian, where she worked, and then just see where the night took her. It had seemed so normal at the time; but now, somehow, even thinking about it made her feel mortified.

She and Rachel walked along the street in momentary silence.

'So,' Rachel said finally, 'how was everything with Mark this evening?'

'Everything was fine. Why?'

'Don't give me that,' Rachel laughed. 'I saw you doing big Ciara-eyes at him.'

'I was not!'

'Whatever you say.'

'He is fit, though.'

Rachel shrugged dismissively. 'If you like that sort of thing.'

'What, funny and good-looking? You'd have to be a bit weird *not* to like that combination. Come on, Ray, he's gorgeous.'

Rachel's eyes flicked quickly to Ciara. 'So you do fancy him? I knew you would; everyone always does.'

Ciara thought she detected a slight tetchiness in Rachel's tone. 'Look, I'm not going to try to get off with him and make things awkward in the house, if that's what you're getting at.'

'I wasn't.'

'Do *you* fancy him?'

'For God's sake, Ciara! No, I do not.' Rachel screwed her face up, incredulous.

'Well, what were you getting at?'

'Nothing. Mark's a bit of a charmer, that's all, and I don't want you getting hurt.'

Ciara raised an eyebrow. Mark was a great bloke, but he was hardly Maurice Chevalier. The truth was that, although he was very fanciable, Ciara didn't think he had that certain something she had seen in Declan when they first met. Maybe this was what she needed, though: someone to take her mind off

Declan for good. And, if Mark was a love-em-and-leave-em ladies' man, maybe he would be perfect. They could have a bit of fun and then go their separate ways – as separate as adjoining bedrooms would allow. 'Don't worry about me, Rachel; he'd have to do something pretty special to hurt me, after the way my life's been going. Shag my dad, or something.'

'That's disgusting!'

'I know; I'm sorry. He's not my dad's type.'

Rachel rolled her eyes. 'Come on; it's freezing out here. Let's go find the others.'

They headed into the bar. Ciara caught Mark's eye and gave him a winning smile. She was beginning to enjoy her new life.

22

It was the end of the day, and the office was deserted except for Becky, who was amending a document that Maeve needed for the following day, and the cleaner. Maeve rubbed the palm of her hand with a tissue before reaching for her office phone again. It was her fourth attempt to dial Catherine's number; each time she reached for the receiver, her nerves overcame her. This time she grabbed it purposefully and punched in the numbers before she had time to change her mind again. Her heart thumped loudly.

'Hello?' a young, quiet Irish voice said. Maeve felt every drop of moisture vacate her mouth.

'Catherine?' she asked. Her heart was pounding

so hard she felt sure it was about to leap out of her chest and land on the desk in front of her.

'Yes?'

'Catherine, it's…it's Maeve.'

'Maeve?' The girl sounded…*What?* Maeve thought. *Excited? Shocked? Disappointed?*

'Yes, it's me. How are you?' Maeve's voice wavered nervously.

'I'm fine. How are you?'

'I'm good – yeah, I'm good.' Maeve winced. She was speaking to her daughter for the first time, and this was the best she could come up with? 'Thanks for your presents. I got them last week. I used the face pack the other day; it's made me look years younger.'

'Good. You sound like you work too much,' Catherine said. She added quickly, 'Not that there's anything wrong with working hard; I just wanted you to have something to pamper yourself.'

'I know exactly what you mean.' Maeve could hear the nerves in Catherine's voice. Nervous though she herself was, she knew she needed to guide the conversation and let the young woman on the other end of the phone know that whatever she said was OK. 'It really was a lovely thought. So what do you think of my accent? A bit different from yours.'

'You sound like that one out of *Footballers' Wives*. You know the really good-looking one? You have a northern English accent, like, but it's posh.'

Maeve laughed. 'Posh? Now that's not something I'm called often. But thanks.'

'I don't like my accent.'

'Why not? You have a beautiful accent.'

'I do not!'

If they didn't change the subject soon, they could spend the next half-hour admiring each other's dulcet tones. 'I've so many things I want to ask you that I don't really know where to start.'

'God, I'm so relieved!' Catherine exhaled loudly. 'I didn't know how you'd feel about talking to me. I mean, I've been so excited about it, but…well, I just didn't know what you really thought. I've spoken to other people who tried to get in touch with their natural mothers and they were just ignored. When I found out you were married – well, I just thought you'd built your own life now, and you might not want to know.'

Maeve felt her heart sink. 'Of course I wanted to know,' she said quietly.

'What does your husband think about all this?' Catherine asked suddenly.

Maeve felt foolish. 'He doesn't know. I haven't told him.'

There was a pause. Then Catherine said tentatively, 'And are you planning on telling him?'

Maeve could tell that she was trying to keep her tone light. She chose her words carefully. 'I am. But we see so little of each other at the moment that the time never seems to be right.'

'Oh,' Catherine said, sounding deflated.

Maeve felt terrible. She didn't want Catherine to feel that her natural mother, while she didn't mind staying in touch for her own peace of mind, had no intention of incorporating her into her own life. 'I'm sorry, Catherine – it's just that things between Michael and me are difficult at the moment. I'm not sure how he would take it. I've never told him about you. That's no reflection on you – it's just that, as I said in my letter, that was how I was told to deal with it: by telling no one. And that's what I did.'

'I know. I understand.' Catherine was still trying to sound upbeat.

'You don't have to understand. It's too complicated for you to understand. I just need a bit of time to tell everyone over here what's going on, if that's OK?' Maeve felt weak. She knew she should be telling Catherine not to worry, that she would sort everything out and it would all be fine; but she couldn't. She couldn't reassure her daughter that everything was going to be OK when she wasn't sure of it herself.

'Yes, that's OK.'

'I just want you to know that it's great to finally talk to you.'

'Yeah, you too.'

'It really is. And it means so much to me that you tried so hard to find me.'

'It's OK.'

Maeve tried again; she didn't want to let Catherine down in their first conversation. 'Look, Catherine, I know you're in school at the moment, but when do you finish for summer?'

'We're finished. We broke up last week. But I'm working over the summer; I won't have any time off until the last week in August. I was meant to be going to London with some friends, but they can't afford it, so I was just going to mess around here for the week.'

'Well…' Maeve paused momentarily. 'Why don't I come over to Ireland? We could spend the day in Dublin – my treat. What do you think?'

'That would be great!' This time Catherine sounded genuinely delighted.

'Why don't I come over on the Wednesday and book into a hotel? Then if you want to stay overnight, you can, but if you decide you want to head home, that's fine as well.'

'That'd be deadly!'

'Great. I'm really pleased.'

'Well, listen, I know you're at work, so I won't keep you any longer… I feel bad that you have to ring me, but the credit would have gone on my phone in a minute, and my mum – Miriam, that is – would strangle me for ringing England – well, not if she knew it was to call you, because they're fine about it, but—'

Maeve laughed affectionately at her confusion. 'It's fine, Catherine; you don't have to explain yourself. How about I ring you again – same time, next week – and let you know what hotel I've booked? Is that OK?'

'Yes, that's great.'

'Good. Well, have a good week, won't you?'

'I will – you too. Bye, Maeve.'

'Bye, Catherine.' Maeve replaced the receiver and jumped from her seat, taking a deep, sharp breath; she felt like yelping with excitement.

She hit the intercom button, and Becky answered quickly. 'Hello.'

'You still here?'

'I might as well bring a tent and camp here.'

'Could you do me a quick favour before you go?'

'Yeah, go on.'

'Can you put me in for three days' holiday in the last week of August? Wednesday, Thursday and Friday.'

'No problem.'

'And remind me to book flights tomorrow.'

'I can book them if you want,' Becky offered.

'No, it's fine – I'll do it myself. I want to check out the flight times; I might as well book them while I'm at it.'

'OK,' Becky said. She didn't ask where Maeve was going, and Maeve knew that she wouldn't. She would tell her in due course, but she didn't want to tell anyone at the moment. She wasn't even sure how to admit it to herself.

23

'I am the dog's bollocks!' Declan was singing to Barry, to the tune of 'I Am the One and Only' by Chesney Hawkes.

'No, you're just *a* bollocks,' Barry said, taking a bite out of his sandwich as they strolled through Didsbury Park.

Declan grinned. 'You're only jealous.' He had spent Saturday night with Ashlyn; then, on Sunday, he and Barry had gone to a bar in town and a girl had given him her number. They had been by the canal in Castlefield – a trendy area of the city centre – sitting outside the bar, drinking beer and watching a disproportionate amount of good-looking women stroll by; the woman in question had approached Declan and asked him if he was in a boy band.

'Jealous? I don't think so. You only spoke to her because you were flattered by the word "boy".'

'You've got to take it where you find it.'

'And you're finding it everywhere, so it seems.'

'Just getting back into practice, that's all.'

Declan had had a great night of guilt-free sex with Ashlyn. The next morning he'd told her that he wasn't up for anything serious; he'd just split up with his girlfriend and he wasn't in Manchester for long… He might as well have added, 'et cetera'. She had seemed a bit miffed at the time, but this morning at work she had been all sweetness and light, so Declan reasoned that he must be forgiven. He was set to meet the boy-band girl, Carrie, in a city-centre bar on Wednesday, and he was delighted with himself. 'What a weekend. It's the Irish charm, Bar; you should try it.'

'Don't give me that. It's because you're trying to prove you still have it, after everything with Ciara.'

'That might be so, but it's working,' Declan said smugly.

'So, changed your mind about Manchester, have you?'

'Not at all. I've booked my flight back to Dublin next weekend. Monday to Friday only in Manchester, from now on. The season's nearly over, so there's no chance of you getting me the star treatment at Old Trafford again; I might as well go home.'

'Fair enough.' Barry lunged after a piece of chicken tikka that had just fallen from his sandwich; it hit the ground and he stood on it, shaking his head. 'Not thought about contacting Ciara, then?'

'And why would I do that?'

'I don't know; I just thought…well, she was your mot for ages and she's just up the road.'

'Yeah, and now she's not my mot, OK? So if we could have an embargo on the mention of her name, I'd be delighted.'

'OK. I just thought it might be an idea to give her one last chance – see if she's calmed down.'

'Oh, yeah, I can see that. Calm is her middle name.'

'Ciara Calm Coffey – that's got a nice ring to it,' Barry said approvingly.

'Shut up, Bar,' Declan said, shaking his head.

24

'Your chariot awaits, madam.' Mark was standing beside his clapped-out Clio. 'It's not exactly an Aston Martin, but it gets me from A to B – well, I usually manage to set off from A, at any rate.'

Ciara laughed. 'Oh, Mark, this is my dad, Sean.'

Sean set the bin-bags containing Ciara's clothes down on the pavement and wiped his hand on his trousers before offering it to Mark. 'Pleased to meet you, Mark. I hope you don't like a quiet house down there in West Didsbury.'

'Dad!' Ciara protested, as Mark laughed.

'Is that everything, then?' Sean asked.

'Yeah. I just need to say bye to Mum.' Margaret didn't like it when her children moved out; she was standing in the kitchen, nursing a cup of coffee, waiting for the last of Ciara's meagre belongings to be taken out to the car.

'Right, Mum, I'm off,' Ciara said. She noticed that her mother was tearful. 'Oh, come on, Mum, I'll only be down the road – that's better than Dublin, isn't it?'

Margaret nodded. 'I suppose. I just don't like seeing bags leave the house.'

Ciara grinned. 'So it's the bin-bags you're bothered about, not me? Well, thanks a lot, Mum.'

Margaret managed a smile and kissed her on the cheek. 'You take care, now.'

'Mum, I'm ten minutes' walk away, at most. I'll be back nicking the biscuits every two days.' Ciara hugged her mother and then, as an afterthought, pulled open the fridge. 'Anything going spare?'

'There's salmon fillets in the freezer, and some Breakaways.'

'Breakaways? I never saw them. Where are they?'

'If you lift the piano lid up, they're there. I hid them from Anthony. That's the last place he'd think to look.'

Ciara rolled her eyes and laughed. 'Are you still doing that?' When her children had been younger, Margaret used to come up with more and more inventive places to hide any food that she thought they might devour within a day. This meant that, after the weekly shop, the only food on show was baked beans and Weetabix. Anything chocolate-coated would be found in the garage under a bucket, or in the attic behind the old dolls' house. (She had also tried to pass off the supermarket's own brands as the genuine article: 'Own-brand cola *is* the same as Coca-Cola. They just put it in different bottles.' Claire had once been sent to her room for replying, 'And they make it taste like shit, as well. Brilliant marketing.')

Ciara raided the fridge and went into the dining room to lift the piano lid. 'Cheers, Mum!' she shouted back into the kitchen, running back out to the car.

Mark had loaded the bags into the boot and Sean was wandering round the car, kicking the tyres. 'Good little motor, this,' he informed Ciara solemnly, as if they were about to drive to the North Pole.

'Yeah, Dad. That's good. Anyway, we're off.' Ciara got into the car.

Mark started the engine. Sean gave the bonnet two forceful slaps, then raised his hand like a policeman stopping traffic.

'Does he want me to stop?' Mark asked.

'No, he's waving goodbye.' Ciara waved back. 'He always does that – slaps the bonnet. And, before you ask, I have no idea why.' She laughed, throwing her eyes skyward.

Ciara hadn't seen Mark since their Saturday night out, but she was fairly sure her flirting had been wholly reciprocated. They had danced together in a bar by the canal until three in the morning, and at the end of the night Mark had asked if she wanted to go back to her new home 'for a nightcap'. Ciara had smiled knowingly and said, 'There'll be plenty of time for that when I move in, won't there?' She had awoken the next morning mortified, the cheesy line ringing in her ears. However, when she had called Rachel to arrange the move, Mark had shouted in the background that he would pick her up, which led Ciara to assume that her cheesiness hadn't had an adverse effect.

The drive to the house took less than five minutes.

'So, any news from your ex-boyfriend?' Mark asked, out of the blue, as he turned onto Burton Road.

Ciara raised an eyebrow. 'And why are you interested?'

'Did I say I was?'

'No, but it's an odd question.'

Mark laughed. 'It is if you want it to be. You just talked about him a lot on Saturday night, that's all. I was wondering if he'd been in touch since he came over here to try to "win you back", as you put it.'

Ciara felt every muscle in her body contract in embarrassment. She didn't even remember talking about Declan. She thought she'd done a great line in cool on Saturday night, but she had been quite drunk by the end of it, so she couldn't be sure. And saying he'd come over to 'win her back', like some Barbara Cartland character...definitely not cool.

'Look, Mark. Declan – my ex-boyfriend – is in my past. I haven't heard from him since he came over, and I don't expect to.' Ciara shrugged and looked meaningfully at Mark. 'And, anyway, I'm back home now and I'd like to move on.'

'Well, that is good news,' Mark said, smiling. Ciara smiled back. He really was cute, she thought; she just wished she could get Declan out of her head. *He cheated on you, you idiot,* she told herself as Mark pulled the car up in front of the house.

Rachel threw the door open. 'I've got the coffee on, your room's clean and aired – and the washer's packed in, so you might want to consider a trip back to your mum's with a bag of laundry by the end of the week.'

'Can't you call the landlord?' Ciara asked, grabbing some of her bags from the boot.

'You'll learn, Ciara.' Mark chucked her under the chin, laughing.

'OK.' She shrugged. 'Listen, I'm going to go and dump my stuff in some semblance of order, and then I'll come down for a coffee.'

'I'll bring you one up in a minute,' Mark offered.

'Oh, you will, will you?' Rachel said. Ciara looked up quickly.

'Yeah, and I'll bring you one in the lounge.' Mark threw Rachel a look that Ciara couldn't quite decipher.

'I'll be about half an hour,' Ciara said, dragging the first of her bags up the stairs.

Mark delivered a cup of coffee, as promised, and admired the room as Ciara tried to make it her own. She put on the burnt-orange bedclothes that her mother had given her, and arranged a few photographs around the room, but this made her feel sad. She had a few pictures of Róisín, Geraldine and Sinéad, but the rest were pictures of her family: all her other pictures from the past six years had Declan in them, and she wasn't about to put any of *those* up in her new room.

'Want some food? I'm making a stir-fry for me and Ray,' Mark said.

'Yeah, that'd be lovely.' Ciara needed to go food-shopping. 'There are Breakaways for dessert.'

When Mark closed the door, leaving her alone, she flopped onto the bed and looked around the room. This was the first time she had had a room of her own in years. She knew this thought should be liberating, but she just felt deflated.

She thought back to when she and Declan had first moved in together. He had just started working as an advertising creative; Ciara had been working in an office in the centre of Dublin. In the evenings they would sit on the floor (they hadn't saved up enough money to buy a settee), drink wine, eat dinner – which Declan had invariably prepared, as Ciara was a dab hand at burning water

– and talk into the early hours of the morning.

Ciara pulled herself up off the bed and told herself to snap out of it. She had a new home and a new life, and she needed to forget Declan. She knew it would take time to banish him to the far reaches of her memory, but banished he would be.

Ciara and Rachel were sitting in the living room, watching TV and laughing at the contestants on a new reality show. Mark brought in the stir-fry and they all tucked in, plates on their knees.

'This is gorgeous,' Ciara said appreciatively.

'Yeah, Mark. You should do this more often,' Rachel said. Ciara looked up to see if Rachel was insinuating that he was only cooking tonight because she was there; but Rachel was staring at the TV.

'Well, I would, if you stopped nicking the food I buy.'

'Ooh, stroppy.' Rachel arched an eyebrow at Mark, but Ciara was relieved to notice she sounded good-humoured. She thought she might have sensed an atmosphere earlier, and she didn't want to live with two people who were at each other's throat.

When the programme had ended and their plates had been cleared, Rachel stood up. 'Well, I'm going out, if anyone fancies coming to the Old House for a drink. A girl from work's coming down with her boyfriend; anyone up for it?'

'Sounds good,' Mark said.

Ciara knew it might be a good idea to go out for a drink with her new housemates, but she was tired and wanted to sort all her stuff out properly. Since returning to Manchester, she had found herself less inclined to be the last person standing. She no longer felt as if she might be missing something if she didn't go out every night of the week. Anyway, when she went out she just found her drunken mind wandering to mawkish thoughts about Declan – and that was the last thing she needed.

'Actually, Ray, I might give it a miss. I was going to stay in and get my stuff sorted – and I was wondering if I could use your computer, Mark? I just want to look for something on the internet.'

'Oh, you're not coming out?' Mark sounded disappointed.

'No. I need to look at the college websites. I'm thinking of trying to get on a degree course – again. I keep thinking about looking for a permanent job, but I think first I need to see if I can get a college to take me on – although I'm not sure anyone'll have me, with my track record.' Ciara sighed.

'Just don't tell them about cheating,' Rachel said.

'No way. If I apply for a course, the first thing I'm going to do is admit what I did in Ireland. I'd rather know there and then that they don't want me than be kicked out halfway through if someone should happen to find out.'

'Very commendable,' Rachel said.

'I try my best.'

'I think I might stay in as well, actually,' Mark said suddenly, a little too casually.

Rachel's face darkened. 'You might stay in? On a Saturday night?'

'Yeah. What's wrong with that?' Mark asked.

'It's a first, that's all,' Rachel said, raising her eyebrows sarcastically.

Ciara suddenly felt uncomfortable. She wasn't sure if she wanted anything to happen between her and Mark – and she didn't think that having a cosy night in with one housemate and not the other was the best way to spend the first night of a house-share.

'Listen, I might actually change my mind and come to the pub.' She tried to sound nonchalant.

'OK,' Rachel said, throwing Mark a triumphant look.

Ciara looked from one to the other, like a piggy in the middle. She wasn't sure what the dynamic was between them, but she was determined to get Rachel on her own and find out.

25

'Well, Declan Murphy, I think you need your head examining. She's a lovely girl. I've a good mind to ring her myself and tell her what a fool I think you are.'

Declan stabbed at a potato and forced it, whole, into his mouth to prevent himself from saying anything he might regret. He was at his mother's in Glasnevin, in Dublin, and he had just informed her that he and Ciara had split up. Aileen Murphy liked Ciara, and she was not about to let her son announce that it was over without telling him exactly what she thought.

'She had spirit, that girl.'

'She was argumentative, Ma.'

'And who wouldn't be, having to put up with the likes of you?'

Declan wished his father were there to side with him, but he'd gone off to play golf at the municipal course with some fella who had got him cheap laminated flooring the previous year – anyone with a bargain was a friend of Declan's father's. 'Ma, will you just get it into your head that Ciara and I are finished?' He put his knife and fork together on the plate.

His mother switched the kettle on. 'So what are you doing in Manchester?'

'Working.'

'Declan Murphy, do you think I came down in the last shower?'

'I am working! Why would I lie about it?'

Aileen sighed. 'Wishful thinking, I suppose. I thought you might be over there trying to fix things up. So what did you do to make her leave?'

'I didn't do anything!' Declan protested. 'Jesus, Ma, you're like the Spanish Inquisition.'

'Does this mean you'll be back here every weekend, touting yourself around the unsuspecting women of Dublin?'

'I don't tout myself around! But, to answer your question, I was going to come back at the weekends, but that's changed. They've told us they'll need us in the Manchester office until at least September, so I've managed to let the flat to make myself a bit of extra cash.'

'What are you at with that? It's not even your place to be renting.'

Declan shook his head. He couldn't be bothered explaining. Barry had told him that he was subletting his flat and making a tidy sum on it, so Declan had decided to put an ad on a Dublin accommodation website to see if anyone was interested in renting his flat for three months. The price he was asking would cover his own rent and make him two hundred euro a month; and, if he wanted to come back to Dublin for weekends, he could always crash at a friend's house. An American girl had replied to the ad almost immediately. She and a friend were spending the summer in Dublin and were delighted to find somewhere central that was the same price as a hostel would have been. He was going to meet his two potential tenants after his mother had finished pointing out where he was going wrong in every aspect of his life.

'Look, Ma, I've got to go; I'm on a flight out of here at half six.' This was true; it was just that the flight was at half six the following morning.

'Well, fine. I'll tell the girls you were asking after them.'

'I've already seen them.' Declan had three sisters who lived around north Dublin, in varying degrees of domestic bliss.

'Well, that's good, at least.' Aileen gave him a hug. 'Now, you swallow that pride of yours and go see Ciara,' she instructed.

Declan nodded wearily. *There's no way that's going to happen,* he thought, as his mother tried to foist a bag of bread on him. 'They have bread in Manchester, Ma.'

'Not my bread, they don't.'

'It's not your bread – it's from Dunne's!'

'You know what I mean.'

Declan raised his eyes skyward. Kissing his mother on the forehead, he headed off into town.

Declan walked into the mayhem of Dublin airport the following morning and decided that, no matter how good a time he had in Dublin, he couldn't cope with this bleary-eyed tussle every weekend for the next few months. Besides, his back was killing him from sleeping on his friend Joe's couch. Joe had said that he could stay any time he wanted, but the tight-lipped smile of his girlfriend, who'd been rudely awakened when Declan's alarm went off, had suggested otherwise.

The previous day, when Declan had seen his two new tenants – Marie and Cheryl – waiting for him, he had smiled to himself: they were both very good-looking. And he had been sure that Marie was flirting wickedly with him as he took their rent and deposit. He'd tried his best to return the compliment. Cheryl, on the other hand, had been brusque with him – which he hadn't minded too much, as he seemed to have Marie's undivided attention.

He had handed over two sets of keys. 'There's a

camp bed in the cupboard – you'll have to fight over the double bed.' Cheryl had thrown Marie a look. Just as Declan was about to leave, he'd decided to ask Marie out for a drink. He knew it wasn't very professional; but then, being a landlord wasn't his profession.

'Here's my number; call me if you need anything.' He had smiled. 'And I was wondering, Marie – would you fancy a drink later?' He had let the question hang in the air, sure she would say yes.

'We're a couple, Declan,' Cheryl had snapped, in her nasal New York accent.

Declan had fled the scene of his acute embarrassment, thinking that they could at least have had the courtesy to have short hair and a fondness for waistcoats. As he waited in the queue to get on the plane back to Manchester, he thought that he might very well stay away for a few weeks; he was definitely having more luck with women on that side of the water.

26

'Michael, have you seen the keys for the car?' Maeve was hopping into a pair of Woolford tights and trying to mentally retrace her steps since she had picked him up from the airport the previous day.

'I haven't a clue!' Michael shouted from the bottom of the stairs. 'I've got to go; I've a client visit at half eight.' Maeve heard the door slam as she desperately wiggled into her favourite Armani suit. *Shit*, she thought. She really didn't have time for this; she had a meeting at half past nine, and it had to be finished in time for her to catch a one o'clock plane to Frankfurt.

'Spare keys, spare keys,' she muttered to herself. *Now where would Michael have put them?* He had a habit of depositing them in the inside pocket of his suit jacket. Maeve lunged for his wardrobe and riffled through his suits. They were all more or less identical, which didn't help. As she felt in the pocket of the tenth suit, she pulled out an airline ticket stub and, unthinking in her haste, threw it on the bed. She found the spare keys in the second to last suit.

As she sat on the bed to put on her shoes, she quickly glanced at the ticket stub. Michael's name was on it, and the destination was Venice. Maeve smiled to herself in surprise: Michael had kept the ticket stub from their honeymoon all this time. Then she launched herself down the stairs, grabbed her briefcase and overnight bag and flew out of the door.

As she threw open the car door, Maeve felt a familiar pang of Catholic guilt: her husband *was* a good man – he did little things like bringing her flowers and making her breakfast in bed and keeping ticket stubs from honeymoons. He didn't deserve the way she was treating him, Maeve thought sadly. He deserved to know about Catherine.

But, as she pulled onto the main road and joined the rest of the irate throng who hadn't bothered to get out of bed when their alarms went off, Maeve knew instinctively that she wasn't going to tell him – not yet. She couldn't. She needed more time to come to terms with it herself.

Flying into the office, Maeve made a mental note to congratulate Ciara on her work. In the short time she had been working at Williams Mackay, Ciara had been a revelation. Maeve had assumed that she would be recalcitrant – if not with the PAs, then certainly with her – but she hadn't been. She had been punctual and organised, Becky said, and had already implemented a new production-line system that cut the shared workload; and her natural charm meant that even the two PAs who were usually truculent were happy to try out her suggestions. Maeve couldn't believe it. Initially, she had been sure Ciara was just being super-organised to prove she could be better than her big sister, but gradually she had begun to realise that Ciara was simply good at adapting to new situations. She had never expected to say this, but her sister would be missed.

Ciara was sitting at her desk at Williams Mackay. She was quite enjoying herself there. In her first few days, she had watched Maeve like a hawk, sure that she was going to put her down in front of other people; but she hadn't. She'd been helpful and kind. Ciara had decided there was no way she was going to come out of this looking like the wayward sibling, so she had undertaken her work with drive and enthusiasm, and had found that she actually quite enjoyed it. She discovered that she could be on time, and that it was actually far easier than running into work late with the tired old line, 'You'll never guess what happened...' And being the sister of one of the partners was more of a help than a hindrance: it meant that she wasn't automatically treated as the coffee slave, and people credited her with slightly more intelligence than a plank of wood.

She was also enjoying finding out exactly what her sister did. She had never thought about Maeve as anything but her older sister who was a stuck-up pain in the bum, but according to Becky, Maeve had forgotten more about accountancy than most of the other partners knew – and, to Ciara's absolute astonishment, she was very well liked at work. The thing that had surprised Ciara most of all was Maeve's sense of humour. She was cheeky and irreverent to the other partners, and she had a twinkle in her eye that Ciara – much to her own annoyance – found herself secretly wanting to copy. She watched with something approaching pride as her sister walked into the office that morning.

Maeve headed for Becky's desk, to look at her diary for the week, and noticed Ciara, who was waving two pink Post-It notes stuck to her hands. They said, 'Hi, Maeve!'

'Hi, Ciara. How's it going?'

'Good, I think.'

'So I hear.'

Ciara raised an eyebrow at the praise, but decided not to comment. 'Michael get back OK?'

Maeve and Michael had been conspicuous by their absence at the Coffey Sunday lunch the previous day. Ciara had been there, but she told herself she would not allow this to become a weekly tradition. She was going to break the apron strings – like Claire, who put in the odd appearance but otherwise insisted on getting on with her own life.

'Yeah, fine.'

'I was saying to Dad, "Who flies from the Cotswolds?"'

Maeve threw Ciara a look suggesting that she didn't want to discuss her husband's movements in an open-plan office. 'The company has a stately home there where they do the training courses, and then he was in London on Friday and Saturday. He flew back from City airport. Let me just sort this out with Becky, and then you can come into my office.'

'Cool,' Ciara said. 'Fancy a coffee?'

She gave Maeve time to settle down at her desk, then brought two cups of coffee into her office.

'Sorry about that,' Maeve said. 'I just don't want the world and his granny knowing my business, that's all.'

'No problem. I keep forgetting that all these people are scared of you.' Ciara smiled.

Maeve's face fell. 'They are not scared of me,' she said in alarm. 'Tell me they're not scared of me!'

'No, they're not scared of you, Maeve! I was only joking. Chill out.'

Maeve sighed with relief.

'In fact, everyone really likes you, which is making my job easy – loath as I am to admit it.'

'What are you after?' Maeve asked.

'I'm not after anything; I'm just saying. God, Maeve, don't be so suspicious.'

'Sorry.' Maeve leafed through the papers on her desk. 'Anyway, I just wanted to tell you that you've been really good while you've been here.'

'Oh, yeah; my filing is second to none, and as for my ability to log on to a computer...well, eat your heart out, Bill Gates.'

'No, seriously. We usually get people who skulk in corners, pretending to work, while they're actually e-mailing their friends and writing the next *Reservoir Dogs* and generally sneering at the other admin staff. I'm not saying that everyone's been like that – it's just that we've had a couple of lads over the last few months, and that's what they were like, and...well, I didn't know if you were going to do the same, but –'

Ciara rolled her eyes. 'Thanks for the vote of confidence.'

'Let me finish. I just wanted to say that you've been really good. Everyone likes you, and I believe you persuaded Mr Carroll to make you a cup of tea last week.'

'Of course I did. I'd made him one.'

'Well, he's one of the senior partners, and rumour has it that he doesn't know the back of a kettle from the front. But he had his secretary send me an e-mail on Friday asking if we could get you to work here permanently – he said he "likes a woman with spunk".' Maeve and Ciara shared a look and burst out laughing. 'Whatever that means.'

Ciara smiled. It felt good to laugh with Maeve for a change.

Becky knocked and opened the door. 'Maeve, I'm sorry to interrupt, but they moved the meeting forward and didn't tell me. They're all in Meeting Room 4, waiting.'

Maeve sighed in exasperation. 'Cheers, Becky. I'll be there in a minute.' She glanced at her sister. 'Sorry, I'm going to have to run. Why don't I take you out for lunch on Wednesday, when I'm back in the office?'

'Yeah, cool; whatever you think.'

Maeve gathered up her papers and set off at full speed for her meeting, and Ciara headed back to her desk.

Maeve flopped onto the hotel bed and listlessly scrolled through the delights that German TV had to offer that evening. There were several music channels, CNN and other assorted news channels, and *Honig, Ich Gerschrumpt den Kinder* on the film channel. She sipped the gin and tonic she had made herself and toyed with the idea of having a sneak peek at the adult channel; but it was showing a film entitled *Dangerass,* and she decided that she might be better off working her way through the mini-bar and leafing through the day's notes.

Maeve was exhausted, but she had to be back in the Zala office at seven in the morning to meet with the chief auditor. She was to give a presentation to the board before heading back to Manchester on the ten o'clock flight, for another meeting with Jack Partridge, who had promised to treat her to a 'proper feed'. He was apparently planning to take her to some greasy spoon on the East Lancs Road. She wasn't sure how she would contain her excitement.

Dragging her presentation file across the bed with her foot, Maeve thought about what she was going to say the following morning. As she twisted her Mont Blanc into action, her mobile began to ring.

'Hello.'

'It's me,' Michael snapped.

'Hi, babe. I'm absolutely whacked; they've had me charging –'

'Don't "Hi, babe" me, Maeve. I've just got in and come up to the bedroom. What the hell were you doing snooping around my stuff?'

'*What?* Why are you ringing me up to shout at me?'

'Because I found my ticket stub on the bed. I bet you were over there brooding about what I was going to say. Well, I'm not going to discuss it, Maeve – not until you get home. You had no right—'

'Jesus, Michael! I might go on at you about hoarding things, but I'm hardly about to take your head off for keeping the ticket stub from our honeymoon!'

There was a moment's silence. 'I…'

'And don't bark down the phone at me as if I were four. I was looking for the spare car keys this morning, and I found that thing in your jacket pocket. I thought it was quite sweet that you'd kept it, if you must know, but now I think you're behaving like a maniac.'

Michael sighed heavily. 'I'm sorry, Maeve – really, I'm sorry. I'm just very stressed, with work and everything…'

'Well, so am I. I've been rushing around like a blue-arsed fly all day, and I just wanted to relax and get myself together. I don't need you barking at me.'

'I know, and I'm sorry.'

'Look, Michael, I'll see you tomorrow night, OK?'

'OK. And, Maeve…'

'Yeah?'

'Nothing. I love you, that's all.'

'Love you too.'

Maeve hung up and sat on the bed shaking her head. *This is why I don't open up to him,* she thought. When he lost his temper like that, she felt as if she were speaking to a stranger. Maybe she and Michael needed to get away, just the two of them, for a week or so. She would suggest it when she got home, she decided. They needed some time together to patch things up.

Pulling her notepad closer, Maeve began trying to make sense of everything she had written that day; but she fell asleep, exhausted, before she had finished the first page.

27

Ciara was in the kitchen, shouting at the oven, which was refusing to work. She really didn't want to resort to Pot Noodles. 'Work, you bloody thing!' she yelled, kicking the rusty, antiquated piece of equipment.

'It's a heap of crap,' Mark said over her shoulder.

'Oh, hi.' Ciara turned around, smiling. 'How was work?'

'Work was work.' He sighed. 'You?'

'Mine's great at the moment. It's really weird working at my sister's place, but it's good at the same time. I thought I'd find out loads of gossip about her, but all I'm finding out – as much as I hate to admit it – is that she's good at her job.'

'Sounds better than my place. Staring at a computer screen all day…it's not exactly riveting.'

'I can imagine.' Ciara threw her frozen cannelloni back into the freezer. 'I give up: I'm going to order a curry.'

'Why don't we go out for food?' Mark asked.

'Well, what about Rachel?'

'What about her? She's got a parents' evening. And, anyway, I didn't mean with Rachel. I just meant me and you.' He looked at Ciara meaningfully.

Ciara reddened, taking a sudden interest in a cobweb hanging from the cornice. She knew exactly what he meant. Mark had flirted with her all weekend. Even she could see that he fancied her – and she usually couldn't tell even if a guy went down on one knee with a bunch of flowers in one hand and a big sign saying, 'I Fancy You,' in the other.

The problem was Rachel. She seemed to watch Ciara like a hawk whenever she talked to Mark. After her warning that Mark was some kind of Don Juan, Ciara could only assume that she was just being over-protective. But Ciara didn't really think Mark was like that – and even if he was, she wasn't particularly bothered. She wasn't having sleepless nights over him; she was just attracted to him.

'OK, but give me an hour or so, will you? I've just got a few things to do. If we head out at seven, is that OK?'

'Fine. I'll be grooming myself for the next hour, should you need me.'

Ciara smiled and waited for him to go upstairs. As soon as he was out of earshot, she rang Rachel.

'Hi, Ray, it's me. I'm not disturbing you, am I?'

'No, the parents' evening doesn't start till seven. Why, what's up?'

'Nothing. I just…well, the thing is…' Ciara craned her neck around the kitchen door to check that Mark couldn't hear her. She flicked the radio on, just to be sure. 'The thing is, Mark asked me to go out for food with him tonight, and – well, I think it kind of means more than food, if you get my meaning…' She paused to see how Rachel reacted. It was hard to gauge over the telephone.

'Yeah. Go on.'

'Well, I was just wondering if you would have any objection.'

'Why would I object?' Rachel said quickly. 'I'm not his mother, Ciara. I told you that stuff about him because I thought you should know that he's a bit of a flirt. But, God, by all means go out. Have a great time.' She was laughing, but Ciara thought it sounded slightly forced.

'Do you think it'll upset things in the house?'

'Ciara,' Rachel replied sharply, 'go out and enjoy yourself. Seriously. I've got more on my plate than my housemates' love lives. It'll be fine – won't it?'

'Yeah, I think.' Ciara was a little confused. She wasn't sure if Rachel was encouraging her or chastising her.

'Look, do you like him?'

'Yes, but...'

'But you're not utterly besotted with him, are you?'

Ciara laughed. 'Not at all! I just fancy a bit of...' She trailed off.

'Well, I'll leave you to decide what you fancy a bit of. Just to let you know, there are condoms in my top drawer if you need them. They're "gossamer", apparently – none of your heavy-duty wellies from the family-planning clinic.'

Ciara blushed, slightly outraged. 'Well, thanks, but I don't know if I'll be needing them.'

'Well, take them anyway, because God knows I don't need them at the moment. And, Ciara?'

'Yeah?'

'Have a good time, whatever happens.'

'Thanks, Ray. I will.'

Ciara switched her phone off and sighed with relief. At least that was cleared up – she hoped.

Ciara and Mark were looking at the menu in the Gurkha Grill curry house when Mark looked over at Ciara and said, 'How do you like this place, for a first date?'

'Is that what this is? A first date? I hadn't noticed.' Ciara realised that all she needed was a fan and a deep-South accent and she could have starred in a remake of *Gone with the Wind*. She cast her eyes back to the menu, making a mental note to be less dramatic.

'Well, I hope so,' Mark said.

Ciara didn't have a clue what to do on a first date. She was so out of practice she was sure she needed oiling. She crossed and uncrossed her legs at least fifty times. She sat with her shoulders back for a while, but switched to leaning her elbows on the table when she realised that was how Mark was sitting. Then one elbow, which had been holding her chin up, slipped off the table with such a violent jolt that her head ended up somewhere in the region of her knees; she managed to concoct some kind of elbow table-dance, as if this was what she had meant to do all along, which manoeuvred her back into the shoulders-back position. When Mark informed her that the restaurant had been renovated fairly recently, she stared at him, wide-eyed, as if he'd just told her the secret to life, the universe and everything.

Ciara wasn't sure, however, that any of this dating behaviour was doing her any favours. What she secretly wanted to do was go to a pub, get a bit drunk, flirt, and end up in Mark's bed as if she had accidentally fallen into it. All this admitting that they were on a date and being super-nice to each other was setting her teeth on edge. Also, her conversation with Rachel hadn't completely put her mind at ease; the odd dynamic between Rachel and Mark was still nagging at her.

'Do you and Rachel get on?' she asked cautiously.

Mark laughed. 'Yes, course we do. I mean, we get

on each other's nerves sometimes, but that comes with living together; I suppose we're like brother and sister.'

Ciara sighed with relief. 'So nothing's ever happened between you two, then?' she asked.

There was a split second where whistling tumbleweed wouldn't have been out of place.

'Me and Rachel?' Mark's eyebrows leapt to his hairline. 'Don't be ridiculous!' He shook his head vehemently. 'God, no – no way. Nothing at all.'

Ciara waited to see if he had any other forms of denial to add, but he seemed to have finished. 'No?'

'Good God, no! I wouldn't – not a chance.'

Methinks the gentleman doth protest too much, Ciara thought. 'Anyway, she's my housemate.'

Ciara bit back a grin.

'Oh, God!' Mark moaned. 'I'm making an arse of myself. Look, I know you're my housemate too, but, well…oh, I don't know.'

Ciara decided it was time to let the poor man off the hook. 'Mark, it's fine. I believe you – not that it would have mattered if you had…' This was excruciating. She hated dates; they could be so forced. She might as well have had a sign on her head saying, 'Dispense with all the niceties; I'll snog you in a couple of hours.'

An hour later, Ciara and Mark were sitting in a nearby pub. They had managed to secure a huge leather settee, and Ciara felt that she could finally breathe again. For some reason, now that there was no longer a table between her and Mark, she didn't feel the need to keep crossing and uncrossing her legs like Cupid Stunt and straightening her back like she'd just spent two years in a Swiss finishing school. She felt relaxed and normal once again.

Over the rest of the evening, they chatted and laughed and drank enough premium-strength lager to warrant a fight and a night in the cells. As the barman called last orders, Ciara was confessing to Mark that she had been uncomfortable in the restaurant; he, in turn, admitted that he had wanted to laugh when her elbow fell off the table, and that he had had no idea what she was doing when she wiggled around pretending it hadn't happened.

They left the pub – and within a split second they went from cheerfully chatting to kissing so enthusiastically that they were drawing stares and calls of 'Get a room!' Ciara found herself down a dark alleyway, much like the ones in the opening credits of *Coronation Street*, with one hand up Mark's shirt and the other down his pants – unlike anything in the opening credits of *Coronation Street*. He pinned her to the wall and pulled at her jeans and jumper.

As Ciara felt her left breast pop out of her bra, she had a moment of clarity. This was not how she had envisaged her first sexual encounter with a new partner in six years. She said to Mark, breathlessly, 'Let's go home.'

They entered the house shh-ing each other and making every drunken effort to be quiet; they would have been quieter had they dropped a set of pans from the roof. They decided to go to Mark's bedroom, as Ciara's was next to Rachel's. Mark hurriedly put on a CD; then he lunged at Ciara again. In his haste, he had chosen 50 Cent, which was slightly disconcerting: Ciara found herself performing her first non-Declan sexual act since she was nineteen while being serenaded about hos, bitches and motherfuckers in general.

Ciara banged her head on the wall. Mark fell off the bed. Ciara, in her drunken state of mind, kept thinking Mark was Declan and then remembering sorrowfully that he wasn't, but she energetically ploughed on. Eventually they both collapsed in a grateful heap.

Mark fell asleep almost immediately. Ciara knew she should really stay awake, letting the Catholic guilt eat at her, thinking about Declan and wondering how she had just managed to sleep with someone who had been her housemate for about a millisecond. Catholic guilt, however, was no match for five pints of Stella, and she was asleep within minutes.

Mark's comedy alarm clock barked Ciara awake at seven o'clock. She felt a familiar dread spread from the tips of her toes upwards. It was the same dread she had experienced so many times, when she had gone out after work and come in drunk and pestered Declan at five in the morning, and woken up the next day feeling ashamed of herself, trying to piece together what she had done the night before. The previous evening was coming back to her in flashes.

She climbed quietly out of bed, not sure how to react to her own nakedness. She wanted to cover herself with her hands, like Barbara Windsor in a *Carry On* film when her underwear has, once again, inexplicably fallen off. Instead she pulled on a T-shirt of Mark's, which was lying on the floor, and tugged it down to cover her bum as she searched for her own clothes.

'Morning,' Mark said lazily, turning over to face her. He pushed himself up on his elbow and watched her rummage around the floor.

'Hi,' Ciara said sheepishly. A flashback of Mark's genitalia rudely forced itself, uninvited, into her mind. She quickly replaced it with a mental image of the top she was searching for.

'I really enjoyed last night,' Mark said croakily.

Ciara laughed, embarrassed. 'Yeah, it was good.' She didn't know if she meant that, but it seemed like the right thing to say.

There was a knock on Mark's bedroom door, and Ciara felt her embarrassment escalate several notches.

'Yeah?' Mark shouted.

'Hi, lovebirds. Just wanted to see if you had a good night.'

'Yes, thanks,' Mark shouted back, without inviting Rachel in.

'Anyone for coffee?'

'Me, please,' Ciara said sheepishly, locating her clothes and dragging them on as quickly as possible. She was mortified at the thought that Rachel might have heard what had gone on last night. They heard Rachel heading downstairs.

'Shit,' Mark said.

'Exactly,' said Ciara. 'I'm just going to go downstairs and see Rachel, before she goes.'

'Check she didn't hear anything?'

'Kind of.'

'And then will you come back to bed?' Mark's embarrassment threshold was obviously far higher than Ciara's.

'I'm in work at nine.'

'I'll give you a lift – that is, if you want one.'

'Em...OK.' Ciara wanted to say no – she wasn't sure if she liked Mark enough to get back into bed with him the morning after a drunken fumble – but she thought that might seem impolite. Ciara was hopeless at saying no. She would have let a rhino sit on her head if she'd thought she might cause mild offence by refusing.

She headed downstairs, hoping Rachel wasn't annoyed or upset. But Rachel was nowhere to be seen. On the table were a mug of coffee and the packet of condoms she had offered Ciara the previous day. Attached to it was a note: 'As you didn't use these, I hope you used *something*!' (They had, as it happened: Rachel might have been avoiding the family-planning clinic's industrial-strength condoms, but Mark obviously wasn't.)

Ciara looked at the note and screwed it up, embarrassed. It might as well have said, 'I know what you did last night.' *Well, she does, and we did,* Ciara thought, grabbing her coffee and trudging back upstairs.

28

It was Friday afternoon, and Ciara was busy typing up minutes. It was her last day at Williams Mackay, and she was surprised by how much she had enjoyed working there.

Maeve sprinted towards Ciara's desk, making her sit up in panic. 'Jesus, Maeve!'

'Sorry – I'm up against it this afternoon. I just wanted to say I'm sorry about Wednesday, and I promise I'll take you out next week.' When Maeve had offered to take Ciara out to lunch, she had forgotten that she had a prior appointment with a fry-up and Jack Partridge. Ciara had made do with a meat pie, which must have been ninety per cent pig's eyeballs, from the pie shop near the bus station. 'Where are they sending you next?'

'I've no idea. Haven't heard anything yet.'

'Well, Becky sent a note to HR to see if they needed anyone, so you might be back here.'

'I'd like that. I've enjoyed it here.'

'I'm glad.' Maeve smiled at her. Actually, this was one of the reasons Ciara had enjoyed herself: she had seen her sister showing signs of humanity in her old age. She was sure that, up until a few weeks ago, she couldn't have prised a genuine smile out of Maeve with a crowbar.

Maeve held out a perfectly wrapped package. 'Anyway, here's a little something from everyone, to say thanks for not doing a Quentin Tarantino in the corner for the last couple of weeks.'

Becky popped her head up over the divider. 'Yeah – thanks, Ciara. You're the first person in months who's done any work, instead of spending the whole day on the phone telling your friends how pissed you were last night.'

In the parcel was a silver pendant in a box. 'It's not Tiffany's or anything,' Maeve said, 'but we had a decent whip-round. People have retired from here after thirty years and not got the collection you had.'

Ciara blushed. 'I've only been here two minutes.'

'Yeah, but you've made quite an impact,' Becky agreed.

'Thanks – it's lovely.'

'Mr Carroll put in half.' Maeve smirked. 'I think you've pulled there.'

'Maeve, give up. I only made him a cup of tea!'

Maeve grinned and hurried away. Ciara was left to stare at her present. She couldn't believe it. When she finished temp assignments, she didn't get presents; she got sacked for not turning up, or for ringing in sick and putting on a terrible pretend-sick voice that fooled no one.

Ciara sat back in her chair and started to type a group e-mail. 'Did everyone put in for it, Becky? I want to send round an e-mail saying thank you.'

Becky stammered, 'Well…em…it was just me, Maeve and Mr Carroll, actually – but Maeve told me not to say anything. She just wanted you to have something nice; it was her idea.'

Ciara looked at Becky. Usually, she would have assumed Maeve was feeling sorry for her, or had some ulterior motive. Instead, she smiled a broad, grateful smile.

'Why didn't she tell me it was her idea?'

'Because she doesn't like taking credit for things, does she?' Becky said, as if this were obvious.

Ciara raised her eyebrows. A few weeks earlier, this would have made her grab the nearest phone and call Claire to say, 'Wait till you hear this. Maeve's got everyone at work thinking she's *selfless* – ha!' But she didn't want to do that. Maeve had been kind to her while she had worked at Williams Mackay. Even though she didn't spend much time in the office, she still sent Ciara e-mails, checking that she was OK.

Ciara unfastened the necklace and put it around her neck. Then she went back to typing the minutes, smiling to herself.

Ciara tentatively pushed open the unlocked door of her new home. It had been less than a week since she and Mark had slept together, but things in the house were beginning to feel slightly strained. Mark had gone out with friends from work the previous two evenings, and Ciara had gone to bed, bolting her bedroom door, before he came in. Last night he had knocked gently at her door, but she had pretended to be asleep. She had tried to talk about the whole thing with Rachel, but Rachel had laughed it off: 'I didn't hear a sound – not above 50 Cent being played at four thousand decibels. Stop obsessing about it.' But Ciara was obsessing about it. She couldn't help feeling that she had gone into a functioning household and put the starving cat firmly among the pigeons.

'Hi!' she shouted into the house.

Mark popped his head out of the bathroom door. 'Hey, how are you?'

'I'm good. How are you?'

'Glad it's Friday.'

'Yeah, me too. I got a present today, though – look.' Ciara held up the necklace like a barrier, hoping it would distract him from more serious topics.

Mark strained his eyes. 'Looks lovely from here,

but it could be anything. I'll come down.' He descended the stairs. A towel was wrapped around his waist – he had obviously just been in the shower – and his trim upper body was bare. *He is really fit,* Ciara thought. Physically, she really fancied him; but there wasn't anything else there. And, as they were housemates, the issue would have to be dealt with a lot sooner than it might otherwise have been. But Ciara just wasn't ready for the conversation at that moment – not with Mark towering over her; not with him taking the necklace gently and inspecting it, his body inches from hers. She looked at him and wondered how she was going to get herself out of this situation.

Instead, she got herself into Mark's bed, for the second time that week. This time, though, it was far better, by virtue of the fact that she could remember and enjoy everything that happened.

As Ciara pushed herself up on her elbow and tried to get her breath back, her clothes strewn to the four winds again, she gazed at Mark and waited for a feeling – any feeling – to wash over her. But it didn't. She knew how men must feel – those men who wander around sleeping with whomever they please and walking away, feeling nothing. *That's me,* Ciara thought. *I'm turning into a gigolo!*

Mark turned over in the bed and met her gaze. 'I've missed you since the other day,' he said.

Ciara felt her toes curl. She didn't want to lead him on, but she didn't want to hurt him, and she had to say *something*. She was sure it was against her biological makeup to hear a statement like that without offering some equally grand proclamation in return. 'I know; I've missed you too,' she said weakly. 'Listen, I'm sorry to run off, but I said I'd be around at my sister Claire's by seven, and it's nearly that now. I've really got to get ready and go.'

'OK, no problem. I'm meeting some friends in town anyway. Will you be back tonight?'

'No, I'm staying over.' Ciara hoped Claire wouldn't mind an unexpected guest.

'Well, I'll see you tomorrow.'

'You will,' Ciara said, leaning over and kissing him. The kiss was nice, but it didn't feel right. It didn't feel right at all.

She needed to extricate herself from this situation as soon as possible. But, for now, she was going to run to Claire's and hide.

29

After being thrown out of Trinity, Ciara spent the next few days moping around Declan's house declaring that her world had ended, while Declan comforted her and encouraged her to think about what she was going to do next. By that weekend, she had become bored of feeling sorry for herself and had decided to drag her sorry backside out of her pyjamas and type up a rudimentary CV. By Tuesday she had work, in an accountancy firm in the IFSC. The Celtic Tiger was in mid-roar at the time, and even a monkey could have found gainful employment if it didn't mind wearing a headset.

With a new job and a new regime that included getting out of bed before midday, Ciara was soon declaring herself a new person. She gave her notice at the bar where she had been working part-time and decided to throw herself into organising her life. She was going to apply for the English course at UCD, she informed Declan. Ciara had always had a passion for literature; she had taken Economics simply because it was the course her father had taken.

By the time she finally appeared back at her house in Rathmines, she had spent over a week running around, filling her time with anything and everything to keep her mind off her expulsion. She was hoping that she and Róisín could forget about the heated words they had exchanged; but when she saw the look on Róisín's face, she realised it wasn't going to be that easy.

'Nice of you to finally put in an appearance,' Róisín said coldly.

Ciara put the kettle on and turned to her. 'Róisín, I was a complete arse last week, and I'm really sorry. What I did was wrong – the exam and everything – but I've been punished for that, haven't I?' She waited for a response; Róisín shrugged. 'And I'm sorry for the way I went off at you, but I was having a hard time.'

'Well, at least Declan thought to ring me and let me know you were OK.'

'I know he did; I asked him to. I just wasn't up to speaking to anyone. I felt terrible – I feel terrible.' Ciara hung her head.

'Come here, you,' Róisín said, holding out her arms. 'I've missed you.' Ciara pulled her tight, relieved to be forgiven.

As she made the tea, Ciara told Róisín how industrious she had been. 'You thought I'd be moping round the North Circular Road feeling sorry for myself, didn't you?'

'Well, I didn't think you'd have a job in an office – put it that way.'

'And something else came up, as well,' Ciara said sheepishly.

'What's that?'

'Well, seeing as I'm no longer a student, I might have to move out of my student accommodation.'

'What – move out from here?'

'Yeah. Me and Dec have been talking, and I think we might rent an apartment together, somewhere near town. It won't be until September, but I just thought I'd better let you know. I'll tell the other two; I just wanted to say it to you first.'

'Oh, my God – you're moving in together? That's serious stuff!'

'Yeah, I know,' Ciara said, 'but it just feels like the right thing to do.'

'Well, that's great news,' Róisín said, smiling. 'A bit of a shock, but great news. I'd better see you, though, Ciara. I don't want you moving out and disappearing off the face of the planet.'

'I'll be here more than I am now. You'll be sick of the sight of me – I promise.'

When September came, Ciara moved her belongings into the new apartment that she and Declan were renting in Smithfield. She was still working at the IFSC – she had been far too late to apply to UCD that year. She told Declan it would give her a chance to save some money; actually, she was relieved not to have to set foot in an academic institution for the time being. She had spent the summer in Dublin, telling her parents she had found a summer job. She didn't feel this was a lie – she had been working and it had been, in fact, summer. She hadn't yet broached the subject of her expulsion with her mother and father; she had decided to tell them at Christmas, when she went home.

But Christmas came and went, and Ciara had such an enjoyable time catching up with everyone in Manchester that she didn't want to spoil it by mentioning the minor detail that she had been unceremoniously kicked out of college. When she told Declan this, he asked her how she was going to get around the fact that she was meant to be having a graduation ceremony in July. She told him she'd think of something.

As the year progressed, Ciara saw less and less of Geraldine, Sinéad and even Róisín. There was something about living north of the river that made the south side seem a million miles away. When she had first moved out, she had made an effort and gone over to Rathmines two or three times a week, and the girls had joined her in town on weekends.

But, as the three girls' final exams neared, the contact between them dwindled. It was more Ciara's doing than theirs: the talk of finals reinforced her feelings of failure.

Ciara found herself scouring the UCD website more and more often; it gave her a nervous thrill to look at the pages on the Arts course that she actually wanted to do. But, every time she picked up the phone to ring for an application form, her mouth would dry up and she would slam the receiver down. By the middle of January she was telling herself on a daily basis that she would definitely apply the following day.

It was around this time that Declan decided that he and Ciara needed to have a serious discussion.

'We seriously need to talk, Ciara,' Declan said, sliding into the bench of the juice bar on Suffolk Street.

Ciara was nursing a mango juice. She had been waiting for him to finish work. 'What about?' she asked innocently.

'About that thing out there.' Declan pointed out the window.

'Avoca?' Ciara asked, looking at the shop across the road.

'Don't be a smart-arse. Not Avoca – Trinity.'

'I don't want – or need – to talk about Trinity, Declan.'

'OK, then how about UCD? It's been months

since you were…' Declan tried to find the right words.

'Kicked out.'

'Well, yeah, kicked out. You keep promising to apply to UCD, but you haven't. When I try to raise the issue, you just body-swerve away.'

'"Body-swerve"?' Ciara raised an eyebrow. 'Is that one of those words they teach you in advertising?'

'Stop it, Ciara; this isn't about me.'

'No, because things are pretty rosy for you, aren't they?' Ciara snapped. Sometimes she couldn't help herself.

'Do you begrudge me that?'

Ciara quickly shook her head. 'No – not at all. I'm sorry.'

Since Declan had started working at JMSS&A, he and Barry had become shining stars in the world of Irish advertising. The economy was booming, and everyone and his grandmother was cashing in on being Irish. Talent that, only a few years before, would have been at best cautiously encouraged over time and at worst allowed to stagnate was being used to its full. Declan and Barry were being given accounts that would have taken them years to acquire in London, and they were doing a better job than their English counterparts: they had an increasingly groaning trophy shelf to prove it.

'It's OK,' he said. 'I just want you to be happy, and I don't think you're happy running that office.'

'Actually, I quite liked it, I'll have you know.' Ciara quite liked her job as much as she quite like getting repeatedly kicked in the temple.

Declan laughed. 'Since when? Your boss is a bitch, and everyone you work with is obsessed with property prices.'

Ciara laughed and fiddled with her drinking straw. 'Yeah, all right – it isn't great, I'll give you that.'

'So I've been thinking. We've been together for almost two and a half years—'

'Oh, Declan, you remembered!' Ciara clutched at her heart with mock gratitude.

'And,' Declan continued, ignoring her, 'we've been living together since September. So I think there's some sort of commitment there – wouldn't you agree?'

'You're not going to propose again, are you? Because I don't have a spare sock on me.'

'Ciara, I'm being serious.' Declan glared, which shut her up. 'I've a suggestion.'

'Go on.'

'I think you should quit the office job, get a part-time bar job again and concentrate on getting into the UCD course. You can spend the summer going through the reading list.'

Ciara furrowed her brow. 'I can't afford to do that, Declan. I've got a bit saved, but it'll only cover the rent for a couple of months.'

'I know that. But I'm earning bin-loads at the

moment; I can easily afford your part of the rent for a while.'

Ciara looked across at him, and a surge of pure love erupted inside her. 'I don't know what to say.' She wanted to jump on the table and shout at the top of her lungs that she had the most amazing boyfriend in the world – but she thought it might be a bit too *Kids from Fame* for the people around her, who were trying to tuck into their mung-bean falafels in peace.

'Just say that you'll hand your notice in to Bitch-Features by the end of the month, and that you'll fill in an application form for the UCD course.'

Ciara pushed her mango juice to one side and leaned over the table, pulling Declan close. She kissed him and sat back down, smiling at him. 'I love you,' she said.

'And why wouldn't you?' Declan winked.

Ciara began working at Barian a few weeks later and immediately remembered how much she enjoyed working in a bar – the laughs, the unintentionally funny regulars, the lie-ins. There was very little petty bitchiness among the bar staff, and they all went out together after work. She walked along the river, looking over at the building where she had worked in the IFSC, and suddenly felt young again.

The thing she wasn't finding so easy was applying to UCD. She wanted to, desperately, but she knew she hadn't a hope of being accepted; they would be bound to find out about her cheating. The thought put the fear of God into her. Declan kept pestering her, and the more he pestered, the guiltier she felt. So Ciara did what she did best: she lied.

'I've got an interview at UCD next week,' she told him.

'What do you mean? You've not been through the CAO or anything.'

Ciara winced. 'Yeah, but because I'm classed as a foreign student I can apply directly to the college.'

A grin broke across Declan's face. 'Really? That's brilliant!'

'Yeah, isn't it?' Ciara tried to sound upbeat, but she felt wretched.

Declan jumped up and kissed her. 'You'd better get reading, then.'

Ciara spent the next week reading over classic texts. Declan was so excited for her that it was heartbreaking. He arrived home one evening with an armful of books – Thomas Hardy, Graham Greene, D.H. Lawrence and E.M. Forster: 'That should keep you busy,' he said, kissing Ciara on the forehead. 'I'll make the dinner; you've got work to do.' Ciara ploughed morosely through the books, wishing she'd never said anything. But she couldn't come clean to Declan, not at this stage; she would just get to the day of the interview, then come home and tell him it had gone badly. He need never know.

On the day of the 'interview', Ciara dressed up in a suit, Declan wished her luck, and then she went to a café and sat there until she knew he would have left for work.

That night, when Declan got home, he asked, 'Well, how did it go?'

Ciara winced under his gaze. 'It was awful. There's no way I'll get in. They grilled me, and I fell to pieces.'

'Really?'

'Yeah. And one of the guys was so harsh...' Declan didn't respond. 'I'm not sure I'd want to go there anyway.'

Declan's fists were clenched by his sides, and his eyes were sparking with anger. "Why are you lying to me?'

Ciara was stunned into silence.

'I went up there to meet you after the interview, as a surprise. The Arts department had never heard of a Ciara Coffey. And no one was being interviewed, because, as I was reliably informed, that's not how it works!' Declan shouted. 'I'd brought you flowers, but I gave them to the secretary; she seemed delighted.'

'Declan, I'm sorry!' Ciara wailed. 'I didn't mean to lie to you.'

'You never mean to lie to anyone, do you? You just do it. And I'm a fucking mug for putting up with it.' He stormed to the door.

'Where are you going?' Ciara pleaded.

'As far away from you as I can get, for tonight. I'll see you later.' He slammed the door, leaving Ciara to slump into an armchair, sobbing.

It took him over a week to calm down. Ciara promised over and over that she'd never lied to him before and never would again. Finally, when she felt he had come around, she told him, 'I've made a decision.'

'Is that right?' Declan asked sarcastically.

'Yeah, that is right, actually. I won't be applying anywhere. I've decided that I don't want you to support me in something I'm not completely sure I want to do, and the fact is, I don't think I want to do a degree.'

This was rubbish, and both of them knew it.

'Of course you do. You just don't want to be embarrassed. That's why you didn't contact UCD in the first place.'

'That's not true. I want to earn some money and enjoy myself, and not do a degree just because everyone thinks I should.'

'No one thinks you should. You just *think* everyone thinks you should.'

'Look, Declan, I don't want to go back to university and that's that, OK?'

'OK, fine – do whatever you want to do. But don't lie to me again, Ciara.'

'I've told you a million times, I won't.'

'Good,' Declan said, pulling her towards him and kissing her for the first time in a week.

30

Ciara spent Friday night at Claire's and then sheepishly returned home on Saturday. She knew that she and Mark would have to cross paths eventually, but she also knew he was visiting a friend in Leeds overnight, so she wouldn't have to confront the situation just yet. She spent Saturday night in with Rachel, watching cheesy 80s films and drinking wine. Ciara mentioned Mark a couple of times, but Rachel seemed completely disinterested, and Ciara didn't feel able to confide that she had made a mistake and didn't know how to get herself out of it. She had talked to Claire, who had simply said, 'Finish it. He's a big boy; he'll live' – which Ciara knew was true, but somehow this solution seemed far too simple to work in practice.

Mark had asked if she would like to do something on Sunday afternoon, but this time Ciara had a genuine excuse to decline. It was her mother and father's wedding anniversary. The Coffeys were celebrating with Mass and Sunday lunch, cooked by the four children and Michael. Ciara was in charge of vegetable-peeling.

Father O'Neill had been invited. Sean took him through to the lounge, while Margaret stood in the kitchen among her children, barking orders. Finally Maeve took her by the shoulders, handed her a dry sherry and ordered her out.

'Thank God for that; I thought she'd never go,' Claire said, checking on the roast.

'What am I doing in here?' Anthony asked.

'Bugger all, from what I can see. Why don't you go and set the table?' Maeve suggested.

'Why don't you shove it up your arse?' Anthony asked sweetly.

'I beg your pardon?'

'You're not my mum, Maeve, so stop acting like you are.' Anthony stormed out of the kitchen. Claire followed him.

Maeve shook her head. 'I don't understand him, I really don't.'

'You're not meant to, Maeve; he's a seventeen-year-old boy,' Michael said.

'I know what he is,' Maeve snapped.

Ciara threw them a look to remind them that

she was there. 'Sorry,' Maeve said, randomly opening and shutting cupboards. 'Where's the gravy powder?' Ciara, knowing she wanted to change the subject, pulled open the correct cupboard and pointed at the packet.

'Listen, Ciara,' Michael said, straining to be light-hearted; he sounded like a voice-over artist who had been told to put a laugh in his voice.

'Yeah?' Ciara studied her work and realised that there was far more carrot in the peelings than in the carrot bowl.

'Did Sally call you on Friday?'

'Sally?'

'Sally-that-I-work-with Sally.'

'Oh, yeah, right. No, she didn't. Why?'

'She had a fantastic job come in – sounded right up your street. But we were pretty snowed under; she must have forgotten.'

'What is it?' Ciara cringed. She hadn't heard anything from Michael's firm, and she'd hoped that she wouldn't – but, of course, she should have known that Sally would make a point of trying to get Michael's sister-in-law a job. She knew that, whatever it was, she would be hopelessly under-qualified for it.

'I'll give her a call now, and you can talk to her.'

'On a Sunday? Won't she mind?' Maeve asked. Ciara looked from one to the other, certain that she could feel tension.

'I could ring her at four in the morning, if it meant adding to her bonus,' Michael said flatly.

Maeve raised an eyebrow and resumed inspecting the gravy packet.

'For what we are about to receive, may the Lord make us truly grateful.' Father O'Neill was saying grace. The food looked great, Ciara thought proudly. Claire had come to the rescue and found a bag of parsnips, so the carrots didn't look so sparse.

'Why should we be truly grateful? Surely access to food is a basic human right.' All eyes shot up from the table and towards Anthony.

'Anthony, I will not have insolence at the table,' Sean said sternly.

'I'm not being insolent; I'm just asking a question. How do you expect me to learn anything if I never ask any questions?'

'I think that Dad is just suggesting that there's a time and a place,' Maeve said, quietly, widening her eyes warningly towards Anthony.

'No one asked you,' Anthony shot back. 'Sorry, Father, continue.' He put his hands together in an affected steeple. Claire kicked Ciara under the table. Ciara knew that their dad was going to hit the roof once the priest had gone. Looking across at her mother, she saw that tears had sprung to her eyes. She felt sorry for her mum sometimes. She always felt she had to back her husband on everything: he had the final say in any matter.

They ate in silence for a moment, and then Sean

began his customary buttonholing. 'So, Ciara, how's work been?'

'Fine. The usual – just temping in town, until something comes along that fits my skills.'

'Working for your sister, no less, I believe,' Margaret piped up.

Ciara put down her knife and fork and threw Maeve an evil glare. *I knew it! She couldn't wait to go telling tales.* Maeve looked shocked. 'Working *with* my sister, yes, but—'

'But she'll soon have a career over here,' Michael interrupted. 'I thought Sally had something for her there, actually, but it's not going to happen. Shame about that one, Ciara.'

'It's OK,' Ciara mumbled.

'It's a great job, but Ciara's over-qualified for it, aren't you?' Michael helped himself to a glass of the Châteauneuf-du-Pape that he had brought as an anniversary present. He was the only one drinking it.

'Yeah; they were after an office-manager sort of person,' Ciara told her parsnips.

'Well, there's no point in taking something that's beneath you,' Sean nodded approvingly. 'Something will come up.'

'Your children are a credit to you, Sean,' Father O'Neill said. 'You must be very proud.'

'I am.' Sean nodded.

'*We* are,' Margaret said tersely. Ciara put her knife and fork together. She didn't feel like eating any more. She was furious with Maeve.

'Father, will you be coming along to the céilí next Friday in the church hall?' Sean asked, ignoring any tension at the table.

'I will, of course. Wouldn't miss it for the world – though I won't be up for much dancing.' Ciara stifled a laugh. 'Are the Kerrymen playing?'

'They are indeed.'

'Great stuff.'

'Dad, could I be excused, please? I have homework to finish,' Anthony asked.

'That's fine.' Sean obviously didn't want the priest to witness any family discord. Anthony hopped from his seat and ran up the stairs.

'I'll get dessert, shall I?' Maeve offered.

Ciara helped clear the table and followed her into the kitchen. 'That is *so* you, Maeve. Nicey-nicey to me all week, and then stab me in the back when Mum and Dad are there.'

Maeve slammed the plates down. 'Look, I didn't tell them that you were working with me. It must have been Michael.'

'Don't make excuses.' Ciara turned her back.

Maeve grabbed her by the shoulder, forcing her back around. 'I am not making excuses. I didn't tell them! What is your problem, Ciara?' she hissed. 'So what if they knew you were working with me, anyway? They know you're temping.'

Ciara's eyes narrowed. 'Yeah, and they also think that you're Miss Perfect. So, if they think I'm playing general dogsbody to you, that makes me look worse and you look better – which is what you want, I suppose.'

Maeve drew herself up to her full five foot nine and stabbed a finger at Ciara's chest. 'Now you listen to me. I have had it with your shit, Ciara. I am far from perfect in their eyes, and the sooner you cop on to that the better. You are twenty-five years old, not fourteen. Now get your arse back out there and play Happy Families. We can continue this discussion later.'

Ciara felt her bottom lip tremble. She was slightly unnerved. There was something in Maeve's voice that suggested she had pushed things too far this time.

She went out of the kitchen and swallowed hard, smiling. 'Maeve's serving up the pavlova. Anyone for coffee?'

'I was just saying what a fine job you've made of things,' Father O'Neill said, as Maeve set out the dessert dishes.

Maeve seemed oblivious of the fact that he was aiming the comment at her. *She would*, Ciara thought, still smarting from her dressing-down. If someone had complimented her on making a resounding success of her life, she'd have cart-wheeled around the room – but not Maeve; she heard this sort of stuff every day.

'Your career and everything… You're a credit.'

'A credit? Am I, Father?' Maeve snapped. 'To whom?'

Ciara's eyes widened, and Claire's jaw narrowly missed her pavlova.

'To your parents, of course.'

'Oh, yeah – to my parents. Right.' Maeve went back to inspecting a raspberry she was balancing on her spoon. Ciara stared; it was like watching a slow-motion car crash.

'They all are, Father,' Margaret said, grabbing her napkin and dabbing her mouth, looking extremely flustered (Ciara would have suspected the menopause if she hadn't remembered her teenage years: HRT tablets left everywhere, and Margaret constantly asking, 'Is it hot in here, or is it me?').

'Yes, I'm sure they are,' Father O'Neill said, digging his spoon into his dessert.

'How's work, Maeve?' Margaret asked, as if she had just been presented with a large crack and been asked to paper over it.

'Work's fine. The weather's been a bit changeable. No, I didn't see that thing about meerkats on the Discovery Channel the other night. Anything else?'

'Chill out, Maeve!' Claire said, shocked.

'What, Claire? Wouldn't you prefer to have a decent conversation about what's actually going on in everyone's life?'

'Maeve!' Sean said sternly.

'Dad!' Maeve met his tone and stare.

'Maeve, come on, now,' Michael said. 'She's been like this all week.' Ciara winced; even she would have known better than to employ such a condescending tone.

'Don't talk about me as if I were somebody's deaf grandmother, Michael. And you don't even know what I've been like; you're never around long enough to find out!'

Claire stared helplessly at Ciara. Maeve put down her spoon and napkin and stood up. 'Look, I'm going to go home. Happy anniversary and everything. I'll just see you during the week.' She looked directly at Ciara, who realised, alarmed, that there were tears in her eyes. Maeve didn't cry – she was the hard-nosed one, for God's sake!

'Well, that's gratitude,' Sean said sharply.

'I'm *eternally* grateful, Dad, aren't I? That's my problem.' Maeve sighed. Then she walked out of the dining room, leaving everyone in stunned silence.

Michael got to his feet. 'I suppose I should go too. I'm really sorry about all this.'

'Don't apologise for me, Michael!' Maeve shouted from the hallway. He shrugged his shoulders and followed her. The front door slammed.

'I really don't know. I give up,' Sean said, shaking his head.

Ciara knew something wasn't right. Her father was incensed – which made sense, after an outburst like that; but he was also acting as if he had spent his life trying to keep his eldest daughter on the straight and narrow.

Margaret, Sean and Father O'Neill spent the rest of the meal exchanging inane pleasantry after inane pleasantry, while Ciara and Claire sat in awkward silence, occasionally kicking each other under the table.

'Are you going to sit there saying nothing all night?' Michael asked. He and Maeve were in the living room; they had just got home.

Maeve sighed and folded her arms. 'I am so annoyed with you – telling my parents about Ciara working with me, when I specifically asked you not to, and then sticking your oar in during dessert.'

'Well, you can stop being annoyed with me, because I am not getting involved in any more of your petty family bullshit.'

Maeve glared at him. 'I *told* you I didn't want my parents to find out that Ciara was working with me. Remember? I said that, for the first time in an age, she and I were getting along, and I didn't want to ruin that.'

'And what was all that petulant rubbish about the weather and meerkats?'

'You just don't listen to me, Michael.'

'You're right, Maeve. To be perfectly honest,' Michael said, rising from his seat, 'most things you tell me about your family go in one ear and out the other.' He picked up the jacket he had just discarded and put it on again.

'Well, that's great to know; I'll save my breath

next time.' Maeve watched him check his pockets for his keys. 'Where are you going?'

'Out.'

'But we need to talk.'

'I know better than anyone, Maeve, that we need to talk. Half the time I don't know where I stand with you; the slightest thing sets you off. You can blame work, you can blame your family, but there's more to it – and, until you're willing to stop lashing out at me and tell me what that is, I'm not going to listen to you. Now I need to clear my head. You can get me on my mobile if you want me.'

Maeve had been sitting in silence for nearly half an hour when there was a knock at the front door. She answered it to find Ciara standing there, with her hood pulled tightly over her head, like Kenny from *South Park*. The sleeves of her jacket were pulled down over her fists, and a bottle of wine wrapped in paper nestled under her arm.

'Oh, Ciara; it's you.'

'Can I come in?'

Maeve sighed. 'I suppose so,' she said, holding the door open.

'Here you go.' Ciara held out the bottle of wine. 'And I got you these…' She rummaged in the deep pockets of her parka. 'Peace offering.' She held out a jar of olives. 'I was in the deli on Burton Road. They didn't have any olive branches, so I thought a jar might be the next best thing.'

Maeve rolled her eyes, but she couldn't help smiling as she closed the front door.

'Where's Michael?' Ciara asked, taking her coat off and slumping into the armchair.

'I'm surprised you didn't pass him galloping along Burton Road on his high horse.' Maeve went into the kitchen and returned with two glasses and a corkscrew.

'Bad mood?'

'That's the understatement of the century. He went out of here like a bear with a sore arse.'

Ciara laughed.

'What?'

'Nothing. I just like your sarcasm – when it's not directed at me, of course.'

Maeve raised an eyebrow at Ciara and handed her a glass of wine. 'Here you go, and I promise I won't be sarcastic to you at all this evening.'

'Good. I wouldn't want to be on the receiving end of what you were dishing out earlier.'

'That was bad of me, wasn't it?'

'Well…I don't know – depends why you did it, I suppose. It was entertaining, though, I'll give you that.'

'Great.' Maeve rolled her eyes. 'I aim to please.'

'Are you all right, Maeve? Really all right, I mean?'

'Yeah, I'm fine,' Maeve said, with mock breeziness.

'Because Dad was really weird when you went out. He was acting like he'd spent his whole life dealing with hassle from you. Now, call me paranoid, but I don't think he was pushed to that by a narky comment about meerkats.'

Maeve shrugged. She tried to compose herself, but the lump in her throat rose and her chest tightened. A tear began to trickle down her cheek.

Instantly, Ciara was out of her chair and over by Maeve's side. 'What's wrong?' she whispered.

'Nothing,' Maeve said, through a sob. 'I've so much on at the moment... I'm just being stupid, that's all.'

'No, you're not being stupid, but you're treating me as if I might be. Come on – there's more to this than Mum and Dad getting to you and you being busy at work. You never, *ever* freak out like that. What's up?'

Maeve tucked her hair behind her ears – something Ciara did as well, when she was nervous – and sat up straight. Ciara ran to the kitchen and came back brandishing a roll of kitchen towel. 'Go on,' she urged, as Maeve wiped her eyes and blew her nose.

'There's no good way of saying this...' Maeve gulped, trying to halt the tears so she could talk. 'I've never told anyone before – apart from Mum and Dad, that is. They know; well, it *was* their idea.'

Ciara hadn't a clue what she was talking about.

'Ciara, you know how you go on about me not coming over to Ireland while you were there?'

'Yeah.'

'Well, I hate Ireland.'

'I know. You've told me.'

'But I didn't tell you the reason. It's not just because Dad goes on about it all the time and we got dragged there as kids.'

'Well, I didn't think it was that. You seemed to have a great time when we went there; you always got to go to the discos, and the rest of us had to stay in and watch *The Late Late Show*.'

'Age difference,' Maeve reminded her.

'Oh, yeah...' Ciara nodded.

'Look, I need to say it now, or I'm not going to say it. You know when I was in sixth form and I went to Ireland for the summer?'

'Yes.'

'Well...' Maeve paused, gathering every ounce of energy she had. 'I know you all thought I was there for some sort of holiday. But I wasn't. I was there because I was pregnant.'

Ciara's eyes widened in shock. 'No,' she whispered.

'I went to Aunt Patricia's in Tullamore, and I had the baby there.'

'You had it?'

'Yes.' Maeve cast her eyes downwards. 'Had *her*.' Her eyes still glistened with tears. 'Her name was Gemma – well, I called her Gemma, but that's not her name now. She's called Catherine.'

'You know what they called her?' Ciara asked tentatively. 'How?'

'Because she got in contact with me. Around the time you came back from Ireland.'

'Oh, God!'

'What's wrong?'

'You've been dealing with this since I came back, and I've been giving it loads, acting like a spoilt little madam – like in the café in Chorlton... I'm mortified.'

'It doesn't matter. Anyway, I've been dealing with it since I was seventeen. It's only in the last two months that I've started to feel better about it, that's all.'

'God, yeah – I suppose.' Ciara said slowly, trying to arrange her thoughts and feelings on the matter. 'Are you going to see her?'

'She's working this summer, so I've said I'll go over to Dublin at the end of August. She lives in Cashel, in Tipperary.'

'Just think – I had a niece in Ireland all the time I was there!' Ciara said in wonderment, before quickly catching herself. 'Sorry, Maeve – there I go again, bringing everything back to me. It revolves around me, you know, the world.' Maeve laughed through her sniffs. 'It does. I could see a man with his leg hanging off, and I'd say, "Could you put that away, please? I don't want to look at it!"'

Maeve cracked a laugh. 'There you go – that's better: you're laughing.' Ciara brushed her sister's hair back from her face. 'Oh, Maeve... What did Michael say when he found out?'

'He doesn't know.'

Ciara's mouth fell open.

'I know.' Maeve nodded. 'Mum and Dad told me that I couldn't tell anyone... When I met Michael, I kept wanting to tell him, but it just never seemed like the right time; and then, after a while, I knew I'd left it too late.'

'Wait a minute – Mum and Dad told you? You mean they knew?'

'Of course they knew. How else do you think I ended up at Aunty Pat's? And that old fucker Father O'Neill knew. He organised things through the Church, told Mum and Dad he could contact the adoption agency for them – it was run by nuns.'

'Oh, my God.'

'I know. I used to ring home and talk to you lot, and you'd all be fighting, and I just wanted to be home being a teenager... It was awful. Pat made me go to church every week wearing a baggy T-shirt because she didn't want anyone knowing I was pregnant. She kept telling all the nosy neighbours that I was there as a treat for doing well in my exams. Some treat! I felt like Mary bloody Magdalene. Dad would ring up and ask how I was and tell me it would be OK when I came home, as long as I forgot about it. He called it my "silly mistake". I hardly even got to see the baby before they took her away.' Maeve's voice cracked with anger. 'Listen, it sounds like something out of *Angela's* bloody *Ashes*, but it was only sixteen years ago. And I know Mum and Dad said they had my best interests at heart – they wanted me to get a good education and all the rest of it – but they wanted what was best for them, too. They didn't want a pregnant sixteen-year-old daughter, and that was that.'

'Maeve, I can't believe it,' Ciara said. She was trying desperately to remember the summer in question, but she couldn't really; she had only been ten at the time.

'No, neither can I. I think about it every day, but I still can't actually believe it.'

'Do you ever talk to Mum and Dad about it?'

'Are you kidding? Not a chance. As soon as I got back over here, Dad sat me down and said, "Everything that happened was very unfortunate and not what we would have wanted for you, but it's over now. You can get your A-levels and go to university, and nobody need ever know." And that's what I did. Like a complete dick, that's what I did.' Maeve rubbed her forehead.

'Who was the dad, if you don't mind me asking?' Curiosity had got the better of Ciara.

'Dale Kay.'

'Really?'

'Well, who else did you think it was going to be?' Dale had been Maeve's first boyfriend. Ciara had liked him; he used to take her to the park and play football with her. But then Maeve had gone to Ireland for the summer, and when she came back Dale had disappeared off the scene, much to Ciara's annoyance.

'Did he know?'

'No.' Maeve shook her head defiantly. 'Dad just told him that he knew what we'd been doing and that, if he caught Dale anywhere near me again, he wouldn't be responsible for his actions.'

Ciara leaned back in the chair and thought about her parents. 'Do you know something, Maeve? I am sick to death of keeping up appearances. I spend half my life lying just to keep them happy – and what for? Fuck all. I feel like going back there right now and telling them exactly what I think of their bullshit. I can't believe they made you give up your child – their grandchild – just so that the hypocritical arseholes they call friends wouldn't talk about them. I swear to God, I am going to read them the riot act.'

'No, you are not!' Maeve snapped defiantly. 'There is no way you're going to say anything until I'm ready. I'm not ready yet. And, anyway, it's not black and white, Ciara. They might very well be hypocrites, but I genuinely believe that what they did with me, they did at least partly for the right reasons.'

'For *their* reasons, Maeve! You said it yourself!'

'Ciara, calm down.'

'No, I won't! I'm as bad as you – doing what they say, toeing the line, pretending that everything in the garden is rosy when actually it's pretty fucked up.' Ciara paused for a moment. 'I've a little secret of my own, actually – nothing like as serious as yours, but still, it's affected everything I've done for the past few years.'

'Really?' Maeve asked, intrigued.

'Yeah...'

Just as Ciara was about to deliver her -- under the circumstances – second-rate bombshell, the front door flew open and Michael marched into the lounge, his head poking over the top of a bunch of flowers. Maeve groaned inwardly. Michael had brought home so many peace offerings recently that their lounge was starting to look like the Chelsea Flower Show.

'Oh...Ciara. I wasn't expecting you.' He looked shocked.

Ciara shrugged uncomfortably. 'I just came round to bring something for Maeve; I'm not staying.'

'Will I give you a lift home?' Maeve asked.

'No, it's fine. I've got Anthony's mountain bike locked up outside.' She quickly pulled on her coat.

'Are you all right, Maeve?' Michael asked, seeing her blotchy face. He looked at Ciara, who shrugged and looked away. 'I didn't mean to upset you.'

'It's fine, Michael, really. I'll just see Ciara to the door.'

At the door, Maeve said quietly, 'Ciara, I'm sorry about this. Do you want to finish what you were saying?'

'No, it's OK. I'll catch up with you during the week. You have more important things to sort out.'

Ciara nodded towards the lounge. 'Has he got Interflora on automatic redial?'

'More like the Esso garage,' Maeve whispered, stifling a laugh. She hugged Ciara tight, then closed the door gently behind her.

Maeve knew that she and Michael needed to have a serious conversation, but she couldn't face it tonight. There was so much to say that, if she started, she feared she might not be able to stop; and this conversation would have to be considered carefully. She would go back into the lounge, accept the flowers from Michael, placate him for the time being and think about what she really needed to say to him.

31

After Ciara lied to Declan about UCD, she managed to convince him that she really didn't want to go back to university, and began working full-time at Barian.

Then, one evening towards the end of May, she received a panic-stricken call from Claire in Manchester.

'Ciara, you have to talk to Mum and Dad. I mean it. I am not lying to them any more for you.' Ciara had told Claire about being thrown out of college and sworn her to secrecy, saying that she would deal with everything in her own time.

'Why?'

'Because Mum's bought a new outfit and she's

working on putting Dad into a penguin suit for your graduation.'

'Shit, shit, shit!'

'Precisely.'

'What am I going to do?'

'Don't ask me. You're the one with the imagination; you think of something.'

'What's that supposed to mean?'

'Easy, Ciara, don't get paranoid. It doesn't mean anything. Just think of something.'

Ciara put the phone down and slapped herself on the forehead.

'What's up?' Declan asked. He had been in the kitchen, preparing a feast of beans on toast for their evening meal.

'Mum and Dad and the graduation! I just forgot.'

'Yeah?' He smiled and passed Ciara a glass of wine. 'I'll just go fetch the grub.'

Ciara balanced her plate on her knee. 'I can't tell them now, can I?'

'Well, you don't *have* to do anything. But if you leave it, I think it'll just get worse.' Ciara grimaced. 'Listen, they'll still love you if you tell them. They're hardly going to disown you, are they?'

'Quite possibly, yeah.'

'You only think that.'

'I only *know* that,' Ciara said glumly.

'Well...there's not really an alternative, is there?'

Ciara slowly looked up from her food, a sudden

simple plan forming in her mind. 'There might be,' she said.

'Hi, Mum, it's me.' Ciara wound the phone wire round her finger and then all the way up her arm. Declan was sitting on the arm of a chair opposite her, holding up two thumbs in support.

'Well, hello, stranger. I was wondering where you'd been hiding yourself; I was saying to your dad that you're probably in the library all the time. How are you getting on?'

'Really well. Look, Mum,' Ciara said briskly, getting herself in character, 'I've heard from Claire that you've gone out and bought an outfit for my graduation, and that Dad's on about bringing the car over and stuff, but no one thought to ask me what I'm doing for my graduation.'

'What do you mean, what you're doing? You're graduating.'

'Well, yes and no.'

There was a pause on the other end of the phone as Margaret tried to recover from having the rug whipped out from under her.

'What do you mean?'

'I mean I'm not going to the ceremony.'

'I don't understand. I just don't understand.'

There was a muffled noise as Margaret put her hand over the phone. Ciara gulped, knowing what to expect. A moment later her father was on the line.

'You're not going to your graduation? What sort of nonsense is that?'

Ciara had decided that the only way to play this convincingly was to have the courage of her convictions and try her best to believe her own lie. 'It's not nonsense – it's just what I want. I don't want a load of pomp and circumstance around this, Dad; it's just showing off for the sake of showing off. So I've decided that I'm not going to attend.' She was quite enjoying herself. 'Nobody goes to graduations these days,' she added, as if they were talking about Bros concerts.

'Well, your mother and I would quite like the opportunity to go to a graduation at Trinity again.'

'Ha!' Ciara spat, getting into her role. 'So it's not about me at all, then?'

'I never said that,' Sean said sternly.

'Well, that's what you implied, Dad.' Ciara paused, drawing breath. When she spoke again it was with well-modulated calm. 'Dad, I don't want a big commotion over this, that's all. Please try and see it from my point of view.'

'If that's what you want, I can't force you to go to your graduation.'

'I just don't want a fuss,' she said, appealing to her father's stoical side.

'Well, I can understand that.'

Ciara sighed. 'I know Mum loves anything like that, but you know me – I just don't like being the centre of attention.' Declan nearly fell off the chair-arm. If Ciara had actually been graduating, she'd happily have cartwheeled through Trinity's Front Square wearing a clown suit and flashing reindeer-antlers.

'I'm not sure I understand,' Sean said quietly. 'But if that's your decision, what can we do?' His voice was long-suffering, as if Ciara were forever disappointing them. 'I'll have a word with your mother.'

'Thanks, Dad.' Ciara put the phone down and breathed a huge sigh of relief. 'I think I've got away with it.' She looked at Declan to make sure he didn't think she was the most scheming, conniving individual he had ever clapped eyes on.

'If you're happy that your mum and dad are happy, then I'm happy. I think,' Declan said. 'Come here.' He opened his arms wide, and Ciara ran over and hugged him. 'And I was thinking that maybe we could go away somewhere together, the week when you would have been graduating; that way there's no chance of them turning up on the off-chance that you might change your mind.'

'That's a great idea,' Ciara said gratefully. She'd been dreading graduation week. Barian wasn't far from Trinity, and she could do without all the happy graduates bringing their proud, beaming parents for a celebratory drink while she shuffled round in the background like Cinderella, enviously looking on. Another important factor was Róisín. Ciara didn't want to have to congratulate her in person on the day. She knew she would explode into self-berating tears.

'Shall we go out and meet the others from work, to celebrate?' she asked.

Declan furrowed his brow. 'I'm knackered.'

'Aw! Come on, Dec; it'll be good.'

'What exactly are we meant to be celebrating, anyway?'

'Well, I just thought…' Ciara hadn't actually thought anything – only that she'd quite like to go out. She'd been quite liking going out a lot recently. She didn't need the prospect of a holiday to celebrate; these days, anything was a reason to celebrate – or, more to the point, a reason to go out and get drunk. If Declan had been sitting quietly, clipping his toenails, Ciara could have found a reason to cheer and open a bottle of wine.

Declan looked at her and smiled, half-heartedly. 'Come on, then. But I'm not staying out late.'

'OK, Cinderella; I wouldn't want you turning into a pumpkin,' Ciara said, jumping up and giving him a kiss.

32

When Ciara left Maeve's house, she cycled to the nearby river. She propped her bike against a tree and sat on the bank, staring at the Mersey as it wound towards the motorway bridge in the distance. Maeve's news had had a resounding impact on her – not only because of what it meant for Maeve, but because Ciara suddenly realised that she wasn't the only one in the family who was living a lie. Most of them were. *Maybe Anthony's really a monkey that my mother found at the bottom of the garden and decided to shave and keep*, Ciara thought, throwing a stone into the river; nothing would surprise her now.

She wanted to call Declan. It would have been stupid and pointless, and she knew she wouldn't do it; but in her head she still played through the conversation they would have had, and it was a warm one. She knew she was deluding herself: any conversation between her and Declan would have descended into a mud-slinging exercise long before she got the words 'Maeve' and 'adoption' out of her mouth.

Instead she went home and spent the rest of the evening with Rachel, watching TV and berating this year's *Big Brother* contestants. Ciara thought about telling Rachel what she had discovered, but she couldn't; she was finding the information difficult to process herself. She went to bed infuriated with her parents. *How could they let Maeve give up her child – their grandchild?* she kept thinking, over and over, until at last she drifted into fitful sleep.

She awoke at six the next morning and was showered and ready for work by half past. She had a new temping assignment, but she wanted to talk to Maeve before work. She sent Maeve a text: 'Would u be able 2 give me a lift in2 town?'

Maeve pulled up outside the house just before seven.

'Well, how was Michael last night?' Ciara asked.

'He was only in for half an hour before he stormed out again.'

'Really? Why?'

'Oh, who knows. I can't remember what it was about. We can't even be in the same room any more without arguing.'

'Where did he go?'

'I've no idea, but he didn't come back until one in the morning and he slept in the spare room.'

'I take it you've not told him, then?' Ciara said. Maeve threw her a look. 'Sorry.'

'It's OK,' Maeve said, putting her foot down and speeding along the near-deserted streets. 'No, I haven't. I can't. He's impossible to talk to at the moment. It's as if he's always looking for something that he can dive on, to create an argument. Like yesterday, at Mum's – I know I was out of order, but Michael's like that all the time.'

They drove in silence for a few moments; Ciara looked out at the shuttered shops of Withington village. 'Look, Ciara, I need to know that you won't tell anyone what I told you.'

'I won't. I promise.'

'I don't want this to get out of hand. I'd like to meet Catherine first and then see how I feel about telling everyone.'

'OK,' Ciara agreed. She didn't know how she was going to look her parents in the eye, knowing what they had done. 'I wanted to call Declan,' she admitted suddenly.

'Really?'

'Yeah. Stupid, isn't it?'

'You're bound to think about him.' Maeve ran her hand along the dashboard, attacking invisible dust.

'Maeve, I can't get him out of my head. I've met this other guy called Mark, and he's lovely and good-looking and funny, but I can't stop thinking about Declan. It's ridiculous.'

'You've not told me what happened between you two.'

'The Coffey grapevine hasn't been up to speed on this one?' Ciara threw her a wry smile.

'Seriously, I don't know why you split up.'

Maeve pulled into her parking space outside the office, and they sat in the car while Ciara told her exactly what Declan had done the night before her return to Manchester. It made her cry.

'I don't know why I'm crying,' she admitted. 'I'm not exactly an angel myself. I've got myself in a right mess with this Mark. I think he really likes me, and I've slept with him – twice.' Maeve raised an eyebrow. 'I know, I'm an idiot.'

'You're not an idiot. It just feels strange to hear you admit something like that to me. It...well, I suppose it feels good that you've told me. That's all.'

'Well, I've got to tell someone. Rachel won't listen; any time I say anything about me and Mark, she shrugs it off. To begin with she was all warnings, telling me what a womaniser he was – and now she's so bloody phlegmatic about it that I feel silly even mentioning it. She's acting like something out of *Sex and the City*, pretending it's *de rigueur* to shag your housemates.'

'Well, maybe she likes this Mark bloke.'

'I've asked her that, and she said no – although I swear there's something fishy there. Anyway, that isn't really why I'm upset. It's because I can't stop thinking about Declan.'

'You need to try to move on.'

'That's what I keep thinking. But then another bit of me thinks that it was my fault – that I made it happen.' Much as Ciara wanted to believe that Declan was the biggest bastard on the planet, she was somehow sure that he had only been unfaithful once.

'Your fault that he slept with someone else?'

'No, I don't mean that – I'm not going all Country and Western on myself. I just think I didn't help. I was making living with me impossible, and I was pushing Declan every single time we argued, just to see how far he could be pushed. I know it sounds fucked up, but in a way I wanted to see if he would finish with me, or if he really wanted us to stay together.'

'What?'

'Does that sound weird? I didn't really want him to end it; I just wanted to know how much he would take. Oh, God, I sound nuts – and maybe I am. I've been acting like more and more of an arsehole lately. Maeve, I was out till four or five in the morning every chance I got; I hardly ever even saw Declan. I was only hanging around with people who would go out on the piss with me, whether I really liked them or not. I let Declan pay all the bills, because I never had money – but if I hadn't been out every other night, I'd have been able to pay my half…'

Maeve sighed, unlocking her seatbelt and shaking her head. Her sister's life was nearly as complicated as her own. 'You need to see him. From what you're saying, you haven't discussed anything – not just the Laura thing, but anything.'

'I can't even make myself dial his number.'

'Then don't dial his number. Book a flight. It's peanuts to fly from Manchester to Dublin. Don't tell him you're going – that way it'll be on your terms.'

Ciara thought for a few moments. 'You know something? You're right. Maybe I'll go over next weekend and just turn up at the flat. If nothing comes of it, then at least I've tried instead of just legging it.'

'I'll give you a lift to the airport if you want. Just text me the flight time.'

'Cheers, Maeve. That's good of you.'

'It's down the road, Ciara; I'm not driving you to Dublin.'

'Still – thanks.' Ciara checked her watch. 'I'd better head; I don't want to be late on my first day.'

'What's the job?'

'Some insurance company.' Ciara made a face.

'I don't want to sound like Dad, Ciara, so if this annoys you, just tell me – which you probably would anyway.' Maeve grinned. 'After having you in the office, I think you could do pretty much anything you set your mind to – and I'm not saying that because you're my sister. I was just wondering if you wanted to do more. I mean, you have a degree from Trinity. Even over here, people know that's good. You could run an ad firm standing on your head. I wouldn't wait around for Michael's right arm Sally to get you a job; get yourself out there.'

Ciara shuffled in the passenger seat. 'Look, Maeve, I'm a bit embarrassed even saying this, in light of what you've been through...but the thing I was going to tell you last night – the secret I was on about – is the reason I can't get a better job.'

'Go on.'

'Well. OK. I haven't got a degree.'

'*What?*'

'I got kicked out. I lied and pretended I'd passed. That's why there was no graduation, and that's why I ended up...well, working in a bar,' Ciara said sheepishly. 'I've never even worked in an advertising agency, except for a few weeks' temping; I just lied because I was too embarrassed to tell the truth.'

'I can't believe it,' Maeve said, open-mouthed. 'In a bar?'

'God, Maeve, I'm such a liar. I've been lying about everything for years...' Ciara was beginning to get upset again. 'I'm so stupid!'

It took Maeve a few moments to take in exactly what Ciara was telling her and the extent of her fabrications. Finally, she shook her head, her blue eyes shining with warmth. 'Come here.' She held her arms open, and Ciara gratefully fell into them. It was a genuine, warm, loving hug. 'You're not stupid; you're not stupid at all.'

'But I am. I lied about everything – my job, living with Declan, cheating in an exam, everything. I ended up with Post-Its by the phone to remind me what I'd told everyone back home – what a psycho... But you know what Mum and Dad are like, better than anyone. Surely you can see why I did it.'

'Yes.' Maeve nodded thoughtfully. 'Yes, I can. But you shouldn't have had to.' She sounded suddenly angry. Ciara pulled her head up to look at her. 'I mean it. How many more secrets does this family have? How much more pretence are we going to put up with, just to show the world what a good Catholic family we are? It's ridiculous.'

Ciara nodded in silent agreement.

'I'm not sure how much longer I can continue to play Happy Families, you know.'

Ciara could tell she meant business. She wasn't quite sure how she felt about rocking the family boat, but she wasn't about to say that to Maeve – not with the angry glare in her eye. She was just thankful there were no sharp objects around.

33

Declan climbed out of the shower and, rubbing a hole in the steam on the bathroom mirror, inspected himself. It was Monday morning, and he was thankful that the weekend was over and he had something to concentrate on, other than his hangover and Ciara.

He and Barry had spent the weekend trying to discover Manchester. They hadn't got very far. Saturday afternoon, which they had intended to spend looking around the designer shops of St Anne's Square and Deansgate, had turned into a messy pub crawl. They had started at Sinclair's, which sold the strongest beer Declan had ever tasted – it had him grinning inanely after three pints – and then moved on to the Living Room, where they had spent a happy couple of hours spotting soap stars and footballers; then they had headed to another bar, about which he couldn't really remember much. He had finally found his second wind at around one o'clock in the morning, when he and Barry had somehow got into a heated discussion about swans with two guys in the Press Club – an all-night drinking establishment, which Declan vaguely remembered reminding him of the last half-hour of a bad wedding. One of the men had been asserting that a swan could break your arm with its wing; Declan had been adamant, to the point of shouting, that if a swan wanted to break your arm it would definitely use its beak.

'Jesus, Dec,' Barry had said in the taxi on their way home. 'There was no need to get worked up about fecking swans.'

'It wasn't swans,' he had said grumpily. 'It was Ciara.' Barry had raised an eyebrow: Declan hadn't mentioned Ciara all night. Back at the hotel, he had thought sorrowfully, *I want Ciara back*, before falling into a comatose sleep.

Declan dried himself and went back into his bedroom. It was a magnificent room. The curtains were great swathes of velvet, the bed was a huge baroque four-poster, and his writing desk looked like something the Marquis de Sade might have used prior to being thrown in the Bastille. But it was still just a hotel room, Declan thought numbly

– a hotel room in a city that wasn't helping him get over his ex-girlfriend.

He slumped down on the bed and ran his hands through his hair. Every time he tried to dismiss Ciara from his mind, another memory jumped up, taunting him. He hadn't thought about her constantly when they were a couple, but now she was haunting him. He thought about the stupid stories she used to tell about the people she worked with; her animated way of gesticulating wildly, like someone bringing a plane in to land. He thought about the way she made him laugh – Declan didn't meet many girls who really made him laugh. He thought about how vulnerable she had looked when she had a particularly severe dose of flu; he had looked after her, bringing her tea and chocolate and magazines…

Declan had found, much to his surprise, that he really liked Manchester; but, with Ciara always looming close by, it wasn't an ideal place to be. He thought about going back to Dublin at the weekend, but that wasn't possible either. He and Barry had the fourth of many deadlines looming on Monday – and, anyway, he had sub-let his apartment. He snapped himself out of his reverie and made himself get ready for work.

Barry was running late as usual. 'Morning,' he said cheerfully, bouncing into the hotel foyer tucking his T-shirt into his jeans.

'It's twenty past nine. Could you not drag your arse out of bed?'

'It's the crack of bleeding dawn.' Barry rubbed his unshaven chin. 'I was up till all hours, trying out tag lines for this fecking dishwater we're trying to sell.'

'They'll have you drinking bitter yet, Bar.'

'They will in me hole.'

They walked the thirty or so metres to work in silence. At the door of the building, Declan stopped.

Barry turned round. 'What you doing?'

'Listen, Bar, I need to know something.'

Barry looked confused. 'Yeah, go on.'

'Well, it's just that I've been thinking a lot this weekend.'

'Yeah, I've noticed. You've hardly said a word.'

'Sorry about that, but... Right, the thing is – well, it's hard for me to ask this without looking like a big girl; you know the way.' Barry was standing, his hands jammed in his pockets, an eyebrow raised, waiting for Declan to spit it out. 'Me and Ciara – you know, when we were together and that – were we...a good couple, like?'

'Yeah, fucking Posh and Becks.'

'Ah, come on, Barry. It's a serious question.'

Barry exhaled heavily. 'This is a fecking minefield. I wish you wouldn't put me on the spot. Do you want me to tell you what I think, or what I think you want to hear?'

'There's no point in giving me a pat answer. I want to know what you genuinely think – as my mate and everything.'

'Right. The truth is I think you drove each other fucking bananas.' Declan nodded sombrely. 'Listening to you over the last few months, before you did Laura—'

'Barry!'

'What? Is she here?' Barry looked around in mock surprise. 'Cop on, Declan; don't get all uppity. As I was saying…it was a nightmare. The way you were carrying on, you should have split up months before.' Declan let out a huge sigh; he knew Barry was right. 'You got the girlfriend you wanted; you just fucked it up because you tried to change her.'

'What?' Declan looked up in shock, the words stinging.

'You asked me what I thought, and I'm telling you. You hear about women trying to change fellas all the time, but you did it with Ciara. And when it didn't work, you started arguing.'

'And?' Declan demanded.

'You want me to go on?'

'You've started, so you'll finish, Barry.'

'Well, that's it, really. Ciara was everything you wanted, wasn't she? Good-looking, funny, smart and up for a good time. But, as time went on, you decided you wanted a "proper" girlfriend.' Barry waggled his fingers in the air to indicate quotation marks. 'One who had your tea ready and nagged you about staying out late and moaned about you going out with your friends – not one who didn't know what time you got in because she was out on the lash herself.'

'That's not true,' Declan protested.

'Isn't it? Look, Declan, in my opinion you were perfect for each other. She was mad about you and you were mad about her. But you had to go and make things difficult by expecting her to settle down. She's only twenty-five, for Christ's sake; it's a bit early for the pipe-and-slippers routine.'

'But you saw what it was like!'

'I did, and that's why I'm telling you what I think. If you don't want to hear it, you shouldn't have asked.'

Declan put his hands to his face. He felt as if someone had told him that the world was flat after all. 'What do you think I should do about it?'

'Ah, here, I'm not getting into that. That's up to you. I've enough trouble trying to get a bird of my own, without sorting out *your* love life.'

'Yeah,' Declan muttered. 'Cheers, Barry.'

'Not at all.' Barry headed into the office. The conversation was closed.

Declan followed Barry into reception and received a lukewarm smile from Ashlyn; she'd been cool to him since it had become apparent that they wouldn't be going out again. He grabbed a couple of the day's papers and headed for his desk.

For the first time, he found himself wondering whether he might have been responsible for some of the arguments. He had always thought they were Ciara's fault – she could goad an argument out of a mute pacifist. He thought back to the first argument he and Ciara had had.

It had been over ice-cream. One Sunday afternoon, when Ciara was still at university, they had decided to go to Howth, a picturesque harbour at the northern end of the Dart line. By the time they got there, the heavens had opened and the yachts were being thrown up and down the harbour by heavy gusts of wind. Ciara had been adamant that she was having an ice-cream, regardless of the weather. Declan had followed her into the ice-cream shop, soaked from head to foot, with a face like thunder. He just wanted to go somewhere warm to dry off.

'Look at Mr Grumpy,' Ciara had said to the owner. 'He wanted to come to the seaside, and now we're here he's nearly crying because it's not the Bahamas.'

'I'm not crying, Ciara,' Declan had said through gritted teeth.

'Do you want chocolate sauce?' the shopkeeper had asked.

'I'd love some. Dec, do you want chocolate sauce?' Ciara had curled a hand into his pocket to take his hand, which was firmly jammed there.

'Does it matter?' Declan had asked childishly.

Ciara had smirked at the owner. 'In the grand scheme of things, probably not, but it tastes nice. Here.' She had thrust the cone upwards just as Declan leaned forward, pushing his face straight into her ice-cream.

'Jesus Christ, Ciara!'

She had looked at him with her lopsided grin and started laughing. As she rummaged around for the money to pay, the owner had winked at her, as if to suggest that she had her work cut out with Declan. This had only infuriated him further. 'What is the point in even being here?' he had snapped.

'Ooh! Steady on, Sartre.' Ciara had pulled up her hood and run across the road towards the harbour wall, in the pouring rain, licking her ice-cream. Declan had stamped angrily after her.

Ciara had turned around, with ice-cream on her mouth and her hair sticking to her face. Seeing Declan's face, she had said, 'Declan, if it's an argument you want, it's an argument you'll get. I just want to have a nice day. I was messing about, that's all. Now, we can mess about in the rain, or we can argue and go home and be pissed off with each other.'

Declan had leaned forward, pulled her towards him and kissed her.

He wasn't about to admit full responsibility for all the rows they had had over the past year – he wasn't even willing to admit that he might have been fifty per cent responsible; but, he realised, he had probably fuelled them. Maybe Barry was right, Declan thought: maybe he had been trying to change Ciara all along.

34

'And I told him, I said, "Look, it's not me that says it's good, it's Jamie Oliver. And if couscous is good enough for Jamie Oliver, it's good enough for you, Lee Mosley." And he storms out, saying he's going to get a bag of chips. By the time he came back, I'd packed his bags.'

Ciara's eyebrow twitched empathetically, but her brain was atrophying. She had been in the offices of Carlisle & Hobart Insurance for six hours, fourteen minutes and counting. She was working on the switchboard, alongside Lindy. 'It's Linda, professionally, but Lindy to my friends – and you can be my friend!' she had announced, with as much gusto as if Ciara had just won an Oscar. The phone lines lit up once every three to four minutes, and the calls took only a moment to put through; the rest of the time was filled by Lindy imparting her life story. Ciara knew that Lindy's favourite colour was cerise, that she didn't like *Bo Selecta!* because she didn't get it but she didn't dare tell Lee as it was his favourite programme, that she had an aversion to whelks but could eat salmon until it came out of her ears, that she drove a Smart car but had reversed it into a lamppost (Lee had commented that that wasn't very *smart*) and that she had a cat called Princess Di. Ciara was bored rigid.

'Oh, Lindy, did the agency tell you that I need to leave early on Friday?'

'Yeah. That's no problem; I can hold the fort on my own, if it's only for a couple of hours.' *She could hold this fort on her own for years*, Ciara thought; it wasn't exactly the Pentagon.

Her flight was booked for five o'clock on Friday afternoon. Maeve was going to pick her up at half past three. By six o'clock she would be back in Dublin, her home for six years; and she was going to face Declan, on her own terms. Ciara's stomach did nervous flip-flops at the thought.

On the way home, Ciara decided that she absolutely had to say something to Mark. She had done a marvellous job of avoiding him all weekend. He had sent her a few text messages on Saturday, but the number had dwindled to one on Sunday, and that had been asking her if the family meal was going well. Her reply had been, 'Yeah, really good, except for another row with sister. Going round to straighten out. Back later. How's Leeds?' She didn't think Mills and Boon would be beating a path to her door for the rights to her steamy text conversations.

She had spent the day rehearsing in her head what she was going to say to Mark. In fact, on a personal level, her work day had been quite productive. She had realised that, if she nodded her head at Lindy and asked 'Really?' and threw in the odd 'I know,' *à la* Sybil Fawlty, she could play on the internet all day, stopping every half-hour to answer the telephone. So she had looked up the English courses at all the local universities. She had enough A-level points to walk onto any of them. She couldn't really afford to go back to university – but then, she couldn't afford to go to the pub on a Friday night; lack of finances had never been a barrier to Ciara doing what she wanted to do. This time, she had decided, she would finance herself. There was no way she was going to ask her parents for money. They had given her enough, over the years; she didn't want to be beholden to them any more.

As she opened the door of the house, she felt almost ready for a conversation with Mark. Her sense of purpose had increased one hundred per cent today, and she couldn't carry on messing him around – it wasn't fair.

Rachel was running up the stairs, screaming as though she were being attacked by an axe-wielding lunatic. At second glance, Ciara realised that the axe-wielding lunatic was Mark, wielding a washing-up-liquid bottle filled with water. He ran past her, shouting, 'Hi, Ciara!' and charged up the stairs. Rachel squealed, 'Give up! Get off me!' but she didn't exactly sound like she meant it.

Ciara felt strangely envious, as if she had just walked in on something that didn't involve her, yet somehow should.

'Mark, you are an arsehole!' Rachel shouted, with such enthusiasm that, if the words 'an arsehole' had been replaced by 'the best', Ciara would have assumed that two people were having energetic sex upstairs.

Ciara wandered through to the kitchen and switched on the kettle. She wasn't about to join in their horseplay. What could she do? she thought. Grab the garden hose, attach it to the bathroom tap and try to join in?

A minute later, Rachel and Mark came back downstairs, giggling like a pair of naughty five-year-olds.

'He just soaked me to the skin!' Rachel announced with mock indignation.

'I can see that.' Ciara nodded at Rachel's white cotton shirt, which was stuck to her stomach and wasn't doing the best job of hiding her nipples. 'You're going to have someone's eye out, Ray.'

Rachel looked down at the soft-porn look she was sporting. 'Oh, my God! I didn't even realise!' She clamped one arm across her chest and hit Mark with the free one. 'Why didn't you tell me?'

'I was quite enjoying it.' He grinned.

Ciara found herself launching teabags into the teapot almost viciously as Rachel ran upstairs to change.

'Good weekend?' Mark asked pleasantly.

'Yeah. You?'

'Brilliant. Leeds was really good. I had a great night out and then stayed up all night talking to Jess.'

'Oh?' Ciara said nonchalantly. She wondered for a moment if they had been talking about her. 'Is he a friend from uni?' She waved a cup at Mark inquiringly.

'Yeah, I'd love one – cheers. Oh, Jess? Jess is a girl – and, yeah, I've known her for years. I used to go out with her.'

Ciara felt suddenly annoyed. She had thought she was in charge of this situation, but now she was somehow losing control of it, and she didn't like it. She felt affronted, but she told herself she had no right to feel this way. She had been coming home to finish things with Mark. But he seemed to be making it clear that there wasn't actually anything to finish.

She handed Mark his tea, poured a cup for Rachel and then went into the living room and switched on the TV. Mark followed her in. He didn't sit on the seat next to her, as he usually did; he perched on the arm of the other chair and stared at the screen. 'So what's the plan for tonight?'

'Nothing, really,' Ciara said guardedly. *Nothing, now I don't need to have a complicated conversation with you.* She couldn't work out why she was annoyed. She was being handed a perfect solution on a plate: Mark seemed to have lost interest in her, so she didn't have to tell him she wasn't interested in him. But suddenly she wanted to say, 'What's wrong with me? I'm perfectly bloody good, you know. Look: blonde hair, blue eyes, all my own teeth…'

'Well, Ray and I were going to go to the Woodstock for food, if you fancy it.'

'No, I'm fine, thanks. I can't be eating out on a school night; my piggy bank will have nothing left in it.' Ciara didn't look Mark in the eye, as she might have the previous week. She was trying her best to be nonchalant, and hoping he couldn't tell it was an effort.

Rachel came into the room, this time covering her modesty. 'Ciara, do you fancy food at the Woodstock? I'm like old Mother Hubbard, and I can't be bothered going food-shopping.'

'No, thanks. I'm going to cook me some nice Pot Noodles.'

'Minging.'

'Yeah, I know, but I'm skint.'

'I'll sub you.'

'No, Ray, seriously – it's fine. You two go out and enjoy yourselves.'

Mark and Rachel stood up. Ciara knew she was being paranoid, but she couldn't help noticing that they hadn't needed much persuading.

As they headed noisily out the door, Ciara's mobile began to ring.

'Hi, is that Ciara?'

'Yes.'

'It's Sally from NPV.'

'Hi, Sally. How are you?' Ciara gulped, sure that Sally was about to run through the specifications of a job that she wouldn't be able to do in a million years.

'I'm great, just great. And you?'

'Yeah, I'm fine.'

'Listen, I've managed to get you an interview next Wednesday. I think you'd be perfect for the job. It's working alongside an account handler at an advertising agency, with a view to becoming an account handler yourself. They offer training – they feel that they work differently from other ad firms. I thought it could be a challenge.'

'So they know I've never done it before?'

'Well, not exactly…but I think if you go in there and play on your strengths, you'll stand a good chance of getting the job.'

'You want me to lie?' Ciara smiled wryly at her own double standard.

'No, no – God, no! Not lie; just tell them what they want to hear.' Sally laughed nervously, making Ciara uneasy.

'Look, Sally, I'm in a bit of a rush.' She just wanted to get off the phone. 'What are the details?'

'It's Mauldeth Hall, Chester Road, Old Trafford, at eleven o'clock. The interview's with Carl Brody. Now, he has your CV, and he thinks you sound ideal.'

Ciara rolled her eyes. 'Right, Sally. I'll do my best. I've got to go now; I'll call you after the interview.' She hung up. She might as well go to the interview, she decided, if they were offering training – not that she had any interest in working in an ad agency, but it was better than nothing. And anyway, what did she have to lose, except her dignity?

When Mark and Rachel got back from their dinner at the pub, Ciara informed them that she was going to Ireland for the weekend.

'Going to see your ex?' Mark asked, a little too casually for Ciara's liking.

'No, I'll leave that sort of thing to you,' she said, smiling serenely. The quip backfired: Mark simply arched an eyebrow and left the room. Ciara didn't see him again until Thursday evening, and then they only exchanged brief hellos before he ran out of the door, heading for the gym.

'What is his problem?' Ciara finally asked Rachel, after Mark had left.

'What do you mean?'

'What I said. He's been funny with me since — well, since the weekend.'

Rachel raised an eyebrow. 'Do you want my opinion?'

Ciara shrugged. 'Why not?' Rachel's opinion, when she offered it, was usually worth hearing.

'Well, when you moved in here, it was obvious that Mark liked you, and I thought you quite liked him. You went out with him, slept with him a few times, and then gave him the cold shoulder.'

'I did not!' Ciara said indignantly.

'Oh...OK. What was Friday night?'

'I was at Claire's.'

'Yeah, but that's your sister; you could have got out of it if you'd wanted to. And Sunday?'

'It was my mum and dad's anniversary. Anyway, he went to Leeds on Saturday night. And how come you know so much about all this?' Ciara demanded.

Rachel sighed, getting up. 'I'm going out. I'll see you when you get back.'

Ciara was left sitting alone, thinking that she needed to have a talk with each of her housemates, one to one, and get a few things straightened out. But that would have to wait. She had bigger Irish fish to fry that weekend.

35

Maeve drove towards the airport with Ciara sitting quietly in the passenger seat, thinking about the weekend ahead.

'How's this week been at work?' Maeve asked, as she pulled up in front of the terminal.

'Torture. I'm working in an office with one other woman, who, when she's not going on about her boyfriend, is going on about her cat – which, incidentally, is called Princess Di.'

'No!' Maeve said in horror.

'Shit! Look at the time! I'm going to have to go check in.'

'OK, OK. You have a great time, and try and sort everything out with Declan. And, Ciara – don't take this the wrong way, but if you want any help with sorting out a course when you get back, I'll help you.'

Ciara grabbed her bag from the boot of the car. 'Thanks, Maeve. That'd be really good, actually; I need a good kick up the arse.'

She hugged her sister again and hurried into the airport. She couldn't help remembering the last time she and Maeve had been at the airport together: Maeve had been the last person she wanted to see. *Claire will have a fit when I tell her I've finally confessed my secret to another member of the family – and it's Maeve! What a difference a couple of months can make, if you let them,* Ciara thought as she found the Ryanair check-in desk.

Walking through the crowds of people at Dublin airport, Ciara felt like a newly arrived ghost. She didn't feel that she belonged there, among the holidaymakers, hen and stag weekenders and businesspeople. She had thought she might feel excited about being back in Dublin, but all she felt was a numbness tinged with dread. As she boarded the bus for the city centre, she wasn't sure that she was doing the right thing at all.

Half an hour later the bus was crawling along O'Connell Street, and Ciara felt a jolt of reality as she looked out at the bustling city. *This used to be my life,* she thought. There was something strange about returning to the place that had been her home, until she had abandoned it so abruptly. Now she was a spectator rather than a participant in Dublin; the reality of the place had nothing to do with her any more. She was beginning to think that she might be having a particularly surreal dream when the bus driver shouted, 'Blondie, you're for O'Connell Street, am I right?' *It's real, all right*, Ciara thought, getting up from her seat.

Walking along Bachelor's Walk towards her old apartment, she felt a giddy excitement building. Suddenly she was dying to see Declan and talk things through with him. She would be able to tell him that things were going well in Manchester, although she would have to refrain from pretending that she was the new CEO of Microsoft. She was going to be straight with him. She was trying to be truthful about things – and, anyway, she had nothing to lie to him about; she just wanted to clear the air.

Standing outside the apartment block, Ciara had to catch her breath. She suddenly remembered the day she and Declan had moved in together; it was more vivid in her mind than anything that had happened between them in the past year, even the Laura episode.

Declan had met Ciara by the Ha'penny Bridge, waving the keys to their new place, and had insisted on giving her a piggyback all the way there. By the time the lift doors opened, he was panting and she was squealing with laughter, but he had refused to put her down until they were over the threshold. 'It's only a piggyback now; I'll carry you over when we're married,' he had said.

'Is that another proposal?' Ciara had asked, joggling up and down on his back.

'Depends if you're saying yes or not,' Declan had said, struggling to get the key into their new door. Finally, flinging the door open, he had charged into the empty apartment and launched Ciara onto the carpet, kissing her and unfurling the sleeping bag he had brought for them to sleep in that night.

Looking up at the apartment building, Ciara felt a flood of nostalgia. She tried to tell herself that was all it was – nostalgia; she didn't want to descend into mawkishness before she'd even had a chance to check if Declan was there. She pushed the intercom buzzer; there was no reply, so she rummaged around in her bag and found her old keys. Nervously she opened the door and went inside. She climbed the stairs, telling herself that what she was doing was perfectly fine; it was her place as much as it was Declan's – or, at least, it had been.

She stood at the apartment door, her heart thumping loudly, and raised her fist to knock; she was so nervous that she pulled her hand away and had to muster up the courage to try again. She knocked softly at first; when there was no answer, she knocked louder. *Where is he?* Ciara thought angrily. He could at least have had the decency to develop his sixth sense and realise that she had travelled over here for his benefit.

Then she did something she hadn't been planning to do: she took the keys out of her pocket again and nervously let herself into the apartment. Once inside, she felt a sudden, resounding sense that what she was doing was wrong. If this were a soap opera, Ciara thought, she would climb into bed, wait for Declan to come home, and seduce him as soon as he stepped through the door to see her enveloped in satin sheets. As it was, he would probably have a heart attack at finding someone in his room, and Ciara would probably get a dumbbell in the face before he realised who it was.

The lounge looked much the same as it had when Ciara had left, except that Declan had taken down the photos of the two of them. This hurt, even though she knew it shouldn't. She tiptoed into the bedroom like Goldilocks; but, rather than finding a vat of porridge and an inviting bed, she was presented with a sight that made her want to run all the way back to Manchester. The room was full of women's clothes. The owner had made herself very comfortable: these weren't the remnants of a one-night stand.

There were framed photographs around the room, and Ciara was about to inspect them when she heard a key in the door. She ran into the lounge, her heart racing; then she froze, rooted to the spot like a doomed private who has just heard the click of a mine underfoot, knowing that she needed to move but not knowing where. The stupidity of what she had done was rapidly dawning on her.

A dark-haired young woman walked in, carrying two bags of shopping, oblivious of her intruder. Then she looked up and, seeing a complete stranger standing in her home, let out a scream that could have warped iron. Ciara raised her hands in a bid to appease her, but the woman shouted in alarm, 'Get out of my apartment or, I swear to God... What do you want? Money?'

Ciara was stunned. She knew she needed to say something, fast. 'I used to live here, with Declan. This was my flat.'

'Well, he never said anything about you. You can't just let yourself into someone else's home! We could have been doing anything!'

The 'we' made Ciara feel ill. 'Well, I wouldn't want to interrupt you!' She tried to glare at the woman, but she felt like a complete fool. 'I'm sorry. I'm going.'

'You don't just break in here and then walk out!' the woman shouted. She had an American accent, Ciara realised. 'I'm calling the police.'

Ciara shook her head; she was past caring. 'Call them if you like; I won't be bothering you again.'

'Come back here!' the woman screamed out of the apartment door, as Ciara ran along the corridor and down the stairs. She kept running until she came to a quiet side-street, where she stopped and put her hands over her face, sobbing broken-heartedly.

Ten minutes later, Ciara was standing in a phone-box beside the Liffey, picking up the receiver with a trembling hand. She had racked her brain, but she was finding it impossible to think of anyone she could call. The people she had socialised with wouldn't want to see a weeping, desperate Ciara; they wanted twenty-four-hour fun that she couldn't deliver. Ciara felt hopelessly lost. It was resoundingly clear to her, as she stood alone in the place that had been her home, that she had let good friendships slide and had given her time to people who meant as little to her as she did to them. She couldn't believe she had been so foolish. And there was no point in calling Declan: even if she had still wanted to see to him, the scene in the apartment had made it perfectly clear that he didn't want to see her.

Ciara pulled a scrap of paper from her pocket and, unfolding it, slowly punched in the numbers. She tapped her foot fretfully against the phone-box door, wanting to hang up almost as much as she wanted someone to answer.

'Hello,' a familiar female voice said.

Ciara swallowed hard, mustering the courage to speak. 'Róisín?'

'Ciara?'

'Hi,' Ciara said meekly.

'Jesus Christ.' There was a pause. Ciara wasn't sure whether Jesus was being brought into it for good or bad reasons.

'Róisín?'

'*Ciara?* Oh, my God! How have you…where have you been? I don't know what to say… Jimmy!' she shouted, away from the phone. 'It's Ciara.'

'Hi, Ciara!' Jimmy shouted in the background. Ciara felt an overwhelming rush of gratitude. They sounded genuinely pleased to hear from her.

'I'm really sorry to just ring up like this, after so long,' she said humbly. 'I know I've been crap, and I was a complete shit last time you saw me…' Róisín let out a surprised laugh. 'But I'm in Dublin, and I was wondering…I know this is really cheeky, but could I come and spend the evening with you? I know you might have stuff planned, and I can stay somewhere else—'

'Not at all. Where are you? I'll come and get you in the car.'

'I'm in town.'

'Will I pick you up at the apartment?'

'Look, it's a very long story, but I don't live there any more.'

'OK, that *is* news – although I did get a call from Declan recently,' Róisín said slowly. 'Look, Ciara, where are you near?'

'I'm by the Morrison.'

'Well, go in and get a coffee. Have half an hour of people-watching and I'll be there.'

'Róisín?'
'Yeah?'
'Thank you.'
'Shut up and get inside. I'm on my way.'
Ciara hung up the phone, smiling with gratitude. She was so thankful that she wanted to cry again.

36

Ciara positioned herself at a table in the Morrison, surrounded by the beautiful people of Dublin – or, at least, those who could afford the clothes, hairstyling and make-up to appear beautiful. She felt like an outcast. She was trying to appear at ease, as if she regularly dragged herself through a hedge backwards and then went to the Morrison for coffee. She knew she could look quite presentable herself, if she put a brush through her hair and a smile on her face; today, however, she'd forgotten her hairbrush, and any attempt at a smile would just end up being a manic *Whatever Happened to Baby Jane?* grin. She warmed her hands on her coffee and settled back in her seat, waiting for Róisín to arrive.

The last time they had seen each other had been at a dinner party hosted by Róisín and her boyfriend, Jimmy. Ciara had helped herself to more than her fair share of wine and asked Róisín, 'How did you become so *staid*?' Looking back, she cringed with embarrassment. *Who did I think I was?* she thought. *Róisín invited me around for a nice meal, and I insulted her.* Thankfully, Declan hadn't been there to witness the embarrassing spectacle, or he'd have shepherd-crooked Ciara out of the building.

Róisín had gracefully said that she wasn't 'staid', she was just very busy at work. Ciara had taken offence to this comment, assuming that Róisín was referring to her work in order to highlight Ciara's failure. She had made her excuses and called a taxi. They had spoken on the phone a handful of times since, but it hadn't felt the same. Ciara had never apologised for what she had said, and contact between them had dwindled to nothing.

Half an hour later, Róisín walked through the door, and Ciara got to her feet with such haste that she banged her shins on the table. She ran towards Róisín, not caring that running probably wasn't the done thing in the Morrison, and swept her into a bear hug.

'You look great!' Róisín's brown hair, which used to be cropped short, was now highlighted and shoulder-length. Her old hippie look had been replaced with a sleeker, more modern style: she was wearing jeans and a fitted brown leather jacket.

'Well, so do you, as always.'

Ciara looked down at her clothes, which she had picked out with Declan in mind. She was embarrassed, now, that she'd made such an effort.

'Look, Róisín, I feel like I just want to apologise over and over again to you, for everything.'

'Shut up and get in the car. We can have a chat on the way over to Lucan.' Ciara hung her head like a chastised child. Róisín, seeing her face, hugged her. 'Come here, you. It's great to see you – and I don't want to hear apologies; we've been as hopeless as each other.'

Ciara knew this wasn't true. Their lives had naturally taken different paths – Róisín had met Jimmy in her fourth year of college, Ciara had moved in with Declan – but she knew there was more to it than that, whatever Róisín thought.

When Ciara came back from her holiday with Declan – the one that he had suggested to take her mind off what would have been her graduation week – she had met up with Róisín in town. She had tried her best to be magnanimous about the fact that Róisín had the degree that she might have had; Róisín, in turn, had made light of the situation, saying that, whatever her qualifications, she was no closer to getting a decent job. Even so, Ciara had felt awkward and a failure.

The next time they met up had been to celebrate Róisín's new job as a trainee accountant. Ciara had told Róisín she was proud of her, but secretly she thought that Róisín was joining the rat race – whereas she, in her infinite wisdom, had decided that she wasn't going to be another corporate monkey greasing the wheels of commerce. She tried to ignore the fact that her job was to serve the corporate monkeys who greased the wheels of commerce.

Whenever they met, Ciara felt a nagging sense of disillusionment. It always faded once Róisín started talking animatedly about the people she worked with; she had such a way with words that Ciara always found herself relaxing and rolling about laughing. But, once she and Róisín said their goodbyes and went their separate ways, she would feel the dissatisfaction descending again.

Not long after Róisín had graduated, she and Ciara met in La Stampa, a beautifully decorated and somewhat imposing restaurant on Dawson Street. The starters cost more than Ciara spent on pasta – her staple diet – in a week.

'It's fine,' Róisín said, seeing her staring at the menu in shock. 'My treat – I've just got my first pay rise.' Ciara shuffled uncomfortably.

As the waiter came over and poured the wine, Róisín asked, 'Ciara, are you all right?'

'Yeah, I'm fine,' she said defensively, pretending to take a great interest in the menu.

'Well, I haven't seen you in ages; and every time I've called you recently, you've been suffering from a raging hangover or on your way out to work. And it's been ages since you've mentioned reapplying to college,' Róisín said gently.

'Have you been talking to Declan?' Ciara snapped. She had been going out after work a few nights a week, and Declan had been complaining as if he were living with W.C. Fields.

'No, I haven't been talking to Declan. I'm just worried about you, that's all.'

'Well, there's no need to worry about me,' Ciara said sternly. She set her menu aside and folded her arms. 'Just because you've got a great – but, by your own admission, boring – job, that doesn't mean everyone has to do the same.'

'I know that.' Róisín sighed. 'Look, you might as well hear what I'm thinking, seeing as you're already crossing your arms and giving me that look.'

'What look?'

'*That* look. The "I'm right, everyone else is wrong" look.'

'Go on, then. Tell me how I'm fucking everything up in a fantastic fashion.' Ciara tried to make her face as neutral as possible, for fear of being accused of having a 'look' again.

'No. No, I won't. I just think that you are very intelligent and very talented, and you're working in a bar.'

'Yeah. And?'

'And that's not what you came to Ireland for.'

'Maybe not, but it's what I'm doing. Can we change the subject, please?'

They had eaten a delicious meal in uncomfortable silence.

Now, as they got into Róisín's car, Ciara wanted to go through everything chronologically and apologise for each mistake. She started by explaining why she had moved back home, and what had just happened in Declan's apartment.

'Ciara, I am so sorry. I can't believe Declan did that.'

'I know. Neither can I – but I heard it, and he admitted it, so that's that. I just feel like such a fool for coming over here, thinking I could just walk back into Declan's life and he'd have me.'

'Why is that foolish?' Róisín asked. 'You were together for years.'

Ciara felt her eyes fill up. What was wrong with her these days? she wondered. She had never been a weepy person, yet now she found herself crying at the drop of a hat. She had even begun sobbing when Ainsley Harriott asked two contestants on *Ready, Steady, Cook* how long they had been together and they had gazed lovingly at each other and said, 'Nearly five years.'

'I just can't believe he's moved that bloody Yank in,' she said.

'God, Ciara, I don't know what to say.'

'Well, he obviously doesn't want to hear from me, does he?'

Róisín sighed. 'It would seem that way.'

Ciara stuck her fingers in the corners of her eyes, willing the tears to go away.

When they reached Róisín's house in Lucan, Jimmy came out to greet them. 'Well, Ciara, how are you keeping?' he asked, giving her a hug that she wasn't sure she deserved, after the last time she had seen him.

'Not bad, Jimmy. You?'

'I'm grand. Come on in.'

Ciara went into the house. 'Wow, it looks lovely in here,' she said, sincerely. They had decorated since the last time she had visited.

Jimmy looked up at the cream walls and said, with a wry smile, 'Not too staid for you, then?'

Ciara felt her toes curl. She had an overwhelming urge to open the front door again and slam it on her head. 'I am so sorry for saying that. Look, I've done a lot of thinking over the past couple of months, and one of the conclusions I've come to is that, for the last while I was in Ireland, I was behaving like a complete dick.'

Jimmy smiled warmly. 'Well, at least take your coat off before you start whipping yourself.'

'Come on through to the lounge and stop apologising,' Róisín said, squeezing Ciara's arm affectionately.

Jimmy left Róisín and Ciara to catch up. Róisín opened a bottle of wine and they talked about Declan for a while; but every time his name was mentioned, Ciara felt sick to her stomach.

'I can't talk about Declan any more, Róisín, honestly,' she said finally. 'It's wrecking my head.'

'No problem.' Róisín looked kindly at her. 'So go on, then – tell me how Manchester's treating you.'

Ciara sat back in her chair. She hadn't really thought about that. Going home had been a knee-jerk reaction; but now she was forced to think about how things were panning out in her home city.

'Good, actually. I've got back in touch with Rachel – you know, the one I used to talk about from school?'

'Oh, yeah. How's she?'

'She's great. I've moved in with her and this guy called Mark.'

'Oh, so you're not at your parents'? That was quick.'

'Not really. One week with my dad's music and my mum's fussing was enough to have me packing my bags.'

Róisín laughed. 'Still the same, are they?'

'Actually, you know, my mum and dad have been OK since I've been back.'

'Yeah?'

'Yeah. I haven't felt as pressurised to act like their performing monkey.'

Róisín paused. 'So...have you come clean with them about what you ended up doing over here?' she asked tentatively.

'I said they'd been OK, I didn't say they'd had

personality transplants.' Ciara saw the look on Róisín's face. 'Maybe I will tell them one day, but I need to feel that I'm actually doing something worthwhile before I break it to them that I've been a lying, cheating, shacking-up-with-boyfriend good-for-nothing.'

Róisín laughed and shook her head. 'Your father is in the Ark if he thinks people don't live together.'

'It's not my dad, Róisín; it's me. I just wanted to be the perfect daughter for my parents. I wanted to look as good as Maeve and Claire. And all I've done is lumbered myself with a pack of lies that I have to haul around like a sack of very heavy shite, everywhere I go.'

'Stop beating yourself up! You are the most self-critical person I've ever met.'

'Am I?'

'Yes.'

'Well, look, while I'm being self-critical, I want to apologise to you.'

'Ciara, stop it! You already have. Look, if you want the truth, when you accused us of being staid, Jimmy and I just laughed about it afterwards. He didn't even know what "staid" meant; I had to explain it to him. Anyway, you were a bit pissed.'

Ciara cringed. That was the story of her life. That would be her epitaph, if she wasn't careful: *Here lies Ciara Coffey – she was just a bit pissed.*

'Not just about that. I want to apologise about everything. We were really good friends, up until I cheated in that bloody exam; but after that, every time I saw you, it reminded me of what I should have been doing. When we went for that meal at La Stampa and you said you were worried about me, I was horrible to you. But the fact was, I was worried myself. I kept telling myself I was having a great time; but it's hardly living the bloody dream, is it – cleaning out ashtrays for a living? So I just went out all the time, to try to forget about what I wasn't doing with my life.'

'You can't beat yourself up about it, Ciara.'

'Yes, I bloody well can.'

Róisín laughed. 'Are you out on the lash a lot at home?'

Ciara set her glass down on the coffee table beside her. 'You know something? I hadn't really thought about it, but no, I'm not. I just go out like a relatively normal person. I mean, don't get me wrong – I'm not tucked up in bed with a cup of cocoa at ten o'clock every night; but I haven't tried to force anyone to find an all-night drinking establishment with me, or jumped back into the clubbing scene like I'm Shaun Ryder or something.' Ciara could see that Róisín was surprised. *Let her be,* she thought; it was fair enough.

'Well, I don't want to sound patronising, but I probably will, so here goes: you really seem to be getting your act together.'

'Well, that's one patronising way of putting it.' Ciara grinned.

'I warned you,' Róisín laughed. 'So I take it men have been at the bottom of your priority list in Manchester, then?'

'You could say that,' Ciara said. She didn't even want to mention Mark. If someone had asked her about Declan when she first met him, they would have had to listen at length to Ciara's 'Why Declan Is Great' list; the fact that she didn't even want to talk about Mark proved that nothing was ever going to happen between them.

Róisín went into the kitchen to rustle up some food, and Ciara's thoughts turned to Declan again. She felt so angry and hurt, all over again, that she just wanted to crawl under a big rock and stay there until she calcified.

Róisín came back into the room armed with bags of Taytos. 'I've put in a pizza. Will these do until it's ready?'

'Yeah, great. Róisín, I've just been thinking…'

'If this is another apology, I might have to thump you.'

'No, it's not an apology. I just want your opinion on something.'

'Yeah, go on.'

'Do you think that what Declan did with Laura was on the cards? You know, do you think I sort of pushed them together?'

Róisín paused for a moment, looking like she'd rather not answer. 'Well, I couldn't really say…'

'Couldn't, or don't want to?'

'It's all in the past, Ciara. There's no point in dwelling on it.'

'So you think I did, then?'

'Put it this way: once you started working in that bar, I don't think you were particularly easy to live with.'

Ciara hung her head, foraging in the bag of Taytos like a horse with a nosebag. She was so ashamed of the mess she had made of her life in Ireland that she thought she would probably spend the rest of it apologising.

37

Declan was standing outside Ciara's parents' house, smoothing down his jumper, as if this would make all the difference in convincing Ciara to talk to him. He had thought about little else all week, ever since realising that he had played a part in their break-up. He wanted one last opportunity to talk to Ciara. It was ridiculous: they were in the same city, and he was skulking around, looking out for her at every turn, yet making no effort to contact her.

As he nervously waited for a reply to his knock, Declan saw the shape of Ciara's father heading towards the door. He gulped. Sean unnerved him because Ciara had always been so reverential towards his wishes. Also, the few times Declan had met him, he'd got the sense that he should feel guilty for not being fully appreciative, twenty-four hours a day, seven days a week, of the fact that he was Irish.

'Hello?' Sean peered around the door. 'Declan,' he said, noncommittally.

'Hello, Mr Coffey.'

'I suppose it's Ciara you're after, is it?'

'Em, yes, it is.'

'Well, she's moved out. Some fella picked her up the other day, and off she went.'

Some fella? Declan thought, his heart sinking. 'Have you any idea where she's moved to?'

Sean shrugged. 'I can give you the address. Wait there while I find it.' He wandered off (*Nice of you to invite me in,* Declan thought) and came back with a scrap of paper with Ciara's new address scrawled on it. 'It's about five minutes from here, along Burton Road, near the Old House at Home pub.'

Declan folded the paper and shoved it into his jeans pocket. 'How's home?' Sean asked.

'Home? … Oh. Home's fine.'

Sean nodded. 'Good, good.'

Declan felt compelled to keep talking. 'I'm living over here, though, for a little while. My boss sent me over to work on a project in our Manchester office.'

'I see. I wouldn't have had you down as one to leave Ireland.' It was an observation, delivered flatly, but Declan couldn't help feeling it was a criticism.

'Well, I'd better head off,' he said, feeling thoroughly unnerved.

'Off you go, now.' Sean raised a hand in acknowledgement. Declan noticed that he wasn't smiling.

As he headed towards the address he had been given, Declan realised why Ciara was scared of her father: he was a very forbidding man in a one-to-one situation.

Declan found Ciara's new house and knocked nervously on the door. Although he had been dismayed to discover that Ciara had been brought to her new abode by another man, he didn't think that meant she was living with this person; he was probably a friend helping out. Surely she couldn't have shacked up with some other bloke already? Anyway, she was far too near her parents for that sort of thing…

Or is she? Declan thought, bristling, as the man he had seen in the pub with Ciara answered the door.

'Hi.' Declan nodded coolly, jamming his hands in his pockets in an attempt to appear nonchalant.

'Hi.' The man looked blankly at him.

'I'm looking for Ciara. Is she in?'

'No, she's not here at the minute. Can I help?'

'I wouldn't have thought so,' Declan, the alpha male, said dismissively.

'OK.' The other man laughed. 'Do you want me to tell her you called?'

'No, it's no bother.' Declan turned to walk away, expecting to hear the door shut behind him.

'Are you Declan?'

'Yeah. Who wants to know?' he heard himself say. He knew he was acting like a fool, but he couldn't help himself.

'Come in for a minute, Declan. I'd like a word, if that's OK.'

Declan sat on the settee and accepted the beer that the man, who introduced himself as Mark, offered him.

'You're Ciara's ex, aren't you?'

'That's right.'

'Well, I just thought you might like to know…' Mark took a swig of his beer and Declan squared himself in the chair, ready to hear that Mark had won the hand of the fair – if argumentative and slightly mad – Ciara. 'We were kind of seeing each other…'

Declan felt as if the wind had been knocked out of him. 'You brought me in here to give me a beer and tell me that? That's big of you.'

'No, that's not it,' Mark said, running his hands through his hair. 'The thing is that, frankly, her heart wasn't in it.'

Declan felt like leaping to his feet and punching the air. Instead he arched his right eyebrow a fraction.

'And…well, she kept talking about you. I don't think she even knew she was doing it.'

Yes! Declan's thoughts screamed. 'Did she?' he asked. His voice came out more high-pitched and inquisitive than he had intended.

'And she's gone over to Ireland this weekend. She said she was going to catch up with old friends, but I think really she was looking for you. So, seeing as you've come over here looking for her—'

'No, actually, I've been working here, in Didsbury.'

Mark went suddenly quiet: what he had taken for a desperate attempt to win Ciara back now appeared to be just a casual call because Declan was in the area. Declan didn't know what to say. He wasn't about to tell this stranger – who, by all appearances, had been sleeping with his ex-girlfriend – that he desperately wanted to get back together with her.

'Do you know when she's back from Ireland?' Declan asked, his mind racing. If Ciara had gone in search of him, she would surely have met the girls who had moved into the flat, and they would have informed her that Declan was in Manchester. He wasn't sure if that was a good or a bad thing.

'Tomorrow, I think. Look…things have been a bit weird in the house, and I just want to straighten things out with her. Could you give me a chance to smooth things over with her – call her Tuesday, maybe, if that's OK?'

Declan wanted to say, 'Why should I do you any favours?' But he reasoned that this guy had done *him* a favour, and he was sure he wouldn't have been big enough to do the same in Mark's situation. 'Tuesday's fine.' He had been in Manchester long enough; a couple of extra Ciara-less days wouldn't kill him. 'Can I get your number here?'

Mark scribbled down the house phone number, and Declan finished off his beer and stood up, sticking his hand out towards Mark. Mark shook it. 'Well...thanks a million,' Declan said, slightly embarrassed. Surely, he thought, he should be slapping Mark across the face with a leather glove and announcing theatrically, 'You, sir – I challenge you to a duel!'

'No problem,' Mark said amicably, sounding equally uncomfortable with their post-modern situation.

38

Ciara and Róisín spent Saturday in Kilkenny; Róisín had decided that Ciara needed to spend as little time in Dublin as possible. They looked around the shops, had tea and scones in the Kilkenny Castle café and destroyed a seminal piece of artwork. There was an art installation at the castle, and one of the pieces consisted of ten lilos propped up against one another to give a tepee effect. Ciara and Róisín stared at it in awe – awe at the fact that someone had had the audacity to label this 'art'.

A man beside them said to his friend, 'An amazing piece of irony. The everyday, mundane object, transformed in such a way that it points the finger firmly at the denial of the ethnicity and birthrights of the Native Americans.'

Ciara dug Róisín in the ribs. She didn't think that many Native Americans would feel the same way about a bundle of inflatable beds. After the men had moved away into another room, they doubled up laughing.

'I don't know which is a bigger pile of shite – what he just said or the thing itself,' Róisín said, clambering over the rope that held back the public's admiring touches. 'It's fecking *lilos*. That's *it*! Some people are complete chancers, I tell you.' She put out her hand to touch one of the lilos, and the entire thing collapsed in on itself like a house of cards. What had been an ironic piece of art, highlighting birthright denial, was a pile of blow-up beds.

'Shit!' Róisín leaped over the rope and grabbed Ciara by the arm. 'Quick, let's get out of here.'

They ran out of the castle and down the street before they allowed themselves to stop for breath. Both of them were laughing guiltily. 'I feel really bad,' Róisín said.

'You do not.'

'I do. I mean, God, it must have taken someone all of three minutes to tie those together like that.'

Ciara burst out laughing again.

'I think we should go. I could be in real trouble,' Róisín said, looking around to see if anyone was watching them with suspicion.

'Come on, you've hardly just drawn a 'tache on the Mona Lisa, have you?'

They drove back to Lucan regaling each other with the tale over and over again – 'The look on your face!' 'The look on *yours*, more like!' – and when they got home, Jimmy was on the receiving end for a good fifteen minutes: Róisín and Ciara were both laughing too hard to compose themselves and tell the story. That evening they went for a quiet pint in Lucan village and were in bed by midnight. 'I think you quite enjoy the staid lifestyle,' Róisín said, smiling impishly at Ciara.

Ciara awoke on Sunday morning in Róisín and Jimmy's spare bedroom. She couldn't get Declan – or the American girl – out of her head, but she had decided to stop talking about it. As much as it hurt her inside, she didn't want to inflict it on Róisín.

Her flight was that evening, but she didn't want to go – not yet. She certainly didn't want to stay in Dublin and risk bumping into Declan, but she didn't want to leave Róisín. She had had a wonderful weekend, considering the circumstances.

Ciara spent the day lazing around the house with Róisín. They had a long, leisurely breakfast and read the papers. By the time they had watched *EastEnders* for two hours, it was time for Ciara to go.

'Jimmy, thank you so much for letting me disrupt your weekend. You're more than welcome to come to Manchester and disrupt my weekends any time you please.'

'Thanks; I might hold you to that,' Jimmy said, giving her a big bear-hug.

Róisín drove Ciara to the airport. 'I'm really sorry about all the shit with Declan, but I am so glad you rang me,' she said earnestly.

'God, so am I,' Ciara admitted. 'It's been brilliant, Róisín, and I just want you to know that I really appreciate everything.'

'Stop; I've done nothing. Now, you have my mobile, my home number and my e-mail address, so there is no excuse for us not to keep in touch.'

'I know.' Ciara smiled. 'And you have to come over to Manchester soon, please.'

'Of course. I think Jimmy was looking at the first week in September. I'll see you then.'

Ciara hugged Róisín warmly, knowing that she would definitely see her again very soon. She wasn't about to mess up a friendship like this a second time.

Claire picked Ciara up from the airport in Manchester. Ciara told her about her weekend, and artfully slipped a question into the conversation: 'Could I stay at yours again tonight?'

'Ciara, for God's sake! If you're avoiding Mark, you're being an idiot. You have to live there. Go and talk to him.'

'Aw! Come on, Claire. Just for tonight.'

'No. End of discussion.'

'You're no fun any more.' Ciara pretended to sulk.

'Maybe not. Anyway, moving swiftly on, I want to hear about you and Maeve. A little bird tells me you're getting on like a house on fire.'

'I wouldn't say a house; maybe a small garden shed.'

'So it's true, then?'

'I told you I quite liked working with her.'

'I know, but apparently you've volunteered to have contact with her outside of work.'

'Who's the little bird?'

'Maeve.'

'And did she tell you anything else?' Ciara said carefully.

'No. Why? What do you mean?'

'Nothing,' Ciara said quickly. Maeve would tell Claire about Catherine in her own time. 'I just want to know what she's said about me, that's all.'

'She said she can't believe how much you've grown up in the last few months.'

Ciara arched her eyebrows defensively. 'And what did you say?'

'I agreed.'

'What?'

'Well, you have. Coming clean to her about the degree, for example – a couple of months ago, you wouldn't have done that to save your life.'

'I wouldn't have told her because she used to get on my nerves, doing the big-sister bit, but she's been OK since I came home.'

'So it's nothing to do with you? You're exactly the

same as you've always been, is that right?'

Ciara stared at Claire's profile. 'All right. You win. I've changed a little bit…but not that much. Look at me: I'm trying to get out of going home because I've shagged my housemate and can't face talking to him. It's hardly the height of maturity, is it?'

'Well, maybe not, but you've got no choice: you have to face him.'

'Thanks.'

'Don't mention it,' Claire said, pulling up in front of Ciara's house. Ciara gave her a quick peck on the cheek and jumped out of the car.

As she came through the hall door, she heard music coming from Mark's bedroom. She took a deep breath and went upstairs.

'Mark?'

The music stopped suddenly, and he threw open the bedroom door. 'Hello. How are you?'

'Look, I need to talk to you,' Ciara announced, marching into his room. She threw her rucksack on the floor and placed her hands on her hips to demonstrate that she meant business.

'Yeah, well, I need to talk to you.'

This threw Ciara somewhat. 'What about?'

'Well, about me and you and all this ignoring-each-other rubbish. I can't be arsed with it.'

'Neither can I,' Ciara said defensively.

'Good,' said Mark.

'Yeah, good,' Ciara agreed, at a loss.

Mark sighed and picked up a CD that was lying

unboxed on his bedside table. He began to spin it absently around his finger. 'The thing is, you go on about your ex-boyfriend all the time.'

'Declan? I do not!'

'You do. You drop him into conversation without even knowing you're doing it. And it seems kind of obvious to me that you're still a bit hung up on him – which is fair enough, but it's a bit boring, if you don't mind me saying so.'

Ciara did mind. 'When do I talk about Declan?'

Mark smirked. 'The night we went out and ended up back here?' He patted the bed, just in case she needed reminding. 'By the end of that night, I knew more about Declan than I did about you.'

Ciara blushed angrily. She couldn't argue, because she couldn't remember much of what she had said; she could have spent the night talking about Ghenghis Khan, for all she knew.

'So I gave you a couple of texts over the weekend, and then I gave up. You're not interested in me, Ciara. You still want to go out with your ex-boyfriend.'

'No, I do not,' Ciara said indignantly. How dared Mark assume that he knew what she wanted?

'Whatever.' He shrugged.

'"Whatever" nothing, Mark. Declan is living with someone else, if you must know, so a reunion is hardly on the cards.'

Mark spun the CD for the last time and threw it on the bed. He looked at Ciara as if he was trying to decide whether to say something or not. 'No, Ciara, he's not. I don't know where you got that information, but Declan was here looking for you the other day. I'm only telling you this because I've got to live with you, and I can only assume it's not the last time I'll see him. He came here to talk to you. He's living here, in Manchester.'

'He's *what?*' This made absolutely no sense whatsoever to Ciara.

'He's working here, and he said he was going to give you a call on Tuesday. That's it. Make of it what you want; I'm just passing on the information.'

Ciara pulled her rucksack up from the floor, dazed. She wanted to ask Mark hundreds of questions – what had Declan said? how had he looked? – but, under the circumstances, it would have seemed highly inappropriate. 'OK. Thanks – I think.'

'No problem. And about me and you…I just couldn't be arsed with any weird vibes between us, so I wanted to say something.'

'Yeah, me too,' Ciara conceded. 'It's good that we sorted it out.' She knew she wasn't being very agreeable, but she didn't care – not now that she knew Declan had been there. *I am fickle*, Ciara thought, quite taken with the calm way she'd managed to handle the Mark situation.

She dragged her rucksack into her bedroom, her mind racing. What on earth was Declan doing in

Manchester? Had he come to the house to try to sort things out with her? But, if that was the case, then who was the screaming American? None of it made sense.

She needed to talk to Declan. She had his e-mail address, but there was something too detached about e-mail. She wanted to see him, hear his voice, get his immediate and truthful reaction when he saw her. She would just have to wait until he called.

39

'This place is absolutely cracking!' Jack Partridge exclaimed, at the door of the little Italian restaurant tucked away down a small city-centre side-street. Putting his hand on the small of Maeve's back, he guided her through the door.

'Mr Partridge! Welcome! Welcome!' The waiter ran across to greet Jack, brimming with genuine glee. 'We have your usual table.' He swept his arm grandly in the direction of a table in a snug corner. 'May I take your jacket, madam?' *He thinks I'm Jack's mistress,* Maeve thought dismally as she took off her coat. 'Make yourselves comfortable; I'll be back with the menus in a moment,' the waiter instructed over his shoulder.

Jack pulled out Maeve's chair, and as she thanked him she surveyed her surroundings. It was a 'traditional' Italian restaurant: dimly lit, with candles in Chianti bottles, pictures of Italian towns adorning the walls and a small overstocked bar with liqueurs of every variety. Even the waiter was the most Italian-looking man she had ever seen outside of a *Godfather* film.

'Never been here before, then?' Jack asked.

'No, I haven't.'

'It's been here years. I used to come here at the back end of the 60s, when it first opened.' Maeve imagined a group of Salford gangsters having a powwow in the corner, drinking sambuca and deciding who needed relieving of his kneecaps.

'It seems very nice,' she said genuinely. It was far nicer than the stark, whitewashed eateries that most of her clients preferred to frequent.

'Glad you like it. Now, sweetheart, I'll take the liberty of ordering the wine, if you don't mind.'

Maeve stifled a laugh and shook her head. There was something about Jack Partridge's bluff misogyny that amused her and, in a strange way, made him a refreshing curiosity. 'No, go ahead. But I'll only be having one glass; I'm driving.'

'Now, now, Maeve, I've got my driver outside. And it's gone two o'clock; don't tell me you were planning on going back to the office.'

'Well, no, I wasn't, but I've got a few things to do at home.' Maeve didn't have anything to do at home, other than cook another microwave dinner and wonder when Michael was going to make an appearance.

'Come on, let your hair down. This isn't a business meeting; it's just a thank-you.' Maeve smiled guardedly. 'Look, if it makes you feel any better, I'm not trying to get into your drawers.' She burst out laughing at his bluntness. 'Seriously, I'm not; I might be daft, but I'm not that daft. I just wanted to bring you out to thank you for a job well done, and to say that you're not full of it, like most people in your profession.'

'Thank you.' Maeve smiled, relaxing.

'No problem. Now that we've got that out of the way...' Jack turned to get the attention of the waiter. 'Colin, can I have a bottle of the '89 Barolo?'

'Colin?' Maeve asked.

'Yeah, why?' Jack replied, scanning the menu.

'I thought he'd be called Marcello or something.'

'You have to stop judging books by their covers, Maeve. He's from Moss Side.'

Maeve laughed, embarrassed.

'Come on, get stuck into the menu; I'm starving,' Jack instructed. Maeve felt herself relax. Whatever could be said about Jack Partridge, there was little mystery to him. It was a long time since she had sat down to a meal, either professionally or privately, without feeling that she needed all her wits about her.

An hour later, Maeve and Jack were making their way through grilled sea bass and *osso buco* respectively. 'So,' Jack said, 'tell me about this husband of yours.'

Maeve rested her fork against the plate, slightly taken aback. She didn't talk about Michael with her clients – but then, Jack wasn't most clients; he had an air about him that suggested that the world of business was just a silly game he had to play. 'Well, he's a recruitment consultant.'

'Much money in that game?' Jack asked, picking the last bits of meat from the bone on his plate.

'Well, we're not on the breadline, if that's what you mean.' Maeve felt uneasy. It wasn't that she minded talking about her husband; it was just that Jack's question reminded her, yet again, of the strained situation between her and Michael. They were arguing constantly now. Michael had not received a bonus for the past two months – even though he claimed he had – yet his spending seemed to have increased dramatically; this contributed to the arguments, but Maeve knew that if it hadn't been their finances it would have been something else.

'And where would a gentleman like your husband meet a lovely young lady like yourself?'

Two glasses of good wine and a full belly meant that Maeve was immune to the 'lovely lady'. 'We met through friends.'

'That's how I met my wife. I was no good at the chat-up when I was a lad. We met when I was nineteen.'

Maeve had never imagined Jack to be married; she had assumed that his edges wouldn't be quite so rough if he'd had a woman to smooth them out. 'Your wife? How long have you been together?'

'Forty-one years. She died from cancer six months ago.' Jack put his knife and fork gently on his plate and looked up at the ceiling, blinking.

Maeve felt suddenly sad. 'I'm sorry, Jack. You never said.' She had had a number of lunch appointments with Jack that year, and he'd always been his usual upbeat, inappropriate self.

'Well, I didn't like to. Anyway, don't be sorry; it's fine, just fine.' Jack raised his eyebrows and exhaled sharply. 'Have you ever been to Italy, Maeve?' He nodded abruptly at a shabby picture of the leaning tower of Pisa.

Maeve would have been happy to talk about Jack's wife, but he obviously wanted a change in conversation. 'I have.' She nodded animatedly. 'Have you?'

'Venice, once; five years ago.'

'Venice. That's where Michael and I went; we were on our honeymoon.' Maeve smiled; but the smile was for Jack's benefit. Remembering Venice made her feel heavy-hearted. She and Michael had had a lovely time; but the feelings she'd had for him then weren't the same any more.

'It's lovely, Venice,' Jack said, as Colin cleared away the dishes.

'It was.' Maeve nodded, remembering Michael commandeering a gondola and singing to her despite the fact that he couldn't hold a note. 'We were there for six days; then we spent four days in a little fishing village by the Adriatic.'

'Is that the same side of Italy as Venice?'

'That's right – about an hour up the coast. But it was handy for the airport. We didn't fly into Venice; we flew into a place called Trieste.'

As she said it, Maeve had a terrible realisation. The colour drained from her face and she felt an overwhelming urge to be sick. The ticket stub she had found in Michael's jacket pocket hadn't been from their honeymoon; it couldn't have been. She had never flown into Venice airport. They always thought of their honeymoon as having been in Venice, as they had spent most of the time there; but they had flown into and out of Trieste airport. Michael had been to Venice again. Without Maeve.

Jack was chatting happily about how much he had enjoyed Italy, and how he wanted to go back there one day. Maeve excused herself, ran to the toilet and heaved the contents of her stomach into the white porcelain bowl.

Her mind was racing. Everything was falling into place. The late nights, the overspending, the time spent away on 'courses', the excessive flower-buying... Even Michael's reaction when she had found the ticket stub suddenly made sense. If she hadn't been in such a rush to get to work, she might have paid more attention to what she had found. But she had been so busy lately that she literally hadn't had time to think. She had been laying the blame for the coolness between her and Michael squarely on her own shoulders; but now all the things that had been wrong suddenly became parts of a glaringly obvious pattern.

As Maeve opened the door of the toilet cubicle and made her way out to the sink, she felt a strange combination of relief and humiliation. She wanted to ask Michael, 'How could you?'; she wanted to find out who had gone to Venice with him, although she had a sneaking suspicion she knew. At the same time, though, she wasn't reacting to the sudden realisation in the way she would have expected. She didn't want to perform any eye-gouging, or take to her bed and be fed through a pipette for the next two months. Maeve was acknowledging something that she had already known, deep down: their relationship had been beyond repair for a long time.

She knew that, if she had been truly in love with Michael, she would have done anything to save her marriage; and she would have been truthful with him about her past from the start. The fact that she saw this discovery as a solid reason to end things, once and for all, made Maeve realise that she hadn't loved Michael for a long time – if she ever really had.

'You all right, Maeve?' Jack asked as she returned to the table, making an effort to compose herself.

'I'm fine, Jack. I've had a lovely lunch, but I really do have a few things to do at home.'

'Come on, now; there's nothing that can't wait till tomorrow.'

'Actually, there is. I've just realised my husband's having an affair,' Maeve said matter-of-factly. 'And I want to find out with whom, before I ask him to leave the house.'

For once, Jack Partridge was speechless.

40

In the weeks before Ciara left Ireland for good, she and Declan argued on a near-daily basis.

'Who the hell do you think you're talking to, Declan Murphy? If it's a mother you want, you've a perfectly good one in Glasnevin.' Ciara glared at Declan.

'I don't want a mother. I just wouldn't mind seeing my girlfriend once every six months, if that's not too much to ask.'

'So why did you just ask me if I'd ironed your shirts? Since when do I iron shirts?'

'Since I pay all the bills,' Declan muttered.

'Oh, throw that in my face, why don't you? You said you were *happy* to pay all the bills. Happy because it gives you something to hold over me, isn't that right?'

'No, that's not right. I said I would pay all the bills when you said you wanted to go back to college. But that was ages ago. You're not going back, are you, Ciara? So what I'm supporting, in actual fact, is you getting rat-arsed drunk nearly every night and trying to pass it off as being cool. I'm sick to fuck of the whole thing.'

'Well, so am I,' Ciara snapped. 'You don't have to pay for anything else for me, Declan. From now on, I'll pay my own way.'

'Good.'

'What's that supposed to mean?' Ciara demanded.

Declan stared at her in disbelief. They had been arguing more and more frequently over the past six months, but for the last two weeks he'd felt as if he couldn't open his mouth without being accused of some awful boyfriend crime. 'Good,' he said wearily. 'It means good. Look it up in the fucking dictionary, if you can still use one.' Then he went out of the apartment and slammed the door behind him. He was at his wits' end. How had they got to this stage?

At the same time, though, Declan knew exactly why he and Ciara were being like this with each other. They were both fed up. Ciara was fed up of keeping up the pretence of having a high-flying life, while doing a job that she didn't like very much any more. But she was too stubborn and scared to admit it. The word 'failure' didn't feature in her vocabulary; only words like 'amazing' and 'great' and 'cool' were in the Ciara Coffey dictionary. She was angry with herself for not doing anything with her life, but whenever Declan tried to broach the subject, the arguments started. Declan was fed up because he felt that, whatever he did, it wasn't right. They had been arguing for so long now that it was his automatic reaction to be as sarcastic as possible, then walk away. Later he would calm down and apologise, if Ciara didn't apologise first.

In Declan's opinion, he had tried everything. He had tried being reasonable with Ciara, trying to convince her to go back to college, to do what she wanted to do. He had tried to be fair when pointing out that he thought she went out too much; he had tried not to appear jealous when she came in reeling off a list of her fellow revellers, who were mostly men. He tried to see her point of view in arguments – but there was something about the way she goaded him that made him see red.

Declan wanted the old Ciara back. *This used to be good,* he thought. They had always had their ups and downs, like any other couple, but they had come through them. And the thing that annoyed him most was that they shouldn't be arguing to start with, because none of it mattered. It didn't matter because he loved Ciara. He was absolutely smitten with her. He had never felt this way about anyone in his life; he had never thought that he could. He knew he needed to rescue the relationship, before it was too late – but he was having problems thinking how, exactly, to do it.

Declan crossed the Millennium Bridge and headed purposefully towards the bar where Ciara worked. Ciara had a friend from the bar, Laura, whom Declan liked; she was straightforward and not as airy-fairy as Ciara's other new friends. If she wasn't at the bar, at least he'd had some air – well, a lungful of car fumes – and some time to think.

Pushing open the door of the bar, Declan saw Laura in a corner, restocking one of the beer fridges. The bar was unusually quiet, but then Declan realised that there was a big match on – and Barian was far too cool to show football.

'Laura?'

Laura turned around, swinging her long chestnut ponytail. 'Declan! Hi, how are you?' She smiled. 'If you're after your other half, she's not here.'

'No, I wasn't, actually. I was after you.'

'Really?' Laura looked pleasantly confused.

'Yes. The thing is, I just wanted to talk to someone who knows Ciara. There's no point in trying to talk to any of her friends from university, because it's so long since she's seen any of them…'

'OK.' Laura nodded slowly, still puzzled.

'I've talked to my mates, but I might as well talk to the wall. Things have been pretty rough between Ciara and me lately, and I just wanted to know if…well, if she'd said anything to anyone here.'

Laura shook her head and pulled a pint of Guinness for Declan; leaving it to settle, she leaned on the bar. 'To be honest, Declan, I'm pretty worried about her. I haven't been out with her in ages – and we used to go out quite a bit. She just goes round with all the media types who come in here talking shite.' Laura looked at Declan and burst out laughing. 'Sorry, Dec – you're a media type, aren't you? I wasn't saying that you're full of shite.' She gave his arm a playful squeeze. 'The thing is – and Ciara's too daft to see it – that most of them are just trying to get into her knickers.'

Declan felt a lump rise in his throat as, for the first time, a tiny doubt popped into his mind.

Laura noticed his reaction. 'Come on, Declan, I don't for a minute think she'd go off with someone else. It's just that she's – how can I put it?'

'A lousy judge of character?'

'Spot-on.'

'She hasn't always been.'

'Well, she decided to go out with you, didn't she?' Laura smiled cheekily.

Declan laughed. 'I suppose she did.'

'Listen, Declan, I have a hundred and one things to do in the back office; the area manager's in tomorrow. I usually finish at seven, but I'm on a bloody double.'

'No problem; fire away.'

'Why don't we meet for a drink – Friday, maybe?

If you're free, that is. You sound like you could do with a good chat.' Laura smiled warmly.

'That'd be great. How about Doheny's? I work around the corner from there.'

'OK. Have a few drinks with your lot from work, and I'll meet you at half seven. How does that sound?'

'That sounds great, Laura. Thanks a million.'

Declan finished his pint and strolled home. When he walked into the apartment, he realised he was alone. The lights were off and Ciara was nowhere to be seen. Declan sighed and flopped onto the settee, his heart sinking.

41

Jack Partridge had insisted on dropping Maeve wherever she needed to be; after a moment's thought, she had asked him to take her to Michael's office. If she had been relaxed enough to take in her surroundings, she would probably have had to stop herself from howling with laughter at Jack's Bentley, with its velvet interior and walnut drinks cabinet; it looked more like a brothel than a mode of transport. As it was, she had sat silently in the back of the car, playing over in her mind exactly what she planned to say to Michael.

She stood on the pavement, looking up at the building where Michael worked. It was nearly five o'clock; *Michael should be inside*, Maeve thought.

She smoothed her chocolate-brown skirt and pulled self-consciously at the collar of the matching jacket. She had checked her make-up in the mirror provided in the back of Jack's car; it was all in place. She had managed to keep the tears at bay, for now.

'Hello,' the doorman said to Maeve as she walked into the foyer. 'May I help you?' He didn't recognise her as Michael's wife. Despite the fact that she and Michael both worked in the city centre, they very rarely visited each other's workplace.

'Hello. I've an appointment at NPV Consulting.' Maeve wasn't sure if she would be allowed to go straight up, or if he would ask for her name and ring the office.

'That's fine, love. Fourth floor. Good luck.'

'Thanks.' Maeve smiled tightly. 'I think I'll need it.'

The first person she saw in NPV's open-plan main office was Sally Thompson.

'Em...Maeve, hi. What are you...I mean, how are you? Are you here to see Michael?'

'No.' Maeve smiled sweetly and pulled herself up to her full height. 'I'm here to discuss the beauty of St Mark's Basilica with you.'

Sally furrowed her brow.

'No? Not ringing any bells? OK, how was the Grand Canal?'

Sally's face dropped so quickly that it nearly sent her desk-tidy flying. 'I don't know what you mean.' She grabbed her phone. 'I'll just get Michael for you.'

'No need.' Maeve leaned across and, putting her hand over Sally's, slammed the receiver back down. 'I'll go through myself.'

'But I...we...we never meant...' Sally's voice dissolved into a strangled cry. Maeve turned to look at her; her eyes were tearful and pleading. It was all the proof she needed.

The others in the office had all stopped working and were staring, transfixed by the drama unfurling before their eyes. Maeve was sure it was better than the usual altercations when someone had been slacking on his lottery subs or hadn't paid for his share of the Mellow Birds coffee. She arched an eyebrow at the snivelling young woman and went to find her equally pathetic husband.

Throwing open the door of Michael's office, Maeve found him on the phone. He looked up, confused, and pointed angrily at the phone, mouthing, 'This is important!'

Maeve leaned forward, knuckles on the desk, and looked squarely at her husband. 'So's this, Michael. I want a divorce.'

Michael looked up from the receiver; the client on the other end was still talking. 'John, something really big has just come up. Can I call you back in ten? Thanks.' He put the phone down slowly. '*What?*' he spat, with utter incredulity.

'I want a divorce. I don't want to be married to

someone who spends my money on holidays to Italy with his secretary.'

'What are you talking about?'

'Michael, I know. I know about you and Sally. Please do me the courtesy of not treating me like a fool – I'm sure you've been doing that for long enough. How long has it been going on?' Maeve was amazed at how calm she was.

Michael put his head in his hands. 'Six months,' he mumbled through his fingers.

'Six months?' Maeve's eyes narrowed; she felt nauseated again. He had been away for weekends and weeks, having sex with someone else, then coming home and having sex with her… 'And you didn't think to tell me?' She sat down in the chair facing Michael's desk. The hypocrisy of her lambasting Michael for keeping secrets wasn't lost on her; but she didn't care. She hadn't come for a heart-to-heart talk. She had come to tell her husband that their marriage was over.

'I didn't think it would last…'

'All that bullshit and flowers and asking me if I was pregnant – and yet you were off fucking some half-bit secretary with a face like a slapped arse.' Maeve heard her voice rise and reined herself in, annoyed. She wanted to be in control, not a neurotic nutcase.

Michael took his hands away from his face. 'She's not a secretary, Maeve. She's a bloody consultant.'

'Michael, I don't care if she's the managing

director of ICI; you were still fucking her behind my back while pretending that everything was fine.' Maeve's voice was measured this time; she looked Michael directly in the eye. 'I'm just glad I was on the pill, that's all I can say.'

Michael's face contorted. 'You were on the pill?' he spat. 'What? You were lying all along?'

'Yeah, I've been lying. We're very good at it, you and I. I think it's the only thing we have left in common.'

'Oh, for God's sake, Maeve, this is ridiculous. We need to talk about this.'

'No, we don't, Michael. We don't need to talk about anything. We've been living in cloud-cuckoo land from the word go. Other people don't go a week without seeing each other, and then make up for it by having a fifty-pound bottle of wine and a brace of pheasant for their tea. That's just you, in some bullshit Didsbury world, and I went along with it because I'm an idiot and I thought I needed to work at our marriage. Well, I can't any more. You can only work at something if there's something to work with – and there isn't, Michael.'

'You can't just leave me, Maeve,' Michael said, sounding suddenly lost. 'I'm sure we can work something out, now that everything's out in the open.'

'I'm not leaving you, Michael,' Maeve said softly, leaning forward to catch his gaze. He looked up, suddenly hopeful. 'You're leaving me.' Her voice turned icy. 'I want you out. I'll be seeing a lawyer in the morning. I'm sure your new girlfriend will put you up – that is, unless she had a glass up against the door just then, listening to you pleading.' Maeve opened the office door, just in time to see Sally hurrying out of the office, clutching her bag and coat. 'Oh, dear, I think she heard you.'

'Why are you doing this? You're acting like a complete bitch.'

'Am I?' Maeve asked calmly, raising an eyebrow. She walked out of Michael's office, pulled the door firmly closed behind her and headed for the lift, between the employees, who were craning their necks for more gossip. Sally was nowhere to be seen.

The lift opened on the ground floor, and the doorman asked, 'How did you get on, love?' Maeve had intended to answer cockily, on the off-chance that he asked, 'I think I did quite well.' But the fact that she had just ended her marriage hit her suddenly, with an almighty thump. She stared dumbly at the doorman.

'Didn't get it?'

Maeve shook her head and ran to the door, her hand trembling as she opened it. She hurried out into the street, tears streaming down her face. She needed someone to talk to. Maeve took out her phone and called the only person she knew who had first-hand experience of what she was going through.

Ciara had finally managed to pen Rachel into a corner. Now that she and Mark had sorted things out, it was time she talked to Rachel.

'Ray, I'm going to ask you something – and, I swear to God, it goes no further than these four walls. I think I've been an idiot.'

'Why?'

'I think something has been staring me in the face and I've been too self-obsessed to notice. Something to do with my two housemates.'

'Nothing's been staring you in the face, Ciara.'

'Rachel, I remember what you were like at school; you were my best friend for years. When you really like someone, you go out of your way to make it look like you don't like him at all.'

Rachel folded her arms and looked defiantly at Ciara. 'Like who?'

'Liam McCarty.'

'What about him?'

'It took you two years to stop slapping him and finally ask him out.'

'What's that got to do with anything?'

'It's got everything to do with everything. You really like Mark, don't you?'

Rachel looked away, unable to meet Ciara's eyes.

'Don't you?' Ciara urged.

'Yes, I do,' Rachel admitted. 'But when I introduced you to him, I knew he'd fancy you. Petite, blond hair, blue eyes – what's not to like? Everyone always fancies you.'

Ciara was floored. 'Don't be ridiculous! They do not. I'm a stumpy dwarf with a funny nose, and you're tall and elegant – so don't give me that crap!'

The frustration on Rachel's face gave way to a smile. 'Stumpy dwarf?' she asked, beginning to laugh.

'Yeah, well, I am. Anyway, never mind my being vertically challenged. Why didn't you tell me you liked Mark? I wouldn't have touched him with a barge pole!'

'He's my housemate.'

'He's mine too, in case you hadn't noticed. Didn't stop me wading in with both feet.'

Rachel shrugged. 'He just thinks we're friends.'

'Oh, yeah. Soaking you to the skin? That's not what male friends do; that's what someone flirting does. It looked like the Playboy Mansion in here the other day.'

'I don't know, Ciara...'

'Well, I do. You need to say something, or else you'll always be wondering if something could have happened between you two. He'll get another girlfriend, he'll propose to her, she'll say yes, you'll end up being best woman – it'll be a disaster!'

'God, I don't know if I'd dare say anything...' But Rachel sounded as if she was coming around to the idea. 'And, anyway, what about you? You've slept with him! Won't that be weird?'

'I'm very modern. It's my upbringing; my parents are hippies – free love and all that.' Ciara's phone rang. 'It's Maeve; I won't be a minute.'

When Ciara got off the phone, she was ashen-faced. 'Look, Ray, could you do me a favour and drop me in town? I wouldn't ask, but Maeve's really upset. I'm not sure what's wrong.'

'No problem,' Rachel said, grabbing her coat.

Ciara gathered her bag and her jacket. 'And I haven't forgotten our conversation. You will say something, won't you?'

'I'll try,' Rachel said, ushering her out of the door.

Ciara looked around the dim, candlelit bar and spotted Maeve huddled in a corner, nursing a glass of wine. Ciara waved as she neared the table, but there was no response.

'Hello! Earth calling Maeve.'

Maeve snapped out of her trance. 'God, Ciara, sorry – I was miles away.'

'What's up?' Ciara asked, pulling out one of the heavy wooden chairs.

'Look, I'm sorry I've dragged you here. You probably think I should have friends that I could tell this to, but the fact is that any friends I have are Michael's friends, and I can't bring myself to call them. I just felt like I needed someone who knew what I was talking about.'

'Well, that's not me, Maeve,' Ciara said. She hadn't a clue what her sister was on about.

'Sorry.' Maeve breathed deeply and smoothed her hands along the table, gathering her thoughts. 'Michael and I are getting divorced.'

Ciara gasped. 'You told him?'

'No. He still knows nothing about Catherine. Michael's been having an affair,' Maeve said matter-of-factly.

Ciara stared at her sister. 'Oh, my God.' She didn't like or trust Michael, and she had painted him as a sleazy Lothario in her own mind, but she had never thought that he would actually cheat on Maeve. She felt suddenly protective of her older sister. She wanted to find Michael and smack his smug teeth down his smarmy throat. *How dare he?* Ciara thought. *He should count himself lucky that someone like Maeve would even look at him!*

She chose not to voice this opinion. 'Maeve, I am so sorry. When did you find out?'

Maeve smiled weakly. 'Just now.'

'Who with?' Ciara said, realising too late that it wasn't the most sensitive thing to ask.

'That silly cow from his office.'

'Sally Thompson? Oh, my God – no way!' Ciara was stunned. *What was Michael thinking?* 'She arranged an interview for me this week; I'm going to fuck it up on purpose.'

'Don't be stupid.'

'I am, I swear. I don't even want the job; I want to go back to college, if anyone will have me…' Ciara realised that she had stopped Maeve in mid-flow. 'Sorry, Maeve; I didn't mean to go off on a tangent. What were you saying?'

'I think it's been going on for a while.'

Ciara remembered Michael and Sally's sickly flirting. She wanted to rewind to that moment and knock their adulterous heads together.

'And, if I'm honest with myself, I think I already knew.'

'Maeve, I'm really sorry.'

'Don't be sorry, Ciara. It's shit, and I feel terrible – but only because my pride is hurt, not because I'm still in love with Michael. And this clears the way for me to get on with my life.'

'I suppose.'

'There's no "suppose" about it. I was just sitting here thinking how feeble I've been. I've clung to Michael, thinking that, as long as we had the perfect life on the outside, everything would come good in the end. But that's exactly what Mum and Dad do: keep up appearances, set unachievable standards for themselves and their family…and for what? For me to have a daughter I've never met. For you to cheat in your exam—'

'In all fairness, Maeve, I can't blame them for that; Dad was hardly next to me, throwing away the answer booklet.'

'No, but you did it because of the pressure on all of us. You know that.' Ciara shrugged half-heartedly. 'Hello! You stuck Post-It notes on the wall so you could keep track of your lies, Ciara!' Maeve reminded her.

'I know. You're right. Are we a set of lunatics, or what?'

'I think everyone's family is mad, to one extent or another; but most people talk. We don't even do that. We just sit around on Sundays, firing roast potatoes into our mouths and trying to impress Mum and Dad with our empire-building. It's bullshit, Ciara, and it has to end.'

'Yes, you're right; it does.'

'I'm going round to Mum and Dad's now,' Maeve said resolutely.

Ciara looked at her, startled. She had known that, sooner or later, Maeve would want to face their parents and get all of the family secrets out in the open; but she hadn't thought it would be immediately. 'Now, Maeve? Are you sure?'

'Sure as I'll ever be,' Maeve said, draining her wineglass. 'Are you coming?'

42

'Shall I call Claire?' Ciara fidgeted in the taxi. She felt as if she were being forced to walk the plank.

'I'm not sure,' Maeve said, nervously tucking her hair behind her ears. 'I think this is about you and me, Ciara. If we drag everyone into it, it could finish up like World War Three.'

'Anthony will be there, though, won't he?'

'He's got kickboxing tonight; he doesn't get home until about half past nine.'

'Oh, so it's just us, then.' Ciara decided that now might be a good time to run away and join the circus.

Maeve took a deep breath as the taxi rounded the corner onto their parents' street. 'Yep, it's me and you.'

Ciara smiled weakly as Maeve paid the taxi driver. 'Here, take this,' she said, fishing out a few pounds.

'No, it's my treat.'

'Some treat.'

Maeve smiled and put her arm around her sister's shoulders as they faced the family home together. 'I've only spoken to Mum twice since the anniversary meal,' she admitted.

'Really?' Ciara said, surprised. Maeve had always spoken to their mother regularly. 'What did she say?'

'She said Dad was disappointed in me.'

'For God's sake.'

'I know. So I told her that, if he was so disappointed, he could tell me himself. But he hasn't bothered. He can tell me now, can't he?' Maeve said, trying to sound brave. She tried the door: it was open.

'Hello!' she shouted into the house. Ciara hung back nervously, hoping that her parents had gone away for a few years and forgotten to lock up. She doubted it: Sean battened down the hatches if he so much as popped out for a pint of milk.

'Hello!' Margaret came out of the kitchen, wearing a tea towel draped over her shoulder like a pashmina.

Sean joined her. 'Nice of you to finally put in an appearance, after your anniversary display.'

Maeve looked at her father, and Ciara could tell her steely resolve was wavering under his gaze. 'Yes, well, I'm only here because I've got something to tell you both. Actually, there are a few things.'

Sean looked sternly back at her. 'OK, come through – and you as well, Ciara. You two are getting on well these days,' he added sarcastically. Ciara stared at the floor to avoid his gaze.

'Do you want a cup of tea?' Margaret asked nervously.

'No, thanks, Mum,' Maeve said, taking a seat in an armchair. Ciara perched awkwardly on the sofa. 'I just want to say what I've come to say.' She was rallying again, much to Ciara's relief; she didn't think she could handle this situation if Maeve went to pieces.

'OK, then,' Margaret said, sounding defeated. 'What have you got to say?'

Sean sat down opposite Maeve, folded his arms across his chest and waited, glaring at her. Ciara found the situation extremely curious. Suddenly, watching her father and Maeve, she realised that her view of Maeve as the perfect daughter was as huge a misconception as her own attempts at *being* the perfect daughter were a charade.

'Michael and I are getting a divorce,' Maeve said. Ciara winced and waited for the fallout.

Sean raised an eyebrow. 'Divorced?' he asked, in mild surprise.

'Yes, Dad.'

'And what have you done to upset him?'

'What have *I* done?' Maeve nearly leapt out of the chair. 'Michael's been having an affair!'

Ciara waited for the shocked reaction, but her mother simply looked away, taking a great interest in a picture on the wall. Sean, equally phlegmatic, took a breath and said, 'And how long have you known about this?'

'I've just found out. Why?'

'Because you should sit down and discuss your problems together – not come flying around here declaring you're getting divorced. There is nothing within a marriage that cannot be sorted out if you just talk it through.'

'Are you insane?' Maeve demanded. Ciara felt as if she were watching the situation unfold in slow motion, observing every detail. '*Talk?* Like we talked about Gemma?'

'Who's Gemma?' Sean asked, genuinely bewildered.

Ciara pulled her shoulders in as though she were preparing for the ceiling to come crashing down around her ears.

'Gemma, my daughter! Your granddaughter! Or Catherine, as she's now called.'

Well, that's that, Ciara thought: *all out in the open.* Illegitimate adopted children, affairs…it made her cheating in an exam look positively third-rate.

Sean's face darkened. 'In this house, we don't talk about what happened back then!'

'Well, fine,' Maeve snapped. 'I won't waste another minute of my time in *this house*.' And she stormed out, slamming the front door.

'OK, if we don't talk about that, do we talk about your reaction to the fact that Michael had an affair?' Sean and Margaret turned from staring after Maeve to staring at Ciara, who had surprised herself by voicing this. 'It's just that you didn't react the way I thought you would. No one seems incensed. Mum, you just look away; and Dad, you get all philosophical about working things out.'

Margaret got to her feet, dewy-eyed. She rubbed her hand on her tea towel and placed it gently on the table; then she followed Maeve out of the house. 'Mum!' Ciara shouted. She heard the door close.

Sean and Ciara looked at each other.

'That is enough, Ciara!' Sean snapped, trying to regain control of the situation. 'Look what you've done now, upsetting your mother like that.'

But it wasn't enough. Ciara looked him in the eye and said boldly, 'I don't think it's me that's upset her.'

'She's upset because everything we've worked for, everything we tried to give you children, is being thrown back in our faces.'

He really didn't get it, she realised. 'Oh, it's all our fault, is it? You know something, Dad? This family is built on lies. We lie to each other all the time. There's a sixteen-year-old girl out there who should be part of our family—'

'We did what was best for your sister!' Sean bellowed.

Ciara wasn't going to be shouted down. 'You did what was best for *you*! You wanted it to go away. Well, it hasn't – *she* hasn't.'

'Whatever your mother and I have done, young lady, it has always been with our children's best interests at heart. And what went on with your sister has nothing to do with you!'

Ciara shrugged in exasperation. 'Yes, it does, because Maeve confided in me. And don't give me "best interests"; you don't even know what our best interests are, because we spend so much time trying to please you! Trying to be the perfect kids, lying to you so we won't upset you… I spent all my time in Dublin making things up to tell you, so you could have the perfect sepia view of life in Ireland—'

'Don't raise your voice to me, young lady!'

'If I have to scream the house down to get you to listen, then I will. Maeve's not perfect, you're not perfect and *I* most certainly *am not perfect*! I haven't got a degree, Dad – not from Trinity, not from anywhere.' Ciara let her father digest the information for a moment. 'And I never told you because I didn't want you to think badly of me.'

'What are you talking about? You dropped out?' Sean asked, incredulous.

'No, I didn't drop out; I was asked to leave. I cheated on an exam – I was an idiot, and I panicked. And, rather than facing it, I've stuck my head in the sand. I lied to you and Mum, and because of having to keep up the pretence, I made things very difficult for Declan, who had to put up with me…oh, because I lived with him,' Ciara said, almost as an afterthought. She had never imagined delivering this piece of information to her father in such a casual fashion; but, after everything that had just been said, his daughter living with her ex-boyfriend was the least of Sean's concerns.

'You cheated?' Sean bellowed. His face was scarlet. 'And that's somehow our fault? You wouldn't have had any pretence to keep up if you'd worked hard! Don't you dare try to blame me or your mother for your shortcomings, Ciara Coffey, because it won't wash. Lying to us – I'm appalled!'

'Have you listened to a word I've said?'

Sean rose from the table. 'Yes, I have, and I've had enough of it.'

'Where are you going?'

'Never mind where I'm going.' Sean grabbed his walking jacket from the cupboard under the stairs and marched out of the front door, slamming it as he left.

Ciara sat for a moment, a lump rising in her throat, staring around the empty house and trying to take in what had just happened. Then she reached for her mobile and called Maeve.

'Hi, Ciara. I'm with Mum in Solomon Grundy's, having a coffee.'

'Dad's just stormed out,' Ciara said quietly. 'I don't know what to think, Maeve.'

'Lock up and come round here.'

Ciara walked the few minutes to the village, looking around for her father, but she saw no sign of him. He was probably pacing up and down in the park, she decided.

Maeve and Margaret were sitting in a corner of the bar; Margaret looked utterly worn out.

'Are you OK, Mum?'

'Ciara, I'm fine. I'm always fine.' Margaret clasped her hands together and pressed her knuckles to her lips.

'She's fine, Ciara.' Maeve put her hand on her sister's knee and mouthed, 'Tell you later.'

'You know, if your dad's out, then I'll go home. He'll calm down soon enough. I might leave you two to it,' Margaret said, getting up from her chair. She glanced at her barely touched coffee. 'You have that, Ciara, if you want it.'

'Are you sure you want to go back right now, Mum?' Maeve asked.

'Yes, I'm sure.' She kissed each of her daughters on the cheek. 'I'll call you both later.'

'Dad's in a right stink with me – and he can stay that way, for all I care,' Ciara told Maeve, as the door closed behind Margaret. 'So come on – why was Mum so upset about Michael's affair?'

'Well…just after you were born, she was feeling

quite low, and Dad was spending a lot of time at work. She thought he was very friendly with one of the female English teachers.'

'Is that it?'

'Pretty much. Mum's convinced herself that nothing happened, that she was just blowing things out of proportion.'

'Do you think…?' Ciara asked incredulously. She couldn't imagine her father – who seemed to spend half his time giving out Communion or doing laps of the Stations of the Cross – having any interest in any woman other than her mother; or even in her mother, for that matter.

'I've no idea. I suppose we'll never know. Did you tell him about the degree?'

'Yeah. That was sort of why he stormed off. But he'll calm down.'

'Or not.' Maeve gave Ciara a wry smile.

'Did you tell Mum you'd been in touch with Catherine?'

'Yeah. I told her I was going to see her. She just kind of raised an eyebrow and went, "Oh, really?"'

Ciara laughed out loud. 'What a rubbish reaction!'

'That's what I thought. She's just in shock; it's going to take a while to sink in. I mean, how much more could we have come out with tonight?'

'Anthony might come back from kickboxing and say he's marrying a horse. That'd just about put the tin hat on it.'

Maeve burst out laughing.

'Fancy something stronger than coffee?' Ciara asked.

'Might as well; it's not like I've anything to go home for.' Maeve smiled sadly. In the furore, Ciara had forgotten that she still had to face the aftermath of discovering Michael's affair.

43

Ciara was having a productive day – although it didn't involve much manning of the switchboard: there hadn't been a single call. She didn't think Lindy would be seeing out her working days at Carlisle & Hobart. Ciara had spent the day applying, through the clearing system, to a number of English degree courses in the area. From what she understood, she would be called in for interviews once this year's A-level results were out and the universities knew whether there were any spare places. If she wasn't accepted this year, she had decided, she would apply through the normal channels for the following year's intake.

Next on her list of things to do was phone Sally

Thompson and tell her she wouldn't be going to the interview. Ciara dialled the number, gearing herself up to give the woman an earful of abuse; if Sally had anything to say about the irresponsibility of only giving a day's notice, Ciara was going to tell her what she thought of her. She was quite enjoying the idea of shouting into the phone, 'And what about your responsibility to not shag my sister's husband?'

Ciara had decided to keep temping through Sureplace. That way, when she was in university, she could keep working whenever she had a free day. There was no way she was getting a bar job again; she might wake up in a gutter in five years' time, wondering how she had got there.

'Hello, NPV Consulting,' chirped the receptionist.

'Hi. Can I speak to Sally Thompson, please?'

'I'm sorry; Sally Thompson no longer works with us.' Ciara was shocked. 'Can I put you through to Michael? He's dealing with Sally's clients.'

Ciara collected herself. 'No, that's fine; I don't need to speak to Michael. Thank you.'

She put the phone down. A part of her was glad that Sally, too, appeared to have left Michael; but she didn't want to talk to him. She never wanted to speak to Michael again.

'Hello!' Ciara shouted into the house. There was no reply; Rachel and Mark obviously weren't home.

There was a note from Rachel on the telephone table: 'Gone to Fellucini's for a meal,' and a smiley face. Ciara hoped this was the start of something beautiful, and not just Mark's attempt at creating a harem. She was rather pleased with her own liberal stance on the whole thing. She really hadn't been bothered about Mark, she realised; if she had, she wouldn't be feeling half so charitable.

The red light on the answering machine was flashing, and Ciara jumped at it. *Could it be Declan?*

'Hi, this is a message for Ciara...'

It was. Ciara felt her throat dry up, and her heart began to thump heavily. 'If you're there...em, I don't really know what to say – I'm chancing my arm leaving a message, because your housemates might hear it first, but anyway, feck it. I'm in Manchester. I'm staying in Didsbury, and I love you. That's it, really. Look, I've booked a table in a restaurant for tonight at nine. It's a place called Piccolino's, near the Town Hall. If you can't make it, give me a call; if I don't hear from you, hopefully it means you'll be there. I'll be there anyway, because I need to get out of my hotel room.' The line began to crackle. 'Anyway, look, give me a call on...hang on; I don't know this number off by heart – I have it...' The message was breaking up. '...ven, nine...en...' There was a muffled 'Bye,' and then the line went dead.

Ciara stared at the machine, but the tape had

ended. 'Shit!' she yelled, and jumped to dial 1471 for the number of the last incoming call.

Just as her hand touched the phone, it began ringing. 'Oh, fuck off!' Ciara shouted: now 1471 would only get her the number of whatever half-wit was calling. She snatched the receiver and snapped, 'Yes?'

'Ciara, it's me, Mum.'

Ciara could have screamed. 'Hi.'

'I just wanted to say – well, about yesterday…'

'Mum, you don't have to say anything.'

'Well, I just want you to know…we always thought about you all, always.'

'I know, Mum. You said.'

'I just don't want you thinking we didn't, that's all. Oh, and your dad told me about the degree.' Ciara cringed. 'You are silly, Ciara; you should have told us.'

Five years of worry and lies, for her mother to say simply, 'You are silly.' *She's right,* Ciara thought: *I am silly. Very silly indeed.*

'I know, Mum, and I'm sorry. Listen, could I talk to you tomorrow? I've had a long day.'

'Of course you can. Bye, then, love.'

'Bye, Mum.'

Ciara put the phone down and rested her head in her hands. She knew her mum just wanted everyone to be happy – but why did she have to call at such an inopportune time? Ciara went into the kitchen, wondering what she was going to do.

There were so many things she wanted to know: what Declan was doing in Manchester, why he hadn't been in contact before, whether he had seen Laura since – and who the American girl was … Ciara grabbed a glass of milk from the fridge and headed upstairs. There was only one way to get her questions answered. She was going to get ready for her night out.

Ciara hopped in a taxi at a quarter to nine, and spent the journey into town trying to calm her somersaulting emotions. She hoped that the effort she'd put into her appearance would go some way towards disguising the fact that she was a bag of nerves. She was wearing jeans, a simple black halter-neck top and black patent high heels, in a bid to be on Declan's eye-level.

In the restaurant, as she waited for the maître d' to find Declan's name, Ciara thought she might be in danger of vomiting on his clipboard with nerves. 'Ah, yes, here we are – Murphy. The table is ready; it's just over here.' The maître d' pointed. 'Would you like me to get you a drink while you wait?'

'I'll have a still water, please,' Ciara said, taking her seat. She was slightly worried that Declan wasn't there, but she decided to use his tardiness to collect herself. She tried to appear poised, but underneath she was panicking, thinking with dread that he might not turn up at all – she would have to pay for her water and make her excuses… Just as she was considering going to the toilet and trying to escape through a window, the door revolved and Declan walked in.

His hair was longer than Ciara remembered, and he looked slightly tanned. Watching him grin at the maître d', she had trouble restraining herself from jumping up and shouting, 'I'm here!' Every drop of love and closeness and happiness she had ever felt for Declan came crashing back to her.

The maitre d' pointed to the table and Declan smiled, his eyes twinkling at Ciara. He walked over and said, almost shyly, 'Hello. Is anyone sitting here?'

'No, feel free.' Ciara smiled.

Declan leaned forward to kiss her on the cheek, but she turned her head the wrong way and the kiss landed on her ear. 'Sorry,' he said nervously, starting to wipe the kiss off her ear.

Ciara looked at him and began to giggle. 'Sit down!' she laughed.

Declan did as he was told. 'How are you?'

'I'm fine. How are you?' Ciara asked. The formality made her feel slightly foolish.

'I'm good.'

'That's good.'

'Yeah, it is good. Yeah.' Declan laughed nervously.

'I met the American girl you're living with,' Ciara said, trying to sound neutral and missing by a mile. 'I was over in Dublin this weekend and I called into the flat.' She knew this was the last thing she should be saying, but she couldn't help herself; she had felt like such an idiot at the time, and it was so fresh in her mind, that she had to say something. She looked fearfully at Declan; she wasn't really sure, any more, that she wanted to know the truth.

Declan looked astounded. 'Living with? I'm not living with her. I'm not even living in Dublin; I'm here. I've got two Americans living in the apartment – Barry gave me the idea: subletting, just making myself a bit of extra cash. You didn't think…?'

'I didn't get a chance to think anything. I still had my old key, so I let myself into the flat.' Ciara glanced down at the table, embarrassed. 'And then she came in straight after me and started yelling her head off, thinking I was there to rob her blind' – Declan began to laugh – 'and then she told me to get out and said, "We could have been doing anything," and I thought "we" meant you and her…'

Declan shook his head, smile playing on his lips. 'Well, it didn't. She's living there with her girlfriend.'

'Girlfriend?'

'Yep.'

'Well, it's nice to know that now, but at the time I was mortified. I ran all the way to the Liffey, rang Róisín and had a great weekend with her, so it wasn't a complete disaster.'

'How is Róisín?'

'She's great, really great. But I'll tell you all about that later. How are you? And what are you doing here?'

'I'm here for work. JMSS&A has an office in Didsbury, and I've been staying there, in a fancy hotel by Didsbury Park.'

'Oh, yeah, I know it. Very nice.'

'And I'm grand.' Declan paused to accept the beer he had ordered on the way in. Once the waiter was out of earshot, he leaned forward and held Ciara's gaze. 'Actually, Ciara, I'm not grand. I'm lousy. I've been over here for what seems like ages, and all I can think about is you. I can't get you out of my head.'

Ciara bit hard on her lip and tucked her hair behind her ears. Encouraged that she hadn't told him to shut up, Declan ploughed on.

'Look, I know we weren't exactly fecking Snow White and Prince Charming – but who is? And I know that we were at each other's throat for a long while there, and that I ended up…well, I was stupid. But I love you, and I'm sorry for everything that happened. I love you and I want to be with you – and if that means here or Dublin, or bleeding Addis Ababa, for that matter, then so be it. We can work it out. If you want to go out a lot, then I need to cop on and remember that that's who you are…' Declan stopped. 'Jesus, listen to me. I'm sorry; I don't even know what you're thinking.'

'Declan, look. I've done a lot of thinking since I last saw you. And you know what? I think I must have been a right arsehole to live with – going out all the time, hanging round with a set of tossers who just wanted to be seen out and about… Don't get me wrong, I don't think it was just them: I was as bad. What was I like? Billy fucking bullshit, that's what.'

Declan let out a burst of shocked laughter.

'I was! Look, a lot's happened in the past couple of months – stuff that's made me realise I was having myself on. And it's made me think about us, and why things happened the way they did.'

Declan nodded, fiddling with his napkin.

'I'm not saying that what happened with you and Laura is something I'll forget; if I said that, I'd be lying. But I think I understand that you did it at a time when I was such a pain in the arse that I probably didn't deserve you.'

'Look, like I said in the letter—'

'What letter?'

'The letter I sent you just after I came over to your parents' house. The one about how much I regretted the whole business with Laura.'

Ciara shook her head. 'I never got it.'

'Shit, I definitely sent it.' Declan's eyes narrowed as he thought back. 'That's strange. I sent it to your mum and dad's; they wouldn't have hidden it, would they?'

'They're mad, but not that mad. Anyway, post is sacrosanct, for some reason – always has been. Any post is opened by the addressee only, on pain of death.'

'That's really odd. I wouldn't mind, only it took

me ages to write and I poured my bloody heart out in that thing.' Declan smiled bashfully. 'Well, anyway, I said in the letter that I was sorry and that I was an idiot.'

The waiter had been lurking by the table for over a minute, notepad at the ready, leaning forward every time Ciara or Declan paused for breath. 'Look, shall we order?' Ciara nodded towards him.

Declan smiled. 'Go on, then. We've got the rest of the evening for me to spend grovelling on my hands and knees.'

Two hours later, Declan paid the bill and Ciara graciously accepted, after only a mild credit-card-wrestling bout and a promise that Declan would allow her to pay for something next time. The prospect of there being a next time made Declan agree readily.

They had spent the evening discussing what they had been doing since Ciara had moved so abruptly back to Manchester, and Ciara couldn't help noticing that Declan had been more than a little shocked to discover that she had not only befriended Maeve, but finally come clean with her parents. There had been another break with tradition, too: Ciara had happily shared a bottle of wine with Declan and then announced that she would head home. Only a short time ago, she would have polished the wine off herself, had a few sambucas and tried to instigate a conga line around the restaurant before dragging him off to some late-night drinking den.

'Look, I'm not turning into Mother Teresa, Dec; I've just got to get up for work tomorrow,' she explained as they left the restaurant.

'I know, I know. It's just – well, weird, I suppose,' Declan admitted. Work had never posed a barrier to Ciara enjoying herself in the past.

'Bad weird?'

'No,' he laughed, 'definitely good weird.'

They crossed the road to Albert Square. It was a warm evening, and they strolled aimlessly under the flower-adorned lampposts and between the statues and Victorian fountains.

'The taxi rank's there. I really need to get going soon.' Ciara pointed to a line of taxis. 'And my feet are killing.' She sat down on a bench, kicked her shoes off and rubbed her feet.

Declan sat down beside her. 'What are we going to do, Ciara?' he asked, instinctively bending forward and rubbing her right foot as she rubbed the left.

'I don't know.' But she did. She had known, the moment Declan walked into the restaurant, that she wanted to be with him. They could put everything else behind them and work something out.

'I do,' Declan said, slipping off his shoes and taking his socks off. He carefully placed them on Ciara's feet.

'Go on, Prince Charming!' a bald, drunken man

shouted from the taxi rank; he was quickly hushed and shoved into a taxi by the woman accompanying him. Ciara began to giggle uncontrollably.

'I don't know what you're laughing at.' Declan smirked. 'He's right: I am. Now why don't you get yourself home? If I remember rightly, we meet up at a designated watering hole tomorrow and I get my socks back. How does that sound?'

'I don't know, Declan.' Ciara shook her head. 'Too much has happened between us over the years for me to just go home and meet you tomorrow.'

Declan's face dropped; he looked like a lost boy. 'OK – well, if you think so…Sorry. I'm really sorry. It was just that I was having such a good evening…'

'So was I. That's why I thought it might be nice if I came back to your hotel.' Ciara broke into a grin. 'You know, just to check out if it's all it's cracked up to be.'

'Fantastic,' Declan said, his face breaking slowly into a grin. 'Let's go!' He threw his arm around Ciara's neck and kissed her deeply. Ciara was so excited she could have yelped.

Declan looked up at the clock of the Town Hall. 'You know something, Ciara? I don't want to jump the gun or anything…' He kissed her on the forehead and turned to face the waiting taxis. 'But I could get used to Manchester.'

Ciara put her arms around his waist and hugged him tightly. They headed for the taxi rank, Ciara tottering along in Declan's socks, her shoes peeking out from the top of her bag. 'Well,' she said, 'I'll help you settle in, if you want.'

Declan opened the taxi door for her and smiled. 'Yeah, I think that could work. What do you reckon?'

'I think we should give it a go,' Ciara said, standing on her tiptoes to kiss him. He pulled her close and nuzzled his face into her hair.

'Hey!' The taxi driver tapped his meter. 'This isn't a bloody knocking-shop, you know.'

'Fair enough,' Ciara said. Slamming the door shut and stepping back onto the pavement, she pulled Declan towards her and kissed him, as the Town Hall clock began to chime midnight. It would have been almost poetic – if the bells hadn't been out of tune on every fourth note. Declan and Ciara ended up doubled over, laughing hysterically, and the kissing had to wait.

Epilogue

By September, Sean had finally calmed down and was – at least in public – on speaking terms with Ciara and Maeve. With no one left to vie for his approval, he had tried to place Claire on the well-trodden Coffey pedestal, but she wasn't having any of his nonsense. Sean had tried complimenting Anthony, in an attempt to implant in him the desire to impress his father; but Anthony wouldn't have noticed a hidden agenda if it came up and sat on him. So Sean was left to try and establish a new, adult relationship with Maeve and Ciara.

'Well, how's Ciara?' Sean said, pulling out a chair in the restaurant Maeve had chosen for Sunday lunch. Since the family had begun to be more truthful with one another, Margaret had delivered a home truth of her own: she hated cooking. She wasn't going to do it any more, she said – only at Christmas, and then only if everyone mucked in and helped.

'Ciara's fine.' Ciara had some good news, actually, but she had promised herself not to blurt it out at the first opportunity. Old habits died hard, though, and she was itching to tell everyone that she had been accepted onto a course at one of the local universities. She had applied through the clearing process and had been interviewed the previous week.

She had walked into the interview determined to tell the truth – and, for once, she had. The tutor who interviewed her had been curious about why she had given up the course at Trinity: 'I assume it was because you realised that economics wasn't for you?'

Ciara had looked him straight in the eye and told him exactly what had happened. 'I'll understand if you don't admit me because of this,' she had said contritely, 'but I really regret what I did, and I wanted to be honest about it so I can put it behind me.'

The tutor had been taken aback. He had never heard anyone openly admit to having cheated in an exam, he said; he would have to find out where the institution stood on the matter. He hadn't sounded hopeful.

Ciara had had to wait two nail-biting days.

When the tutor had called and said that he was pleased to offer her a place, she had nearly fallen off her chair. When he informed her, 'We made the decision to admit you based on your enthusiasm for and understanding of the course, and on your mature approach to admitting your former failings,' she had thought she might have to be sedated.

Claire leaned towards Ciara and whispered, 'Well done.' Ciara hadn't been able to resist ringing her as soon as the tutor got off the phone.

'Thank you.'

'When are you going to tell them?' Claire asked.

'After the meal. I'll take Mum and Dad to one side and tell them.'

'What, no big announcement?'

'No. It's the new, don't-need-to-make-a-big-song-and-dance-out-of-everything me.'

'Very commendable.' Claire nodded, impressed.

'I know.' Ciara smiled. 'We'll see how long it lasts.'

'Where's Maeve?' Sean asked sharply, looking at his watch. 'She was meant to be here by now. She booked the table for one o'clock and she can't even get here herself.'

'Dear God,' Ciara muttered under her breath. 'She'll be here in a minute, Dad. Her plane was delayed; you know that.'

Maeve had gone to Dublin to see Catherine, for the second time. The first time had only been for the day. They had been nervous about meeting each other, but they had found that they got on very well. Maeve had also met Catherine's adoptive parents, who had dropped her off in Dublin; she had been worried that she might be hurting them by suddenly intruding upon their lives, but Miriam and John had been so welcoming that she had felt comfortable suggesting that she and Catherine spend a bit more time together. This time they had spent three whole days in Dublin.

'Glad to see Dad's his usual comfortable self in a restaurant,' Claire said, looking over at her father, who was busy tucking his napkin into the top of his shirt. Claire, when she heard about Maeve's past, had been her usual laid-back self: she had never expected perfection, so she wasn't completely shocked by the revelation. As it was the summer holiday, she had offered to go over to Dublin with Maeve for moral support, but Maeve had wanted to go on her own. She would introduce Catherine to the family when Catherine was ready, she said. Anthony, on the other hand, had been freaked out by the notion that his sister had a child the same age as him; in the past week, though, he had come around to the idea a little. It gave him much-needed ammunition against his father whenever Sean tried to preach about honesty.

'I know,' Ciara agreed. 'Eating out does his head in.'

'Is he still in a strop with you and Maeve?'

'Only when he remembers to be.'

Claire smiled and looked over at their father. 'Excuse me! Could we have some bread, please?' Sean barked at a passing waitress, in the tone that an angry drunk might use to ask, 'Are you looking at my bird?'

'I think he's doing very well, for someone who ruled you lot with an iron rod up until a few weeks ago,' Declan said, smirking. 'Give the fella a chance. What's he supposed to do – start giving you big hugs and telling you he loves you for who you are?'

'Shut up, Dec.' Ciara nudged him affectionately.

Ciara and Declan had begun the slow job of patching things up. At first they had decided to see each other only twice a week, to give themselves time to re-adjust. But Ciara had found herself making up excuses to go to Declan's hotel – she knew she was scraping the bottom of the barrel when she found herself there because they had run out of toilet roll at her house. In the past week, Declan had decided to rent a flat in Manchester. He would give notice on his flat in Dublin; the two American girls were only there for another month. Ciara wasn't going to move in with him; she was happy living with Rachel and Mark for the time being, now that she had ironed things out with them. (Rachel – after a number of tongue-tied attempts – had finally managed to inform Mark that she liked him, with predictable results. They had been acting like two teenagers, coyly pussyfooting around each other by day and sneaking in and out of each other's bedroom by night. Ciara was happy for them; there was a tiny Catholic part of her that thought the whole situation was a little bit *too* Generation X, but she was only admitting that to herself.)

'Ah, here she is now,' Margaret said, standing up and waving to Maeve.

'Sorry I'm late, everyone.'

'No bother; sit yourself down,' Sean said, as if he hadn't been fussing and complaining for the past fifteen minutes.

'So how was the weekend?' Ciara asked. She saw Sean flinch and Margaret lay a hand on his knee.

'It was great.' Maeve smiled. 'Really great.'

Maeve was still trying to get used to a house and a life without Michael. When she first discovered his affair, there had been so much else going on that it hadn't quite seemed real. But, as Maeve had watched Michael mournfully remove his belongings from the house and heard him tell her that he had never wanted this to happen, she had suddenly realised that a large chapter in her life had ended. She told Ciara that getting over this was probably going to take more time than she had initially bargained for. At least, thought Ciara, she hadn't wavered and considered going back to him; she deserved someone with more integrity – and more hair. Looking at Maeve today, though, Ciara realised she seemed really happy.

'What's she like, then – my niece?' Anthony asked Maeve.

'Anthony!' Margaret said. Ciara felt the old pangs of mortification coming back as her mother and father cringed visibly.

'What? She is, isn't she?' Anthony was enjoying himself. 'It's weird, isn't it, Mum? One week we're like the Von Trapps, the next we're like something off *Trisha*.'

Ciara was sure that Sean was going to overturn the table, like Jesus in the temple, and run from the restaurant roaring in anger; but instead he said, 'Very good, Anthony. I wouldn't have thought you'd know who the Von Trapps were.'

Everyone laughed. Ciara smiled, relaxing. It seemed that her father was beginning to understand that, if he couldn't beat them, he might have to join them.

'Dad, you used to make us watch *The Sound of Music* every time it was on,' Anthony said, rolling his eyes.

'I think you'll find that was your mother.'

'Don't blame me!' Margaret exclaimed.

'No one's blaming you, Margaret. You've just got terrible taste.'

'Sean Coffey!' Margaret cried in mock disgust. 'I married you, didn't I?'

Ciara looked around the table; her eyes fell on

Declan, and she smiled happily. He smiled back, seeming to know what she was thinking. For all their faults and foibles, this was her family, and she loved being part of it. And anyway, she decided, she'd rather be a Coffey than a Von Trapp any day.

**Just finished a great book and dying to dive into another?
Don't know where to start looking?**

Visit gillmacmillan.ie/readers for

Sneak peeks
Read a chapter from our books before you buy

Reading guides
Download a guide for your book group

Author interviews
Get the chance to ask our authors your burning questions

Competitions
Win books and advance reading copies

Book news
Get the news on the latest launches and events

All this **and** 20% off every order!

www.gillmacmillan.ie/readers

get more from your reading

Also by Anne-Marie O'Connor

A lively rollercoaster of a comedy based on the theory that everyone in Dublin has met Bono. For all fans of the Man Himself, and for everyone who loves a good laugh.

On the mother of all Mondays, Aoife finds herself broke and homeless when both her boss and her landlord tell her it's time she moved on. After the obligatory night in Dublin's watering holes drowning her sorrows with best friend Rory, he makes her a proposition she can't resist. If she can engineer her very own encounter with Bono, followed by a suitably impressive Bono Story, he will give her €5,000. Aoife accepts the challenge with relish — but after dressing up as a nun, staking out Dublin Airport and getting drugged by rival fans, she's still no nearer her goal. Time is running out, and Aoife's life is getting complicated, so just how far will she be prepared to go to get her man?

'Hilarious romp' *Books Ireland*

Available wherever books are sold or order online at **www.gillmacmilllan.ie** to save **20%**